J.A. KERLEY

THE APOSTLE

HARPER

Harper
An imprint of HarperCollins*Publishers*
1 London Bridge Street,
London SE1 9GF

www.harpercollins.co.uk

A paperback original

1

First published in Great Britain by
Harper, an imprint of HarperCollins*Publishers* 2014

A catalogue record for this book
is available from the British Library

ISBN 9780007493692

Set in Sabon Lt Std by Palimpsest Book Production Ltd, Falkirk, Stirlingshire

Printed in Great Britain by
Clays Limited, St Ives plc

MIX
Paper from
responsible sources
FSC
www.fsc.org FSC™ C007454

FSC™ is a non-profit international organisation established to promote the responsible management of the world's forests. Products carrying the FSC label are independently certified to assure consumers that they come from forests that are managed to meet the social, economic and ecological needs of present and future generations, and other controlled sources.

Find out more about HarperCollins and the environment at
www.harpercollins.co.uk/green

To Floyd and Addie Richardson –
And the house where the trains rolled by

Thunderous accolades as always to the splendid folks at HarperCollins UK, with special shout-outs to Sarah Hodgson, Anne O'Brien and the graphics staff. Thanks also to Lucy Childs of the Aaron M. Priest Literary Agency. And special "high-five" gratitude for technical input goes to Officer Kyle Shipps of the Prairie Village, Kansas, Police Department.

1

"I'm putting in the last of Christ's blood."

Raoul Herrera studied the slender needle for a long moment, assured himself it was the right choice, then bent forward, his skilled fingers guiding the needle into flesh, adding a bright highlight to a plump drop of red dripping from a thorn. Herrera dabbed a cotton ball in antiseptic, blotted his client's scapula, then leaned back and studied his work.

"Done," he said.

Herrera flicked off the instrument and admired the most fantastic tattoo he'd ever created, a masterwork of detail that had stretched his talent to its limits, making him develop new ways of adding depth to color, motion to stillness, beauty to horror.

Yet all the tattoo consisted of was the back of a head. Not inked on the back of a head, an illustration of the back of a head.

The client had entered Skin Art by Raoul six weeks ago. The tattoo artist was alone in the back room, sanitizing equipment and preparing to close for the evening when he'd walked into the reception area. Though the door rang when opened, the bell had not sounded. Yet a man stood in the center of the Oriental carpet, utterly still, eyes staring into Herrera's eyes, as if knowing the precise space the tattooist would occupy.

Herrera's heartbeats accelerated. There was nothing but night outside his window and the neighborhood was dangerous in the dark. He kept a .38 pistol in back and Herrera mentally measured his steps to the gun.

"I'm closed," he said.

The man seemed not to hear. He looked in his mid-thirties, hard-traveled years, lines etched into his angular face, his eyes tight and crinkled, as though he'd spent a lifetime squinting into sunlight. He was small in stature, wearing battered Levis and a faded Western-style shirt with sleeves rolled up over iron-hard forearms. His face was small and flat and centered by a nose broken at least once, the hair a tight cap of coiled brown that fell low on his forehead and gave a simian cast to his features. His eyes were the color of spent briquettes of charcoal.

"I said I'm done for the day, man," Herrera repeated. "Come back tomorrow."

Again, the man seemed deaf to Herrera's words.

Work-hardened hands unfolded a sheet of paper and held up a richly detailed illustration of Jesus inked into a man's bicep, a work by Herrera that had been featured in a tattoo artists' publication.

"Did you do this?" the man said. "Do you claim it yours?"

"It's my work. Why?"

"It ain't quite real yet, is it?"

Despite his uneasiness, Herrera felt his ability challenged. "You won't find better, mister. Not that I figure you could afford it."

The man balled the page and tossed it to the floor. "It ain't there yet. It looks like Him. But He ain't in it."

Meaning Jesus.

"Use the door, mister," Herrera said. "I'm closed."

Eyes locked on to Herrera, the man turned to the sign switch and flicked off the neon display. He pushed the door closed and set the lock. Herrera inched closer to his gun. The man lifted his hands.

"I mean you no harm. Look here . . ."

The man eased a hand into his pocket and produced a roll of paper money. He crossed to the artist, took Herrera's hand and pressed the roll into his palm.

"Count it up."

Herrera did. Over five thousand dollars in fresh, clean bills.

The new client pushed through the beaded curtain to the work area in back and the tattoo artist followed. The man withdrew his tails from his pants, unbuttoning the shirt and throwing it to the floor. He turned to display his back, wide at the shoulders, narrow at the waist. When he moved, the muscles twitched with sudden electricity, as if hidden power had been awakened. The man sat in the tattooing chair and stared over his shoulder at Herrera.

"Turn a mirror so I can see. This time you gonna get it right."

Herrera shook his head. "That's not how it works. I make drawings. Get your approval."

The man closed his eyes and retreated inside his head. After several long moments he nodded. "That makes sense."

"You want me to do Jesus, I take it?" Herrera asked.

"The back of His head from the bottom of my neck down. His exact size and as real as His tribulation."

"How do I know if I'm representing the, uh, subject correctly?"

"He'll guide your hand," the man said, meaning Jesus.

Herrera had felt no hand but his own on the needles through a dozen sessions, but something seemed to have driven him to a greater height of art than ever before. The back of Christ's head appeared dimensional, a tumble of brown and shadow starting at the base of the client's neck and feathering out on his lower spine. The crown of thorns seemed so real that wearing a shirt would be impossible, the fabric tearing on the horrific spikes, stained by the bright blood dripping down curling locks of tangled hair. The project was beautiful and awesome and terrible in equal measure.

4

And now it was complete.

The man stood from the chair and reached for his shirt. When he turned toward Herrera the tattooist's breath froze in his throat. A gulley had been cut into his customer's chest, an inch-wide strip of flesh and tissue running from below one flat nipple to the other. It was a recent wound, the furrow red and puckered and weeping yellow fluid. Herrera swallowed hard, wondering if the visor-like cut went all the way to bone.

"Um, what happened there?" he asked.

The man pulled on his shirt and left the top half unbuttoned, the raw slit visible in the V. His dead-charcoal eyes bored into Herrera and he shook his head like the tattoo artist was the village idiot.

"He's gotta be able to see out now, don't He?"

Meaning Jesus.

2

Mobile, Alabama. Mid May

"Carson. Yo, brother. Wake up."

"Mmmf," I said, trying to slap a big hand shaking my shoulder. I missed and slapped my own cheek.

"Come on, Cars . . . time to get hoppin' and boppin'."

The only reason I opened my eyes was because I smelled bacon. Say what you will about alarm clocks, bacon is better. I looked up and saw blue sky filtered through tree branches. I tried to sit up, made it on the second try. I was in a lounge chair on Harry Nautilus's back patio. The picnic table beside me looked like a launching pad for beer bottles. A pedestal fan on the patio was blowing air across me. Harry switched the fan off.

"Good morning, merry sunshine."

I studied the chair beneath me, gave Harry a look.

"You fell asleep there, Carson. I kept the fan on you to keep the skeeters off."

"A polite host would have carried me to a real bed and tucked me in."

"A smart host would have coffee. And these." His right hand held out a steaming mug and his left opened to display a half-dozen aspirin. I grabbed both, chewing the pills and washing the paste down with New Orleans-style coffee, brewed black with chicory and cut with scalded milk.

"Want a bacon-egg sandwich?" Harry said.

I shot a thumb up as Harry retreated into the kitchen and the previous night returned to me, the major scenes at least. Flanagan's bar decked out for a party: blue balloons, two long tables weighted down with cookpots of chili and sandwich fixings – ham, turkey, barbecue, cheeses – plus bowls of chips and nuts and pretzels. A twelve-foot banner over the bar said simply, *436 is 10-7*.

It meant badge number 436 was out of service. Harry was badge number 436.

It was his retirement party. A surprise, Harry lured there by me and Lieutenant Tom Mason, our long-time leader and apologist. I don't often get misty-eyed, but when we'd walked into Flanagan's and I saw the sign, it got a little blurry.

Harry was my best friend and had been my detective partner for years. It was Harry who'd convinced me to join the force when I was a twenty-seven-year-old slacker wondering what to do with a Masters Degree in Psychology gained by traveling to every max-security prison in the South and interviewing homicidal maniacs.

Harry was ten years older than me, a year and some shy of fifty. He'd started on the force young, and when adding in unused sick and vacation days, plus time credits when he'd been injured in the line of duty, it added up to thirty years in service, all but five of them in Homicide.

The bash at Flanagan's had been an alcohol-fueled semi-riot. Harry was a legend in the MPD, and his friends had come to see him off, his enemies to make sure he was leaving. We'd stayed two hours, neither big on shoulder-to-shoulder crowds, slipping away to Harry's place on the near-north side of Mobile, a trim bungalow in a quiet neighborhood overslung with slash and longleaf pines and the snaking branches of live oaks. His back yard was slender and long and landscaped with dogwoods and banks of azaleas. It was centered by a looming sycamore, from which Harry had strung a half-dozen bright birdhouses.

He'd fetched bottles of homebrew from his closet, channeled mix-tapes of Miles and Bird and Gillespie through the speakers, and we'd sat beneath a fat white moon and had our kind of party, long beer-sipping silences broken by stories from the streets, good and bad and blends of both.

Harry stepped out and handed me six inches of warmed French bread filled with scrambled eggs, bacon, melted

8

cheddar and heavy lashings of Crystal Hot Sauce, and I went to work supplanting beer with food, something I probably should have done more of last night.

Harry's eyes went to the bottle collection on the patio table.

"Happy to see you liked my homebrew."

When I'd accepted the position in Florida, Harry'd started brewing beer, saying he needed something temperamental to work with now that I was gone. I'm pretty sure it was a joke.

"Great stuff," I said. It truly was, but Harry mastered anything he did. "How much kick is in that freakin' stout?"

"It's about eight per cent alcohol."

I shook my head. My brain didn't rattle, the aspirin kicking in, along with snatches of last-night's conversation.

"You're really thinking about the job?" I asked, recalling one of our conversations. "You retire one week, take a new job the next?"

Harry slid a chair near and sat. He was wearing an electric orange shirt and sky-blue cargo shorts. His sockless feet crowded the size-thirteen running shoes, yellow. The colors were strident to begin with, and seemed neon against skin the hue of coffee with a teaspoon of cream.

"It's hardly a job, Carson. I'll be driving a lady around when she wants to go out. Sometimes her daughter comes along. It's maybe ten hours a week. Did I mention the gig pays twenty clams an hour?"

"For turning a wheel? Now it's making more sense."

"Mostly it's taking the lady shopping. Or to church, the hair stylist, doctor, stuff like that. The lady lives in Spring Hill, just a couple miles away. She calls, I'm there in minutes."

"You didn't say who the lady was."

Harry's turn to frown. "Can't, Carson. It's confidential, part of the agreement."

"She's in the Mafia?"

"It was her husband who hired me, actually. And no, he's sort of on the side of the angels."

"Who you think I'll tell?"

"Sorry, Carson. I gave my word I'd be mum."

That was that. Harry's word was a titanium-clad guarantee of silence. I switched lanes. "The wife unfamiliar with the operation of automobiles?"

"I guess she can drive, but doesn't like to."

"Damn," I said, "Harry Nautilus, chauffeur."

"Driver," he corrected.

3

I bought a *Miami Herald* for the flight and returned to Miami. The headlines hadn't changed much since Friday: "*No Progress in Menendez Murder*" blared the main story, with another headline, inches below, saying "*Miami Mourns Loss of Favored Daughter*".

Last Thursday had been a horror for local law enforcement. Roberta Menendez was an MDPD administrator who'd started as a beat cop, putting in eight years before a fleeing felon's gunshot shattered her hip. Undaunted, she worked a desk at the department while pursuing a degree in accounting – delighted to find an unrealized ability with numbers – and becoming a supervisor in MDPD's finances department. Balancing books was work enough, but Menendez gave her remaining time and talent to a host of social and charitable organizations throughout the region, helping volunteer organizations manage their finances on a professional level.

I'd met Roberta Menendez a couple of times, a stout and handsome woman with an unfailing smile and sparkling eyes. She had a gift for public speaking and was a flawless representative of the department.

Then, in the early hours of last Thursday, someone had broken into her home in the upper east side and put a knife in her upper abdomen. Robbery was ruled out because nothing seemed missing. The perp simply entered, killed, retreated.

It was a tragedy and I read for two minutes and set the paper aside, knowing the frustration taking place in local law enforcement, news outlets screaming for meat, leads going nowhere as live-wire electricity sizzled down the chain of command: *Get this killer; get him now.*

I hit Miami in mid afternoon, stopping at the downtown Clark Center before heading home to Upper Matecumbe Key. My boss, Roy McDermott, was at his desk rubber-stamping paperwork.

"Hey, Roy. Anything happening on the Menendez case?"

My boss frowned, a rare look; Roy normally resembled a magician who'd just finger-snapped a bouquet from thin air.

"Nada, Carson. MDPD's working double shifts. They're angry."

"No doubt. We in?"

Roy tossed the stamp aside. "I've got Degan and

12

Gershwin working with the MDPD, but everyone figures it's MDPD's baby, one of their own gone down. Even if our people figure it out, we'll dish the cred to the locals. They need the boost."

"You want me on Menendez?" I asked.

"You're on something else," he sighed. "Call Vince Delmara."

Vince was a detective with MDPD, an old-school guy in his early fifties who believed in hunches and shoe leather. My call found him working the streets on the Menendez case and he asked could I meet him briefly at five, which meant Vince needed a Scotch.

We met at a hotel bar in Brickell, Miami's financial district. Vince was dressed as always: dark suit, white shirt, bright tie and a wide-brimmed black felt Dick Tracy-style fedora, which he wore even when the temperature was a hundred in the shade. It kept the Miami sun from his face, Vince regarding sunlight as a cruel trick by the Universe. The bartender saw Vince and began pouring a Glenfiddich. I studied the taps and ordered a Bell's Brown Ale. I started to pull my wallet but Vince waved it off.

"I've run a tab here since the Carter administration. You're covered."

I followed Vince to a booth in a far corner. There was a middling crowd, men and women in professional garb, dark suits prominent, few bodies overweight. The women tended to pretty, the men to smilingly confident. It reminded me of the book *American Psycho* and I wondered who kept an axe at home.

We sat and Vince set the fedora beside him on his briefcase. His hair was black and brushed straight back, which, with his dark eyes and prominent proboscis, gave him the look of a buzzard in a wind tunnel.

"You read the paper day before yesterday?" he asked.

"Out of town."

Vince popped the clasps on his briefcase and handed me a folded *Miami Herald*.

"Page two, metro section."

The table had a candle in a frame of yellow glass. I pulled it close to read five lines about a twenty-three-year-old prostitute named Kylie Sandoval found dead along a lonely stretch of beach south of the city.

"Sad, but not unusual, Vince."

Vince rummaged in his briefcase and passed me a file. "Story's missing a few details, Carson." The file contained photos centering on a tubular black shape on sand studded with beach grass.

"Is that a cocoon?" I said.

"If so, this is the butterfly." Vince passed me a second photo and I saw a woman on an autopsy table. Though her skin was charred, I discerned a caved-in cheekbone and a depression in the left temple.

"The cocoon was a thick wrapping of cloth. It was doused in accelerant and set ablaze. She was alive at the time."

I grimaced. "She looks beat up. What's the autopsy say?"

"Scheduled for tomorrow. The techs spent ten hours unwrapping charred strips of cloth from the corpse."

I studied the photo. Burned alive. I had half my beer left and ordered a double bourbon chaser.

"How'd you make the ID?" I asked.

"One hand was balled into a fist, which protected several fingertips from the fire. Kylie Sandoval had a record of hooking, shoplifting, two possession busts, one for crack, one for heroin."

"What are you looking at, Vince?" Meaning which direction was the investigation headed.

"Nothing right now."

It took a second to sink in. "Every investigative resource is on the Menendez case."

Vince's eyes were hound-dog sad. "I've never seen a shitstorm like this, Carson. The press is shitting on the Chief, the Chief's shitting on the assistant chiefs, the assistant—"

"Been there. And it's all landing on the detectives."

"No one's gonna give a dead hooker a second glance until Menendez gets cleared. Can you help me here?"

"Who'll I work with at MDPD? You got a detective ready?"

When Roy created the agency a few years ago, he wanted to avoid the antipathy between law-enforcement entities often arising when one swept in and took over, the hated FBI effect. To ameliorate some of the potential conflict, the FCLE always tried to partner with the local forces and detectives.

Vince said, "Investigative's not going to spare an investigator for Sandoval right now."

"I'm gonna need a liaison to MDPD, a detective."

Vince sucked the last of his Scotch, rattled ice as his brow furrowed in thought. "I got an idea, Carson. If it works you'll have a face in your office tomorrow. How well do you speak English?"

"Uh, what?"

But Vince was up and moving back out into the Menendez *merde*-storm.

Hoping to put something inside my head besides photos of a young woman's fiery end, I pulled my phone, fingers crossed.

"Is this my personal detective?" said Vivian Morningstar in a pseudo-sultry voice that always quickened my breathing.

"Ready to detect anything on your person," I acknowledged. "I'm in town. Is tonight a good night?"

The lovely Miz M had been my significant other – if that was the parlance – for almost a year, a record on my part. Until eleven months ago Vivian was a top-level pathologist with the Florida Medical Examiner's Department, Southern Division, which basically served the lower third of the state. She'd had an epiphany and decided to "work with the living". Much of the past year had thus been crammed with courses at Miami U's Miller School of Medicine, where she was working on a specialty in Emergency Medicine.

"I'm an intern, which means rented mule. I finished day shift, now I'm on night shift. You're staying at my place tonight?"

Vivian had recently commenced her residency at Miami-Dade General Hospital, where the 65,000-square-foot emergency center treated upwards of 75,000 patients annually, the work often involving thirty-plus-hour stints, catching sleep on a tucked-away gurney. Between the haphazard hours of our jobs, we managed to see one another about twice a week, me generally staying with Viv in the city.

"Got a case I need to hit hard in the early a.m. You don't want details. You off tomorrow night?"

It seemed tomorrow would work out fine and I drove to Viv's home, a lovely two-story in Coral Gables, the walls' white expanses broken by vibrant art and photography. When we'd began dating, I'd figured her home shone with so much life because her work held so much death.

I started to pull the case files again, but their horror seemed discordant in Viv's home, so I mixed a drink and reviewed them beneath a lamp in the back yard, nothing above but the lonely stars, which I figured had seen it all before.

4

Harry Nautilus was half-reclined on his couch and listening to a YouTube upload of a performance by jazz great Billie Holiday and thinking her voice was a trumpet, the words not sung as much blown through that life-ravaged throat, some notes low and growled, others bright as a bell on a crisp winter morning.

Fifteen years ago, give or take, Nautilus had sat in this same room with a half-baked man-child named Carson Ryder when the kid had asked Nautilus why he listened to "all that old music". Nautilus had dosed the kid with Waller, Beiderbecke, Armstrong, Ellington, Holiday, Henderson . . . they started at sundown and met the morning with Miles.

Along with the intro to jazz, Nautilus convinced the kid his degree in Psychology and eerie ability to analyze madmen would be a gift to law enforcement. The next week Carson Ryder signed up at the Police Academy, blowing through it like a firestorm, impressing many, pissing off as many more. He'd put in three years on the street before solving the high-profile Adrian case, advancing to detective and Nautilus's partner. They'd been the Ryder and Nautilus Show for over a decade. But today Carson was in Florida and Harry Nautilus was a retiree.

The show was over.

And tomorrow morning, Harry Nautilus was going to the home of Pastor Richard Owsley to meet the man's wife and try for a gig as a driver. Last week's interview with the Pastor had taken all of fifteen minutes, the man like a thousand-watt bulb in a room that only needs about a hundred, pacing, smiling, gesturing . . . all assurance and zeal and – like Southern preachers everywhere – stretching one-syllable words into two and often using larger words than called for, which Nautilus ascribed to latent insecurities perhaps caused by going to schools like West Doodlemont Bible College rather than Harvard Divinity School.

It had all happened so quickly that Nautilus realized he knew little more about Richard Owsley than the stacks of books he saw at local shops, the man smiling on the cover with bible in hand.

He took another sip of brew, set his computer on his lap, and checked YouTube for the Pastor's name. There were several dozen hits, sermons, it seemed. In his youth Nautilus had been dragged from church to church by a procession of severe but well-meaning aunts, and figured he'd had enough sermonizing for a lifetime. He continued scanning the videos until he found a six-minute piece titled, *Highlights: Richard Owsley on Willy Prince Show*. Prince had a talk show out of Montgomery and was a regional favorite, a smug little fellow in his forties with shaggy, fringe-centric hair, and a slight mouth permanently puckered toward sneer.

Nautilus hit Play and the screen showed two men sitting at a round table in a television studio dressed with a pair of bookshelves and artificial plants. Nautilus figured someone once told Prince that slouching would make him look more like William F. Buckley, so he resembled a boneless puppet dropped into a chair. Prince sat on the left and was speaking.

". . . then to recap, Reverend Owsley, you hold that Jesus wants people to have fine cars, boats, luxury items?"

Pastor Owsley was to the right, a dark-suited figure with narrow shoulders and a touch too much weight at his waistline, slightly pearish. His round and cherubic visage was topped by back-combed black hair. He looked pleasant and not particularly commanding, a small-town insurance salesman whose ready smile is part of the tool kit.

"Jesus wants people to enjoy abundance, Willy," Owsley said in a Southern-inflected tenor and pronouncing the word in three distinct syllables, *a-bun-dance*. "In biblical times, abundance might mean having a donkey, chickens and a warm hearth. Today, it might be a new pickup truck and a house with a white picket fence."

A chorus of handclaps and *Hallelujahs* from the audience. A raised eyebrow from Prince.

"Or a Mercedes-Benz and a mansion in Miami Beach?"

"If that is your yearning and you honor God, God will hand you the keys to the Benz, the keys to the mansion and then, finally and best of all, the keys to His Kingdom. It's in John 10:10: 'There I am come that they might have life, and they might have it more abundantly.'"

The audience again expressed satisfaction with the answer. "Perhaps the abundance comes in the afterlife, Reverend," Prince said. "In Paradise."

Owsley nodded vigorous agreement. "Our prosperity in Heaven is boundless, Willy. We're also supposed to taste of it in this life. Proverbs 15:6 . . . 'In the house of the righteous is much treasure.' Then there's John 1:2 . . . 'Beloved, I wish above all that thou prosper and be in health, even as thy soul prospers.' When your soul prospers, so shall *you*."

"So why did Jesus hang around with poor people, Pastor Owsley? I mean, Jesus wasn't prone to spending his days with the wealthy, right?"

"Of course not, Willy. He treasured the poor."

"But you just said—"

"Jesus Christ loves the *faithful*, Willy. If you have ten billion dollars and believeth not in the Lord, you are as poor as a cockroach. Conversely, if you have nothing and turn yourself over to the Lord, you have wealth beyond measure."

21

"But you're still poor, pocket-wise."

"'Keep therefore the words of this covenant, and do them, that ye may prosper in all that ye do.' That's Deuteronomy 29:9. It's said even more directly in Proverbs 28:20: 'A faithful man shall abound in blessings.' Do you know the Greek translation of the word 'blessings', Willy?"

"Oddly enough, no."

Owsley's pink hands came together in a thunderclap. "*Happiness*! Blessings are happinesses. God wants His faithful children to abound in happinesses. It's a three-step process, Willy. One, surrender your soul to Christ. Two, cast your bread upon the water. Three, watch the bread returneth a thousand-fold."

A chorus of amens and hallelujahs. Prince studied the audience and turned to the preacher with an uplifted eyebrow. "You have a lot of followers here tonight, Reverend. Did you pack the crowd, as they say?"

A split-second pause from Owsley, followed by *who-me?* innocence. "I noted on my website that I was to be a guest. That's all."

"Really? I'd like to go to some video we took earlier in the day outside the studio, if that's OK with you."

"It's your show, Willy," Owsley said. The smile stayed as toothy as a beaver, but Nautilus detected irritation as the screen behind the interview table filled with two large buses emptying to the pavement a block from the studio, an attractive woman with a haystack of blonde hair organizing the passengers into a queue.

22

"All those folks went directly from the buses to the studio. I'll ask again: Did you pack the crowd, Reverend?"

Murmurs of irritation from the audience. Owsley replayed the innocent face. "All I can say, Willy, is that I'm delighted so many faithful Christians chose to honor me with their presence."

Applause. Whistles. Amens.

Prince tented his fingers and frowned in apparent confusion. "Faithful Christians, you say, Reverend Owsley. But what about people of other beliefs? Can they not be equally faithful to the creator of the universe?"

Owsley smiled benignly. "I can only preach the gospel of the Lord Jesus Christ, who I hold to be the creator of all that is and ever will be."

"So other religions are wrong?"

"I judge not, lest I be judged, Willy."

Prince shook his head. "You're a hard man to pin down, Reverend."

"No, Willy, I am not. It's all in my owner's manual."

"Owner's manual?"

Owsley reached to his side and picked up a bible, holding it high with both hands, the thousand-watt grin ramping up another hundred.

The audience went wild.

"Thanks, Mama," Teresa Mailey said, patting her child on his pink forehead as her mother pulled the baby blanket closer around Robert, just seven months old the day before. "It might not be like this much more."

23

Jeri Mailey thumbed graying hair back under the red headscarf and smiled. "Like I care, baby." Her voice was husky, a smoker's voice.

"Me waking you up at four thirty in the morning when I come to pick Bobby up?" Teresa said.

"Hush up that stuff. I go right back to sleep." Jeri paused as her smile shivered and her eyes moistened. "I never thought I'd have days like this, baby."

"Come on, Mama, not again," Teresa said, her voice gentle.

Her mother brushed a tear from the corner of an eye. "I'm sorry, baby. It's like every day has been a gift this past year. Taking care of you and Bobby is a gift from God."

Teresa kissed her mother's cheek. "It'll keep giving, Mama."

Teresa's mother nodded and pulled Bobby tight as she crossed to the door. "See you later, baby. Have a good one."

"Thanks, Mama."

The door closed and Teresa Mailey was alone in the tiny first-floor apartment, the bulk of the rent paid by a charitable organization that helped the fallen regain their feet. She looked out the window and watched her mother put Bobby in the child seat in the rear of her blue Kia Optima and snug him tight. Just before her mother closed the door, Bobby waved goodbye.

OK, only a waggle of his arm, but it looks like he's waving bye-bye to his mommy.

Teresa went to the mirror and straightened her uniform, the fabric flat and wrinkle-free, the uniform immaculate. Satisfied that she was a suitable representative of her employer, she glanced at the clock, 9:32 p.m., and headed to the door. Pausing, Teresa ran back to her bedroom and grabbed her necklace, a tiny gold chain holding a small cross, and put it around her neck.

I'm ready for this again.

Teresa exited to a third-hand Corolla. She had to be at work at ten, and the Publix was twenty minutes distant. She was to do night restock until four a.m. Yesterday her supervisor had spoken of moving Teresa to daytime as a permanent deli worker. Permanent!

"*You've gotten noticed by a lot of people upstairs, Teresa*," the super had said. "*Your attitude, work ethic, ability to shift positions . . . we'd like you as a permanent member of the team.*"

The year had been a gift, Teresa thought as she drove through the warm Miami night. *Of finding out who am I, and that I have worth.*

The traffic was thick with homecoming day workers, but Teresa pulled into the Publix lot with eight minutes to spare, aiming toward the far edge where the employees parked. She grabbed her purse, exited the vehicle, and started for the store when she felt a tingle on the back of her neck, like eyes were watching.

Teresa turned to see a light van parked three slots distant, a hard-worked vehicle judging by the dinged body and dented hood. A man was sitting in the driver's

25

seat, face hidden behind a newspaper, the halogen-lit lot bright enough for reading. He was tanned and ropy and shirtless, a line running across his upper chest, a weird tattoo.

No . . . not a tattoo . . .

A nasty, puckery scar.

The man shifted in his seat and the scar stared at Teresa. Feeling an odd void in the base of her stomach, Teresa turned and hustled toward the supermarket.

5

It was eight a.m., the oblique sun lighting a soft mist that rose from a brief morning rain, giving a ghostly cast to the tree-canopied streets of Spring Hill, Mobile's finest old neighborhood, many of the homes dating back to ante-bellum times. Harry Nautilus pulled to a two-story house set back a hundred feet from the avenue, a square, white, multi-columned Greek Revival monster Nautilus thought as charmless as it was large, redeemed by the landscaping: oaks and sycamores standing in hedge circles further bordered by azaleas and bougainvillea. Lines of dogwoods paced the high fence of the side boundaries.

He blew out a breath and pulled into the long drive. His red 1984 Volvo wagon had recently expired at 377,436 miles and he'd found a 2004 Cross Country model truly owned by the little old lady who only drove it on Sundays, the odometer registering 31,000 miles.

Nautilus parked behind a gleaming red Hummer with smoked windows and was rolling his eyes when he realized it was probably what he'd be driving. He exited the Volvo wearing the suit he'd worn to the interview with Richard Owsley, coal black, the suit he wore to court and funerals. His shirt was blue with a button-down collar and the tie a red-and-blue rep stripe. The whole drab get-up was already beginning to itch.

Nautilus patted his hair, a one-inch natural with a sprinkling of gray, licked an index finger and smoothed his bulldozer-blade mustache, took a deep breath and walked to the front door. The knocker was a cast-iron version of the three crosses of Golgotha – currently unoccupied – hinged to slam the base. Nautilus gingerly lifted a thief's cross and let it drop.

A harsh metallic clank. Nautilus stood back as the door opened to reveal one of the most impressive stacks of hair he'd seen in years, a cascade of blonde-bright ringlets that bounced atop the shoulders of a slender, and apparently confused woman in her early forties. Her make-up was old-school-thick, early Dolly Parton, but her face was model-perfect, with high cheekbones, a pert nose and lips like pink cushions. With her dress, white and embroidered with creamy flowers, she looked part porcelain angel, part country singer from the seventies. Nautilus immediately recognized her from the Willy Prince Show, the woman organizing the bused-in audience.

"Mrs Owsley, I'm Harry Nautilus. You're expecting me, I'm told. Or hope."

The woman stared, as if Nautilus was a unicorn. "Mrs Owsley?" Nautilus said, resisting the impulse to wave his hand before her wide, blue-shadowed eyes. "Did your husband tell you I'd be by today?"

"You're black," she said, just shy of a gasp.

"Since birth. Is something wrong?"

A brief pause and the woman's startled expression flowed effortlessly into a glittering smile, teeth shining like marquee lights. "Goodness, no," she said, reaching to touch Harry's sleeve and tug him over the threshold. "It's just such a surprise. All my other drivers were, well . . . do you folks prefer the term white or Caucasian?"

"It doesn't really matter, ma'am. It's more what you prefer to call yourselves."

She canted her head in thought, followed with a tinkly laugh. "Of course. Come inside, Mr Nautilus, please."

She led Nautilus through the wide entranceway and into an expansive living area, the walls a soft peach, the French Provincial furniture having matching cushions and looking delicate and expensive. The room was vaulted, twenty-feet tall, a pair of ceiling fans whisking high above. One wall held family photos, one the front windows. The third held a cross of dark and rough-hewn beams, a dozen feet tall, eight wide. It had been thickly coated in shellac or varnish and gleamed in the in-streaming sun.

Nautilus said, "You have a beautiful home, Mrs Owsley."

"God gave it to us," she said, looking to Nautilus as if expecting an amen.

He said, "Indeed and fer-sure, ma'am," and found his voice failing. "Might I trouble you for a drink of water? I seem a bit dry."

"Right this way."

The kitchen was straight from *Architectural Digest*: beaten copper sinks, twin refrigerator-freezers, an island with a maple chopping block. The countertops were richly textured marble. Above, an eight-foot rack was hung with cooking implements.

"There's water, of course," Celeste Owsley said. "I also have sweet tea."

"Tea then, please."

A crystal vase of tea was produced from a refrigerator seemingly sized to hold sides of beef. Celeste Owsley poured a glass and handed it to Nautilus. He sipped and studied the vast kitchen.

"You must truly like to cook, ma'am."

The woman frowned at the rack festooned with pots, pans, colanders, whisks. "They all do something, but I've no idea what. Thankfully, our cook likes to cook. You'll meet Felicia, I expect. She's a precious little Mexican girl."

"Girl?" Nautilus asked. "How old is she?"

Ms Owsley canted her head sideways, perplexed. Somehow the huge beehive 'do remained centered. "I never asked," she said, a scarlet talon tapping a plump lower lip. "Forty? Fifty?"

Girl, Nautilus thought, holding back the sigh as Celeste Owsley gestured him toward the wide staircase. "Now let's meet our daughter and see how she is today."

Owsley clicked the high heels across the floor to the foot of the broad staircase and clapped her hands as if summoning a pet poodle. Seconds passed and Nautilus heard a door opening upstairs, looked up to a teenage girl staring down, her brown hair shoulder length and a pouty look on an otherwise sweet face.

"What?"

"Well, come on down."

The girl sighed dramatically and headed down the steps. Nautilus knew she was sixteen – research again – and her name was Rebecca. Owsley's face lit to a zillion watts as she pointed to Nautilus like he was door number three on a game show.

"This is Mr Nautilus, hon. He's our new driver."

The girl scowled. "But he's bl—"

"He's your Papa's choice," Owsley interrupted, "and that means he's the best there can be."

The girl stared at Nautilus. A smile quivered at the edge of her bright lips.

"Fuck," she said.

"Becca!" Owsley snapped.

"Fuck fuck fuck," the girl said, looking pleased. "Fuck fuck fuck fuck fuck fuck fuck fuck . . ."

"Get upstairs! Now!"

The girl slowly climbed the stairs, repeating her mantra until it ended with the slamming of a door. Owsley sighed and turned to Nautilus.

"I'm sorry. It's a stage. I can't wait for it to be over."

The meeting seemed to have reached a conclusion,

Owsley leading Nautilus back to the front door. Her hand was on the knob when she turned, her eyes searching into Nautilus's eyes.

"You have been saved, of course, Mr Nautilus."

The same question had been asked by Reverend Owsley, early in their meeting, as if, answered improperly, the interview would be over. Ten years back he and Carson had been chasing a trio of murderous dope dealers through a dilapidated warehouse, their leader a psychotic named Randy Collins. Nautilus had been following Collins down a rotting flight of stairs when they collapsed, Nautilus tumbling ten feet to concrete, gun spinning from his hand as the maniac spun and lifted his weapon, the nine-millimeter muzzle staring straight into Nautilus's chest as a tattooed finger tightened on the trigger.

Until the front of Collins' face disappeared, Carson firing from forty feet away, a perfect shot in the shadowed warehouse.

"Yes, ma'am," Nautilus replied, just as he'd done with the mister. "I was saved years ago. It was a beautiful day."

Nautilus returned to his vehicle thinking about his interview, the written part and subsequent face-to-face sessions with Owsley. A good third of the questions had – in veiled fashion, mostly – been about his discretion, the ability to handle secrets. He'd answered truthfully, meaning that he didn't disburse private information. There would have been other vetting, he now realized – probably a private-investigation firm – but even his enemies would have said something akin to, "Harry Nautilus doesn't carry tales."

Twenty bills an hour, he told himself as he buckled into his car. *Drive 'em around, stay uninvolved, cash the checks. The gig is worth it, right?*

6

I awoke at eight twenty with the vague recollection of dreams made of flames and punctuated by screams. Breakfast was strong coffee and stale churros and I was at the department an hour later, hungry to track down the maniac who'd killed Kylie Sandoval. Roy was in his office, the muscular Miami skyline looming outside the windows of his twenty-third-floor office, Biscayne Bay visible to the east.

I gave him an *anything happening?* face, meaning Menendez.

He shook his head. "I figure this will be solved by snitches and shoe leather. It'll come. Like Tom Petty said, the waiting is the hardest part." He gave me a curious look. "I take it you haven't been to your office yet."

"No, why?"

He closed his eyes and began whistling "Rule Britannia".

Wondering if my boss had gone around the bend, I headed down the hall to my office, finding the door ajar. I used to share space with Ziggy Gershwin, but Zigs had impressed Roy enough to get his own office and assignments last month, so I was the sole occupant, generally leaving it unlocked.

I pushed the door open quietly, seeing a light-skinned woman of African heritage sitting in the chair opposite my desk, her back to me. She was leafing through a book I had contributed to some years ago, *The Inner Cultures of Sociopaths*, more for academic than general audiences. She wore a taupe uniform and though only a small portion was visible, I recognized the shoulder patch of the Miami-Dade PD.

I cleared my throat and she jumped, the book skidding from her lap to the floor.

"Bloody hell," she said, standing. "You scared the piss out of me."

Her voice sounded closer to London than Miami. I scooped up the book from the floor and set it back on the shelf, then sat, head cocked. My visitor was a petite woman in her mid-to-later twenties, brunette hair tugged back in a ponytail. Full lips framed a small mouth that was now pursed tight. Her eyes were large and brown and watching me as intently as I was watching her. I had the feeling I was being weighed.

"And you would be?" I ventured.

"Holly Belafonte. I'm an officer with the MDPD."

I didn't point out that, as a detective, I'd already deduced it by the uniform, though the accent seemed misplaced. "Did I mis-park my car, Officer Belafonte?" I said, a shot at humor that went wide, judging by the narrowed eyes.

She nodded to the chair. "Can I sit?"

"I suspect you can, since you were sitting when I entered."

The stare again. Humor didn't seem her métier. "Please," I sighed. "Sit. And tell me why you're here."

She sat tentatively, reached into her purse and pulled out an envelope.

"I'm told this will explain things."

I opened the envelope and saw Vince's card clipped to two sheets of paper, the top one in his jagged handwriting.

Hey Buddy – Meet H. Belafonte, your official departmental liaison on the Sandoval case. She's all I could scratch up on short notice and I picked her because she knew the vic personally. I cleared this with the Chief – at least I shoved it under his nose while he was screaming at everyone. The head of Investigative signed off as well, so you're clear to proceed and I'll lend a hand whenever possible. This place has gone nuts.

The second sheet of paper was typed:

This document authorizes Of. H. Belafonte to serve as official contact between the Miami-Dade Police

Department and the Florida Center of Law Enforcement in duties relative to Case 2015/6 –HD 1297-B.

Below that was a hastily scribbled signature, the line tailing off the paper, like the signer was running while signing. Even the top brass at MDPD were in sprint mode due to Menendez.

"You know what this stuff says?" I asked Belafonte. "The notes?"

A prim nod. "We're to work together on the Kylie Sandoval murder."

I stared at the face; handsome but expressionless. "How long have you been with the force, Officer Belafonte?"

A frown. "Long enough."

"I'm talking about measured quantity, as in time."

She stared evenly without speaking.

"Well?"

"You asked, so I'm thinking." Five more mute seconds passed. "One hundred and sixty-seven days. I'm counting days on duty but not counting today yet. Tomorrow will of course make one hundred and—"

I held up a hand to cut her off, barely resisting banging my head on my desk. Instead of working with the typical seasoned investigator, I'd be dragging around a uniformed newbie a half-step above writing traffic citations.

"We're done here," I said, standing.

That put expression on the stone face. "You're bloody dismissing me?" she said, eyes wide. "Just like that?"

"I'm dismissing nothing," I said, giving her a come-hither jerk of my head. "We're adjourning to the coffee shop in the atrium. I need a triple espresso. Or maybe a shot of whiskey."

We reconvened below, where I ordered my coffee, Belafonte a tea, declining to allow me to pay for her tinted water.

"That's not a typical Miami accent," I noted. "At least not in MDPD."

"My childhood was in Bermuda. It's a British territory."

"Oddly enough, I knew that."

"I've met people who think it's one of the fifty states, along with Puerto Rico and Nova Scotia."

I started to laugh, then realized she wasn't making a joke, just transferring data. "I lived in Hamilton," she continued, "the capital, until I was twenty-one, when my father and I moved to Miami."

"Why here?" I said. "Both to the US and Miami?"

"Shouldn't we be discussing the Sandoval case?" she said.

So much for get-acquainted talk. "You knew her, I take it?"

"I work out of South Division and arrested Kylie twice for prostitution. And nearly a third time but, but . . ."

She paused with tea in mid-air and set it back on the table, her eyes serious, as if looking inside her head and not liking the pictures there. Belafonte swallowed hard and turned away. I realized I'd seen a glisten of tear in the expressionless eyes.

"Take your time," I said.

"The third time I arrived as a john propositioned her, an obese businessman who stank of gin and sweat and had greasy hair and vomit on his lapels. When I told the arsehole to bugger off he gave me a big smirk like *Big deal, copper, I'll go find another one*. I cuffed Kylie to a pipe, followed Mr Businesspuke around the corner. I let him get in his car and turn the key and busted him for drunken driving."

"And then took Kylie to the lockup."

"Actually, I took Kylie to an all-night diner and bought her a meal." She paused. "My shift was over, of course."

"I don't care about your timecard, Belafonte. But why the kindness, may I ask?"

She looked out the window a long moment. "The john was a disgusting lump of ugliness, like some hideous disease taken human form. I then realized how these girls . . . don't simply sell their bodies. They have to pretend to like these scumbags. I was new to that world and wanted to understand how they did it time and again, night after night."

"Drugs," I said. "It shows their power."

Belafonte nodded. "At first Kylie played the hardcore working girl, every third word a curse. But subsequently, as I was driving her back to her cheap flat, I saw tears rolling down her cheeks. Kylie broke down like a, like a . . . little girl dressed in hooker clothes. I realized many of them are little girls in hooker clothes. Childhood doesn't end when they go on the street, it gets packed away under layers of numbness. But sometimes it breaks out. And there's nothing before you but a terrified little girl."

It was beginning to seem Belafonte wasn't quite the robot she'd initially appeared. "You befriended her, right?"

A sigh. "I tried to get her into therapy, but the free clinics are booked for months. I brought her home with me, told her to stay until she got herself together."

"How long did it last?"

"Three days. Kylie had had something broken inside her, Detective. I don't know what happened, but someone or something had torn everything from her, every bit of self-worth. Kylie lived with a horrific hurt buried inside her and I pray she didn't die in pain."

I fished the investigative reports from my briefcase and reluctantly handed them over. My day was about to reach its low point.

7

Teresa Mailey opened her eyes. Or had she? The dark with her eyes open was darker than the dark behind her eyelids. Her head ached and she felt her stomach tumble and pushed herself up from what felt like a hard dirt floor, a wave of dizziness too much for her stomach to handle and she vomited between her hands.

What happened?

Pictures began to return to her head: Working until four and walking out to her car. As she departed the lot she noticed the road seemed darker on the right. She stopped and discovered a shattered headlamp, a thoughtless shopper had backed into her car. She'd headed to her mother's trailer court to pick up Bobby, winding down the road from the main highway, darker than usual, like the streetlights had all burned out at once. She'd reached the final turn to find a tree branch in the center of the road and crept to the ragged limb, sighing. Teresa had gotten out, road dust blowing into the beams of her headlamps and dragged it to the side of the road. Until . . . until . . .

Footsteps somewhere in the dark.

"Hello?" she had called in the enveloping darkness. "Is someone there?"

Until hands like steel covered her mouth and tape covered her screams and a cloth bag fell over her head.

And now she was here, wherever *here* was, stinking with a smell of burned meat and motor oil, lightless, as black as death. She could feel flies lighting on her bare arms.

"Please . . . who's there?" Teresa called out, her mouth so dry the words came out as a rasp. "What do you want?"

"*Sinner . . .*" The words a hiss. "*Jezebel . . .*"

The sound of footsteps again. Her head jerked to the sound, but all Teresa saw was black. "I have a baby," she pleaded. "He needs me to take care of him."

The footsteps again. Hands held before her, Teresa walked until stopped by a wall, rough and wooden and she felt her way along its surface, trying to hold her breath and keep her feet from making sounds. *Get out!* her mind screamed. *Find a way out.*

The footsteps again.

"HELP!" Teresa shrieked into the darkness. "SOMEONE HELP ME!"

The whispering voice moved closer, the words becoming a growled sentence. "*For he is the servant of

God, an avenger who carries out God's wrath on the wrongdoer . . ."

Heart pounding, like a hammer, sweat pouring down her covered face, Teresa retreated down the wall until her flailing hands found the shape of a window, but wood where glass should be. A shuttered window? Her fists pounded the wood like a drum.

"SOMEONE PLEASE HELP ME!"

Bam. The wood answered back with a single staccato sound. Had someone heard her?

"I'M IN HERE," Teresa yelled. "HELP ME!"

Bam answered the wood. Then again, *bam.*

An object hammered her side and she grunted with pain. Something skittered across the floor. "HELP!" she screamed again. "PLEASE HELP M—" A punch to her sternum knocked the words from her mouth. Again, she felt the breath of something moving past her head. She dropped to a knee and held her hands against whatever seemed to be hitting her. The footsteps again, the hissing, poisonous voice . . .

"Then the LORD rained upon Sodom, And upon Gomorrah brimstone and fire from the Lord out of heaven . . ."

Something struck Teresa's face and she tumbled backwards in a spray of blood and pain. Her hand went to her nose but it was no longer there, just a flat lump of shrieking pain. When she fought to her knees something hit her in the side of the neck and the blackness turned red, then white, then black again.

8

Belafonte stared into her Earl Grey. I think it's where her eyes needed to rest after studying Kylie Sandoval's morgue photos.

"Who'd do such a thing?" she said.

I pushed my remaining pastries aside. Seeing the shots again had killed my appetite. "Maybe the perp thought burning the body would hide Kylie's ID, or destroy evidence of his involvement. Or it could be darker."

The eyes lifted from the mug. "What does that mean?"

"The burning satisfied a psychological need. There was also damage to the skull and the face. The postmortem will tell the full story."

"When's that?"

I looked at my watch. "Forty-seven minutes. We've got a ringside seat."

She froze, eyes wide. "I've never, uh . . . do I have to be present?"

"I can go it alone, but one of us should be there." I stood and shuffled the photos into my briefcase, clicked it shut. "I'll get in contact later in the day and let you know what we found."

Belafonte and I walked back through to the atrium where she went her way, me mine. I had no ill feelings toward Belafonte for leaving me alone with the post. Harry hadn't cared much for the procedure himself, part of our division of labors: I took the bulk of the autopsies, and Harry handled the majority of courtroom work, testifying in cases we'd worked. It was a perfect division since he resembled a mustached James Earl Jones down to a bass rumble of a voice and, when it came to resembling actors, I'd been more often aligned with Jason Bateman. My courtroom testimony tended to meander into concept and supposition, while Harry's sounded like a pronouncement from Zeus.

And, truth be told, I liked to look into the machinery that was *us*, the bags and tubes and glistening orbs of multicolored meats that formed our engineering. I was fascinated by the intricacy of the systems and at the same time awed that this assemblage of material – not much different from the systems that powered pigs and cattle – had managed to create glorious paintings, send men to the moon, discover subtle mathematics, build towering structures, create majestic symphonies . . . There was something different in the *us*. I had no idea what it was, but suspected we contained more than complex chemical engineering in bipedal configuration.

Those weren't, however, my thoughts as I pulled into the morgue lot, the sun high in a sky of scudding cumulus, the advance ranks of a nearing shower; I was thinking only of a dark cocoon found on a lonely strand of beach, stinking of scorched meat and chemical accelerant and sending some poor beachcomber screaming back to his hotel, pausing only to vomit in the sand.

Dr Ava Davanelle was on duty and I found her preparing in an autopsy suite, pulling the blue gown into place. The body was on the table, a mosaic of red flesh mingled with char, the burning uneven. Ava looked up, saw me, registered surprise.

"I thought I'd see someone from Miami-Dade."

"They're busy."

It took two beats to register. "Menendez," she said.

"The cops are running full-tilt boogie."

"I met Ms Menendez a couple months ago at a city-county function. She seemed both smart and sweet, a lovely person."

"She had a lot of friends," I said, looking down at the corpse. "But this girl had very few, I think."

"But she now has you," Dr Davanelle said quietly, picking up a wicked-looking scalpel. I walked to a chair against the white wall and sat. My history with Ava Davanelle had started a dozen years ago in Mobile, where she had been my girlfriend, a newbie pathologist with lyrical hands and a fierce addiction to alcohol. She was drawn into a case I was working and almost killed. Ava had also met my brother Jeremy back then, when he was incarcerated at the Alabama Institute for Aberrational Behavior and being studied by Dr Evangeline Prowse, who was fascinated by my brother's brilliance.

Time and events travel roads we can never suppose. Jeremy had escaped from the Institute years ago, placed on every *Wanted* listing between Mexico City and Nome, Alaska. Last year a man of Jeremy's height and weight had been pulled from a river in Chicago, the corpse's DNA matching my brother's. He was now dead and long gone from the listings.

Or maybe not.

In reality, my brother – after a lengthy hiding-out period in an isolated cabin in the Kentucky mountains – was now living in a huge house in Key West and picking stocks based on a simple but bizarre equation developed during his years in hiding: The financial market had but two true states, scared child or blustering drunkard, all else just states of transition.

He'd made millions from his insight.

And the DNA sample taken from the corpse in Chicago? It had been supplied by the pathologist performing the autopsy, one Dr Ava Davanelle, who had been my brother's secret girlfriend for years, though both Jeremy and Ava disdained the characterization, saying their relationship was far more complex.

"Interesting," I heard Ava say, looking up as she leaned over a resected section of upper arm, the bicep splayed open as she studied through a magnifying lens. She cued a communications link to the room where the techs worked. Seconds later a ponytailed young woman in a lab jacket whisked through the door and nearly ran to Ava, who handed over bags of labeled tissue.

"Stain and check these for hemorrhage, Branson. I'm also looking for differentiation between intravital and postmortem trauma. Look close."

"You found something?" I said.

"Just a supposition," she said, turning back to her work.

After an hour – Ava slicing, weighing organs and calling for more tests – I went outside to breathe an atmosphere not thick with the smell of death and antiseptic. The rain had passed though, leaving only small patches of cloud in the eastern sky, clear blue above. In the distance the jagged Miami skyline seemed to glisten in the renewed air and I walked the grounds and the nearby streets for an hour, grabbing a coffee from a street vendor and sipping it beneath a tall King palm in a tiny streetside park, the fronds swaying and rattling against one another.

When I returned, Ava was closing the body, the heavy stitches straight from *Frankenstein*. The top of Kylie Sandoval's head lay beside her on the table.

"Well?" I said.

Ava replaced the bowl of skull as she spoke. "I've identified four sites struck by a blunt instrument, two on the head, two on the body. I suspect it was one of these blows that broke her nose, another that shattered the left temple, creating intercranial hemorrhaging. I think I'll find more."

Ava shed the gown and mask and I followed her to her office, utilitarian, shelves of medical and forensics texts and a simple desk and chair. There was a single large painting on one wall behind her desk, a streetscape of Key West in thick swaths of impasto oil, the houses dark and hunkered shapes, the twilight sky dappled with fierce strokes of orange and red, one slender palm bridging earth and sky, as still as a patch of paint can be, yet somehow moving within the frame of the picture.

It was a stunning work and my brother had painted it, claiming his move to Key West had brought out his artistic side. I had never been able to fathom the inside of his head, and his sudden ability to paint further scrambled my understanding.

Ava studied her notes. "I need analysis from other tissue samples before I confirm my suspicions of multiple trauma sites. Should take a few hours, same with the tox screens, and I'll call you with the results. They might be quite interesting."

9

I was crossing the parking lot when my phone rang: Belafonte.

"Can we speak?" she said.

"We are."

"I mean . . . meet somewhere? I really need to talk to you, hopefully today."

"Where are you?"

"Flagami, tracking down information on Kylie."

"Gimme an address. Preferably a bar where I can get a decent beer."

"I'm, uh, in uniform."

"Go home," I told her. "And await further instructions."

I hung up and pressed the fifth number down on my speed dial. Three rings.

"Carson, what's up?" Vince Delmara. He sounded beat.

"What did you do to me, Vince?"

"Belafonte? She's all I could find, Carson. Really. Every detective or soon-to-be detective is beating the streets on Menendez. Did you see any news show last night? All they talked about was lack of progress. We're in crash-and-burn mode here."

I sighed. "OK, Vince. But I gotta problem with Officer B."

"I figured. She's smart like a whip, but I think she was born with a broomstick up her—"

"Not that. She's in uniform."

It took a second for Vince's frazzled mind to grasp. "Shit, of course. I'll get her reclassified as undercover. Anything else?"

"Call and tell her when it's done. I'm not sure she likes the sound of my voice."

Twenty minutes later my phone rang, Belafonte. "Detective Delmara just phoned. He said—"

"I know. Jump into street clothes and let's reconvene near a beer tap."

I drove over and parked outside a decent-looking place in West Buena Vista named the Sea Breeze – something of a stretch, since the bay was about fifteen blocks distant, but perhaps they meant during hurricanes. Belafonte pulled in two minutes later, driving a venerable Crown Victoria, a former cruiser, given that I could see the logo beneath the fading paint job supposed to cover the previous usage. I stepped out as she did, finding she'd transformed from officer to female, the creased brown uni now blue slacks and a white safari shirt buttoned to the top. Both the slacks and shirt had been pressed rigid. Her shoes were pumps with a two-inch heel. She looked like an advertisement for Sears, except Sears models tended to look happy.

I passed by the bar, the woman behind it offering a smile and a "What you folks need? I'll bring it over."

I glanced at the taps and I ordered an Eldorado IPA from the local Wynwood Brewing Co. Belafonte said, "A glass of water, Pellegrino if possible."

The joint was mostly empty and I angled toward a booth in a far corner, sat as Belafonte followed suit. I stared at her and offered my widest smile, receiving only an anxious look.

"There's something I wanted to say, Detective Ryder."

I stuck my fingers in my ears.

"What are you doing?" she said.

"I can't hear you. My fingers are in my ears."

"Have you gone daft?"

"I'm not going to listen until you order a freaking drink, Belafonte. Unless you're a confirmed teetotaler or a recovering alcoholic, we're going to sit here like two standard-issue cops and sip an honest and refreshing beverage while we talk."

"It's not professional to drink during duty," she said.

"You're now plainclothes, Officer Belafonte. It's not professional to get drunk on duty, or otherwise impaired. I expect this case to take us to some pretty low places.

We can't go into a joint where people are banging down whiskey shots and order Pellegrino."

The big eyes challenged me as the waitress arrived with one beer, one fizzy Italian H_2O. "Will that be all?" she asked.

"I've changed my mind," Belafonte said, the eyes holding on me. "Please be so kind as to bring me a Rum Collins, light."

"Atta girl," I said. "Now, didn't you have something to discuss?"

The big eyes dropped, came back up. "I should have gone with you to the procedure, Detective Ryder. I know nothing of autopsies. And never will unless I attend one."

"Stop by the morgue any day and tell Dr Davanelle I sent you. Now, what do you know about Kylie? Did she have a pimp?"

A nod. "It may have been why she needed to get back to the street. Fear of the guy. Or maybe he had the drugs."

"Did she, Kylie, mention a name?"

"Someone named Swizzle. Should we go out and try and find him?"

"We don't go out, not yet. First we ride on the coattails of others."

My call went to Juarez, a detective with Miami Vice. He was dedicated and bright and a favorite of Vince Delmara.

"Swizzle?" Juarez said. "You're probably talking about Shizzle, Shizzle Diamond. Real name's T'Shawn Matthews.

Collects runaways and confused girls from the streets and bus stations. He's good at being what they need, uncle or daddy or friend, then takes a few weeks to feed 'em and fuck 'em and hook 'em on heroin."

"I think there's a rap song there."

"I ain't writing it. Matthews – I ain't using that idiot pimp name – rides his herd hard and moves them around, sometimes as far north as Orlando. But mostly it's Liberty City or the sadder parts of Flagami and so forth. He might run 'em over to the Beach, but he tends to venues with dark alleys and cheap motels, usually watching from a car or the window of a bar, sipping brandy while his sad little troupe services johns."

"Any idea where I can find this particular bag of garbage?" I asked.

I heard a hand cover the phone, a question yelled out. After a minute the hand fell away. "Feinstein says he saw Matthews a couple days back at Black's Lounge, lower Liberty, probably got his crew working there for a while."

I thanked Juarez and pocketed the phone. "Drink up," I told Belafonte. "We're going hunting."

We headed outside and I saw the Crown Vic. "Who gave you that junker? I can see the goddamn cop logo under the paint."

"Motor pool. It's all they had."

"We'll use my wheels," I said. "Jump in."

I drive a green Land Rover Defender with every possible option for safari use: racks, grille and headlamp shields, spare tire bolted to the roof, heavy-duty suspension. It had been confiscated from a dope dealer and though it rode a bit rough, it was, I figured, the only veldt-ready copmobile in the country and if a case ever took me to the top of Kilimanjaro, I was ready.

Night was deepening as we went to the corner where Shizzle Diamond had been spotted. It was not a neighborhood Miami would feature in a tourist ad, unless the tourists were looking for peep shows, strippers and the uglier side of street life, as demonstrated by the wino puking into the gutter as we passed.

"Get close to me," I told Belafonte. "Whisper in my ear and play with my hair."

"*What?*"

"We need to look like a guy who's just picked up a woman. Or maybe a guy and a woman wanting a third hand at cards."

"Cards?" She thought a moment. "Oh."

Reluctantly, she scooted as close as the shifter allowed. Her hand patted my head like I was a Welsh Corgi. "Try for passion," I said.

She moved her head closer and twirled a lock of my hair. "Is this how you behaved with your male partners?"

"When it was necessary."

Which was true. Harry and I had several times gone hand-in-hand into gay bars or situations to hunt for a perp or gather information. In one memorable instance I had donned a dress and wig to play a cross-dresser,

Harry dubbing me "the ugliest woman he'd never been with".

Thus engaged in mock passion, Belafonte and I cruised toward one of the bars supposed to contain the pimp. There were two damsels of the dark on the street, but there were recessed doorways in the buildings and alleys and I figured there might be ladies back there, either waiting or working on a customer.

"There's a bottle under your seat," I told Belafonte. "Grab it."

She reached down and found a half-full pint of bourbon. "You're going to drink?"

"Pop the cap and bring it to your lips. You don't need to open your mouth, but we need to look like we're partying. Hurry. If we're made they'll slide back into the shadows. Or Matthews might pull them off the street."

She screwed the cap off the bottle, appeared to take a hit. She passed the bottle over and I did the same and pulled to the curb beside a small alley. Across the street a woman of Latina extraction – girl, really – in gold lamé shorts, a top little more than a black bra and net hose studied us. I gave her a wink and took another pull from the bottle. She waved with three coy fingers.

"Now what?" Belafonte whispered.

"According to Juarez, these are some of Matthews' girls, and that means he should be in one of these bars."

"Why then are we here?"

I kept my eyes on the hooker as if appraising her, talking to Belafonte with as little lip-motion as possible.

"I don't want to brace him on his turf. I want him out here."

"How's that going to happen?"

"I'm gonna run a play on these folks," I said.

"A play?"

I winked, time to show the kid how the pros did things. "Stay put, watch how it's done. I'll have Shizzle-boy out here in two minutes."

I half climbed, half fell from the Rover, recovered and meandered toward the hooker. "Hey, babuh," I slurred. "My fren' and I are looking for a li'l spice."

A smile below the street-wise eyes; in this area I figured alley stand-ups and front-seat oral was more the norm. "I can party with y'all," she said. "Two hundred an hour."

"Hunh-unh," I said. "I just need you to tell us where we can find a pretty white lady. We're not into spicks."

"You ain't into *what*?"

"But you ain't too shabby for darker meat. Tell you what, I'll give you ten for a hummer . . . as long as my lady can watch."

The eyes turned to slits. "Get the fuck outta here, asshole."

"Don't be mean, chica," I said. "What else you got goin' on?"

"FUCK OFF!"

"I'll make it fifteen. Where you from, little mama? Haiti? Honduras? Fifteen bucks is like, what, a year's pay over there?"

"GET LOST!"

I was betting one of Matthews' other products had run to his hidey-hole to report a problem. I backed the girl against an abandoned storefront.

"Twenny, chica . . . all right? But you gotta do my lady, too."

She tried to slip by to my right, I was in front of her. Darting left did the same. I was a fast drunk. I saw her eyes look past my shoulder and go from scared to relief.

"Yo, muthafucka," said a voice from behind me; Shizzle, no doubt, out of his hidey-hole and protecting the merchandise. I spun. He was tall and in full-length leather topped with a wide-brimmed white hat, furious that I'd pulled him from the comfort of his brandy cavern.

I was about to cool him out with the shield but my eyes burst into flames. A fist caught me in the throat and sent me to the pavement on hands and knees, rolling away when a kick caught me in the gut and knocked out my breath.

"Muthafucka, you gonna be pissing blood for a week."

Gasping for wind, I was too concentrated on warding off the next kick to try for the piece in my waistband. Plus I was near blind.

"Excuse me?" I heard a polite feminine voice say. It was followed by a sound reminiscent of a hammer striking meat and a simultaneous scream. Shizzle Diamond's hatless head slammed the pavement beside mine and kept screaming, rolling on his back and pulling his legs to his chest.

I blinked through tears to see Holly Belafonte

silhouetted against a streetlamp, a collapsible nightstick twirling through her fingers like a drum majorette in a holiday parade. She helped me to my feet. Matthews was still on the concrete, teeth clenched in pain. It seemed the hooker had pulled pepper spray from her purse and blasted my eyes. Belafonte had trotted over armed with the nightstick kept in her purse, and whipped it behind one of Shizzle's legs. It hurt like hell.

I held my shield in Matthew's face, then dragged him by his shirtfront into the alley where I patted him down, tossed the belt knife to Belafonte, and held the pimp against the building.

"You ain't vice," he said.

"FCLE."

Confusion. "A state guy – why?"

I leaned close enough to let him smell my breath. "A pity the fabric burned but not the skin, T'Shawn. You left two perfect finger prints on her body, bud. It'll go easier if you start talking."

His eyes went wide and the pimp persona dissolved into cold-sweat fear. "Body? B-body? WHAT THE FUCK ARE YOU TALKING ABOUT, MAN?"

"You know, bitch."

"NO I DON'T! TELL ME WHAT YOU'RE TALKING ABOUT!"

"You beat Kylie to death and set her on fire."

"I D-DON'T KNOW WHAT THE FUCK YOU'RE TALKING ABOUT, MAN. SHE'S *DEAD*? OH JESUS. OH MY FUCKING GOD . . ."

I didn't see knowledge or evasion: I saw stark terror. Ten years in the detective game, the last five so experienced from the first five that I knew the scumbucket had no idea what I was talking about.

"Tell me about Kylie," I said, the hands loosening on his shirt.

"I-I ain't seen her in four days. I figured she booked."

"I think I believe you," I said. "So right now I need the whole ugly truth, T'Shawn. Anything less, I'll take you downtown and sweat you all night. Your choice."

He'd probably have done a *go-right-ahead* bit if I'd been MDPD, but the FCLE had arrived in his squalid little world, which meant things were serious.

"Anything, man," he said. "But you gotta know, it wasn't me."

I asked questions, he provided answers. Matthews had found Sandoval on the streets seven months back, drunk. He'd brought her to one of his two cribs, babied her. He also traded out the booze for H and put her on the street.

"What'd she do before she got to Miami?" I asked at one point.

"She never talked about that, man. Never. Like she'd shut it off. Bad shit at home, maybe. You wouldn't believe what got done to some of these girls when they lived at home."

In the end Matthews knew almost nothing of Sandoval; little more to him than an ATM, and as long as she kept pumping out money, he was fine with it. I shot a glance at Belafonte. Her eyes were expressionless but her nose looked like a sewage field was nearby.

"Beat it," I said, releasing the pimp. Matthews ducked low past me and went to pick up his hat but Belafonte was standing on it. He gave her a wide berth and retreated down the street as we climbed back into the car to press onward into the unrevealed world of Kylie Sandoval. I took a deep breath and rested my head on the steering wheel. My cheek was sore from the punch and my side ached from the kick.

"Quite the interesting play," Belafonte said, giving me my first-ever sample of what amusement sounded like in her voice. "Your take on Richard III, perhaps?"

"My kingdom for a nightstick," I sighed.

10

I dropped Belafonte off at her car and headed to Viv's. The place was deserted and my heart sank. I gave her a call.

"I'm running a half-hour late . . . be home in twenty minutes. I'll make a food grab on the way in. Miguelito's?"

"Olé."

Viv arrived minutes later with burritos, chips, salsa and guacamole from a favored tacquería. She grinned as she scampered by to warm the chow and I used the time to admire Vivian's slender form bending to put the food in the oven. She wore a simple blue skirt over improbably long legs and a gray blouse. The kicks were dark athletic shoes which looked out of place, but were the requisite wear for long hours of hard hospital floors.

We feasted on burritos – chicken for Viv, goat for me – washed down with Negra Modelo. Our conversation veered briefly into the sadness of Roberta Menendez's loss, then, happier, into a recap of my weekend with Harry and his new prospects.

"Harry's driving someone around?" Viv said. "He's already bored with retirement?"

"Harry felt he could stash some playtime cash. And yes, Harry needs to be doing something or he gets mopey."

"Mopey?"

"That time he got his head bashed in and spent weeks in the hospital? He hated TV so he tried crossword puzzles. Doing them bored him after two days, so he started making them. I remember one had the word 'heimidemi-semiquaver' crossing the word 'subdermatoglyphic'."

"What the hell do those mean?"

"The first has something to do with music, the second concerns fingerprint patterns, and is the longest word where every letter is used just once, the reason Harry wanted to use it. It took him a month to build that damn puzzle but when he was done it made the *New York Times* Sunday version look like it was written by a ten-year-old."

Viv gave me a look. "You miss him, don't you?"

I made a smile happen. "We had some good times. But the world moves on."

Another look, then a change of subject. "Harry thinks he'll like being a chauffeur?" Vivian asked, curling the long legs on to the sofa.

"Driver," I corrected. "We'll just have to wait to find out."

"I guess we will," she said, standing and angling toward the stairs. "But until then, I know something that can't wait much longer." She winked.

I was off the couch like a shot.

Viv left for MD-Gen before six a.m. and I awoke at eight twenty with the vague recollection of a fleeting kiss. Breakfast was leftover frijoles refritos and chips and I was ready to attack the Sandoval case when my phone rang: JEREMY.

"There's a huge commotion down the street, Carson," my brother said before I could speak. "What is it?"

I suppressed a moan: My brother always wanted something.

"A commotion?"

"An ambulance, a quartet of cop cars. A news van. There's a goddamn circus out there. What the hell is going on, Carson?"

"Why should I know that?"

"You're a big-league detective, right? Find out."

"Jeremy, I'm—"

"It's a distraction. I can't concentrate on my work."

I figured Jeremy had been up at daybreak studying the morning's financial indicators from Asia, preparing for the day's buys and sells. I'd seen what a trading floor looked like and assumed part of Jeremy's success in the market came from years in an institution for the criminally insane.

"What do you want me to do?" I said. "Drive out and shoot them?"

"How much do you pay in rent, Carson?" He hung up.

Through a Byzantine set of manipulations, my brother was my landlord and I paid a hundred bucks a month to live in a home that should have cost three grand. I stared at the phone, sighed, and made a call to King Barlow, an investigator with the Key West PD.

"I got a weird call, King. From a friend, sorta, that lives out there. He says there's a commotion down the block. He's kind of a crank, and thought I could assure him it's not an alien invasion or whatever." I gave King the block number and he blew out a breath.

"You'll find out soon enough, Carson. Gonna be on the news any minute, I expect."

"What is it, King?"

"Amos Schrum has come home to die."

A picture immediately came to mind: a man of towering height with his face looking hewn from flint, all angles and hollows. His eyes were squinty small and peered from the cave of his brow, and his curling, snow-white hair flowed back from his high forehead like a foaming wave. Schrum's stentorian voice had once been compared to "a trumpet calling the righteous to battle".

The Reverend Amos Schrum had been a fixture on the religious scene since I was a kid, my mother dragging me to one of his tent revivals thirty-something years back. Schrum would have been in his late forties at the time, and though I recalled not a word of his message, my child's eyes were riveted to the figure on the distant stage: diamond-bright in cones of light that seemed aimed from the heavens. People were *Amen*-ing and *Hallelujah*-ing. Some wept openly. A black woman beside me began babbling nonsense. A white man fell to his hands and knees and started barking like a dog. Throngs rushed the stage to be saved.

If there were more than a few people who conflated Amos Schrum with God Almighty, I could almost understand.

"Schrum's from Key West?" I asked.

"Lived here until he went to bible school. He felt close to the place – family home and all – and kept the house. He's had a caretaker living there, though Schrum hasn't visited in years."

"What's wrong with the guy?"

"Supposedly the old ticker might blow at any second. His people told us Schrum was arriving today around daybreak, and when the news got out we'd need crowd control."

"Schrum's that big a deal?"

"The guy's network broadcasts into over seven million homes a week. He carries a big stick in conservative and evangelistic religious circles."

"So I should tell my br— . . . friend that his neighborhood's gonna be chaotic for a while?"

"There'll be church buses hauling in the faithful to pay respects, prayer vigils, TV vans, that kind of thing. At least until the bucket gets kicked."

"Thanks, King. I'll pass it on."

I channel-surfed news outlets, stopping on a woman

backgrounded by a photograph of Schrum and I upped the volume.

"... *seventy-six-year-old evangelist and creator of the Crown of Glory television empire, is reportedly gravely ill and has moved from his home in Jacksonville, Florida, to the house in Key West where the influential pastor spent his early years ... wife of thirty years died five years ago from ovarian cancer ... no details on his illness are available, though a history of heart problems ... pacemaker implanted in March ..."*

I called Jeremy and told him to get used to crowd scenes.

"It's already started," he moaned. "Four more news vans and two dozen halfwits weeping in the street. One lunatic is dressed in sackcloth and dragging a wooden cross. Maybe I'll saunter over in a devil mask and tap the window. Give Schrum a heart attack so I can get some peace."

"Stay away, Jeremy. Crowds are potentially dangerous."

"You said my visage no longer graced the halls of police departments. I'm a free man."

A year after being identified as dead and removed from *Wanted* listings, I was less fearful of my brother being identified with old photos than of his need to meddle and manipulate. Despite his claimed need for peace, a crowd of emotionally distraught mourners would fascinate my brother.

"Stay inside and let it blow over," I said. "Promise me you'll ignore the commotion."

"Can you believe this," he said – and I knew he'd been looking out his window – "a guy with a bullhorn has started ranting about homosexuals. Interesting."

"Stay inside," I told him. "Promise me."

"Yes, yes, of course . . ." he said, hanging up the phone, suddenly distracted.

11

Frisco Dredd sat naked save for a T-shirt and briefs in the tiny room on the southern edge of Little Havana, watching the traffic crawl down Highway 90 through a dirt-hazed window. The bathroom was a filthy toilet and a dripping sink, the shower a two-by-two recess in the wall, the plastic curtain half hanging on the broken-tile floor.

The rooms rented by the week, mainly to the desperate, downtrodden and addicted. But the hotel-apartment was anonymous, the other dwellers transient and acknowledging Dredd with a fast nod and averted eyes, if at all.

I live amidst the wicked until my tasks are finished . . . Dredd thought. He closed his eyes and recalled a passage from Malachi: "*And ye shall tread down the wicked; for they shall be ashes under the soles of your feet* . . ."

The room came furnished with a beaten couch, a lopsided chair and a wooden table. The bed was in an alcove and Dredd had stripped off the threadbare cover and stained sheets and put them in the garbage, buying a sleeping bag to put atop the mattress and a fresh white sheet to cover his body. He'd also purchased a small refrigerator and a cheap set of weights to keep his body strong.

His body needed to stay fit: It carried precious cargo.

Dredd started to stand, but his knees quivered and he sat heavily. When with the Jezebel last night, the power had flowed through him brighter and purer than the sun and while he worked the holy symphony sang in his head. But after he'd finished, his energy had drained away, leaving him weak as a kitten.

Dredd looked at his briefs and saw the purple stain of dried blood. He'd been so wearied he'd fallen asleep before removing his wire. He winced as he eased the underwear down and over his animal. Dredd fought his way to standing and limped across the room to the kitchen drawer he used as a tool box. He pulled it open: hammer, vise-grips, duct tape and – tucked in back – the spool of .32 gauge copper wire and the snips. He grabbed the snips and returned to the bed, sitting on the edge with his legs spread wide, picking gingerly at the base of his animal, grimacing as he pulled up a knotted loop of thread-thin brass wire, snipping the strand. Teeth clenched against the pain – *nothin' compared to your pain and tribulation, Lord, forgive my weakness* – he slowly unwrapped the biting wire from his animal, fresh blood seeping from cuts inflicted when the women were close and his animal awakened and hungered for them. But the constricting wire stopped that, the fierce pain reminding him of his holy mission.

Gasping, Dredd dropped the crusted wire to the floor. He fell back to the mattress and began to sing in a high and whispery voice.

*"When the Bridegroom cometh will your robes
  be white?
Are you washed in the blood of the Lamb?
Will your soul be ready for the mansions bright,
And be washed in the blood of the Lamb?"*

Dredd stripped off his shirt to let the Lord see that Frisco Dredd had again fought his animal and won.

*"Lay aside the garments that are stained with sin,
And be washed in the blood of the Lamb;
There's a fountain flowing for the soul unclean,
O be washed in the blood of the Lamb . . ."*

After several verses, Dredd gathered his strength, pushed from the bed and went to the bathroom, dropping to his knees beside the sink. The pipes went into a jagged hole in the wall. Dredd snaked his arm through the hole until his fingers withdrew a leather rectangle with a silver cross of duct tape.

Dredd returned to the bed. From the leather holder he withdrew a black notebook. His missions, his holy crusades, were listed within, along with valuable information: times, dates, locations, employers, routes traveled, maps, photos . . . Time to prepare for the next mission. Dredd thumbed open a page, a list of names. Who would be chosen? Who was next?

Dredd held the notebook inches above his bleeding animal, showing it to the gaping wound.

The choice was His to make.

12

Jeremy Ryder's Key West home sat toward the rear of a long, palm-studded lot abloom with bougainvillea and myrtle, the front yard picket-fenced with ficus on both corners. Pastel yellow with white accenting and a deep porch, the house stood two stories tall plus an attic story beneath a high-pitched roof, a rounded tower twelve feet in diameter comprising the southern corner of the home and ending with a third-story projection with cupola. The majestic dwelling had been built in the early 1920s, when ceilings were a proper height, twelve feet. The original owner, Mr Tobias Throckington, had made his fortune during Prohibition, running liquor from Cuba to speakeasies as distant as Galveston.

It was the top story of the tower where Ryder currently stood, his office, a burled-oak desk curved to fit the wall below one of the wide windows. On the desk were the six small displays of his Bloomberg terminal, his link to the financial world. On the other end of the desk was his personal computer, a large-screen iMac. The Bloomberg monitors danced with charts and graphs and streaming numbers, the personal computer was dark.

Pushed to the desk was a Hermann Miller chair, black and expensive and purchased for comfort, as Jeremy Ryder sat in it several hours daily. A richly detailed oaken wardrobe sat across the room, outfitted to hold files and office supplies. Jeremy Ryder hated file cabinets: they reminded him of institutions.

Three windows faced outward, the northernmost angling toward the re-occupied Schrum edifice. The home had always been well-kept, but lifeless for the most part, a crew arriving every second summer week to keep things tidy, diminishing to every three in the cooler months. The only vehicles in regular attendance belonged to either the crew or tourists gawking at the architectural excesses on the broad avenue. They paused before his home, mouths drooping, cameras ticking.

But now the street resembled a parking lot: news vans, cop cars, the gathering crowd. *A catastrophe*, Jeremy Ryder thought.

But an interesting one.

A hundred people now, up from fifty just minutes ago, not including the news types. Some stared mutely at the Schrum house, others knelt and prayed. From nowhere a man had appeared wearing a coarse robe and dragging a wooden cross up and down the street.

Jeremy started to draw his blinds, but stared down the street, unable to pull the cord.

Why are they there? What do they see? What can a dying man give them?

No . . . what do they think *a dying man can give them?*

The sound of an incoming Skype. Jeremy flicked his personal computer into life. The screen filled with the image of Ava Davanelle in a green surgical gown, her shoulder-length hair snow white though she was in her late thirties, her skin fair, her green eyes sparkling with amusement.

"How goes the day, boyo?" Davanelle said. It amused Jeremy Ryder that her hair was as white as that of the glum Schrum supposedly withering away down the street. Ava was calling during her morning break at the South Florida morgue. She was its newest pathologist, hired last year from her post in Chicago.

Jeremy smiled and leaned the wall across from the camera with arms crossed. "I was checking Baltic shipping rates, but got distracted by the Mongol hordes."

Davanelle sipped from a coffee cup. "Strom Thurmond served in the Senate until a hundred years old. His last years he resembled a drooling puppet carried into the chamber by his aides."

"Meaning?"

"Schrum's a tough and driven old buzzard. Driven types don't die easy."

"I can't work," Jeremy said, scowling out the window and noting church buses pulling to the Schrum house. "Maybe I'll saunter over and inspect the carnival."

An arched eyebrow from Davanelle. "That so?"

"Carson advises me to keep distant from the spectacle, Ava," Jeremy said. "What's your advice?"

She smiled. "When it rains, use an umbrella."

Davanelle blew a kiss and the screen went dark. Jeremy changed his khakis and sport shirt for a sky-blue seersucker suit, cream shirt, red-accented tie, slipping bare feet into cordovan loafers, stopping at the entryway closet to select a cream Panama and large sunglasses. He opened the door to a day bright with promise, and walked toward the milling crowd. The police had blocked half the thoroughfare to give people room for their various enterprises, from open-mouth stares to prayer to lugging a wooden cross. There were impromptu singings of hymns, prayers, candles dribbling wax all over the street. Jeremy watched until bored, ten minutes. He yawned and started back to his house, but paused as a stretch limousine with blackout windows passed the cross street at the end of the block. Normally, a stretch limo was not worth a second glance, another celebrity vacationing in the Keys, but this one was pulling an eight-foot trailer.

A limo with a trailer?

Jeremy reversed direction, jogging down the street to

see the vehicle pull into the gated drive of a house two doors down, the house directly behind the home where Reverend Schrum lay. Two men stepped from the vehicle, dark suits, sunglasses, sized like football linemen, one was a buzz-cut redhead, the other had dark hair and Jeremy knew he was seeing bodyguards, security, whatever. Small minds, large muscles, no creative resources.

The day was getting brighter.

Jeremy retreated around the corner and stationed himself midpoint on the block, looking down the back yards. After ten minutes his conjecture was rewarded. The new arrivals at the house whose backyard abutted the Schrum backyard were now crossing between houses.

Why not park in front? Jeremy wondered. *The crowds a problem? Or did they not wish to be seen?*

Jeremy saw the two security types, plus another of the same rugged stature, a third who doubled as a driver, perhaps. With them were two others, one a man in a motorized wheelchair with tall tires – obviously carried in the rental van – and an auburn-haired woman, tall and slender and walking precariously between the yards, the effect of high heels sinking in to sandy ground. At one point she teetered sideways and when the red-haired bodyguard put out his hand to assist, she slapped it away.

Though Jeremy had seen the wheelchair man and auburn-tressed woman for three seconds and from two hundred feet distant, he knew their names and occupations.

13

Eliot Winkler's motorized chair buzzed to the bottom of the steps to the back porch of the Schrum residence. The rear door was opened by Andy Delmont, a gospel singer and one of the Crown of Glory network's most popular celebrities, his five albums in wide distribution. Delmont was in his early thirties, with red-blond hair, emerald-green eyes, freckle-dappled cheeks, and a bright, engaging smile that bordered on childlike. As always, Delmont looked dressed for a performance, white country-and-western-style suit with embroidered lapels and mother-of-pearl buttons, sky-blue shirt with a bolo tie, silver-tipped leather straps through a silver, cruciform fitting.

"Mr Winkler. Ms Winkler," Delmont said, his face eager to please. "So good to see you. We didn't have time to install a ramp, but I'm sure a couple of your men can lift you up to—"

Winkler scowled and pressed a lever on the wheelchair's arm, the customized Viking all-terrain-wheelchair climbing the steps as the seat adjusted to keep Winkler upright. He reached the top and rolled across the threshold, Delmont having to jump back to keep his toes from being run over.

"Where is he?" Winkler demanded as he whirred past. Vanessa Winkler followed, then paused at a full-length hallway mirror to freshen her lipstick and pat her elegant coif.

"The Reverend is upstairs," Delmont said, stepping quickly to catch up. "The doctor is with him." Delmont nodded to a latticed metal door down a short hallway. "There's an elevator, sir."

Winkler rolled to the metal grate, pressing the button and rolling inside before the door was fully open. He craned his head toward his sister.

"You coming, or you gonna primp all day?"

Vanessa Winkler dropped the lipstick into her purse. "You don't have to do this, Eliot. Let's get back in the limo and—"

"Get in the elevator, Nessa."

An audible and dramatic sigh and Vanessa Winkler entered, pressing between her brother and the operation panel. Winkler grinned wetly and nodded toward the rounded feminine derriere at eye level.

"You reckon that's a good ass, Andrew?"

Delmont looked stricken. "Pardon me, Mr Winkler?"

"You think Vanessa's ass is a nice one? Speak up, son."

Delmont colored with embarrassment and forced a smile to his face. "I . . . uh . . . don't believe I should be the judge of—"

"Closing in on fifty," Winkler continued, "and she wears pants tighter than wallpaper. How much it cost to keep that butt so high up, Nessa?"

"I'm not listening, Eliot."

"Nessa could buy her own gym, Andy boy – hell, a hundred of 'em – and keep that machinery tuned up in private, but instead she goes to some sweaty club. Why, you ask. Cuz Nessa loves showing off for the young bucks. Now and then she brings one home and drains him dry."

Vanessa Winkler remained expressionless. "You're reaching new levels of disgusting, Eliot."

A bell bonged and the door slid open. Eliot Winkler rolled out into a hallway, followed by his sister and Delmont. "Where you got him hid?" Winkler said, looking both directions.

"To the left, Mr Winkler. Toward the front."

Winkler passed through a set of wispy curtains, pushing them aside and finding a small room holding a half-dozen mismatched chairs.

"He ain't here."

"That's the visitor's waiting room, sir. Keep going."

A door on the far side was open and Winkler's chair rolled into a large, high-ceilinged room, his sister in his wake. Just inside the room was a desk with a computer monitor and several files. Dr Roland Uttleman, the preacher's private physician, was at the desk. A slender, sixtyish man with thinning salt-and-pepper hair and round silver-framed glasses, he stood and nodded at the incoming trio.

"Hello, folks. How're you, Eliot?"

"What's this set-up?" Winkler said, pointing at the desk. "Checkpoint Charlie?"

"It's my medical station, Eliot," Dr Roland Uttleman said, coming around the desk with outstretched hand. Winkler ignored the gesture, rolling past, the chair's rubber tires hissing over the polished wood flooring.

The room was cavernous enough to echo, nearly as long as the house was wide. One entire wall, door to sitting area, was lost behind flowers, some thrusting from vases, others foam crosses abloom with buds. Inscriptions ran from *Get Well Soon*, to *Our Prayers Are with You* to simply *Love*. Two folding tables had been brought in, pots of bloom atop and below. At the far end a sitting area was in place: couch, low table, a pair of large, soft chairs, a fifty-inch flat-screen television on the wall. The window behind the area was closed with a heavy drape.

Centering the long room was a king-sized mechanical bed flanked by medical monitors, and centering the bed was the long form of Amos Schrum, his robe thick and dark and running from his shoulders to his calves, the white bouffant of hair like a soft snowdrift over a pitted crag of flint.

Winkler rolled to the bed where Schrum appeared to

82

be asleep, though when his eyes blinked open they were strangely bright, and focused immediately on Winkler.

"Hello, Eliot," Schrum rasped, elevating the top third of the bed to sitting position. "How's my old friend?"

Winkler reached out and took Schrum's hand. "I got a lot on my mind, Amos. How you doing?"

"The good Lord granted me another sunrise. I'll take it."

"He does it because He loves you, Amos. You've carried His sword into great battles."

Schrum coughed and Uttleman appeared with iced water. Schrum sipped and cleared his throat. "His . . . full glory will soon be . . . mine to behold, Eliot."

Winkler's chair spun to the others in the room. "How 'bout you people leave us be? Go get coffee, or food, or maybe Nessa will show you her butt. Me and Amos need some alone time."

Delmont almost ran to the elevator. Uttleman looked unhappy, but followed. Instead of departing, Vanessa Winkler strode forty feet to the balcony window and yanked open the drapes. Light poured inside, and with it the low murmur of prayers and hymns from the street below.

Winkler glared at his sister, shook his head, and turned to Schrum. "You've come back from these heart things before, Amos. He needed you here and He touched you with healing."

"That was years ago, Eliot. Perhaps my miracles are all used up."

83

Winkler leaned forward. "I pray that's not true. But you have one miracle yet to grant: My miracle."

Schrum's wide shoulders drooped. "Eliot . . ."

"I've done many great things for you, Amos. All I ask is one great thing for me."

"I think about it all the time, Eliot. It's just, just . . ." Schrum seemed overcome by the effort and his head fell back to the pillow, eyes closed. Breath rattled in his throat and his head drooped to the side.

"Amos!" Winkler screeched, grabbing at Schrum's hand. "AMOS!"

Schrum's eyes batted open. "I'm fine, Eliot. I'm just . . . so tired."

Eliot Winkler's face, a visage that cowed Titans of industry, crumbled into that of a child lost in the dark. His hands tugged at Schrum's robe. "Amos . . . you promised. It was your idea that day when I was in . . . when I realized my soul was in jeopardy. You said, you promised, that you had a way, that there was a way . . ."

"I've been working on it, Eliot. But I . . ."

"You *promised* you'd do it. Please . . ." Eliot Winkler started weeping.

Vanessa Winkler turned from the window to her brother. "Jesus, Eliot. Don't embarrass yourself."

Winkler's head spun to his sister, eyes bright with tears and anger. "I'm trying to save my soul. I'd save yours, too, if it didn't already reside in the Pit."

Vanessa Winkler rolled her eyes. Her brother turned

back to Schrum. "Amos, I need you. I've never needed anyone more."

Schrum's hand found Winkler's. "Finish the project on your own, Eliot. It's nothing to someone with your resources."

"I CAN'T, AMOS! Without your blessed presence, it's unsanctified. You told me that the event is stuck in time, waiting only to be released. Its release has to be engineered by a man of God."

"I can't even stand up, Eliot."

"The project doesn't need you to stand, Amos. You just have to be there to make it real. YOU HAVE TO DO IT, AMOS. IT WILL CHANGE THE WORLD!"

"Oh, for shit sakes," Vanessa Winkler muttered.

Schrum started to lift his head, but it fell back into the pillow. "The *daily* stress of the project . . . it's not something I can manage, Eliot. Not on a *daily* basis . . . All I have is the power of my faith in God."

"He listens to you, Amos!" Winkler beseeched. "Beg Him for strength."

Schrum coughed and his eyes fell closed. Uttleman appeared, his face dark. "You have to leave, Eliot. The stress will kill Amos."

Tears staining his cheeks, Eliot Winkler whirred reluctantly to the elevator. Vanessa followed, high heels ticking the floor like tack hammers. Uttleman saw the pair to the first floor, riding down in silence.

"Andy," Uttleman said to the singer, sitting at the kitchen

table and arranging sheet music, "would you escort our guests across the yard?"

Delmont scurried to catch the Winklers, now exiting the back door. When it closed, Uttleman took the lift upstairs, where Amos Schrum was sitting up in the bed. The doctor frowned at the open drapes, crossed the floor, and pulled them tight.

"He's gone?" Schrum said.

Uttleman went to his desk and tapped keys on the desk monitor to see live video from six cameras. "Heading through the yard."

"Where's Andy?"

"Walking beside the Winklers and chattering like a magpie while they ignore him."

"Think he's coming back today?" Schrum frowned. "Andy?"

Uttleman shrugged. "What's so important about Andy?"

"He sings and prays and doesn't require anything." Schrum narrowed an eye at his physician. "It's a nice change."

"We're alone, Amos. And we need to talk."

Schrum stood and angled toward the sitting area at the front of the room. "Later. I'm gonna go watch some television."

"It's important, Amos."

Schrum grabbed a pint bottle of cough syrup from his bedside table and poured two ounces into a glass as his black leather slippers padded to the sitting area. He sat on a lounger, crossed his legs, tipped back the glass and finished the syrup – cherry vodka actually – in a single swig. Uttleman followed and sat on a wooden chair.

"Eliot won't be mollified, Amos," Uttleman said. "You better get used to him."

Schrum started to respond, but only sighed. A sound of singing drifted from the street below. Schrum stood, crept to the front window and furtively peered around the edge of a drape. "My lord, Roland. There must be three hundred souls out there, all waiting for me to die."

"All hating that you might die, Amos. They love you."

Schrum's face was impassive. He frowned toward Uttleman.

"How did I get to this point, Roland? Hiding in Key West like a schoolboy feigning the flu?"

"You were being kind to an old friend and one of your greatest backers over the years. You offered hope, was that so bad?"

Schrum held up the glass of flavored vodka. "I'd been drinking. I might have even been joking."

"You can still pull it off, Amos. Eliot needs it bad."

Schrum didn't seem to hear, head canted to the choir singing to him from below. He again peered around the drape.

"Come away from the window, Amos," Uttleman said. "They'll see you."

"And?"

"And they may think you're not as ill as reports are suggesting."

Schrum sat back down on the chair. He picked up the remote and turned on the television, Uttleman noting the selector set on a small religious cable channel out of Alabama.

"I'm starting to feel better these last couple of days, Roland. Maybe even able to return to the Jacksonville studios in a couple weeks."

"Before that, uh, blessed event happens, Amos, I'll need to prepare from a . . . a medical standpoint."

Schrum looked tired of the train of conversation and waved Uttleman from the room. "I'm feeling an upturn, so start preparing. If you see Andy outside, tell him I could use a little entertainment. And a ham-and-cheese sandwich."

14

The FCLE comprised two floors in Miami's towering downtown Clark Center. Though it was the hub of municipal government, I suspected the politically attuned and sporadically Machiavellian Roy McDermott was the reason our agency had been allocated such prime airspace. The admin and upper-level investigative and legal types occupied the twenty-third floor, with the one below the province of pool investigators, support, and record-keeping.

When Roy had moved Ziggy Gershwin from the tight back room of my office to his own space, he'd kept the kid on the twenty-third floor, claiming there was no room downstairs, but I knew it was because Roy figured Gershwin was a future star, proving himself in the cases we'd closed.

Gershwin's office was small and windowless and down

a long hall past the legal team. He was at his desk, tipped back in his chair and studying reports. We'd spent a lot of time together and he seemed to have adopted some of my traits, trading in the former skate-punk garb for summer-weight jackets over T-shirts and jeans, and wearing dark running shoes, which beat the hell out of hard soles on the occasions when you had to chase lowlifes down alleys and over fences.

He looked up and grinned. "S'up, Big Ryde?"

"I need a listing of sex offenders in a fifty-mile radius, Zigs, especially those recently released from prison. Got a couple trainees you can use?"

My worst fear was that the perp had settled an old score with Sandoval, but had more scores to settle. We needed to take this monster down fast.

"Uh, no problem."

"You sound hesitant."

"Just thinking who I can put on it. Roy's got me on the Menendez case, kind of on the QT."

"Menendez? Like what?"

"The lady's a saint, right? So no one's looking past that. Roy wanted me to take a tiptoe through her history."

Meaning dig into Menendez deeper than others were doing, but leave a light footprint, if any. All cop agencies have biases toward their own, and it was best outsiders handle such things.

"Understood," I said.

"But no problem with checking the pervs," Gershwin

assured me, picking up his phone. "I'll put Wagner and Brazano on it. They're new, but good."

"Gracias, amigo."

I was thinking about Menendez as I returned to my office. It was the worst type of case: a beloved and talented public figure killed for apparently no reason, knifed down in her prime in her own home, not a shred of evidence to be found. I was pitying every MDPD detective when my cell rang: Belafonte.

"Good morning," I said, trying for jovial to balance out my dark musings on Menendez. "How's my favorite MDPD liaison today?"

"She just heard about a body found in the waterway in Golden Glades," Belafonte said quietly. "She's hearing 'wrapped in a burnt sheet'."

So much for starting the day on a high note. With siren and flashers pushing aside traffic, I raced there in fifteen minutes, a retiree-oriented neighborhood shaded by palms and garnished with tropical foliage. The street was blocked by a white-and-green MDPD patrol car and I continued to a brick home fronted by another cruiser, an ambulance, and mobile units from the Medical Examiner's office and the Forensics team. Anxious residents stood at the curb and beyond them I saw Belafonte beside the canal a hundred feet behind the house, part of a highway of water running from the glades to Biscayne Bay.

The body had been bobbing at the water's edge, but was now ashore, a charred husk shaped like a mummy.

Belafonte was talking to a distraught-looking elderly guy holding a Chihuahua to his breast. I figured he'd found the horror. The scene tech was a friend, Deb Clayton.

"This no place to leave a corpse, Carson," Deb said. "The perp would have to cross the yard, set off a half-dozen yappy dogs. Seems more likely it was dumped upriver."

I looked upstream and saw Dixie Highway bridging the canal, the traffic a line of fast metal. I heard the roar of heavy trucks and motorcycles. Belafonte saw where I was looking.

"Even at night, there's a lot of traffic on Dixie. Better would be Ponce de Leon Boulevard, just past Dixie. Traffic's lighter. But she could have been dumped anywhere above here."

"Wonder what the flow rate is?" I said, studying the waves.

Belafonte bent to the water's edge and found a sodden cigarette butt. She flipped it into the canal and watched it float lazily away.

"The water's moving a quarter-mile an hour, give or take."

"How'd you know that?"

"Bermuda's a dot in the Atlantic. You get to know water. This close to the Bay there'd be a tide effect. Charts might help. I'll make a few calls."

"First we got a date at Missing Persons."

The Missing Persons department at MDPD was overseen by Rod Figueroa. We'd had a rocky start a year ago, but he'd overcome some personal demons in the interim and was now a solid cop. Figueroa was tall and well-built, with long blond hair over an attractive but slightly lopsided face, the result of a jet-skiing accident when he was a teenager. He was also openly gay, another difference from last year.

I laid out our story. All we had on the body was an approximate height since, like Kylie Sandoval, the corpse was charred and covered with burned fabric. Figueroa opened a file and nodded as he flipped through pages.

"We had a woman in first thing this morning, Carson. Said her twenty-five-year-old daughter was supposed to pick up her kid a bit past four in the a.m."

"Four a.m.?"

"The daughter does night stock at a Publix. When the daughter didn't show up, Mama called the store. The night manager said the kid, Teresa Mailey, left on schedule. According to the mother, you could set your watch by the daughter."

The mother lived in Allapattah, on a decent street in a blue-collar community. The house was small and well-kept, with a blue Kia in the flower-bordered drive beside several bags of fertilizer, a coiled hose and a wheelbarrow holding a rake and shovel. The yard was ablaze with blooms and I figured Mother Mailey was something of a gardener.

I knocked and a stout woman with graying hair and anxious eyes appeared at the door carrying a drowsy child. I'm poor at judging ages on kids, but it looked fairly fresh. We displayed IDs.

"The man at the police station . . ." Mailey said, confused. "He said nothing could be done for twenty-four hours."

"Officer Belafonte and I are sort of a special team. We want to get right on these things."

"Thank God. Please come in."

We sat in a small but tidy living room with inexpensive furniture, K-Mart Colonial.

"Has this happened before?" I asked. "Teresa not showing up?"

She swallowed hard. "It was drugs. Teresa was in and out at all hours. Then she ran away three years ago. I-I didn't know it at the time, but the man I lived with, I thought him a fine and honorable man, a hard worker, good Catholic ways, devoted to his m-mother . . ." She broke down.

"He abused Teresa," I said.

"I worked two jobs, happy he could be there to care for Teresa. She ran away, got trapped into selling herself."

I looked at Belafonte: prostitution. We had a link to Kylie Sandoval, small, perhaps circumstantial, but at least a path to walk.

"Then, seven months back, Teresa showed up at the door, pregnant, filthy, sick, lice in her hair. But I made her well. She got her GED and then a job at the Publix last year. They're going to make her full time."

Belafonte stepped up. "When Teresa was on the streets . . . do you know where, Ms Mailey?"

94

"She never speaks of it, though I think she traveled to Orlando."

"How do you know that?"

"We never went up there until four months ago. We got low on gas. Teresa told me to turn off the highway at the next exit, that there was a Marathon station there."

I put it in my notebook: *Teresa – familiarity with Central FL? Orlando region?*

Before we left I asked to borrow one of Teresa's hairbrushes, assuring Ms Mailey it was just a precaution. She handed over a little pink thing with ample hair for a DNA test. We assured Ms Mailey we'd do all we could and started for the door. The kid awakened and his grandmother bobbed him in her arms, cooing and kissing his forehead.

"The child," Belafonte asked quietly. "Bobby. Do you know who the father is?"

"It was a man Teresa spent very little time with. The boy knows nothing of his mother's lost time, will never know. His road will be perfect."

"The boy's not a link to . . . Teresa's difficult past?" I asked, taken with her love for the child.

"Every soul is a fresh soul. Bobby is clean. Please find my baby."

It was a difficult trip to the hastily scheduled postmortem. Either the victim was Teresa Mailey, a terrible thing, or it was another young woman, an equally terrible thing.

95

But we now knew Teresa's situation: a comeback from drugs and prostitution, a child, a loving mother, a future, and both Belafonte and I were hoping someone else was dead, a disconcerting feeling to have.

I told Ava to start the dance without us, and she was in the belly cavity when we arrived, the medical and forensics techs having delicately removed the strips of cloth doused in accelerant and set ablaze.

Ava looked up and saw us. She flicked off the audio recording system so the transcriptionist wouldn't have to wade through chit chat. The eyes went to Belafonte.

"Hello, Holly."

I turned to Belafonte. "You two know each other?"

She cleared her throat. "I, uh, took your advice and . . ."

"Officer Belafonte was here at six thirty this morning," Ava said. "She wanted to see a postmortem."

"Six-freaking-thirty?" I said, looking at my temporary partner.

"I didn't know when business commenced, and didn't want to miss anything."

"How'd it go?"

"To begin with my knees felt weak, the left, especially. But soon the procedure became extremely engaging."

Ava set aside a kidney and turned to me. "I sent you additional forensics reports on the wrapping and accelerant. I take it you haven't seen them yet?"

I shook my head. "Probably in my email."

"It's fascinating reading, Detective Ryder. The

wrapping is strips of wool. The accelerant appears to be a mixture of naphtha and olive oil."

"Wool? Naphtha? Olive oil?" I'd expected strips of bedsheet and gasoline.

"How's that for an odd trinity?" Ava said.

"Does wool burn well?" Belafonte asked.

Ava shook her head. "It's actually a poor choice. Difficult to light and burns slowly. But naphtha burns fast and hot."

"And the olive oil?"

"Olive oil ignites at 435 degrees Centigrade. It would burn, but . . ."

"A can of motor oil would do a much better job," I finished.

"Olive oil. It's a riddle."

Belafonte and I stayed until the end. Though fire had eradicated the fingertips, tissue DNA had been sent to the new "instant" DNA analyzer in Forensics. A forensics tech entered the suite as Ava was stitching the belly shut.

"We have a match from follicles on the brush. It's Teresa Mailey."

"Bloody hell," Belafonte said, walking to the far end of the room.

"There's more," Ava whispered.

"What?"

"The lungs have heat damage, Carson."

Mailey had also been alive when she'd been set ablaze. I saw an image of a Medieval witch burning, a woman tied to a post as flames devoured even her screams, and forced the sight from my mind.

I took a deep breath. "How about trauma sites beneath the char?"

"Looks the same as Sandoval: Randomly distributed injuries inflicted before death."

"Locations?"

Ava held up a page holding anterior and posterior outlines of a body. She'd inscribed X's at sites she found or suspected she'd find trauma. I saw nine marks: Two on the head, three chest or left side, four upper back or right side.

"Note there are as many posterior strikes as anterior."

"Usually when someone beats a woman, it's from the front."

Ava nodded concordance. "Unless she was surrounded by assailants. I've never seen anything quite like this. And I've seen a lot of beatings."

"Got a conjecture, Dr Davanelle?" I said.

She stared between the actual body and the X-marked outlines as her brow furrowed in thought.

"Offhand, Carson, it looks like she ran a gauntlet."

15

A cobalt-blue Towne Car with smoked windows entered the drive of the house behind the Schrum residence The owner was a retired timber baron from Vancouver who occupied the home November through March, leasing it out the remainder of the year. The spacious home was now the province of a half-dozen administrative workers from the Crown of Glory network, those in the public relations department, mainly, and several of the upper-level financial and accounting types essential to a business deriving the bulk of its operating expenses from donations.

The vehicle stopped behind the impromptu operational center for the COG network and a powerfully built driver exited to open the rear door. A man in a smoke-gray suit emerged, slipping on sunglasses against the raw morning sunlight. His name was Hayes Johnson, and though the most fervid viewers of the network would not have recognized Johnson's name, it often crossed the lips of network employees, though rarely louder than a whisper.

Another man emerged from the other side of the vehicle, small and round, his blue suit rumpled, brown eyes squinting against the sudden sunlight. He patted his balding head and sneezed, stopping to dab his nose with a tissue. He frowned as if forgetting something, then reached back into the vehicle to retrieve a slender briefcase.

"Got everything, Cecil?" Johnson called across the roofline. "The numbers?"

The round man nodded, lifted the briefcase, and sneezed again. Hayes Johnson bent to the passenger window to address his driver, Hector Machado, now cleaning his nails with a knife, the five-inch switchblade looking like a penknife in Machado's huge and tattooed hands.

"Get coffee if you want, Hector. I'll be a while."

Hector Machado's eyes scanned up and down the street, taking stock of the neighborhood. "If you're here, Jefé, I'm here."

Johnson nodded and angled toward the back yard leading to the Schrum house, crossing the yards with surprising litheness for a man of his size, the round man trudging several steps behind, the briefcase tucked to his chest.

Hayes Hayworth Johnson was the CEO of COG Enterprises and credited with turning the network into a conservative broadcasting powerhouse. Johnson was fifty-five, an ex-college lineman, and ducked to enter most doors, the only person in the network taller than Amos Schrum. An ordained minister, Johnson had failed at several businesses before creating a line of vitamins and herbal supplements in a tiered distribution system often derided as little more than a pyramid scheme, but heavily promoted in the Bible Belt as a way to create a second income. He'd sold the business after eighteen years for a profit of eleven million dollars.

The round man, Cecil Brattson, was Johnson's half-brother, different mothers producing sons of surprisingly different physiognomy. Brattson was the accountant at Hallelujah Jubilee, a Christian theme park near Lakeland, Florida. Listed as a non-profit "educational" entity, Hallelujah Jubilee had been started by Amos Schrum and was overseen by the Crown of Glory network. Brattson had held the job since Hayes Johnson took the helm of the network.

The door was opened by Roland Uttleman, gesturing the men to the expansive main room, a light and airy space with high ceilings.

"Good to have you here, Hayes. Where you staying?"

"I'll be keeping a suite at the Marriott until this, uh, event is over. Cecil has the latest numbers. He's heading back to the park this afternoon."

Uttleman raised a questioning eyebrow at Cecil Brattson's briefcase. "Good month?" he asked the accountant.

"Donations are up thirty-seven per cent. I attribute it to the Reverend's illness."

Hayes Johnson took the briefcase from his half-sibling. "I'll take it to the Reverend in a bit, Cecil. Could you give Roland and me some time to discuss, uh, health matters?"

Cecil sniffled away, muttering about pollen. When he was out of earshot, Hayes Johnson turned to Uttleman. "You look worried, Roland."

"It's Amos. He's—"

Uttleman broke off as a trio of young staffers at the network, arms piled with work materials, entered from the front door. When the newcomers saw Uttleman and Johnson they stopped in their tracks, eyes wide. "Sorry," one woman whispered, a mortal in the presence of Titans. "We didn't mean to disturb you."

Johnson crossed to the woman, pretty. His hand took hers as the other found the small of her back, his finger tracing a line down her spine.

"Not a problem, young lady," Johnson said. "We were about to pray for Reverend Schrum. Let's bow our heads and lift our words to God."

"We never stand so tall as when we bow to God," the woman said, awed at being allowed into a prayer circle with the man one step below Amos Schrum at the Crown of Glory network.

The prayer over, the staffers continued to the solarium to meet and work. Johnson's eyes following the young woman as she walked away. "A lovely child," he said, turning back to Uttleman. "Is she from the park?"

"I don't know, Hayes," Uttleman said, irritation

creeping into his voice. "It's not big on my mind right now."

"What were you about to say about Amos?"

"He's morose, peeking out the window and muttering to himself."

"He's got himself to blame. Have you tried to talk to him about—"

"Eliot Winkler was here this morning. He's staying in Key West. He's not happy."

Johnson grimaced. "And?"

"Amos told Eliot he couldn't handle the project. He was too old and sick."

"Too fucking hungover, maybe. He'll change his mind, Roland. He'll get tired of hiding after a few days. You wouldn't believe how much money is coming in. That should cheer him up, make him want to—"

"He's adamant about not completing 1025-M, Hayes."

"The damn thing is halfway there. Why kill the project now?"

"The size of it, maybe. The need for secrecy. That and the whole idea is just so . . ." Uttleman threw out his hands. "Maybe Amos figures he finally got in over his head."

"I give it three days. He'll have an epiphany . . . and then a Heaven-sent recovery." Johnson grinned and winked. "Just like before."

Uttleman walked to the window. "Something's different, Hayes. I haven't mentioned it, figuring it'd go away, but it started after the heart attack, the operation, got worse

103

after the promise to Eliot. It's like Amos has become, I don't know . . . reflective."

"The Reverend's getting old, Roland. It's natural to reflect on his life."

"He's only seventy-six, and his mind is sharp as a tack. There's something else at work. It could even be . . ." Uttleman paused, as if fearful of using a taboo term.

"What?"

"Guilt."

Johnson's face darkened and he selected his words like a surgeon choosing the perfect scalpel. "And why do you think such moments of, uh, reflection might make Amos morose, Roland?"

Uttleman answered by peering over the tops of his glasses.

Johnson sighed and shook his head. "He's had these little depressions before, Roland. The mind of a man as, uh, pious as Amos will at times gravitate to . . ." Johnson again struggled for words. "To moments when his feet were in the clay."

"It's worse this time. He's drinking more. When he drinks too much he loses, uh, his perspective."

"What's Amos doing now?"

"Being a pain in the ass. When I left a half-hour ago he had the door closed and locked, no one allowed in but Andy."

Johnson rolled his eyes. "The cowboy man-child. What's he do in there?"

"Sings hymns. Prays. Babbles. Amos finds it soothing."

Johnson thought for a few seconds. "Maybe we can have an event that will make our reflective and, uh, sick old friend feel better about himself."

"What?"

"Give me time to think."

16

The door of the Mailey household opened, Mailey holding the child. Belafonte and I stood motionless on the stoop, side by side, the angels of death. Our faces told the truth before our voices could.

"NO!" Mailey wailed as her knees buckled.

Belafonte grabbed the child as I jumped to Jeri Mailey's side, holding her up and moving her to the couch. As if knowing, the child began crying.

I'd made such terrible visits many times before, but Belafonte had not. She rose to the moment, her composure solid as she offered a comfort I could not, perhaps because she was a woman. We stayed until a neighbor arrived, a kindly and older woman who helped Jeri Mailey to her bed and sat beside her, Bobby in her arms.

Belafonte and I crept softly away. "Is that the worst?"

she said, sitting beside me in the car, meaning the worst aspect of police work.

I blew out a breath, felt my hands shaking. I'd been in gun battles with crazed felons, my hands as steady as an anvil, but relaying the news of death went somewhere deeper.

"The absolute bottom," I said. "I wouldn't fault you if you want to take the rest of the day off."

"I need to find the monster doing this."

Belafonte and I returned to the street, dark above, the stars blotted out by the flashing lights of used-car lots and strip joints and fast-food outlets. The pressing task was to connect the deaths of Kylie Sandoval and Teresa Mailey. Both were prostitutes, both had been killed in Miami. That's all we had, so we needed to dig deep into their pasts. When I told Belafonte we were paying a second visit to Shizzle Diamond, né T'Shawn Matthews, her nose wrinkled, but she said nothing.

We went to his current turf, the bar-filled block near Liberty City. Matthews was in a sky-blue suit and leaning against the nose of his ride, a Jeep Cherokee with spinners and a custom paint-job, a cobalt metalflake that looked three inches deep. Behind him a bar window blazed with neon logos of beer brands. We pulled to the curb and walked up, me in the lead, Belafonte two steps behind, the nose still wrinkled.

"How you doin', T'Shawn?" I said.

He decided to play it cool, staring through the opaque shades. "Yo . . . You peoples owe me for a hat."

Belafonte stepped forward. "Be glad you still have a head to put one on, Mr Matthews. We need to talk more about Kylie."

"I tol' you all I know. She showed up, I gave her a place to stay and put some food in her mouth. That's it."

"We need you to put more effort into your recollections, Mr Matthews. It's very important."

He peered above the shades at Belafonte, then turned the gaze to me. "Where'd you find this one? A high-yellow that talks straight outta that *Down-town Abbey*." He winked in her direction. "You can come over and change my sheets anytime, baby."

Out of nowhere, BAM! Belafonte's got the folding nightstick open and wreaking havoc on the Cherokee's hood. BAM BAM BAM . . . loud as gunshots.

"My fuckin' paint!" Matthews shrieked. He started toward Belafonte with malice-laden eyes, but she spun and whipped the tip of the baton about ten centimeters in front of the wide-open orbs.

He stepped back, hands in the air. "All right. Shee-it. Just stop fuckin' drummin' on my lacquer, right?"

A small crowd started gathering, mostly drunks who'd seen the show from the bars. Belafonte narrowed her eyes and tapped the baton into her palm. "Beat it, arseholes," she said, giving them flint eyes. They turned away like reprimanded children. Matthews patted the hood of his ride, looking about to cry.

"It's like a fuckin' hailstorm hit it."

"It's just one panel," I commiserated, adding, "But you have others."

"What the fuck you want to know?"

"Kylie ever mention knowing a Teresa Mailey?" I asked.

"Yeah. One day I axed her to tell me everybody she ever knew. I think May-lee was like five hundred on the list."

Belafonte said nothing, leaning to run a finger over an unmarked panel on the pimpmobile. Matthews sighed. "No. I ain't never heard the name before. Why?"

I thought a moment and ran to the car. "Where he goin'?" I heard Matthews ask Belafonte.

"Put a cork in it," was her response. I rifled through my briefcase for photographs of Kylie Sandoval, both in her charred wrappings and on the table in the morgue.

"I never showed you what happened to Kylie," I said, handing him the shots. "Take a look."

I saw the eyes widen, the hard, dry swallow. "Muuuuthafuck," he whispered, turning away.

"We have two girls killed the same way. And probably more to come. You get that, T'Shawn? We need your help. Did Kylie have any enemies . . . or mention any weird trade?"

"Naw, man . . ." Matthews said quietly, the attitude gone. "Kylie usually worked the street. If anyone got freaky, she'd yell and I was there to chill the fucker out."

"She talk much about the past?"

The lips pursed as he thought. "Mos' girls open up with me about past shit, like they need to tell. Kylie kept her past tight, like she'd been born the week I found her."

I recalled Jeri Mailey's comment about Teresa seeming to have been in Central Florida at one point in her journey from hookerdom to salvation.

"Did Kylie ever mention being in Central Florida?" I asked.

Matthews frowned. "Where's that?"

"The center of the damned state, T'Shawn: Ocala, Orlando, Lakeland . . . hell, throw in Melbourne and Tampa."

His high brow creased in thought. "Where that Disneyland at?"

"Disney World. It's in Orlando."

"I think she mighta worked there a while."

"How so?"

"One day I was feeling like some fun and told my ladies maybe we should head up to Disney-town and I'd pay for everyone to ride on Mickey Mouse or whatever the fuck you do there. They was all yellin' like 'Thank you, Shizzle, we love you' an' all that – all 'cept Kylie. She was shakin' her head. I said, 'What's wit' you, girl? Doan you wanna see Donald Duck?'" The forehead creased again.

"Keep going," I said.

"I'm fuckin' thinkin' . . . uh, she said something like she'd seen enough theme parks to last a lifetime. I said,

'What? You work up there?' She nodded yes and started laughing . . . real weird laughing, too, like she was choking." He shrugged. "That was about all we ever talked about her past an' shit."

"How was Disney World?" I asked. "You and the, uh, ladies enjoy it?"

He yawned, patted his mouth. "I fell outta the mood. We never went."

It was suddenly half past nine. Neither of us wanted to stop, but neither of us had the energy to keep going. "We got to bag it," I said. "I'm running on one calorie and two neurons."

I put the Rover in gear as Belafonte stared into a street crowded with traffic, bars, cheap food joints, men looking for women, women looking for men . . .

"He's out there," she said softly. "On the prowl."

"I know," I said. "We'll get him tomorrow."

We drove in silence to Belafonte's car and I assigned her the morning task of checking with Disney World to confirm Kylie Sandoval's employment She started to step from the Rover, paused, turned back.

"Today . . . telling someone a loved one is dead. Do you have to do that often?"

"Seventeen times in my career. Today was actually a better one."

She stared, uncomprehending, until she doped it out. "Mailey saw us and knew. You didn't have to speak the words."

111

I nodded. Belafonte slipped quietly from the Rover. I waited until she was safely in her car then headed toward Viv's for another solo night, she back on night shift. Over the months we'd been a couple I'd come to understand that a major component of our relationship was we both dealt with horror, she in the emergency room, me on the streets, and when the stack of misery grew too high to bear alone, we could talk to one another, lay our burdens down, so to speak.

I unburdened alone at Viv's as best I could, which meant setting my briefcase and files in the closet where it couldn't urge me to continue the day, mixing a bourbon and soda, and sitting in her back yard beneath the swaying palms.

My cell phone rang and when I saw it was my brother, I shook my head. "I still can't do anything about the ruckus down your block, so don't ask."

"I'm actually starting to enjoy the show, Carson. Buses of sad-eyed pilgrims basking in the fading aura of a dying saint. It's medieval, Chaucerian. I've even noted a couple of pilgrims that I knew, a surprise."

"Who's that?"

"You've heard of Eliot Winkler? Vanessa Winkler?"

"The former . . . some sort of wealthy magnate?"

"Winkler wrings every cent out of his businesses. Not afraid to fire the deadwood or negotiate down a pension. I'm not big on buy-and-hold, Carson, but I have longer-term positions in several Winkler companies . . . nice dividends, constant steady growth."

"You know him personally?" I asked. "This Winkler?"

"Goodness no. I've seen him on financial shows and in *Forbes* and *Fortune*."

"And the lady?"

"Vanessa, Winkler's younger sister and a major stockholder in the enterprises."

"Why would Winkler visit Schrum, do you think?"

"He's become quite the religious fellow, I've heard. Opens every business meeting with a prayer. Some companies give out hams as Christmas bonuses. Winkler passes out autographed bibles – his signature, not God's."

"And Winkler's in Key West because . . ."

"Schrum's a religious major-domo. I expect Winkler's saddened by the impending demise of the great Holy Man, perhaps come to gnash his teeth and rend his garments. And maybe get in a few bonus points with the Almighty."

"Money and God . . . the themes seem contradictory."

A chuckle. "The Winklers of the world are egomaniacs, Brother, picturing themselves as the anointed servants of God . . . risen above the rabble on a staircase of gold, chosen for mighty tasks. They are rich because they have been Friended by God."

"And the poor?"

"Are philosophical and theological annoyances. I don't give a whit about Winkler's dogma, Carson. I want him to make money because it makes me money."

"You've been out in the crowds, haven't you?"

"My own little pilgrimage. It seems the house behind the Schrum death-watch palace is the province of busy worker bees and the gun-totin' security types. Perhaps they're there to keep Schrum from drowning in flowers. He's quite the bonanza for local florists, trucks arriving every half-hour or so laden with more posies. If Schrum is dying, that is."

"What makes you say that?"

"The reports make mention of Schrum's bedridden status. I'm sending you an email as I speak. It'll be there anon."

I sighed and headed to Viv's office, her desk and computer, lecturing as I went. "Listen, Jeremy, you shouldn't be milling around. Let the old guy teeter off the mortal coil without you." I sat and opened an email to see a grainy photograph of a face peering out through a draped window. I scrolled downward to see a half-dozen other such shots.

"Who's the window-peeper?" I asked.

"The bed-ridden Amos Schrum had a miracle, Carson. He has risen. Not to Heaven, but to his window. I'm four hundred feet away and on eye level, so I can see his pensive face with my trusty Celestron. There's a balcony outside the window, so the teeming rabble below can't easily watch him watching them. He's at the window quite a bit."

"Schrum's watching the people who've come to see him – so what?"

"I did a touch of research on Saint Schrumly of Key West. This guy's spent his whole life basking in adulation,

Carson. Give him a crowd or a camera and he's fulfilled, the center of attention."

"Am I missing a point?"

"Schrum can obviously stand on his own. He's got a balcony to step out on, he's got a crowd ready to cheer and hallelujah. Why is he hiding behind the curtain?"

"Maybe he thinks he's the Wizard of Oz. Or maybe he's too sick to speak."

"Methinks a miracle is about to bloom."

"What are you talking about?"

"Let me take you to the thrilling yesteryears of the Reverend Amos Schrum – seven, to be precise. He died back then, too. Or almost, that is . . . a very close call. Except Schrum was back on his feet in no time and proclaiming he'd been the recipient of a healing miracle. Naturally, this increased his already-high standing among the faithful, always buoyed by divine interventions. More cynical types noted that before his illness Schrum had overextended himself to upsize his network and the creditors were ready to call in the notes."

"Money came pouring in."

"A pasty-faced and tremble-voiced Schrum did on-air entreaties from his bed, urging people to donate to continue his work after his death. Three weeks later Schrum was in fine fettle, having had his miracle . . . or perhaps a pair of them, since the creditors were suddenly paid in full. Water into wine, death into dollars."

17

Roland Uttleman parked at the house behind the Schrum residence and strode through the yards, entering the home. He nodded at Andy Delmont, now sitting in an alcove beside the kitchen and staring out the window. Uttleman forced a smile to his face.

"How's our friend, Andy?"

"I think he's sleeping, Dr Uttleman."

"I'll go and give him a check-up." Uttleman started away.

"Doctor?" Delmont called. Uttleman turned.

"What is it, Andy?"

Delmont looked side to side to make sure they were alone. "You know I've been with the Reverend a long time . . ."

"Amos discovered you when you sang at one of his traveling revivals, correct?"

"My family sang, all seven of us – Mama, Daddy, me, my sister, two brothers and a cousin. We'd been on the church circuit near a dozen years, bringing the songs of the Lord to people needing to hear them. Reverend Schrum was preaching at a big revival up by Hattiesburg, Mississippi. His singers were coming in from Jacksonville, but their bus broke down. We was playing at a church nearby and got called to fill in. We got there to see twenty thousand people in a stadium and we'd never sang to more'n a couple hundred. It was like God had lifted us up and shown us how things could be."

"And that's when it all started for you? Your career?"

"The Reverend, bless his soul, asked me to stay on with his choir. Wasn't long later he made me part of the network. The day I met Reverend Schrum was the greatest day of my life, letting me serve the Lord and His holy messenger here on earth."

"And the rest of your family?"

"They went their own ways."

"How long, Andy . . . since the Reverend plucked you from the crowd?"

"I was eighteen, Doctor, fourteen years ago. I owe everything to Reverend Schrum. He's made my life a blessing."

"You've paid him back by becoming one of the bright lights of the network, Andy. Now I've got to go and check on—"

"I know Reverend Schrum sometimes uses liquor," Delmont said.

Uttleman froze. "What?"

"I don't think anything of it, Doctor. Ain't none of us perfect but God and Jesus. And the bigger a man is in the eyes of God, the bigger the tribulations Satan throws at him. Satan needs to bring him down so he can steal the souls that Reverend Schrum wins."

The kid was as simple as a rock, Uttleman thought, but a true believer. He affected his most sincere look and put a hand on the singer's shoulder. "Shouldn't you be back at the studio in Jacksonville, son? Getting ready for a performance?"

"I'm proud to say the Reverend's asked me to stay here, sir. He says I'm a . . ." Tears began to well in the singer's eyes and his voice wavered. "I'm a . . . comfort in his illness."

And an on-call entertainment system who asks nothing, Uttleman mused, can talk for hours without saying anything, fetches what's needed, and is utterly loyal. Not bad.

"Bless you, Andy. You'll be rewarded in Heaven."

"I'm rewarded every day I'm with the Reverend."

Uttleman patted the singer's shoulder before heading to the elevator. Upstairs, he found Schrum up and peering through the front drapes. "A big truck just pulled up, Roland. They're unloading a portable stage and lighting."

"The network's doing a remote broadcast, Amos. A tribute to you, broadcast to twenty-one million of the faithful."

"Hayes' idea, no doubt. Cash in on my infirmity."

118

Uttleman raised an eyebrow behind the wire glasses. "I can call Hayes and have it cancelled, Amos."

Schrum pretended to not hear, peering round the curtain, a half-full glass of "syrup" in his broad hand. He studied the crowd for several minutes as the verses of "Shall We Gather at the River" drifted up from the street, then pushed back the shock of white hair and turned to Uttleman.

"Maybe I am dying, Roland."

"Please, Amos. We've been through this before. You have a mildly enlarged heart, early congestive failure. It's easily managed and I expect you to be complaining ten years from now."

Schrum leaned unsteadily against the wall and drank. "If I'm not dying, Roland, then maybe I'm decaying. Like a tree rots from the inside out."

"You're feeling sorry for yourself, Amos. There's no reason for it."

Schrum glared, but said nothing. He picked up the glass and the remaining liquid diminished by half. "I'm stuck here," he said, changing course. "Why did I agree to this?"

"Because you told Eliot Winkler you could—"

"Yes, yes . . . I know. I ran from the project like a scared cat, fleeing a promise made in a moment of . . . What the hell is that fancy word for encompassing pride, Roland? I can't remember anything any more."

Uttleman sighed. "Hubris."

Schrum poured the remainder of the liquor down his

throat. He reached to place the glass on the table, missed, the glass falling to the floor.

"Sit down, Amos," the physician said, anger in his voice. "You're getting inebriated. Mistakes can happen."

Schrum's head flashed to the doctor. "What's that verse again, Roland?" Schrum hissed, the famous voice as cold as death, a sound never heard by the faithful. "Something about sins and stones? What's the fucking phrase, Roland? I need to hear it."

Uttleman looked down, his voice diminished to a whisper.

"Let he who is without sin cast the first stone."

Schrum stared with barely veiled condescension. "Exactly, Roland. Maybe it's best we both remember it, right?"

18

Roland Uttleman turned into the parking lot of the Key West Marriott at ten p.m., finding a dark Towne Car parked near the door and pulling into the adjacent spot. The windows on the car were darkened, but Uttleman knew he had been watched from the moment his vehicle had entered the lot.

He exited and knocked on the window of the Towne Car. It rolled down.

"Good evening, Hector."

"Buenos noches, Señor Uttleman."

"How long has Hayes been here?"

Machado looked at his watch, Rolex, a recent gift from Johnson. He held up a hand, thick and powerful fingers spread wide. "Five minutes, sir."

"Hayes tells me you found a new home for your sister, Hector."

Machado froze for a split second, nodded. "It is a good place, Señor Uttleman. The people there are making her comfortable."

Uttleman started to turn away, but paused. "The place she was before, Hector . . . did I not hear of roaches? Rats, even."

Machado's eyes fell to the floor. "It is past, señor. Juanita is safe now."

"It's what we do for family, Hector. Good care is expensive, but keeping our loved ones safe is a duty we are handed by God Almighty."

Uttleman stared into the dark eyes of Machado, waited for the flicker of assent, then turned to the door of the hotel, entering the lobby and looking into the lounge. A hand waved from a booth in a far corner and Uttleman angled that direction, sitting across from Hayes Johnson. A waiter appeared and Uttleman ordered a Scotch. Johnson had half a martini in front of him to accompany the lone candle on the table. Alcohol was not condoned by the Crown of Glory network, but few of the viewership would be among the Marriott's customers and wouldn't have known Uttleman and Johnson from Adam. They looked like a pair of businessmen planning sales strategies over cocktails.

"I was watching the news earlier," Uttleman said. "It's as full of stories about Roberta Menendez as it was last week. Non-stop. Every few minutes they ask for information on one of those anonymous tiplines."

"A sad case," Johnson said. "Tragic."

"I saw Hector outside," Uttleman said, peering over the top of his glasses. "How's he doing these days . . . with the sister problem and all?"

"It's no longer a problem. His sister moved from a rathole nursing home in Homestead to one of the finest facilities in Orlando. She's getting the best care available and Hector's a grateful man."

Uttleman absorbed the information. "Good to hear."

The doctor's drink arrived. Johnson let Uttleman take a long pull before speaking. "How's our old friend doing, Roland? What you wanted to talk about, right?"

Uttleman looked side to side, as if fearful of spies, voice lowered. "He's no longer sneaking drinks, he's pounding them. Christ, even the choir boy's noticed."

A frown. "Any problem there with Delmont, uh . . ."

"He'll never breathe a word. The kid worships Amos."

"Has Amos said anything more about completing 1025-M?"

A snort. "He's currently pretending it doesn't exist."

Johnson leaned forward. "Eliot Winkler called. He's been thinking about what Amos said, about lacking the strength to handle the daily requirements of the project. Eliot says the words gave him a revelation."

"A revelation?" Uttleman shook his head. "Eliot wants an understudy?"

"He thinks another man of God might take over the, uh, assembly of the event."

"I thought Eliot believed only Amos capable of such a thing."

"Eliot's desperate. He now thinks a lesser man of God can assemble the event. When it's ready, Amos steps in and blesses the project. Displays the miracle to God, so to speak."

"Does Eliot have someone in mind to supervise the project? Did that arrive with the revelation?"

"Eliot's thinking about Galen Mobley."

Uttleman stared. "The lunatic from Tennessee? Mobley started off handling snakes, for crying out loud."

"The Reverend can manipulate Eliot to a different choice, Roland. It's what he does. Eliot gets his event and Amos gets to stay in Key West. He steps in for the finale, and it's done."

Uttleman gazed into his drink for a ten-count, nodding as a half-smile came to his thin lips. "Eliot might have actually stumbled on to a rather tidy solution."

Johnson lifted his glass in toast. "All we do is sell it to the Reverend."

19

Bass-throbbing dance music filled the Overtown strip bar, deep notes rattling the bottles on the shelves. Darlene Hammond spun twice more around the pole, bouncing the boobs for the droolers drinking below, several there since the joint opened at eleven a.m. The music raged to a concussive conclusion and Darlene – Delilah Dawn when she was working – unwrapped from the pole, put on her most salacious, lip-tonguing smile, and bent to gather tributes from outstretched hands: ones from the pikers, here and there a fiver and a twenty from Billy the Voice.

"Thanks, Billy," Darlene whispered to the patron, an overweight man in his early forties dressed, as always, in a blue seersucker suit straining at the seams, his multiple chins quivering as he blushed at the glancing whisk of her finger across his cheek. "You're the best."

Darlene straightened, picked up the slinky outfit she'd shed during the act, waved to the patrons and gave a sly wink to Billy the Voice, her only friend in the audience, the rest a bunch of scumbags and scuzzers, their peckers tapping the underside of the bar while they thought filthy things about Darlene and the other girls. Her shift was over and she could head for home, pop an oxy, and wash the stink from her skin.

She was stepping from the stage when a man approached, a yokel in a cheap brown suit and a tie the color of baby shit that was knotted like a length of rope. His hair was combed and parted and shiny with gel. He was drenched in old-timey slop like Aqua-Velva or Old Spice.

"I'm off the clock, hon," she said, trying to keep her nose from wrinkling. "Next act starts in ten minutes. Get a cocktail and get seated."

"I come to give you this," the yokel said, holding out a folded bill. Darlene snapped it from his fingers to find five hundred dollars.

"I don't do that, mister," she said, reluctantly returning the money. "I just dance, see?"

"Oh my gosh no, Miss Hammond. I meant nothing like that."

She looked at the bill and gave her visitor a dubious eye. "Then you must really like my dancing."

"The money's not mine. It's from someone says you used to know her."

"Who?"

"Sissy Carol Sparks."

Darlene froze at the sound of the name, only then realized the yokel had used her true name, Hammond. Customers never learned it; only Billy the Voice knew. She stared at the bumpkin, prickles rising on the back of her neck.

"How do you know about—"

"I met Sissy in church. She told me your name, that you'd be here. She told me a lot of stuff."

"Church? What the—"

"I preach the Word. Don't worry, I ain't about to start spoutin' gospel. But preachin's how I met Sissy."

Darlene gave the man hard eyes. Religious types were bad enough, but preachers were the worst of the lot. "You must be kidding, mister. If Sissy Sparks went near a church it'd get struck by lightning."

"There was a time that might have been true, ma'am. But Miss Sissy found the spirit, praise God."

Darlene stared. Was this strange, monkey-faced man telling the truth? "Jesus . . ." she said. "I mean, I'm . . ." *fucking shocked? Blown-the-shit-away?* Darlene fought to find words that didn't contain swearing. "I'm surprised, mister. But what's all this have to do with me?"

"Sissy wants to see those she's wronged. To unburden her soul."

"Listen, mister, the last person in the world I want to see is Sissy Carol Sparks."

The man nodded. "Then that's all I need to hear. I'm sorry for taking your time, Miss Hammond." He turned for the door. Darlene watched as he shuffled away. For a bible-thumper he seemed decent enough.

"Wait, mister . . ." Darlene called. "She . . . Sissy . . . she's truly changed?"

The man turned. "Far along the road, Miss Hammond. I guess you remember how Miss Sissy used to be, probably the same the last time you heard from her."

Five months back, Sparks bumped into Darlene at a grocery, talking about doing outcalls, escorts. Making fun of Darlene for dancing in clubs and living in the same fleabag walkup while Sissy had moved into an apartment in Wynwood. *Wynwood*.

Bitch.

"Last I saw Sissy she hadn't changed, mister."

"That was her old life. She's even moved into an apartment in the church, small but clean. You're prob'ly thinking when she still lived in . . ." the man snapped his fingers, trying for the answer.

"Wynwood. She was in Wynwood."

"That's right. Over on uh . . ."

"Twenty-ninth Street. The Reef condos."

The man closed his eyes like stashing something in memory. "That's it. Like the coral stuff. Reef."

"Sissy always came out on top, mister. Even when everyone else came out on the bottom."

"Like I said, she's not there no more. She's living behind the church and giving her life to the Lord. She feels the call to make amends. Money don't mean a thing to her no more."

Money?

The yokel started away again. "Hang on," Darlene said. "Amends? Money? What does that mean?"

"Sissy made a lot of money in her . . . other life. Now she thinks it's the Devil's money. She tried to give me ten thousand dollars for my ministry."

"Hah! The Devil let you take it, I hope."

"I let Miss Sissy buy new pews. If the money does good it burns the Devil's hands."

"Sissy's giving away cash? Am I getting that right?"

"To those she thinks she wronged." The odd preacher looked at his watch. "Anyways, that's the story. I'll tell her you said thankee, but no thankee."

"No thanks to *what*?"

"She's making amends to those she wronged. You were one of them. I heard that she was like your boss at—"

"Where's Sissy now?"

"My humble church, just a few miles yonder. She's praying my mission will be successful."

"I think I'd like to see her."

"You don't have to do that, Miss Hammond. Miss Sissy understands many folks can't stand the sight of her."

"No, I mean it, uh . . . what did you say your name was?"

"Dredd. Pastor Dredd."

"Lemme get changed, mister. Sissy's handing out cash . . . what did you call them, *amens*? I think I'd like to see her."

*   *   *

Roland Uttleman entered the Schrum house, nodding at the security guard on the back porch, less to keep overzealous faithful from trying for an impromptu meeting than to keep lower-level workers at the network from finding the great man wandering drunkenly in his underwear.

The house was quiet. Uttleman took the elevator to the third floor. He stepped into the hall and listened. Was Schrum asleep?

No . . . beneath the muffled outside prayers and singing he heard footsteps. Schrum was up and pacing. Uttleman tried the door to Schrum's sanctorum, locked. He rapped it with his knuckles. The door opened, Schrum leaning into the opening, the white hair tipping sideways. The television at the far end of the room was turned to a YouTube offering, Uttleman recognized a face on the screen.

"Willy Prince? Don't tell me you watch that gasbag, Amos."

"I want to be alone, Roland."

"Cut the Garbo. Hayes and I may have found a path out of this mess."

Schrum switched off the television and turned to Uttleman with a *keep-going* eyebrow. Uttleman sat at his desk, fingers tented before him.

"The project continues without you being a part of the daily operation, Amos. Hayes and I think we can get Eliot to accept a, um, site manager. Someone there every day to put his hands on the materials, to . . ."

130

"To speak mumbo-jumbo into the air," Schrum grunted.

Uttleman's hand slammed his desktop. "Dammit, Amos, you built this shitpile. We're trying to shovel it away gracefully. Give us a fucking break, will you?"

"Sorry, Roland. I'll listen."

"A specially selected construction manager handles the daily needs of the project. When the event is ready, you arrive and give your blessing. Twenty minutes and it's over. Eliot will be happy and you can return to the living."

Schrum took a pull from the syrup bottle and wandered to the far end of the room. "I'm assuming Eliot has someone in mind to be this, this . . . manager."

"Eliot's thinking Galen Mobley."

For the first time in weeks, Uttleman saw Schrum laugh. "Not gonna happen, Roland. Mobley's as mad as a hatter."

"Who would you pick, Amos? You know the, uh, spiritual requirements of the project."

Schrum crossed to the tables of flowers and displays, plucking dead blossoms and tossing them to the floor.

"Can we get rid of some of this crap? It's stifling."

"Stay on task, Amos. We need to get this past us."

Schrum continued to pick at the flowers. "How about that guy from Mobile – Owsley?"

"Owlsley who?"

"*Ows*-ley. Richard Owsley." Schrum nodded toward the television. "You should do more market research, Roland."

"Eliot's gonna want a religious leader, not some no-name upstart."

A quiet smile graced Schrum's lips. "Then I'm the one to make Owsley's case. I think when Eliot hears Pastor Owsley's theological leanings, he'll give the fellow a chance."

20

Celeste Owsley's call had come at seven a.m.

"Mr Nautilus, can you come here at nine? There are things to be discussed."

Harry Nautilus drove to the Owsley home figuring he was about to be fired. Three days and two trips . . . one taking Celeste Owsley to a hairdresser to have the bouffant puffed and the claws buffed, then to a mall where the woman had shopped for two hours. The next day he'd driven mother and child to the local Cheesecake Factory and waited for them to emerge an hour later.

Celeste Owsley barely acknowledged Nautilus, yakking on her phone with scarcely a breath between calls. When he'd hauled mother and daughter to the restaurant they stayed in separate worlds, Mama sawing with an emery board, the girl texting.

The Hummer had a first-rate sound system and Nautilus

had stashed several CDs in the glove box, mostly jazz mix-tapes, but also a copy of Gershwin's *Rhapsody in Blue*, which Nautilus considered the quintessential portrait of America, the urban side anyway, the pioneer spirit residing in Copeland's *Rodeo*. Glancing into the rear-view, Nautilus had switched on *Rhapsody*, the swirling, sinuous clarinet opening filling the car.

"What's that stuff?" the girl had yelled, looking miffed at being jolted from her phone.

"A famous piece of music by a man named George Gershwin. It's called *Rhapsody in Blue*."

"It's weird," the girl demanded. "Turn it off."

"You should try it out. It's very alive. It's some of the most alive music I know."

"That's stupid. Music's not alive."

"We'll compromise," Nautilus said. "I'll turn it down."

The girl huffed and crossed her arms and so they continued for ten minutes, Celeste Owsley shooting cryptic – angry? – looks at the back of Nautilus's head. When the Owsleys departed, Nautilus turned off the music and got in his Volvo. He was reversing when he saw the girl approaching the car. "Yes, Rebecca?" he'd asked, rolling down the window.

"That stuff?" she asked, pretending to stifle a yawn. "That music. What was it called again?"

He'd relayed title and composer and she'd turned and walked away, tapping at her cell phone.

Fourth day in the job and fired, Nautilus thought, pulling into both the present and the Owsley home's driveway. Carson would get a kick out of that. But when the door opened, it wasn't an angry Celeste Owsley on the threshold, it was an anxious one.

"Richard had to fly to Key West on business. He might be working in Central Florida for a while. He needs me, I mean us, there. What I need . . . if you can, is to come along and continue your services. For Richard, too. He'll be needing a driver. It might be for several weeks."

She tried a smile, but it wavered. *Not fear*, Nautilus noted, thirty years of reading faces in play, *it's something else. Anxiety, yes, and . . . excitement?*

"Where in Florida, may I ask."

"In Osceola County. You'll stay in the finest available lodging, Mr Nautilus."

Nautilus liked his own bed. His refrigerator. His music. Plus there was a brown ale fermenting in his closet.

"To be honest, Miz Owsley, it's not really my kind of—"

"Richard said you'll be considered to be working ten hours a day, Mr Nautilus."

Nautilus paused in mid-refusal, and drove home to Art Blakey's "A Night in Tunisia", the wild drumming paralleling his heart: two hundred smackers a day! There was only one catch to Owsley's request: Nautilus had to be ready to leave in ninety minutes. But he didn't have to drive, at least.

A private plane was flying them to Florida.

21

"Get this fucking thing off my head!" Darlene Hammond screamed.

Frisco Dredd watched the woman yank at the black hood cinched beneath her chin. She'd been awake for ten minutes, coming out from under the chloroform after being semi-conscious through the night.

When she'd climbed into the van she'd been all dazzle eyes and non-stop questions like "Where's Sissy?" and "How much money is she giving out?" and Dredd knew she had taken some filthy drug in her dressing room.

Dredd knew drugs. Satan had fed them to him for years.

When he'd pulled behind a strip mall she'd gotten jittery, "*Sissy Carol Sparks is really giving away money?*" turning to "*LET ME OUT!*"

She'd escaped, opening the door and jumping to the

pavement, but he grabbed her and put the wet rag over her face and held her until she was just a limp shape in his arms. The heat had come over him – searing and vile, ancient snakes escaping from a locked basket – and he'd almost pulled into the woods to lose himself in her flesh, but the wires around his animal tightened and the lust turned to pain, letting him take her to the place of atonement.

"Are you there, you hillbilly bastard?" Darlene yelled, head snapping one way, then the other. She stumbled into one of the support posts in the old warehouse, then spun and ran into the wall. Like Teresa, she patted her hands along the bricks until coming to a boarded-over window.

"HELP!" Hammond screamed, fist pounding the plywood. "HELP ME!"

Frisco Dredd stared from two dozen feet distant, just inside the tight cone of yellowed light from a single bulb strung from a crossbeam in the old dirt-floored barn, its two windows freshly boarded with plywood, the rickety door loose on rusted hinges. The barn, a relic of a farm fallow for decades, was isolated in an empty field, far from prying eyes and listening ears. The nearest dwelling was three hundred feet away and posed no threat.

"YOU FILTHY FUCK!" Hammond screamed. "LET ME GO!"

Dredd held a bulging canvas sack in his arms. It clicked as he lowered it to the concrete floor. Dredd stared at the woman, the pointy, bouncing breasts, the long legs that had clutched legions of innocent men in their grip, draining their fluids and stealing their souls. The snakes began to writhe through his loins, his animal starting to awaken, to swell against the wires.

"Jezebel," he whispered, the pain rising. "Whore."

Hammond spun. "I HEAR YOU! TALK TO ME, YOU PERVERTED BASTARD."

Frisco Dredd fell to his knees and prayed, feeling his animal dwindle, its pain lost beneath an energy greater than any earthly power. It quivered through his body and dropped his jaw in awe. Jesus was taking his place inside Dredd. Spittle frothed down Dredd's chin and he fought to keep his eyes from rolling back in his head.

"*Then the LORD rained upon Sodom,*" he whispered, tearing open his shirt. "*And upon Gomorrah brimstone and fire from the Lord out of heaven . . .*"

Dredd stood unsteadily, opened the sack and reached inside. "*For he is the servant of God, an avenger who carries out God's wrath on the wrongdoer . . .*" His hand returned clutching a smooth stone the size of a baseball. "*The God of peace will soon crush Satan under your feet,*" he said. "*The grace of our Lord Jesus Christ be with you.*"

"WHAT THE HELL ARE YOU BABBLING ABOUT?"

Dredd threw the stone. It whizzed over Darlene's shoulder and hit the wall. *BAM.* "*And the great dragon was thrown down, that ancient serpent, who is called the devil and Satan, the deceiver of the whole world – he was thrown down to the earth, and his angels were thrown down with him . . .*" Dredd plucked another stone from the bag and put his whole body into the throw.

The rock slammed a shoulder blade. Hammond screamed and twisted away, one hand grabbing at her broken bone, the other trying furiously to peel the bag from her head. Dredd reached down, came up with a stone in each hand. "*If there be found among you one that hath gone and served other gods, and worshipped them . . . Then shalt thou stone them with stones till they die . . .*" The first stone slammed the woman's side and she screamed wildly, waving her hands against blows she couldn't hope to fend. The second stone hit her upper back, knocking her into the wall. She spun, crouched, screaming NO NO NO as Dredd grabbed two more rocks. "*For he is the servant of God,*" Dredd hissed. "*An avenger who carries out God's wrath on the wrongdoer . . .*"

The first stone struck Hammond in the mouth and knocked her backwards into the wall and she fell to hands and knees, spitting blood and teeth into the bag covering her head. The second struck behind an ear and she collapsed to the floor, her body twitching as her brain began to misfire.

Frisco Dredd kept reaching into the bag.

22

The plane that came for Nautilus and the Owsleys was a Beech King 350 turboprop with a haloed golden crown on the fuselage encircled by the words *Crown of Glory*. It seemed a typical business-style plane save for bibles in the seat-back pouches. Nautilus hoped it wasn't a comment on the pilot's skills.

"You said we're going to Lakeland, Mrs Owsley," Nautilus asked, strapping in. Lakeland was in Central Florida.

"That's where the airport is," she said, holding a pocket mirror and picking at her hair. "We're staying fifteen minutes away, by Hallelujah Jubilee, the Christian park. There's an ark and everything."

Nautilus had driven past Hallelujah Jubilee a couple times, hard to miss with the huge cross at the entrance. "I've always wanted to see the place," he lied, then figured it might be interesting. Nautilus turned in his seat, Rebecca hunkered down in the last row, chewing gum and tapping at her phone. "How about you, Rebecca? You going to check out the park?"

The kid cracked her bubblegum and went back to ticking on the phone. Seconds after the plane had set down, Nautilus saw Richard Owsley crossing the tarmac, hand waving, white teeth flashing like landing lights. He directed them toward a waiting limo, workers transferring luggage. Nautilus watched Owsley close the door on the limousine, then walk his way, pulling a set of keys from his pocket.

"A black Hummer's in the front row of the lot. My family and I have a suite at the Radisson. The people at Hallelujah Jubilee secured you lodging at their Jacob's Ladder motel, the most comfortable of their choices."

"I'm sure it will be fine," Nautilus said, thinking of living from a suitcase and again repeating his mantra: *two hundred dollars a day*.

Nautilus found the motel a half-mile short of the looming cross designating the Hallelujah Jubilee entrance, two hundred feet of burnished steel glowing in the day's hard sun. His lodging resembled most semi-upscale motels, brick and glass surrounded by an asphalt parking lot. Only instead of Holiday Inn or Marriott, the sign proclaimed Jacob's Ladder. He recalled the original ladder as a dream the biblical patriarch Jacob had of a stairway to heaven. This Jacob's Ladder went up four stories. Nautilus shook his head at dwindled expectations and went to check in.

"We've been expecting you, Mr Nautilus," the teen male clerk said. Nautilus turned to see his luggage whisked away by a young bellhop dressed like it was Vegas in the 1950s.

"There's a message for you, sir," the clerk said, handing over a folded note.

Nautilus followed his suitcases upstairs. The room was suite-style, a small living room and TV viewing area, a short hall holding closet and refrigerator on one side, bathroom on the other, with the bedroom area in the rear. He was pleased to see a sliding door that led out to a balcony. When the bellhop had departed, Nautilus opened the note.

Please call me was the message. "Tawnya" was the sender. Nautilus dialed, heard a voice that split the difference between chirpy and sultry. "I'm Tawnya, Mr Nautilus, with Hallelujah Jubilee. I'm making sure everyone in Pastor Owsley's party has a wonderful time. I wanted you to know you can tour the park anytime and I'll be your personal guide. Everyone should see Hallelujah Jubilee."

Nautilus thought a moment. This might be his sole chance to see what lay in the shadow of the huge cross.

"Now a good time?" Nautilus asked.

"It's always a perfect time at Hallelujah Jubilee," Tawnya gushed.

The entrance to the park was a four-minute drive. Instructed to park in the VIP lot beside the office, he passed the rank-and-file lot, acres of shining vehicles. Next was the bus lot, at least two dozen of them, some emblazoned with the names of churches from as far afield as Scranton, Pennsylvania, and Oshkosh, Wisconsin.

Nautilus pulled into a VIP slot and had one foot from the vehicle when he heard his name and looked up to see a twentyish woman in a blue skirt and white blouse striding his way and waving. She was slender and shapely, full breasted, long legged. Though the day was already warm, the young woman wore full-length sleeves, buttoned at the cuffs.

"Tawnya?" he guessed.

"I'm so pleased you could visit, Mr Nautilus," she purred, the voice husky. Her bright smile dazzled, her coiled blonde curls bounced on her shoulders.

"Last name?"

"We go by first names, sir. Are you with Reverend Owsley's ministry?"

"I suppose so," Nautilus said, following the woman through the entrance, a wide opening in a rock wall meant to resemble biblical-era construction. There were a half-dozen ticket booths along the corridor; Nautilus noted that an adult single-day pass was forty-seven bucks. Youths and children got in for twenty-five. But if you were lucky enough to be under age four, you could take it all in for free.

Tawnya took Nautilus to the side as visitors streamed

past, taking a photo with her phone and sending it somewhere.

"I'll be right back, Mr Nautilus. Three minutes."

Tawnya entered a door and was back in two fifty-eight to hand Nautilus a clip-on square of laminated paper with his photo.

"What's this?"

"A special pass to the park, Mr Nautilus. It's good for your entire stay."

Nautilus stared at the laminated card. "What's the big *J* mean?"

"You've been designated a Joshua-level visitor, the highest. Everyone with Pastor Owsley is Joshua level. Everything is free, so you can take your meals here, enjoy the sights, anything." Tawnya's smile seemed to reach an even greater height of buoyancy as she bounced the golden curls. "Ready for the tour, Mr Nautilus?"

Nautilus turned to see a bearded young man in a rough-woven gray robe holding a shepherd's crook as a crowd of visitors took snapshots. This was getting weird.

"Let's hop and bop, Tawnya."

The pair climbed into a golf cart with a Hallelujah Jubilee logo, Tawnya moving expertly through milling visitors strung with cameras – "*Excuse me, coming through . . . bless you!*" – passing through another clay-resembling wall into a large opening surrounded by mangers fronted with counters and signs touting food and drink in pseudo-Hebraic lettering.

"The food court, Mr Nautilus."

Nautilus deciphered the goofy typeface. "Pizza, burgers, pasta, oriental . . . you've got the bases covered."

"These are fast-food choices. Over there are two sit-down restaurants where you can have the full dining experience. One seats two hundred guests at a time, the other seats over four hundred. Plus there are five coffee and snack shops throughout the park."

"How many guests visit annually?"

Tawnya didn't seem to hear and buzzed Nautilus through a miniature Holy Land, the streets cobbled, the walls of stone and clay. Throngs of awed visitors clicked cameras and phones as folks knelt to pray. There were dozens of actors in period costume: a young man riding a burro, the Magi, a Joseph and pregnant Mary, a muscled youth Nautilus took to be Samson, the hair phase. The actors were a big draw for photo ops, probably not a bad gig if you could deal with people hanging off you all day long.

They passed a vast bowl half sunk in the ground, above it a rubberized fabric stretched tight by ship-weight cables. At the far end was a broad stage and lighting system.

"An amphitheater," Nautilus said.

"It seats twelve hundred guests. We have three plays daily, ending with the Passion nightly at seven. Tickets sell out in advance, but I can get you comps."

"Is there normally a charge?"

145

"Twelve-fifty for adults. But that's for the Passion. The other plays are five dollars."

Tawnya reached for the steering wheel and Nautilus shot a glance toward her long-sleeved arms, a theory forming in his mind. The streets entwined and led different directions, and then they were past and into a grove of compact and silvery leafed trees.

"Olive trees?" Nautilus said.

A hair-bouncing nod. "Olive trees grow particularly well in the Florida climate. At the peak of ripeness the fruit is pressed into oil. It's available for sale and most people find it perfect for anointing. It's very blessed since it comes from the heart of Hallelujah Jubilee."

As he had several times before, Nautilus had the impression of hearing words read from a script. The cart continued for several hundred feet, stopping before an artificially constructed hillside, a mound rising fifty feet above the flat terrain where a massive wooden boat was nestled into the ground, over two hundred feet of steep wooden hull with a single-story structure on the deck high above. Nautilus saw a door in the side of the hull and a beaten path leading from the door into the fenced pasture beyond, the grass as green as a golf course in spring. A throng of visitors ringed the attraction, gawking and taking photos.

"The Ark," Tawnya said needlessly. "There's a daily parade of animals from inside. It's like being there when it really happened. People get so overcome with the Spirit that they faint."

Nautilus looked out into the pasture and blinked in disbelief. "Uh, there's an elephant in the field."

"That's Ezekiel. We have three elephants. Look past the trees over there . . . that's one of the donkeys, I can't tell who. Everyone loves it when the animals come two-by-two from the Ark. Twenty-one species, including elephants, camels, donkeys, zebras, horses, dogs and cats. The parade is the first attraction of the morning, at nine, the costumed handlers bringing the flock from the Ark to the ground of Ararat."

Nautilus pictured being shut inside the ark with a horde of stinking, braying, spitting beasts and figured he knew why it was the first attraction of the day. He looked a half-mile into the distance, surprised to see a tall and slender building, five stories at least, looking like a mine tipple from eastern Kentucky or West Virginia. It was as tall as the cross.

"That strange skinny building . . . is it one of yours?"

"It's on the property, but it's not part of the park experience yet. The administrators are always developing new attractions and I know it's going to be something really exciting one day."

If the distant building was on the property, Nautilus realized, the park had to be over a mile in each direction.

"Who owns the park, Tawnya?"

"Reverend Schrum started it to give families a place to visit where their values were respected. It's a non-profit organization, an educational institution. Any fees are for the upkeep, which is ongoing and always a challenge, given the amount of attractions."

Rote recitation again. Tawnya continued her packaged soliloquy as they passed various replicated sites: ". . . *a representation of the Wailing Wall . . . the Church of the Annunciation . . . the Mount of Temptation . . . the Garden of Eden . . .*"

She returned Nautilus to the entrance and handed him her business card. "Anything you need, Mr Nautilus, call me. I'm here to make your stay as perfect as it can be."

His fingers seemed to bobble the card and it flapped to the ground. The lithe young woman reached to the concrete, pulling her sleeve two inches higher. Nautilus smiled to himself, his suspicions confirmed, the girl's wrist encircled by a tattoo of barbed-wire. It explained long sleeves on a hot day: Tattoos were not an image the park endorsed.

And maybe the lovely young Tawnya had a sportier past than the *aw-shucks-gee* act suggested.

Tawnya waved and zipped away in the cart. Head reeling with odd images, Nautilus headed to the parking lot, passing by the gift shop at the exit. In the front window were small tear-shaped bottles, beside them a sign: *Hallelujah Jubilee Anointment Oil, from olives grown in America's Holiest Site!*

You could buy an ounce of the pale yellow fluid for $39.99. Though on the bright side, Nautilus thought, a park-logoed cap was only $19.99. He walked outside as a trio of buses were unloading, happy pilgrims exiting and streaming through the gates, wallets pulled, bills waving, credit cards shining in the sun.

Hallelujah, indeed.

23

Judge Hubert Hawkins turned his jowly visage to me. "You can step down, Detective Ryder."

I exited the witness stand, shooting a glance at the jury box where a dozen faces weighed my testimony. I shot a look toward the defendant, a mercurial little psychopath named Hugo Valenciana, his face coated with tattoos, like he was going trick-or-treating as a sketchpad. He gave me dead eyes and I gave him a smile and turned my next glance to Ronnie Billings, the prosecutor from the DA's office. He shot me a wink and tapped his thumb to his lips, Ronnie's sign for *You did a great job, go grab a drink*.

I left the courtroom, happy to have finished a day of testimony and full-bore cross-examination by Valenciana's ruthless lawyer, but bemoaning a lost day for the Sandoval and Mailey cases. The Valenciana case had been looming for months and my presence was absolute, since I'd been the lead on the investigation.

I stood in the Halls of Justice and looked at my watch: 4.30 p.m. A voice called from behind.

"How'd it go, Detective Ryder?"

I turned to Holly Belafonte, dressed in a blue blouse and pressed denim jeans, a light jacket with a simple pin, a cloisonné conch.

"Valenciana's toast. How'd your day go?"

She nodded, as prim and businesslike as ever. "Several things were accomplished, I believe. I checked the flow rate."

"Pardon me?"

"In the canal. Where Teresa was found . . . you asked me to—"

I'd forgotten, the thought lost in mental minutiae. "Sorry. What do you have?"

"Slack tide that period, with outflow beginning near dawn. Absent rainfall in the previous twenty-four hours, the flow was approximately nine hundred feet per hour."

I smiled. "Pretty precise. You toss two cigarette butts in the water this time?"

She dug in her bag for a notepad, flipping through pages of tiny, perfect script. "I obtained concurring opinions from the US Meteorological Service, the US Geological Survey, the Everglades Protective Association, and the Metro Miami Water Authority, which monitors four electronic stream-flow meters on the canal, situated approximately one-point-three miles apart and stretching from—"

I held up my hand to cut her off and recalled the interstate near the site where the body was found, Highway 441 upstream of the interstate. "If I remember, that would indicate the body could have been dumped from the 441 bridge – your original conjecture. But there's another highway crossing the waterway, plus a large lake further upstream."

She shook her head. "Not if we assume the body was placed in the water after midnight, which keeps to approximate time of death per the postmortem. It's either the always-busy interstate or the less-traveled 441, at least at that time of night."

I thought it through. She seemed right. But she had more.

"I also spoke to several of the odious T'Shawn Matthews' stable, if that's what it's called."

"You talked to Shitzidoodle's girls? By yourself?"

She nodded to the courtroom doors. "You were busy."

"Was Matthews there?"

She leaned the wall and crossed her arms. "He crawled from under his rock. I asked if he was going to intrude, and if so, it would be best to hold off on repainting his vehicle. He returned to his pub, looking out the window and pulling rude faces."

"How many girls did you interview?" I said, hoping she'd managed two or three.

"Eleven."

"*Eleven?*"

"One led to another. Most knew Kylie hardly at all,

just another working girl. None of the girls knew Teresa, I showed a photo."

"Anything from the interviews?"

"Kylie was quite the close-mouthed girl, but one of her companions shared a flat with her for a few weeks. They used to get high together. The roommate, Candi Fyne – I do believe it's fake, don't you? – recalled the pair talking about how they'd fancied going into acting when younger. Miss Fyne laughed about how the only acting she'd done was in a low-level porn film, fornicating for drugs, she called it."

"She really said fornicating?"

"No. Anyway, Kylie had told Miss Fyne that she'd spent five months acting and had even gotten paid for it."

"Porn as well?"

"Miss Fyne didn't think so. But that was the extent of the conversation, since they shot up subsequently."

"We'll have to look into the various perform—"

She was flipping pages again. "Performance unions, yes. I spoke with Actors' Equity, Screen Actors Guild, the American Federation of Theatrical and Recording Artists. All had no records of Kylie ever being a member, and that's from a national database. But those tend to be professional organizations; there are many amateur venues and others that simply disregard union membership."

It was a helluva day's work, the work of two. Or three. But Belafonte had more to come.

"From there . . ." she said, gesturing me to her vehicle,

"I proceeded to Kylie's apartment, a rather sordid little place. I did find this . . ." She opened the car door and came up with a large square of rough cloth, gray, two meters by a meter. I rubbed a thumb over its nubby surface.

"What is it?"

"No idea. The size of a scarf, but too coarse to be comfortable. What made it unusual is where I discovered it . . . in a plastic bag inside a paper bag, the paper bag jammed in the back of a closet with a board over it. It was like Kylie needed to keep it, but at the same time didn't want to keep it, so she did rather a bit of both."

I studied Belafonte. She had to have been in constant motion, and the eyes showed it, darkened beneath. The usually perfect hair was limp, strands hanging loose. I even spotted nascent wrinkles behind the knees of the flat-pressed slacks. While I'd spent a day in a courtroom, she'd made strides that would have been a good day's work for the both of us, an amazing day's work.

"I'm bushed and you look the same," I said. "Let's get a night's sleep and start afresh in the morning." She nodded agreement and started away.

"Hey!" I called after her, shooting a thumbs-up. "Helluva job, Belafonte."

She stared. "What happened to 'Officer'?"

"Consider my newfound familiarity a promotion," I said, turning toward the street.

"So my next advancement is when you call me 'fonte'?" she called back.

154

It took me a second to realize it was meant to be humorous. I turned to see what she looked like when joking, but she was walking away.

I made a mental note to turn faster next time.

24

Nautilus was in his hotel room sipping a bottle of Edmund Fitzgerald Porter and watching *Jeopardy*. A contestant called for the category "Ships". The answer was revealed: *Freighter that sank in Lake Superior in 1975.*

"*Edmund Fitzgerald*," Nautilus whispered, glancing at the bottle of brew; weird coincidence, Carson was gonna like hearing about it.

"The *Edmund Fitzgerald*," the contestant said, adding four hundred bucks to her pile. A knock echoed in the room. Nautilus switched off the television and opened the door to find Richard Owsley framed against the hushed and carpeted hall.

"May I come in?"

Nautilus waved entry, glancing at the porter and figuring he should have tucked it back in the fridge. It was the first time Nautilus had seen his employer suitless, now in pressed green chinos and a polo shirt, argyle socks, tasseled cordovan loafers.

"Can I get you a refreshment, Pastor?"

A frowning glance at the porter. "No, thank you. I'm fine."

Nautilus sat as Owsley paced the room, stopping at the window and looking toward the cross.

"How can I help you?" Nautilus said.

"I'm afraid I invited you here under something of a, uh, mischaracterization, Mr Nautilus."

"Interesting. In what way?"

"I preach a doctrine that some call materialistic and selfish. That's far too . . . *reductionary*, simplistic. I postulate that believing in Jesus Christ the Redeemer results in rewards in the here and now. The faithful don't have to wait for Heavenly remunera-*shun*, the payback for righteousness." He paused and raised one eyebrow. "Do my words make sense to you?"

Nautilus was on the verge of saying "*No, Mista Owzley. Ise jus' a simple country boy, I is,*" but changed it to, "I think so."

Owsley jammed his hands in his pockets and rocked on his heels. "It's a different way of interpreting the gospel than the *quotidian*, the everyday. People need hope."

"Sure," Nautilus said, wondering how much the guy spent on *Word-a-Day* calendars.

"But it's wholly in the vision of Christ," Owsley said. "He came to bring hope to the downtrodden, the

157

neglected. There are people that don't comprehend, find it beyond their ken. People become frightened by what they don't understand, and anger is a stepchild of fright. Simply put, some people are angry with me, resentful." Owsley bowed his head, as if unable to comprehend such thinking. After a suitable pause he lifted his eyes to Nautilus and changed track. "How many years were you with the Mobile police force, Mr Nautilus? Did you say twenty?"

"Almost thirty."

"May I ask, did you ever have protection duties, like when a celebrity came to town, an important personage?"

"Now and then."

"Because there were people who resented the celebrities, their success, their popularity . . . maybe even wished them bodily harm?"

Nautilus laced his fingers behind his neck, wondering where this new road would end up. "That was the general concept."

"An hour ago I received a phone call. A man called me an apostate, Mr Nautilus. Do you know what that means? It's a person who has lost his way, turned from the truth."

Nautilus had known the definition of apostate since he was as tall as a parking meter. But he simply nodded.

"The caller told me I should repent and ask God for forgiveness. And if I didn't . . ." Owsley paused, as if replaying the call in his head.

"Go on."

"That I'd be sent to Hell in flames and smoke."

"Anonymity means people can say anything," Nautilus said. "They vent, they put down the phone, they finish eating their Spaghetti-O's."

"I've had people differ with me on a theological level, Mr Nautilus. This was different. It was venomous, frightening. The man sounded insane."

He is *frightened,* Nautilus thought. Under the façade of being scared, Richard Owsley actually was scared.

"And what you want from me is . . .?"

"I want you to be my driver, as agreed. But I also want you to be my bodyguard. To keep an eye out for those who might do me harm."

"I'd pretty much do that anyway," Nautilus said. "It's visceral."

"Vizral?"

"*Vis*-cer-al. As in felt in the viscera, the internal organs. Simply put, I operate on a gut feeling. My guts, my intuition, often spot trouble before it begins." He paused to enjoy the moment. "Do you understand what I'm saying?"

"That . . . you have a feeling for these things?"

Nautilus pretended to lick his thumb and pressed it toward the preacher. "You get a gold star on the forehead, Pastor Owsley. And yes, I'll take care of you."

Owsley's thousand-watt smile returned to his face. He put his hand on Nautilus's shoulder and gave it a squeeze. "Hallelujah, Mr Nautilus, you are surely a gift from God."

Nautilus had no response to his sudden beatific status. He simply nodded and pictured himself as glowing.

"I have to fly to a crucial – and very hush-hush meeting in Key West tomorrow morning," Owsley continued. "I can then depend on you to be with me, Mr Nautilus?"

He needs me, Nautilus thought, recalibrating the employer–employee relationship; the weight had just shifted. He crossed his legs, picked up the Edmund Fitzgerald and slowly finished the bottle, nodding at Owsley as he set the empty back on the table.

"Depend away, Pastor."

25

The six-hundred-dollar Ferragamo slings of Sissy Carol Sparks clicked the Miami Beach sidewalk like castanets. A pair of middle-aged businessmen turned to watch the leg show, Sparks's skirt inches above the compact knees and rippling seductively in the light breeze smelling of salt water, a Victoria's Secret bag in her hand. She watched the businessmen watching her through her outsize Raybans, noting the name tags on the lapels of their suitcoats.

Hello, my name is . . .

Conventioneers. Money on the hoof.

The sun was hidden behind the tall downtown buildings, falling in the west and turning the twilight sky into a glowing blue promise of a gentle night ahead. Sissy walked to Lincoln, crossed to Meridian and headed south, entering a street-level bar in an upscale hotel. Taxis swept past.

Sissy went to the bar and sat, feeling the eyes. Two-thirds of the tables were filled, mostly men, mostly smiling or laughing. Getting hammered in Miami Beach, beautiful women on every corner, Mama and the kiddies back home in East Backwater.

The thirtyish, Hispanic barkeeper had a napkin and a soda water and lime in front of Sissy within ten seconds. He gave her a wink. She smiled back and nodded to the full tables.

"My, aren't we busy tonight, Julio."

"A car dealer convention in town, Sis. Not the chumps on the floor, the owners. But you know that, right?"

All Sissy had to do was check the Miami Beach Convention Center's website to see conventions due in town. To see if it was her type of clientele: men away from home with money to spend.

"Thursday through Sunday," Sparks said. "The business news expected over eight hundred dealers in town, a biggie."

Sissy Sparks worked under the name Cecily Silk and charged eight hundred dollars a session. Six minutes or six hours, it was eight hundred bills. The average gig ran five hours and fifteen minutes. Fifty went to Julio if he set the job up, and another fifty went to whoever was handling hotel security that night. That left seven. Twenty went for a new black silk thong, since she threw the old ones away, not wanting to wear clothing that one of her clients had removed – either with hands or often with teeth – or held his slop.

162

That was disgusting. Washing them out would be worse.

Another twenty gone. Then there was cab-fare from her Wynwood digs to downtown, thirty round-trip, tip included. Manicures, pedicure, tanning and incidentals . . . another hundred a week.

So five bills a gig times the seven gigs she worked weekly, averaged over the last seven months. Thirty-five hundred a week, a bit under two hundred grand a year. Not bad for a twenty-five-year-old woman from rural Ohio. And it would only get better as she developed repeat clientele and didn't have to rely on the Julios of the world or her miserably expensive escort service.

"You got eyes on you, babe," Julio whispered. "One guy looks like he's about to wet his undies. You want to take a walk?"

Sissy set the half-finished drink on the bar and headed to the restroom. Hopefully one of the dealers was now talking to Julio.

"The lady at the bar . . . is she . . .?"

"If you leave me your room number, sir, I can have her visit, if that is all right with you."

It would be, and if lucky, Julio might score another fifty. Sissy gave it ten minutes. Her phone rang, Julio.

"He's a guest here. Room four-twenty-seven. The guy's a bit tipsy, but has diamonds in his cuff links and five hundred bucks on his feet. I saw him pull his wedding ring before he talked to me."

"Isn't that sweet," Sissy said. "I think I'm in love."

26

Nautilus had Owsley at the airport by seven and they were in the air ten minutes later. The rental Towne Car was ready in Key West and Nautilus drove a pensive Richard Owsley across the island.

"It's a house behind the Schrum home," Owsley said, consulting directions on his smartphone. "We're to pull into the drive."

Nautilus swerved into the wide driveway as a gray-haired and bespectacled man exited the house waving. On his heels was a large man, Nautilus gauging his height at over six and a half feet.

"I don't know how long I'll be, Mr Nautilus," Owsley said, opening the door.

"I'll keep the meter running."

Introductions and handshaking over, the trio crossed the yards to the Schrum residence. Nautilus stepped to the sidewalk, walking around to the end of the block where the Schrum house was located.

Several hundred people were out front, some milling and holding signs proclaiming their love for the ailing minister, others singing, or on their knees at the curb, praying behind lit candles. A wild-haired guy was dragging a six-foot wooden cross down the center of the street. Police cruisers were parked at both ends of the block, allowing residents entry. Two news vans were on site, uplink antennae raised like diabolical engines. The porch of the corner house was occupied by a dozen laughing folks wearing colorful garb and funny hats, drinking Bloody Marys and applauding when one of the choirs finished a song.

Nautilus sighed . . . Key West.

He turned away and walked another two blocks, finding a corner store where he purchased a newspaper and headed back to the car.

Richard Owsley paused at the door and smoothed the front of his dark suit, straightened his tie. He took a deep breath and shot a look at the man beside him.

"It's all right, Pastor Owsley," Hayes Johnson said, patting the youthful pastor on his back. "He's expecting you."

"Yes," Uttleman parroted. "He's delighted you're here."

The doctor ushered Owsley into Schrum's room, the fabled preacher propped up in a king-size bed, robed as black as a Supreme Court justice, the crest of white hair rising from his head like a halo. Owsley's feet malfunctioned until Uttleman's nudge propelled him forward.

"It's a blessing to meet you, Reverend," Owsley said, his voice cracking.

"You too, son," Schrum said. They clasped hands. Schrum nodded to the bedside chair. "Take a load off."

Owsley sat. "You've been my life-long inspiration, Reverend Schrum. I remember the first time I saw you live, it was at a revival in Tuscaloosa and I was just ten years old and my mama had taken the family to—"

Schrum's hand raised. "Hold on, son, you're talking like you got to get it all out before I die on you . . ." Schrum sputtered and coughed. "But I ain't plannin' to go out this morning. Fact is, I'm feeling pretty feisty, given all the trouble my body's been dealin' me."

"Wonderful news. Praise God."

"Now don't get me wrong, Pastor. I ain't outta the woods. I'm still weaker'n an hour-old kitten, and likely to stay this way for another two–three weeks." He paused, seemed to catch his breath. "If I make it, that is . . ."

In the corner of the room, Uttleman started to roll his eyes. Schrum saw, shot a hard glance past Owsley. Uttleman looked away.

"I'll pray continually for swift recovery," Owsley said.

"Lord willing, I'll get back to my work. My only regret is having to abandon my daily pastoral responsibilities, and several projects that I've had to delay."

"I have no doubt you'll soon be back doing God's labors, sir."

Schrum blew out a breath at the enormity of it all. "It's a large undertaking. Especially the media end. Are you on the television, Pastor Owsley?"

"Twice a week in Mobile. The show is rebroadcast on the Alabama Christian cable channel."

"How many of the faithful watch?"

"Sixty or seventy thousand."

"The Crown of Glory channel is seen in twenty million homes a week. What do you think of that, son?"

"Those are some numbers, sir. A lot of souls."

"You probably passed Andy Delmont outside, Pastor, my stalwart companion."

"His voice is a gift from God, Reverend. My wife has all his albums."

"I discovered young Andrew over a decade ago, a singer in a family gospel choir and unknown outside of his small congregation. Now Andy's albums sell in the hundreds of thousands. We all need exposure, wide audiences. Larger ministries bring in more donations and do more good."

"Yessir," Owsley said. "I understand."

"I want to get back to my first point, my unmet responsibilities. Let me ask a personal question, Pastor Owsley, if I may."

"Of course, sir."

Schrum studied the ceiling as if looking beyond for guidance. The eyes returned to Owsley. "Did you ever over-promise, Pastor?"

Puzzlement. "Like how, Reverend?"

"Let's say it's the end of a life and you're called to the hospital. You know in your heart the person is soon destined for the arms of the Lord. But because of their love, the despairing family isn't ready to let go yet. Have you ever offered hope in the face of the actual reality?"

"With faith, there is always hope."

"So you hold out hope to the family . . . even knowing the inevitable, that God's will is about to be done. Because you love the family. And you want them to feel better?"

Owsley nodded slowly, uncertain of where the conversation was heading. Schrum took Owsley's hand and drew him closer. "I want to speak next on the subject of hope and promises, Pastor Owsley. Just me and you, two men of God in a quiet room. Will you grant me that?"

"I will give you anything you ask, Reverend Schrum."

Schrum nodded to Johnson and Uttleman who crept from the room and closed the door. Uttleman turned to Johnson. "Do you think Amos will convince Owsley?" he said softly.

Johnson looked over his shoulder at the closed door. "You never know what Amos will do, only that in the end, it will be perfect for Amos. You, me, Eliot Winkler . . . we're all made to play along."

"You're saying—"

"Remember when Amos met with Eliot . . . Amos gasping, on his last breath, claiming he didn't have the strength to complete the project? Not on a *daily* basis . . . remember? He said it twice."

"I remember, but—"

168

Johnson continued down the hall, shaking his head. "Amos just got himself out of a lunatic promise and passed it over to Owsley. He can now relax in Key West, drink his fill, have one of his little guilt-wallows, and let Delmont play him pretty songs all day. Not bad, right?"

"You mean he's jerked everyone around from the start?"

"Wake up, Roland. It's what Amos Schrum does."

27

Frisco Dredd crouched inside the windowless van and sucked from a bottle of water, his eyes again searching the cream apartment complex on the south edge of Wynwood, the property bordered by tall palms and bright flowers. Thanks to Darlene Hammond he now knew the address of Sissy Carol Sparks, whore and destroyer of great and Godly men. Hammond, another whore and temptress, was currently answering to God for her sins, the ashes of her earthly body lying beside a little-used road at the edge of the Everglades.

He'd done what he could for Hammond, made the preparations, used the correct materials, sending her soul to Heaven with crackling flames and a cloud of dark and holy smoke. Weeping on his knees and asking for his own forgiveness as he asked for hers.

"... *for unto you, Lord, I make this sacrifice in Your*

holy name and beg for her forgiveness for her sins and blasphemies . . ."

The whore might still be saved. The Lord was merciful.

A car turned the block and Dredd's senses pricked up. But it was a pair of hipster males in a red Miata convertible who continued down the block, aiming for downtown Miami.

Dredd again slumped low in the seat and drew another drink from the water bottle. He knew where Sparks lived and how she made her money. He'd wait all day and all night, if necessary.

Time meant nothing to a warrior for God.

Owsley had been in the Schrum house for forty minutes when another vehicle swung into the drive, a limo pulling a trailer. The car pulled past Nautilus to the parking pad in back, Nautilus repositioning himself to watch two burly men remove an elaborate motorized wheelchair from the trailer. They were obviously private security, which piqued Nautilus's interest.

The beefy boys helped an elderly man into the chair. Though looking frail, he seemed resolute, advancing full throttle for several feet before jerking to a halt, one of the tires jamming into a fissure in the patio.

Nautilus watched as the security types struggled to free the wedged tire while the chair's occupant cursed and pressed controls, the chair's power belt shrieking. Powering the motor would burn it out, but neither of the hired hands looked ready to explain that to the boss.

Nautilus jogged over to lend a hand. "Easy on the power, buddy . . ." he said to the chair's occupant as he bent to add his hands to the task, "you're gonna wreck the motor. Lay off the juice and we'll get you free."

The man's face spun to Nautilus, his eyes pinpoints of fury in the wizened face. "Get the hell away from me, boy," he hissed. "I got all the help I need."

"Boy?" Nautilus said. It had been a long time.

The others gave a grunting thrust and the chair lurched free. Without thanks or a backward glance the man accelerated across the yards, the security guys hustling to catch up.

Nautilus dismissed the old crank. He opened the newspaper and read in the warm sunlight, happy to be alone.

He'd read for ten minutes, then heard a "Hello" from the sidewalk. He turned to a man in his mid forties, slender and attractive and dressed in an ice-cream suit with a jaunty Panama on his head. Though the pedestrian wore sunglasses, he did Nautilus the courtesy of removing them to speak, his blue eyes sparkling as if alight with secret knowledge. There was something familiar about the visage, but it eluded Harry Nautilus, who flicked a lazy salute.

"Good morning."

"Anything interesting in the paper?" the man said.

"Usual crapola," Nautilus said, holding it up. "I'm done. You want it?"

"That's very kind of you." The man approached and took the folded paper. If anything, the proximity enhanced Nautilus's feeling that he'd met the man before, but he also knew he hadn't.

Weird.

The elegant man spun on his heels like a dancer, a move so smooth it was disconcerting. He continued down the block whistling, "Can't Take My Eyes Off of You".

Bemused by the encounter, Nautilus was trying the tune himself when Richard Owsley returned in the company of the big man and the mousier guy in glasses. They had shaken hands politely when Owsley had arrived, but they embraced upon departure, exchanging broad smiles and happy words. The cranky old fart was still inside the Schrum house.

The trio dropped their heads in prayer for several seconds before Owsley came to the car, sitting tentatively in the rear seat, as though dizzied by the previous hour.

"I trust your meeting went well, Pastor," Nautilus said when Owsley closed the door.

"I, uh . . . what?"

"I said, I hope your meeting went well. That you accomplished all you wanted."

Owsley gave Nautilus a distracted nod and they headed to the airport, Owsley making a phone call to his wife. Nautilus had long ago stopped feeling guilty about eavesdropping, simple human curiosity, and pretended to be absorbed in his driving as Owsley made the twenty-second call.

"It's everything we've wanted," the preacher said, his voice a mix of fear and elation. "And something you won't believe."

28

The head was encased in a gray Fiberglass shell, the eyes hidden behind a rectangular screen the size of a pack of cigarettes, hard and shiny and as black as black is allowed to become. Every few seconds the screen filled with sizzling white light, like angry comets were trapped inside.

The screen turned black for several seconds. Then again burst into sparking comets.

"Joe!" a voice yelled. "JOE!"

The comets died in the black visor as Joe Grabowski snapped off the welding torch and pushed back the helmet, turning to see Walt Hillenbrandt, his supervisor on the project. Hillenbrandt was in his early fifties, thick in the waist, with a round face and thinning red hair.

"Yeah, Walt?"

"It's 1025-M. We gotta finish the project ASAP. Can you work tonight? Pull double shifts the next week?"

Grabowski pulled a pack of Marlboros from his pocket, lit one. "Tonight's my monthly poker game, Joe. You know how I like my—"

"Triple pay for overtime, Joe. Instead of waiting for all the sub-assemblies to finish, we're gonna ship them out the second they're ready. This one goes out soon as you're done. The semi's in the yard, set to go. Driver's supposed to drive all night."

"Jesus . . . what's the sudden rush?"

Hillenbrandt shrugged. "They haven't said shit about hurrying, now they want the project last week."

"Triple overtime, you said?"

"Plus a thousand-buck bonus for each day we beat the deadline."

"Fuck poker." Grabowski leaned back and studied the long sleek tube. "What the hell is this thing, Walt . . . 1025-M? You been told?"

The alphanumeric was the project's designation, all anyone knew about the assignment, outside of exact specifications. The project had arrived at Chicago Metal Fabrications as no more than a blueprint.

Hillenbrandt shrugged heavy shoulders. "I'm a fuckin' mushroom, Joe. Kept in the dark and fed bullshit. But by my thinking, we're not the only ones working on 1025-M."

Grabowski sucked in a lungful of smoke. "What makes you think that?" he said, a blue plume following his words from his mouth.

"'Cus even when you put the parts together, the fucking

thing just ends, but something has to go there. A base of some kind, maybe."

"Or an engine, you think? The goddamn thing looks like it's ready for a mission to Mars." He paused, assembling the parts in his mind. "Jesus, Walt . . . you think it's some kind of weapon? A missile, a bomb?"

Hillenbrandt chuckled. "I checked the freight bill for yesterday's shipment. I think we can rule that one out, given the destination."

"Where's it going?"

"That bible park down in Florida. Hallelujah Jubilee."

29

Jeremy Ryder continued through the neighborhood for another hour, holding his excitement in check. He'd never met the man, but had heard the stories – all that Carson had chosen to tell. All Jeremy had to go on was a mental picture bolstered by a few grainy shots in newspapers.

Which was a good place to start looking.

He blew a speck from his crisp Panama Borsalino and flicked it a dozen feet to the hat rack where it caught on a hook, spun twice, and stayed. He smiled to himself and hung his jacket carefully in the closet before climbing the stairs to his office in the third floor of the tower. It was a spare setting, a large desk rounded at back to fit the curved wall, polished-oak floors, a circular and red-intensive Oriental carpet on the floor, the stubby round telescope on its eye-height tripod,

178

currently aimed out the wide window toward the Schrum home.

Jeremy sat in his Hermann Miller chair. The Bloomberg terminals on his desk danced with an array of facts and figures from the global markets but he ignored them to turn on his personal computer, tapping into the archives of the *Mobile Press-Register* and inserting a name into the *Search* field.

Searching . . . the screen said as the word appeared with ellipses blinking behind. *Searching* . . . *Searching* . . . A list of hits filled the screen, seven in all. Jeremy scanned the descriptions, finding one titled *MPD Names "Officers of the Year"*. It was eight years old but how much could a man change? Jeremy tapped the link.

Searching . . .

After several moments an article appeared, Jeremy was after a photograph. The article jumped to the side and an empty box appeared, words beneath the box, the original caption from the newspaper.

OFFICERS OF THE YEAR HONORED – Mayor Lyle Edmunds presents Mobile Police detectives Carson Ryder (left) and Harry Nautilus (right) with Officers of the Year awards at the Mayor's annual Recognition Breakfast . . .

The photograph began to load, slowly filling the box from left to right. Five seconds later Jeremy saw the face of his brother, Carson, dark hair overly long and looking like his barber preferred tin-snips to shears, the knot of his tie an inch below the unbuttoned collar, his false smile more akin to a deer in headlights. He was holding some ridiculous plaque, sideways of course, being Carson. At least it wasn't upside-down.

He sighed as the second human image filled in, an older gray-haired man in a dark suit behind a dais, his mouth wide with vaporous natterings, a politician, naturally. The Mayor.

The third form began appearing, a large man, black, shoulders at the height of Carson's nose, heavy arms bunching the fabric of a tan suit. Jeremy turned away to let the image arrive, counting down as he waited for the entire photo.

. . . three . . . two . . . one . . .

He turned back to the picture to see the third figure, clutching its own plaque – right-side up, thankfully – looking into the camera with an expression that read *This is all bullshit but I'll play along*. He had a large, square head. Intelligent eyes holding a touch of dare, wide forehead, a trim square mustache.

Harry Nautilus. Carson's partner for years . . . And the man who, minutes ago, had been reading a newspaper behind the Schrum house.

Jeremy picked up his phone, tapping the first number on speed dial. Carson answered on the third ring.

"Can't talk now, Jeremy. I'm on the road and heading into work."

"I thought I'd deliver an update on the Schrum death

festival. I'm thinking about renting a cart and selling hot dogs. Or do you think loaves and fishes might be more appropriate?"

"Busy here, Jeremy."

"Don't be snippy, it's discourteous. I'm organizing my drawers. Not pants, the one where I keep memorabilia. I have several articles about your career over the years, newspaper stories. Your manly, thrilling exploits. I'm making copies. Would you like a set?"

"Uh . . . sure."

"Some make mention of your old partner, Harry Nautilus . . ." Jeremy paused as if stifling a yawn. "Whatever became of him, by the way?"

"Harry just retired. He's in Mobile and I saw him only last weekend."

"Mobile?" Jeremy said. "You're sure he's not gotten religion and is traipsing around Florida looking for holy sites?"

"Religion? What are you babbling about? Listen, Jeremy, I'm really—"

"Busy, yes, I know. I'll drop these things off next time I'm by your place, probably soon."

"Soon?" An anxious pause. "What? When?"

Jeremy hung up, crossed his arms and stared out the window. Carson had no idea his old pal was right now in Key West, leaning against a big bright Hummer and chatting with passers-by.

Why?

* * *

181

It was minutes past noon when the Ferragamo slings of Sissy Carol Sparks again ticked across the pavement of Miami Beach, her client snoring naked on the carpet beside the bed, a fifth of Pappy Van Winkle dead on the floor. Sissy could smell the guy's nasty, overmusked cologne rising from her breasts and she grimaced as she hailed a cab to take her back to Wynwood, another thirty bucks shot.

It had been a standard night, Mr Car Salesman trying to shape Sissy into configurations he'd seen in porn vids, getting a cramp in his leg at one point, howling and limping across the floor, his pink dick flapping pathetically between his thighs. He'd gotten progressively drunker, passing out at four in the morning. Sissy had slept until ten – the guy a beached whale drooling on the carpet – then called room service for coffee, juice and a fruit plate. He'd paid to have her stay until noon, but snored through what he'd expected would be breakfast in bed, so to speak.

As she waved down a taxi, Sissy winced at a memory, the john patting her hair like she was a show poodle and babbling that she was the *mos' beautiful woman he'd ever seen* and how he'd like to take her home and show her off to everyone in Kokomo or wherever.

Sissy had started life in her own Kokomo, a tiny town in rural northwestern Ohio, aptly named Hicksville, and wasn't going back. It had been a hard climb, chased around the house by her uncle – and occasionally caught – starting when she was fourteen, seduced by a music

182

teacher when she was sixteen, a next-door neighbor at seventeen, passed around by a succession of boyfriends, mostly college types, who promised the world and married women who didn't talk with a twang and live in a trailer park.

Sissy learned two things from her early life: One, men want one thing, and two, men want one thing *only*.

She'd ditched Hicksville at nineteen, trading a meth head mother and winters so cold they broke pipes under the trailer for the bright-future sunshine of Florida. There had been only one problem: Sissy arrived on the Trailways bus with one-hundred-seventy-seven dollars in her backpack, tucked within the make-up and the few clothes she could fit in the pack.

She found the cheapest motel in the Orlando area, hoping to work at Disney World, which she'd heard hired attractive young people to perform for tourists. Only one problem: the goddamn place wasn't hiring.

She started looking south. Then, the ad . . . in the local paper, small and headlined, CHARACTER ACTORS NEEDED. It promised a good steady job, good money, even a place to live. All you needed was to be "responsible, energetic, outgoing and . . ."

And *blah, blah, blah*, Sissy thought. What a fucking bust that turned out to be, at least as far as acting. After a strange interview she'd been made an immediate manager and given special duties, finding that beneath all the promises and glittery up-top bullshit it was just another Hicksville, dark and ugly and full of streets that led nowhere. But she had a feel for the work and the money was good, so she stayed a year before getting bored and bolting south to Miami. She'd intended to sign with an escort service, but fucked up and immediately acquired a heroin habit which detoured her career to a massage parlor, cranking out handjobs like Dunkin' cranked out donuts.

She fell to the bottom, again. Hicksville with hand towels.

Then the cops raided the place and hauled off all the illegals, leaving only one US citizen: Sissy. She'd called a bail bondsman, got a hard-talking dyke named Michaela. With a bit of subtle encouragement, Mick got the drools for Sissy and ended up paying the percentage and all court costs, then sat up three days while Sissy moaned and puked and trembled the H from her system.

Another lesson learned: Fuck with drugs and they'll fuck you back harder.

Sissy stayed clean and started exercising, spurred on by Mick, who did a minimum ten hard hours a week at a health club and fronted Sissy the membership fee.

Sissy 2.0 arrived. With Mick's reluctant help – "This is what I'm gonna do, Mick, you got that? Help me or get the hell out of my way" – she finally signed with a low-rent escort service and began doing outcalls at fifty bucks an hour, half going to the service. She found a better service, moved up, and began trolling the street in her own time, targeting horny johns before they could call a service.

The money was starting to roll in.

Which was why Sissy didn't much care when the cab-fare was thirty and she tipped the guy ten . . . Sissy Carol Sparks had figured out how the game worked.

Sissy exited the cab and smiled at her apartment building, a ten-unit rehab in a gentrifying neighborhood, her neighbors young professionals who thought the beautiful young woman in 22-A was a medical-equipment salesperson who took a shitload of overnight sales trips. The men initially buzzed at her like bees, but Sissy bought a flashy diamelle engagement ring to back the story of an engagement to a Delta pilot, the marriage at some nebulous point in the future.

All worked out.

Sissy crossed to her unit to shower the stink from her skin, hit the club for a workout, then take a facial and manicure. She'd had gigs for four days in a row – the convention – and was looking forward to curling up in a terry robe and watching *West Wing* episodes on Netflix . . . the call girl in that show made three grand a night!

Something to aspire to.

A flash of motion caught Sissy's eye and she turned to a white van parked on the street, eyes reflected in the large side mirror, gray eyes tracking her every step across the pavement. Normally she would have put a little more sashay in the trim rear to give some poor working stiff a couple seconds of the show. She was, after all, Sissy Carol Sparks, moving up and moving fast.

But this guy was scary, his eyes horny-hot, sure . . .

but angry at the same time. And why was the looney fuck holding his shirt open to show some purple tattoo or whatever? Her internal alarms went off and Sissy nearly ran the last few feet to her door.

30

Miami-Dade PD dispatcher Talia Ocales sat in her semi-circular workstation surrounded by monitors and an impressive array of technology. A light flashed on her board and she shifted the headpiece to take a fast sip of coffee, then flicked a switch.

"This is 911," she said, the address registering on one of her monitors. "What is the nature of your problem?"

"*I want to report a freak scoping out the neighborhood. He's sitting in some piece-a-shit van, staring at women. He's got some weird-ass tat or whatever on his chest. He's got sicko eyes . . . trust me, I know what they look like.*"

"*Your name, ma'am?*"

"*It ain't important. You'll send some uniforms to roust this perv, right?*"

Tania Ocales assured the caller action would be taken and switched off the call. "*Uniforms? Roust this perv?*" The caller knew cop jargon. Ocales checked for active units in the area.

"Ten-Charlie-three, you there?"

"*Runnin' south on Northwest Fifth,*" returned the voice of Patrol Officer Jason Roberts. "*Just passed Robert E. Lee Park.*"

"Got a complaint about a suspicious individual . . ." Ocales told him the address.

"*Anything more to go on?*" Roberts said.

"Old van. Creepy-looking guy."

A chuckle. "*That narrows it down. On the way.*"

Frisco Dredd started the van. The engine turned over, coughed, died. He pumped the gas and fired it up again, pulling from the curb when he heard the *whoop* of a siren and saw flashing blue in his rear-view. His fingers rebuttoned the front of his shirt. Jesus didn't need to see this meaningless distraction.

The cop came to the door, a younger guy wearing one of those cop smiles that ain't a smile, eyes like they was weighing you.

"Good day, sir. May I see your license and registration?"

Dredd's hands moved slowly because cops got testy when you moved too fast. "I just fixed that taillight. I hope it ain't broke again."

The cop studied the papers. "We had a call about

someone sitting here for a while. Someone looking a bit out of place."

Dredd laughed and slapped his knee. "I guess that'd be me, officer. There's so many good-looking young folks around here an ugly ol' mug like mine prob'ly seems way out of place."

The cop handed back the papers. "What brings you here, Mr Dredd?"

"I'm just a guy looking for work, passing out my hand-bills." Dredd reached to a rubber-banded stack of copies on the dashboard. "Here . . . mebbe you could use some fix-up around your place. I'm really good. Bonded, too."

The cop studied the flyer: *A-1 Handyman Services*, said the banner, underscored by a listing of services from light carpentry to painting to plumbing.

"It seems you've been here a while, Mr Dredd. Take that long to hang a few fliers?"

"I passed out some handbills and then parked and had lunch. It's a pretty neighborhood."

Dredd side-eyed the cop, seeing him spot a crumpled fast-food bag and a bottle of water on the passenger seat. The cop re-studied the flyer.

"Mind if I look inside?"

Dredd felt anger rise in his throat like bile. Whores and infidels roamed the streets, but this Roman had to bother a God-serving Christian. Dredd wanted to rip his shirt open and let Jesus see the injustice.

Instead, he tightened his hands on the wheel. "It's unlocked."

The cop opened the side door and saw the two metal toolboxes, a pair of collapsed sawhorses, scraps of wooden molding, cans of paint and drop cloths. He handed back the flyer.

"I suggest you move along, Mr Dredd. Folks get nervous about strangers."

Dredd willed compliance into his voice. "I surely will, Officer. Bye now."

Frisco Dredd clenched his teeth in smile and waved as the cop returned to his car. He set the handbills on the dashboard. Having the things made up was real smart, foxy, like keeping tools and stuff in back. He was done here for the most part anyway.

The next time he passed through it would just be for a minute, and he'd be leaving with a wriggling package on the floor of the van, rolled in the first of two wrappings. The first would be a drop cloth or rug, the second would be of the lamb.

It was 4.30 p.m. Belafonte and I were in Forensics for the report on the length of gray-brown fabric she'd found hidden in Kylie's closet. Dayla Hidalgo, in her thirties with red-accented hair and eyes the size of saucers, set the bagged cloth on the lab table and read the analytics.

"It's a coarse-weave linen," Hidalgo said, tapping the bag with a purple fingernail. "Made with short tow fibers, as opposed to longer line fibers."

"Usage?"

"It's not dress linen. Being rough, it's often used

190

for wallcoverings, upholstery and the like. But micro-analysis showed a lot of breakage in the fibers, characteristic of repeated bending and washing. We also found two small hairs stuck in the weave. Donkey hairs, oddly enough. This Sandoval woman . . . she ever work at a zoo?"

I was about to answer when my phone rang – Vince. "We just got a call from an airboat guide service in the Glades, Carson."

My heart fell. I'd known Vince long enough to read the tone in his voice.

"Don't say it, Vince."

He sighed. "Sorry. But it looks like burned woman number three."

"Gimme the location," I said, snapping my fingers. Belafonte turned to the sound. I pointed to the phone and mouthed *three*.

She looked sick.

I put on the screamer and light show and did Daytona 500 driving for twenty minutes, five of them skidding down a single fire lane of sand that wound between canals and swampland. A Seminole guide had been piloting an airboat with four tourists through the sawgrass and lilies when he spied a log-like shape half-submerged in the thick green water. Thinking gator, he'd eased the passengers closer and the visitors now had a memory of Florida they doubtless wished to erase.

We reached the terminus and Deb Clayton waved us to a parking spot beside the medical van. The body had been pulled from the water and now lay on shore wrapped in charred strips and reeking of smoke, burnt meat and accelerant.

Deb walked up. "Three burned women, Carson."

"I can count, Deb."

A scene tech waded ashore with an evidence bag in hand. "We just found this. A cross made of scraps of sawgrass."

"Get photos for size," Deb said.

The cross measured forty-seven centimeters in length, twenty-nine in width, or about eighteen by twelve inches. It was crude, slender reeds knotted in the center to fashion a lopsided X-shape.

"It was floating," the tech said. "Over at the far side of the channel."

"There were no religious symbols at the other scenes," Belafonte said.

I looked out over the water, dark and slow-moving, dense with bass and sea trout and snook and dozens of other fishable species. I figured the cross had been fashioned by an idle angler, not even a cross, just knotting together reeds for something to do.

"Think it's significant?" Deb asked.

"Doubtful," I said. "But toss it in the mix." I turned to Belafonte. "Let's haul-ass back to Miami, push through the autopsy on Burning Woman Three, and review the previous scenes. Something's gotta give, and fast."

*   *   *

192

We returned to HQ. Belafonte went to her space and I called Ava. "Another burned woman," I said, oddly enough in a tired old man's voice. "Heading to you."

A pause. "You all right, Carson?"

"We've been running full-tilt into walls. Listen, can you possibly—"

"I'll schedule it ASAP, tomorrow morning."

I thanked her and crossed the room to fall on the couch and catch my breath. We'd been on the case for four days, but it seemed like weeks. Fourteen-hour days and nightmare-interrupted sleep will do that. I loosened my tie and closed my eyes.

Five minutes later I heard knocking and Belafonte's voice. "Detective Ryder? Are you in there?"

My eyes opened to note that the hard sunlight over the skyline of downtown Miami had softened into twilight. I checked my watch and discovered what felt like a five-minute respite had been a three-hour nap. My door opened slowly, the entry filling with Belafonte's anxious face.

"I'm so sorry to disturb you. I've been putting some things together in the meeting room and thought you should have a look."

"Coffee?" I said, not knowing I'd said it until I heard it. Sometimes autopilot does that.

"I just brought up fresh from the shop below. I figured by your snoring you'd appreciate caffeine."

Shooting a drowsy thumbs-up, I followed Belafonte's blue slacks and white blouse down the hall, passing

193

Gershwin's empty office, his bulletin board holding a single 8 × 10 photo: Roberta Menendez. But in the meeting room Belafonte had configured for our case there were three 8 × 10s: Kylie Sandoval, Teresa Mailey and our latest addition, Jane Doe. They were on the bulletin board, case material on a long adjoining table. I couldn't look in that direction.

"I got you two large bolds with three shots of espresso," Belafonte said, handing me the blessed cups. I nodded thanks, took a chair, and drank, feeling the magic elixir nudging the cobwebs from my brain. By the time I was opening the second cup, I felt conversant in my native tongue.

"You wanted to show me something?" I said, scanning the twin whiteboards for new additions, seeing only our same old scribbles.

"Not show, tell. While you were resting I started thinking about the odd materials used in burning the victims. I began to Google various sites."

"And you found . . .?"

"Nepthai," she said, holding up her tablet computer.

"An Egyptian queen?"

"The biblical term for Naphtha."

"Wait . . . naphtha's in the Bible?"

"Nepthai was thick water that burned and scholars now think it to be the flammable rock oil called naphtha."

I put aside my coffee and sat forward; this was getting interesting.

Belafonte wiped to another screen on her tablet and

read: "And thou shalt offer every day a bullock for a sin offering for atonement: and thou shalt cleanse the altar, when thou hast made an atonement for it, and thou shalt anoint it, to sanctify it."

"Anoint?" I said. "Altar?"

"And you shall say to the people of Israel, 'This shall be my holy anointing oil throughout your generations. It is holy, and it shall be holy to you.'"

It hit me. "Anointing oil is olive oil."

"Sometimes it was fancified with cinnamon, myrrh and so forth, but olive oil was the most common. Now think about sheep."

I tented my fingers, sat my chin atop them, and did so for a full minute.

"Sheep and lambs are a common biblical theme, Belafonte. Wool is sheep upholstery."

"Now consider sacrifice," Belafonte said, tapping the pad. "Genesis 22:7 to 8 – 'Isaac said to his father Abraham, "Father?" "Yes, my son?" Abraham replied. "The fire and wood are here," Isaac said, "but where is the lamb for the burnt offering?"' Then Abraham answers, 'God himself will provide the lamb for the burnt offering.'"

I felt my heart rate jump; not the coffee, but hope mingled with anxiety. We had a potential connection: Biblical themes and imagery.

"The cross of grass," I said. "We have to check the other murder scenes."

Feeling fresh wind, we pulled photos and reports from our towering files, starting with the scene photos from

Kylie Sandoval's lonely stretch of sand. Detritus found by the techs included a Miller Lite can, a Dasani bottle, the butt from a Salem, a crumpled bag of Doritos and a frayed length of boat rope.

No religious imagery.

"Let's try the video," I said.

I put the disk in the computer and watched until the removal of the body, gloved techs moving the charred tube to a gurney. Through the sound of wind we heard a whispered *one-two-three* and the husk was lifted from the sand to a carry board.

"Back up," I said, staring at the screen, blinking like it would bring it into better focus. Belafonte replayed the segment until I again yelled stop. I traced my finger across the screen.

"There's a line here, maybe one intersecting."

She was dubious. I moved to the next series of photos, taken while the photographer was straddling the impression and shooting down.

"There," I said. "You can just barely make it out."

We studied the sand where the body had been removed. You had to squint, but it was there.

"A cross," Belafonte said. "Before it got flattened by the body."

"Made by a stick, a piece of driftwood. Or just dragging a toe through the sand."

"Where was the cross with Teresa?" Belafonte asked.

"It went into the water with her and drifted away. We'll never find it. But if there were two, there were three."

196

I went to the window, put my hands in my pockets and looked out into the night sky to recall writing a widely ignored article proposing that religious zealotry was the most dangerous of the psychopathic aberrations.

The non-religious psychopath carries some constraints in the avoidance of capture and imprisonment. The constraints may be few, but they exist. There are no constraints on the religious psychopath. Cornered, they delightedly fight to the death, as it leads to Heaven and the rewards for battling in their god's honor. Fly planes into buildings, give a thousand followers poisoned Kool-Aid, pull a lanyard that blows a crowded café into shreds and voilà, you awaken in Paradise with God.

It always seems an angry god, needy and tyrannical and demanding unyielding allegiance. And blood. Always the blood.

The ascendant traits of faith, in my mind, were humanizing aspects. Providing awareness of the frailties of oneself and others and viewing oneself as other than the center of the universe. Of giving purpose, or reason. It's the opposite with religious psychopaths, their version of God sucking away everything alive, leaving only vindictive robots that wander a monochromatic landscape with swords in hand, hacking at all that offends them until the earthly landscape is as empty and desolate as the sword-wielders themselves.

I stared into the night until Belafonte cleared her throat behind me.

31

"Can you be ready in twenty minutes, Mr Nautilus?" the voice on the phone said.

Harry Nautilus blinked his eyes at the bedside clock: 6.43 a.m.

"I'll be outside your hotel, Pastor."

Nautilus was beneath the hotel portico in nineteen minutes, Owsley out five minutes later in a coal-black suit with a white shirt unbuttoned to his chest and carrying three ties as he jumped into the back seat.

"I, uh, can never figure out what to wear with what," Owsley said, holding up the silken trio. "Celeste usually does that. Do you mind, uh . . ."

Nautilus turned in the seat. "What effect are you trying for?"

"I'm not quite sure."

Owsley looked lost. Nautilus said, "Give me two descriptive words, Pastor. What do you want?"

"Conservative and, uh, authoritative."

Nautilus scrutinized the ties: dark mud, darker mud and darkest mud. He stripped off his own tie, the most conservative in his collection, burgundy, but at least it had color.

Owsley looked dubious. "Don't you think it's a bit bright?"

"Not for anyone still breathing."

Owsley tied the neckpiece as Nautilus drove, shooting glances in the rear-view. This was not the prancing, up-tempo, thousand-watt Richard Owsley. This was an uncertain man. A confused man.

Maybe even a frightened man.

They drove southwest as Owsley pointed out the direction. "To the right, that tall building. We're to wait for a delivery."

"Like UPS?"

"A tractor-trailer rig."

The road was pitted asphalt paralleling a drainage ditch. In the distance the tall cross blazed in the rising sun, below it the apex of the roller-coaster track. Most of the pilgrims were probably still asleep.

A tall cyclone fence appeared in snatches, sometimes beside the road, sometimes lost in the tangle of gnarled trees and scrub vegetation. The fence was new, the clods of dirt at the base of the posts not yet beaten down by rain.

They turned hard left and came to a wooden guard-house peering from the fencing, its rear end passing through another tall fence topped with razor wire. They were at the structure that had reminded Nautilus of a mine tipple, five or six stories high, fifty feet on the sides and jutting from one end of a rectangular base. Nautilus figured the architect designed it by taping a vertical shoebox atop a horizontal one.

The facility looked hastily assembled, corrugated metal sheets attached to an internal framework, some sheets shiny new, others corroded and miscolored and salvaged from elsewhere, a motley skin over wood-beam bones. A utility building sat to one side, along with elephantine tanks labeled *Water* and *Diesel Oil*. Sections of crane boom were stacked behind the tanks and alongside a Caterpillar 'dozer. The hodge-podge construction site reminded Nautilus of a military installation from early Cold War days, a missile stash in a Third World country.

The sole anomaly was the shiny Kenworth semi-tractor rig idling beside the building, on the flatbed trailer a single large crate, twenty feet long and eight wide, loading hooks affixed to the top side.

"What is this place, Pastor?" he asked.

Owsley hesitated. "It's, uh, where I'll be working for the next two or three weeks." His tone said no more would be forthcoming, and Nautilus parked outside the guardhouse as a guard appeared from the shack, a man needing a shave and wearing the nondescript tan of the park's security staff, more forest ranger than state trooper. He approached Owsley with a smile and outstretched hand.

"Howdy, Pastor Owsley," the guard said in a lazy drawl. "We was told you were coming." He checked his clipboard and looked into the Hummer. Nautilus saw his eye light on the photo shot at Hallelujah Jubilee. The guard nodded and Nautilus nodded back.

"Is Mr Winkler here yet?" Owsley asked the guard.

The guard looked down the road and pointed. "I do believe that's your other party now, Pastor Owsley."

A long limousine pulled beside the Hummer, the glass as black as obsidian. Owsley took a deep breath and exited the vehicle.

"You can return to the park, Mr Nautilus. I'll call if I can't get a ride back."

Basically dismissed, Nautilus retreated down the road, turning the corner. He was another eighth of a mile down the lane when curiosity pulled the Hummer to the side of the road. Nautilus jogged back to the first bend and peered around a ragged pine.

As he'd surmised, the second arrival was the cranky old fart who *boy*ed him in Key West. The wheelchair was out, the two security bulls putting the old codger into the chair. He rolled toward Owsley, stopping four paces distant, the men nodding without handshakes. After a few seconds each seemed to disappear into himself and they turned to look down the road as if awaiting a sign. Nautilus saw the old man shoot sidelong and unhappy glances at the Pastor, as if finding himself in possession of a product he would soon return.

Nautilus heard the sound of a heavy engine as the driver in the long Kenworth rumbled forward to the closed door of the corrugated monstrosity, then exited to loosen the tie-downs holding the crate in place.

When the crate was unhitched, the driver turned and looked down at Owsley. Grumpy Gramps looked at Owsley. The security guy looked at Owsley. Nautilus looked at everyone, then at Owsley.

Everyone seemed to be waiting for the Mobilian pastor to do something, but no one seemed quite sure what, especially not Richard Owsley, nervously tugging the burgundy tie. After a halting step, he clumsily hoisted himself on to the bed of the trailer and took a bible from his jacket. He set the bible atop the crate, having to stand on tip-toe. He lowered himself back to the ground.

The old man didn't look impressed.

A mobile crane emerged from the structure and hooks were attached to the top of the wooden crate. The crate was lifted from the trailer bed, shifting enough to send the bible into a slide, falling from the crate to the dirt, landing with the sound of a wet rag hitting concrete.

No one moved. It was like the air had frozen and time had stopped. Seconds passed.

The man in the chair went apoplectic, pointing, screaming, his face red with anger. No one moved, especially Owsley, who appeared terrified into catatonia.

"*Do something*!" Nautilus heard the man scream at Owsley. "*DO SOMETHING*!" The man sounded on the verge of insanity.

Then, like an actor who realized he'd missed a cue, Richard Owsley jolted into motion. He strode toward the bible, not so slow as to diminish urgency, not so fast as to seem ruffled. He walked like a man on center stage, the spotlight snapping on, about to deliver the soliloquy of his life.

The man in the wheelchair stared as Owsley crouched and retrieved the bible from the dirt. He appeared ready to dust it off, but paused as if taken by a better thought. Instead of patting the book clean, he thrust it into the dirt, rubbing it furiously against the ground.

The old man's mouth dropped with horror.

Owsley pulled the book from the dirt and fanned its pages open with one hand while the other threw dirt between the pages. As he packed the book with soil, Owsley's eyes rolled back in his head and he began babbling nonsense.

"*In the name of Walalalalballummmashabba, I beseech you Almighty God to allullalllahtendonanan . . .*"

Glossolalia, Nautilus realized. *Speaking in tongues.*

Twitching like a spastic and ululating like a drunken auctioneer, Owsley stumbled in widening circles, shaking dirt from the pages into the air, into the building, across the bed of the trailer, over the swinging crate.

"*Alileelalahilalahiateshanonana . . .*"

Owsley spun to the half-mile-distant cross at the park entrance and dropped to his knees, tipping forward until his forehead thumped the ground.

"*A-shallalalaballacallahadalla . . . balacabatedah . . . nomomo . . .*"

Face in the dirt, bible clutched to his chest, Owsley seemed to wind down. Long seconds passed before he stood unsteadily and shook a trance-like expression from his dusty face. He walked to the suspended crate and pressed the bible against its side. The crane rumbled toward the building at a snail's pace, Owsley walking beside and keeping the bible in firm contact with the crate.

Owsley consecrated the dirt, Nautilus realized. Patting the dirt from the bible would have been the expected move, removing defilement from holy scripture. But instead, Owsley had rewritten the script on the fly, removing the taint from the dirt, consecrating it, making the ground holy. Making the site holy.

And maybe making himself holier in the process . . . a man connected to God?

If so, it seemed a master stroke, at least in the eyes of old Crabby Appleton, suddenly looking at peace and

32

Roland Uttleman stood in the sun-dappled backyard of the Schrum home, cell phone to his ear. He said, "I'll tell him, Hayes. I'll go up there now."

Uttleman entered the house, quiet, the only occupant Andy Delmont, sitting at an upright piano and playing a one-finger melody.

"You been upstairs recently, Andy?" Uttleman asked.

"I sang him some hymns and we prayed. Then I ran to the pizza place down the street and got him some food."

Uttleman rode the elevator up and tried the knob. Locked. They should have taken the damn lock off before Schrum arrived.

"Let me in, Amos."

"I'm not in the mood."

"Hayes talked with his eyes at the site, Amos. The

truck arrived with section one. Pastor Owsley and Eliot were there when it was transferred inside."

The door opened, Schrum's wary eyes peering out.

"How'd it go?"

Uttleman walked into a room reeking of dead flowers and Italian sausage, half a pizza on the floor beside the bed. Uttleman sat atop his desk and crossed his arms. "Pastor Owsley put a bible atop the crate as it was being lowered from the truck. But the crate wobbled and the Good Book fell into the dirt."

Schrum looked sick. "In the dirt? Lord Jesus, Eliot's demanding I return and take over, right? I know how he translates these things."

Uttleman's face brightened into a broad smile. "Good news, Amos. Pastor Owsley seized the moment and turned a shitstorm into roses. The man has the instinct. I don't think you'll be needed until the final event."

"Praise God," Schrum said, shoulders dropping in relief. "I think we need to celebrate."

Schrum went to the closet and retrieved a bottle of single-malt Scotch. He poured two fingers in a pair of glasses and handed one to Uttleman. Uttleman sloshed the fluid in his glass and studied Schrum.

"How'd you know, Amos? How'd you figure it out in one meeting?"

"Figure out what?"

"That Owsley could pull this off?"

Schrum finished the liquor and held the glass out for a refill.

"I saw the hunger in his eyes, Roland. It looked familiar."

"It's the same thing, Detective," Dr Ava Davanelle said, bending low to study a resected section of muscle. "Trauma, blows to the body hidden under char. Other blows were immediately evident, a heavy object striking the victim's mouth, breaking off several teeth."

We'd started in the morgue at seven. I'd slept in town last night, figuring that would be the pattern until these cases got solved. Ava had begun the autopsy while I sat in the utility office and had coffee and a bacon-egg biscuit grabbed from a corner market. Belafonte didn't seem able to eat with a body being dissected twelve steps distant.

Ava nodded to an evidence bag holding teeth, broken and whole. "Maybe forensics can figure the composition of the object that struck them. At least we'll know if it's metal or wood, pipe or ball bat or whatever. It might help me figure out the source of the random trauma points."

"Like a gauntlet, you said with Teresa Mailey. That might indicate several assailants."

"The blows come from every angle. I've found them as low as an ankle, and as high as the suture between the occipital and parietal."

"Behind the ear," Belafonte said.

Ava nodded as Belafonte's phone beeped. "Got to take this," she said, stepping from the room.

"You getting anywhere on this, Carson?" Ava said.

"Belafonte figured out a possible religious angle, some symbolism with the olive oil, naphtha, and wool. They have Biblical connections."

Ava's eyes flickered to the corpse, the skin burned and charred, the face a hideous and misshapen mask.

"You mean like a sacrifice or something?"

"Maybe. But if it's a religious psycho, the process could mean anything. Their brains are a slurry of twisted symbols."

We turned to the sound of the door, Belafonte entering. "That was Human Resources at Disney World getting back to me."

I nodded. "Kylie seemed to know the area, at least according to her mother. Anything?"

"Kylie worked at Disney World for six weeks. It was just over four years ago. She was a character in biblical settings until she showed up one day acting oddly. A mandated drug screen found cannabinoids in her system and she was terminated."

"You checked—"

"Yep. Teresa Mailey never worked at Disney World."

I stared down at the tormented body. "I wonder what we'll find from Jane Doe here?"

"She won't be Jane Doe long, Carson," Ava said. "Not if she's in the system. Like Sandoval, she clutched her hands tight and I sent an unscorched print to forensics a half-hour ago."

"You didn't think to tell me?"

"You were eating. I didn't want to disturb you."

33

Not a minute after Ava mentioned sending the prints to the lab, we were called over by Nancy Amante, a tech in Latent Prints. Latents was at a far corner of the main lab, a section devoted to fingerprints – known as friction ridges in the trade – and their esoterica. There was chemistry-set gear for raising and enhancing prints, and a computer terminal linked to IAFIS, the Integrated Automated Fingerprint Identification System, the world's largest biometric database and the friction-ridge repository of over a hundred million people.

I hadn't seen Nancy in a couple months. "Been busy?" I asked.

"Last week alone we processed nearly three hundred latents."

"Menendez," I ventured.

"Every print found in her house, garage, vehicle and vacation house."

"And found nothing," I said. Even the smallest lead would have been leaked to the media.

Nancy simply blew out a breath. "Your case was easier, Detective. We isolated and enhanced a section of the right index and got an arch pattern with some distinctive bifurcations and ridges."

"You got a hit?" My heart rate seemed to double.

"We got seven hundred and ten possibles."

I muttered an expletive, wanting to pick up the nearest beaker and fling it against a wall.

"That's nationwide though. Filter for gender, age and locale and we're down to three possibles in the Miami area."

I mentally set the beaker down. "And the winners are?"

Nancy tapped the keyboard. "One, Linda Quinell, Lauderdale, twenty-three, arrested two years ago for stealing an iPhone at her sorority house."

The sorority-girl aspect was an outlier. "Number two?"

"Dashelle Wilson, passing bad checks. Claimed she did it to make the payment on her Beamer, about to be repossessed."

I frowned. "The Beamer doesn't fit, not that it means anything. Next?"

"Darlene Jean Hammond, age twenty-five. Busts include shoplifting, drugs and paraphernalia, public lewdness, failure to appear on warrants, a DUI, and five prostitution busts in the last four years."

"Bingo," I said. "Low-level crime, street-corner hustling. It fits with Kylie and Teresa."

Nancy continued reading. "It seems Ms Hammond found other employment. Her last prostitution arrest was eleven months ago."

"Maybe she got faster running shoes," I said. "Or went the outcall route. She listed as a Missing?"

More keystrokes. "Nope. But if she was abducted and murdered in the last few days . . ."

"She wouldn't be listed. Got her last-known address? We gotta start somewhere."

We drove to east Miami Gardens, where Hammond had lived in a shabby apartment building with a dozen units, double locks on the doors and steel grating over the windows. The manager was Letha Driscoll, a woman fighting middle age with the full arsenal: make-up applied with a trowel, jet-black hair dye, the over-reliance on Botox that turns a face into an expressionless mask. She wore a white tube top and red Spandex slacks, poor choices given the effects of time and gravity on human tissue. But I expect Miz Driscoll saw something completely different in the mirror.

She was one of those smokers who stick a freshly lit cigarette between their lips and don't remove it until ember touches filter, gray tubes of ash falling to the floor as she led us down the dank hall to Hammond's apartment.

"Excuse me, ma'am," Belafonte said, "but you're dropping ashes."

Driscoll turned to me, like Belafonte was invisible. "Darlene's been on the street," she said, pushing the door open. "That was over a year ago. It made her sick and she got out."

We entered an apartment so small that *cell* seemed more apt, the wallpaper a bilious green, one water-damaged section peeling away. The window air conditioner sounded like a blender full of marbles. The only reading material was pulp astrology mags sold in supermarket check-out lanes.

"You know where she works now?" I said, raising my voice to compete with the AC as Belafonte went to inspect the bedroom.

"Exotic dancing," Driscoll said, smoke pluming up as ashes tumbled down. "Call it stripping, you want. If you're not selling yourself, it's a better way to live."

I leaned the wall, arms crossed. "Tell me about her."

"Kept to herself. Live that kind of life, you always got a head full of stuff make a regular person throw up."

"She have a pimp when she was hooking?"

"A sicko named Flash. I took it he got hisself shot. If so, the best thing that guy ever did was dying." Driscoll's coffin nail was done. She pulled the butt from her lips and looked for a place to stub it out.

"I'll take that," I said. Forensics needed to get here fast.

She handed me the butt and jammed another cigarette

between the red-caked lips. I could have told her not to smoke, but then all she'd be thinking about was getting another hit of the blue drug. I held the smoking butt above my shoulder, looking like the Statue of Liberty. Belafonte exited the bedroom shaking her head, finding nothing.

I handed Belafonte the butt. "Do something with this."

"Do what?"

"There's a whole world outside the door."

She gave me a glance and went out to toss the smoke away from the potential-evidence field.

"You know where Darlene danced?" I asked Driscoll.

"The Velvet Pony in Hialeah. Some places take all your money, but Dar made enough to get by."

Belafonte returned holding a beer can found on the ground and handed it to Driscoll. "Try using this, ma'am."

"I own the place," Driscoll snapped, ashes crumbling from her mouth to the floor. "I'll goddamn do what I want."

I realized her odd anger had nothing to do with smoking procedure and everything to do with the request coming from a woman having youth and beauty. Belafonte affected her best Concerned Public Protector face.

"In a teensy bit, ma'am, our evidence unit will be here. They're a meticulous lot, and will find ashes on the floor. They'll want to make sure they're your ashes and not from the person who harmed Miss Hammond. You'll

216

have to undergo a hemochromatic nicotinic analysis. Have you given blood before?"

Even the Botox-relaxed features of Driscoll crinkled into fear.

"It takes *blood*, this hemo-whatever?"

"Hardly any. The only problem is, the blood has to come from your lip because that's where the cigarettes are." Belafonte smiled sweetly.

Driscoll couldn't grab the can fast enough. "Will I still have to do that, that *thing*?" she said, eyes wide.

Belafonte's big browns scanned the carpet. "I don't believe you've reached critical ash mass yet, Ms Driscoll. You should be fine."

I started to laugh, but twisted it into a throat-clearing sound. "Was Darlene smart, would you say?" I asked, resuming my questions.

Driscoll carefully tapped ash into the can before answering. "Poor Dar wasn't the sharpest tool in the shed, tell the truth. She didn't finish high school, always talking about getting her GED. Never would have happened." Driscoll paused to think, and I saw sadness reach her eyes. "Dar was the kind of girl always hoping for something better, and wanting it so badly that anyone who come along and promised it . . . well, she'd fall right under their spell. Innocent, in her own way."

We got all we could get from Driscoll and left, after getting her to promise to lock the apartment until scene forensics came by later in the day. Our next stop would be the Velvet Pony.

"Hemochromatic?" I side-mouthed as we headed back to the Rover. "Critical ash mass?"

"The stinky old bag was dripping bloody ashes everywhere. I had to do something."

I laughed, a moment of mirth in a long and dark day.

34

We pulled into a parking lot of broken asphalt with weeds pushing from cracks, cans and bottles and debris strewn about. Shadows owned the inside of the Velvet Pony, the sole light above the unoccupied stage, one side fronted by the bar area, a smattering of men hunched over drinks. My nose wrinkled on entrance and I recalled Harry Nautilus's take on the smell: "*Every strip joint in the country is connected by tubes pumping fumes of stale beer and dead cigarettes back and forth between them, Carson. They been pumping this same air since 1953 and no one ever thinks to change it.*"

The barkeep made us as cops within an eye-blink, and stifled a yawn. "We're here about Darlene Hammond," I said.

"She ain't showed up for two days."

"The owner around?"

"Lives in Jacksonville, comes in once a month. You want to talk to Monica Dwell, the club manager." He nodded toward a back booth holding a woman in a blue pantsuit going through what appeared to be receipts and clicking on a calculator. The woman was in her forties, bone skinny, with a tiny mouth and bulgy eyes that made her look like a mix of human and insect. The extra mascara calling out the eyes didn't help. Neither did the frizzed-out hairdo. Or the tattoo encircling her neck, two strands of barbed wire.

"Yeah?" Dwell said in a nasal voice, not looking up. "What's Miami's Finest need?"

I showed the gold.

"FCLE? What the hell you think we did?"

"We're here about Darlene Hammond. I'm sorry to say she was found dead. Murdered."

The calculator was pushed aside. "Oh fuckin' Jesus . . . How?"

"I can't comment yet. How long did Darlene work here?"

A shrug. "Shit, I dunno. A year, more or less."

"Did she appear frightened of late? Nervous?"

A head shake. "Darlene came in, did her shift, boogied. Nothing seemed off."

"Have you seen anyone suspicious about?" Belafonte asked. "Suspicious for a strip joint, that is."

"It's not a strip joint," Dwell frowned. "It's a gentleman's club."

Belafonte looked toward the bar: one guy in farmer's

overalls, two in white tees and jeans, a broken-down iron-pumper in a sleeveless black sweatshirt, and an obese guy in a blue seersucker suit jamming potato chips into a wet mouth. Overalls said something presumably amusing to Iron-pumper, who slapped the bar and accidentally tipped his beer into his lap, jumping from his stool to grab at his sodden crotch and yell "MotherFUCK!"

Belafonte nodded. "And a fine lot of gentlemen they are, ma'am."

Dwell's insectine features tightened into a buggy scowl. "Listen, lady, I don't know where the hell you're from, but—"

"Bermuda, it's a—"

I pushed between Belafonte and Dwell. My partner didn't appear overly charmed by venues where women removed their clothes and swirled on shiny poles. "Have any of the, uh, gentlemen seemed particularly worrisome of late? Maybe focused on Darlene?"

A nod toward the bar. "If Darlene did have anyone she talked to regular, it's that big guy at the end of the bar, Billy the Voice. Sometimes after she got off they'd sit in the corner and talk."

She was indicating the fat guy in seersucker, the seams straining with his weight, perched on the stool like a teed-up golf ball. He was holding a beer mug in one hand, the other ramming potato chips between purple lips like they were his last meal.

"Billy the Voice?" I said.

"He's here three–four times a week. Comes in at eleven,

sits that stool, orders a Michelob Light, a bowl of chips, and watches the dancing. Always polite, too . . . not like a lot of these losers – manners like fuckin' animals."

Ten seconds later we were at the guy's shoulder. He felt our presence and turned, a chip falling from his mouth to his lap. He brushed it away with a plump paw and when he said "Yes? May I help you folks?" my jaw nearly dropped. The guy had a voice like Johnny Cash bred with James Earl Jones.

He'd seen the drop-jaw look before. "I do voice-over work," he explained. "Some commercials, but mainly documentaries and audio books. The name's William Sutherfield."

Belafonte stepped up with the photo. "We're seeking information about this girl, Mr Sutherfield. We're told she was a favorite of yours."

A frown. "Not a favorite as a dancer," Cash Earl Jones rumbled, "but as a kind of friend. Is Darlene in trouble?"

"She's dead, sir," I said. "Unfortunately."

I watched his expression. Shock, yes, sadness, yes. Surprise, not so much.

"Oh, my Lord. What happened?"

"We're not yet at liberty to say, sir. It's still under investigation. You knew Darlene well?"

"Sometimes we'd take a table in back and have a drink. Or hit the coffee shop a couple blocks over."

"Were you her confidant?" Belafonte asked.

The sadness again. "Darlene never let anyone that close."

"Sounds troubled," I said.

"Trapped by circumstance and limited education," the big voice sighed. "She fought back by becoming hard, but sometimes the act failed and she was just a lost little girl."

Music started blasting at jet-engine volume and a woman in a faux-fur bikini sashayed onstage in sequined shoes as tall as the first rung of a stepladder. Silicone had inflated her upper superstructure to soccer-ball dimensions and it strained at the fur. She licked her lips like there was jelly on them and tottered toward the pole.

"How about we repair outside?" Belafonte said. "I'm pretty sure I don't need to see this."

"Repair what?" Billy the Voice said. "Is something broken?"

I made the translation and we adjourned to brighter light and fresher air. William Sutherfield didn't seem the average strip-club patron, but I'd found there was no average, only a bell curve measuring loneliness.

A convertible full of fraternity types blasted by, one kid yelling, "Hey fat-ass, try dieting."

Sutherfield sighed. "I lost a hundred-fifty-seven pounds three years ago and my voice raised a half octave. I can't tell you how many jobs that diet cost me."

"What struck you most about Miss Hammond?" I asked, leaning the wall.

Sutherfield gave it a full minute of thought, as though getting it exactly right was important. "The depth of her anger," he said quietly. "At men, mainly, but a surprising

223

amount aimed at religion. Maybe not anger so much as bitterness. She went out of her way to mock people of faith . . . idiots, she called them."

"She piss anyone off by mocking them?" Belafonte asked.

"It wasn't to their faces. Just to me."

I asked about threats, boyfriends, lovers. I also wondered if Hammond had made any sideline money in her off-hours.

"Prostitution? I don't think sex was her thing. She made money by showing her body, not selling it. But maybe she had in the past."

"What makes you think that?"

"She told me stripping was the cleanest job she'd had, called it a factory: 'Put in your time, go home and wash off.'"

"She do drugs?"

A sad nod. "Sometimes I could see them in her eyes, hear them when she'd laugh. Darlene wanted to be happy. She just didn't know how."

"So nothing out of the ordinary happened recently? Everything seemed as always?"

Sutherfield nodded slowly, like processing a memory through a haze. "A man came in the last time I saw Darlene. A hard-looking fellow with a flat face and nose. He was in a suit, cheap and baggy. They were at the end of the stage. I was trying to hear, but the music was loud."

"You heard nothing?"

"I heard the word *Sissy* twice. *Church* once. Darlene started off looking at him with disgust, like she wanted nothing to do with the guy, but then she seemed to become interested in what he was saying."

"They leave together?"

"I'd, uh, had a drink or two too many. I don't recall. But I do remember there was something about the guy that made me keep looking at him."

"How so?"

"Like I could imagine heat pouring off his body. Does that make sense?"

Harry Nautilus sat on his balcony, beer in hand. He had seen something truly weird that morning. But what?

After Owsley had entered the building, Nautilus had returned to the motel. At noon Owsley called to say another shipment was due and he'd be gone all day. The Pastor had a ride back to Hallelujah Jubilee and Nautilus had the day to do as he wished. Evidently the missus and kid were being flown back to Mobile to gather additional clothing and necessaries.

Nautilus had driven up to Orlando and wandered the town until finding a decent gumbo joint for lunch that also served local microbrews. But try as he might, he couldn't shake the morning's events from his mind: the bible tumbling to the ground, the screaming old man, Owsley breaking from frozen fear and turning in a performance that fell somewhere between ecstasy and lunacy.

It was all weird, Nautilus thought, cracking a bottle

of beer and sitting a lounge chair on the balcony, looking toward the park, the huge tract rides and attractions and the looming cross. The whole treated-like-royalty shtick at the motel and park, the private audience with the ailing Schrum, the aircraft of a multi-million-dollar broadcasting network seemingly at beck and call. All for a small-time preacher from Mobile.

Sure, Owsley had a book out and made television appearances, but the book was regional and the broadcasts were on a cable network confined to the Deep South. It stood in stark contrast to the Crown of Glory network.

And what the hell was in that tall, slapped-together building where Owsley had spent the day?

The sun was dropping in the west and the huge cross of Hallelujah Jubilee – either majestic or intrusive, depending on your point of view – was backlit, the shadow falling eastward across the green field where the Ark's denizens pastured. Nautilus was again running the morning's pictures through his mind when a brittle voice intruded.

"I see you up there."

Nautilus paused in mid-sip. He looked down three stories to see a crinkle-eyed woman in a formless dress staring up at him, her hair to her waist and a stubby finger pointing like an indictment.

"Excuse me, ma'am?" he said.

"I see you drinking up there. You shouldn't be using alcohol. It's a sin."

"Didn't your mother ever tell you not to talk to strange men?" Nautilus said, sitting back and resuming his thoughts.

Joe Grabowski waited for the forklift carrying a load of steel panels to roar past, then pulled a walkie-talkie and keyed it. "Got one more done, Walt," Grabowski said. "Welded the seams, burnished the surface."

"Be right there, Joe."

A minute later Hillenbrandt buzzed up in a golf cart, the fastest way to travel the vast building where crews were building bridge sections, water towers and a host of custom steel assemblages. Machinery grumbled, sparks fell from welding torches, overhead cranes carried beams or partially assembled structures.

Hillenbrandt jumped from the cart. "I'll call the shipper. That just leaves two more and 1025-M is finito."

"We'll have 'em done by next week," Grabowski said. "No prob."

"Five big shiny tubes," Hillenbrandt said, revisiting the original order as he walked the length of a polished steel tube he could have stepped into without ducking. "One with a taper and end cap. Good work, Joe, we'll all make money on this one." He peered inside the fifteen-foot long metal tunnel. "Brackets all in place?"

"Per specs. Ready to lock together. Ever figure out what it is? Or what goes inside?"

Hillenbrandt started to rest his palm against the tube, stopped himself. It needed to be wiped down with an anti-corrosive, then wrapped in plastic to keep the surface bright and unmarred.

"Not mine to ask, Joe. Especially something this hush-hush."

"All sections go to that Hallajubilee or whatever?" Grabowski said. "The religious park?"

"Yep. But I got no idea what it's supposed to be."

Grabowski reached into his pocket for his pack of smokes. He grinned and nodded at the hollow metal cylinder. "It's empty inside now, Walt. But what if they put an engine in it?"

"Engine? For what?"

"A rocket engine. So they can fly to Heaven."

35

Nautilus was outside Owsley's hotel at nine a.m., leaning against the vehicle and sipping tasteless motel coffee. The door swept open at nine ten, the Pastor looking harried, though it was only in the eyes, the smile a luminous crescent of teeth.

"Celeste and Rebecca returned from Mobile last night, Mr Nautilus. Celeste wants to spend the day visiting her sister in Tampa, shopping, girl stuff. My problem is Rebecca. I know she's sixteen and all, but . . ."

"She's been practicing her independence."

"It's the internet and Tweeter, Mr Nautilus, the misinformation and assault on Christian values from every quarter. Children today have forgotten to honor thy father and mother, as stated in, uh . . ."

"Ephesians," Nautilus said. "Something in the sixes."

"Ah yes, 6:2. Anyway, uh, Celeste and I would appreciate it if you could, uh, watch Rebecca today."

The word *babysitter* flashing in his head, Nautilus raised an eyebrow. "You won't be needing me, Pastor?"

"I'm flying to Key West today. I need you to drop me off at the airport in a few minutes. Celeste wants to head to Tampa pretty soon. Could you possibly . . ."

Nautilus glanced up at the Owsleys' window and saw a part in the curtain, the kid looking down.

"Becca hasn't experienced the park yet," Owsley said. "As a saved man you understand that she should see the multifold glories of Hallelujah Jubilee."

Feeling his eyes start to roll, Nautilus closed them instead. "Sure, Pastor. I'll watch the ki— . . . Rebecca."

Owsley laid his hands on Nautilus's shoulders as if conferring magical powers. "You're a blessing, Mr Nautilus. A gift from God."

Nautilus dropped Owsley at the airport and returned to the motel. The kid was in the lobby, slouched in a chair and staring at the ceiling. She was wearing a white tank top and blue miniskirt and Nautilus figured they weren't the clothes she'd been wearing the last time she saw Daddy. She'd affected more make-up than seemed necessary for the clear skin and pretty features but, given Celeste Owsley's usage, maybe was genetic.

"I should check with your mother," Nautilus said. "Tell her we're—"

"Mama left for Tampa," Rebecca yawned. "*You're* keeping me prisoner today."

"I hope it will be more fun than that."

The kid unfurled from the chair, her face a mournful pout. "You're supposed to take me to Holey-Moley land, right?"

"Wait 'til you see the Ark," Nautilus said, aiming the kid toward the door. "It makes people faint."

The first glimmer of interest. "Like fall over and hit the ground? Cool."

The park opened at ten and they were through the gate a minute later. Tawnya appeared to have been tipped off, rolling into the parking lot in her golf cart before Nautilus set the parking brake.

"A blessed morning to you both," Tawnya chirped. "This must be Rebecca. We're so glad you could join us . . . Is it Becky?"

Rebecca grimaced.

"Rebecca! All right then! Do you still have your pass, Mr Nautilus? Good-good. And here's yours, Rebecca. Anything you want, need, think of . . . it's yours. Hop in!"

"I think we'll walk, Tawnya," Nautilus said, staring at the baby-blue cart emblazoned with logos.

The ebullient Tawnya waved, dashed off, turned and waved a second time. The pair went through the gate wearing the Joshua-level passes. Whatever the thing meant, it was heavy mojo, evoking immediate respect from park workers, like they were backstage passes to the Ascension. Nautilus figured there weren't a lot of J-level passes issued.

231

The kid was quiet as Nautilus took her past the initial flurry of vendors and down the long esplanade into the park, the road branching right toward the rides and games, left into the biblical attractions.

"There's an amusement park over there," Nautilus said, nodding right. "Even a roller-coaster. You want to ride the coaster?"

"The last time I rode one I puked my guts up."

Nautilus veered left. The concrete pathway turned to sand and cobbles as they walked backwards in time, the structures brown brick and rough timbers, Middle-eastern architecture circa zero AD. Actors in period garb wandered through the crowd, a kid leading a donkey, a girl carrying a basket of olives, a bearded youth pushing a handcart. Cameras clicked as delighted visitors – "guests" in park parlance – snapped pictures or posed beside the actors. Nautilus heard the awed comments: "*Like walking with Jesus.*" "*I can feel the Spirit.*" "*That donkey is* sooo *cute.*"

"What do you think, Rebecca?" Nautilus said.

"Lame. Can you take me to Disney World instead?"

"If your parents say you can go, I'll be happy to take you. Until I get their permission . . ."

The girl stopped dead in her tracks, scowling. "Yeah, I'm screwed, like always. They treat me like a baby."

"They're concerned for your well-being."

The kid crossed her arms and glared. "You said you don't have kids. How can *you* know anything?"

Nautilus spotted an ice-cream vendor and pointed. "Hey, want an ice cream, Rebecca?"

"Don't change the subject. I want an answer."

Nautilus led the girl away from the incoming stream of wide-eyed pilgrims clicking cameras in every direction, taking shelter beneath a palm. "I have nieces and nephews and I worry about them. I'm transferring that feeling into the feeling parents have for their children. Ergo, I think your parents are concerned for you."

"Air-go?"

"E-R-G-O. It means 'therefore', or 'it follows that'. I have a feeling of love and protection toward my family, therefore I think that's what your parents feel for you."

The kid looked dubious. "When can I see people faint?" she said.

They continued down the lane to the Ark, perched on its grassy rise, the crowd ten deep at the perimeter fence. The show was about to start.

"*God saw how corrupt the earth had become,*" a stentorian voice intoned from hidden speakers, "*and was full of violence, for all the people on earth had corrupted their ways. So God said to Noah, 'I am going to put an end to all people, for the earth is filled with violence because of them. I am surely going to destroy both them and the earth. So make yourself an ark of cypress wood; make rooms in it and coat it with pitch inside and out . . .'*"

Many in the crowd followed along in bibles. If you

didn't think to bring one, there was a fine selection in the gift shop, starting at $19.99 for the pocket version, ranging up to $389.95 for the leather-bound version autographed by Amos Schrum. "*Reverend Schrum's Choice: A Bible That Does Everything!*" the sign assured. Nautilus wondered if it scratched your back and made toast.

". . . *For forty days the flood kept coming on the earth, and as the waters increased they lifted the ark high above the earth . . .*"

Sound effects were added: thunder, crashing waves. Some in the crowd began weeping, others fell to their knees.

"No one's fainting," Rebecca Owsley said, disappointed.

"Maybe the day has to be hotter," Nautilus said. "But it's warming up. Have hope."

". . . *Then God said to Noah, 'Come out of the ark, you and your wife and your sons and their wives. Bring out every kind of living creature that is with you – the birds, the animals, and all the creatures that move along the ground – so they can multiply on the earth and be fruitful and increase in number.'*"

The huge door in the side of the vast timber structure creaked open. Two by two the animals exited with their handlers – Noah's family, presumably – sheep, goats, horses, zebras, dogs, cats, a pair of parrots on an actor's arms, the pair of camels – one balking and whipping its head as the handler struggled to keep it under control, the animals notoriously temperamental, Nautilus recalled, mules with humps.

The elephants were last, trunks swaying as they ambled from the doorway to thunderous applause. Another crowd began queuing in front of a kiosk selling 8 × 10 photos of the Ark with animals disembarking, $18.95, or the poster-sized version for $49.95.

Rebecca stared at the Ark, then turned to Nautilus. "Did you know there are over five thousand kinds of mammals in the world?"

"I knew there are a lot. I never knew how many."

"Guess how many kinds of snakes there are."

"Ninety-eight-point-six?"

"That's body temperature. Stop being goofy. There are almost three thousand kinds of snakes. Species, they're called. And since they were two-by-two, that makes ten thousand mammals that would have been on the real Ark and almost six thousand snakes."

"The math is correct."

"And there are like a bazillion kinds of bugs. Were they all in there? Where did they put them? And didn't the snakes freak the other animals out?"

"I'm sure, uh, accommodations were made and—"

"There wasn't room," the kid said. A sly smile crossed her face. "*Ergo* it never happened, right?"

"Hey, want an ice cream?" Nautilus pointed to another vendor beside the photo kiosk.

"You're really pushing the ice cream today, aren't you?" Rebecca Owsley said.

36

I spent a solo night at Vivian's, she on her third all-nighter in a row. I couldn't sleep, bedeviled by pictures of young women burned alive, so I found a cell-phone app offering sleep-inducing sounds, like white noise, rain, waves, water-falls, and so forth. I used the white noise, fearful my weariness and the sound of running water might make me wet the bed. I had a meeting with the department attorneys on another case, which took ninety minutes, with me mostly sucking down coffee and confirming the account of events.

I had fully awakened when I hit the office at 10.30. Belafonte was in the conference room poring over the cases like they were the Dead Sea Scrolls. I was barely in my chair when my cell went off, the call from Dr Ukulele Johnson, an expert in trace evidence. Johnson was Jamaican, about eleven feet tall and, though he'd left behind his Rastafarian religion when he entered college, he'd kept the goofy pot grin and dangling dreadlocks. As for the name, his mother liked Hawaiian music.

"Where you at, Uke?" I yawned.

"The morgue, helping set up new equipment. Got something for you to think about, maybe."

"On my way."

Belafonte and I headed to meet Ukulele under a sky so richly blue it couldn't have heard of the murders. We met in Ava's office, a modest room with two chairs, a desk, and a wall of handbooks and tomes. Like my pathologist friend Clair Peltier back in Mobile, Ava favored a vase of flowers on her desk, something bright amidst all the death and decay. Ava had a superbly analytical mind, and I wanted her in on anything to do with forensics, medical or otherwise.

Ukulele – pronounced *ookoo-lay-lay* – was already there, his elongated frame seated on a cushioned chair, hair cording down his back, legs crossed at his ankles. He wore bright pink slacks and a Hawaiian print shirt under the lab jacket and I figured that's how Harry would have looked as a forensics expert, just a bit shorter and sans the dreads.

Ava was at her desk, Belafonte took the other chair, I closed the door and leaned against it. Ukulele pulled reports from a manila envelope and passed them around. "We started with the standard microscope," he said, his voice rich and musical and with a reggae backbeat. "Then moved to the scanning electron scope, then to various chemical analyses. We found carbonate stone on four of the teeth. And, in one broken-off tooth, an actual piece of carbonate stone about the size of a grain of sand."

"Carbonate stone?"

"Limestone's the most likely source, Carson. Gypsum, perhaps. Or dolomite. Found anywhere there's Karst geology. One big indicator of Karst is sinkholes."

"Which are everywhere in South Florida," Belafonte said.

I shook my head, perplexed. "You're saying she was hit in the mouth with a rock, Ukulele?"

"With enough force to break four teeth off at the gumline."

My mind saw a tomahawk, the kind in the old Westerns, a stick with a stone axe-blade lashed to one end. Then I recalled Ava's use of the word "gauntlet", which gave me an even worse image, the victims forced to run while someone or *someones* thudded at them with a tomahawk.

"We found black cotton fibers on two teeth, microscopic," Ukulele continued. "It's possible they came from a gag." He paused and thought. "Or a cotton wrapping on her head."

"If cloth was over her mouth," Belafonte said, "how did the rock get on her teeth?"

Ukulele punched himself in the mouth in slow motion. "The rock hits the mouth and the teeth tear through the fabric. Like I said, we just have trace."

Ukulele had to resume his work, the installation of

radiology equipment. He unwound from the chair and headed back to his task.

"Limestone?" I said. "Rocks? What does it mean?"

Ava put a finger to her lips, the sign she was in deep thought. After several moments she grabbed a sheet of paper and a pen, scrawling for a few seconds. "A basic schematic of the tissue-damage sites . . ." she said, displaying a drawing loosely resembling a target, the centering circle fully shaded in, the next lighter, the third and outside circle lighter still. "The center represents the highest amount of broken vessels, capillaries, hemorrhage. The next circles represent diminishing damage."

Belafonte stared at the shapes. "Always rounded?"

"Generally a circular or ovoid configuration. And in this general size as well. Think about it."

Belafonte figured it out and sucked in a gasp.

"What?" I said, my sleep-deprived mind running at sixty per cent.

"The Bible," Belafonte said. "Think punishment."

It took a three-count.

"She was stoned," I said. "Pelted with rocks."

Nautilus and Rebecca lunched al fresco in the shade of a wide sycamore and ate lamb kebabs from the park's Jerusalem Café. They were almost alone outside on the picnic tables, the day having climbed into the upper eighties and most of the faithful preferring the air-conditioned version of the Holy Land.

"Do you think this is where the lambs from the Ark

go when they've misbehaved?" Rebecca said, twirling a cube of meat in her hand.

"I doubt it," Nautilus said. "This is not bad lamb."

It took the kid a moment to get the joke and she laughed. "This is more fun than I thought it would be."

"There's actually a lot to see. Like the—"

Rebecca shook her head. "Not because of all the Bible stuff. Because I like how you look."

Nautilus set down his skewer and raised an eyebrow. "Pardon me?"

"When I look at your eyes I see you looking all around, like your eyes are taking pictures." The kid demonstrated, eyes flashing side to side, seeming to linger on something for a moment, moving on.

"I'm simply observing," Nautilus said. "This is a different experience for me and it makes me think."

"I like to observe," Rebecca said. "I like to think, too." She paused. "But whenever I do, I get in trouble."

"Which probably indicates that you're thinking correctly," Nautilus said, then wondered if he should have said it.

"What do you mean by that?"

He'd used up the ice-cream shtick. "I've got to hit the restroom," Nautilus said. "I'll be back."

The restrooms were at a far corner of the food court. As he got to his feet, Nautilus saw Tawnya talking to a woman dressed in a rough-spun cowled robe. They were standing beside a pair of large trash containers on the far side of the restroom building, away from the walkways.

He was almost at the restroom door when he saw Tawnya's hand slash out and slap the woman's face. Nautilus moved closer, using a large bush as cover and pausing two dozen feet from the mini-drama.

"Shut up, bitch," Tawnya said, not wearing her toothy, sun-bright *Welcome-to-Hallelujah-Jubilee* face. This one was screwed up in anger.

The other woman said something back. Tawnya's finger jabbed toward the woman's eyes. "Fuck that. You do what I say or I'll have your sorry ass on the bricks."

Mumbled response. Some kind of challenge.

"You can try," Tawnya said. "Who's gonna believe a stupid hillbilly? WHO?"

More mumbles. The other woman sounded like she was crying.

"Leave?" Tawnya spat. "Be my guest, bitch. There's the fucking gate. See how long you can make it on the street. I'm happy to have your sorry ass gone."

More crying. Apology. The voice of subservience.

"That's what I thought," Tawnya said, in the cold voice of someone in total control. "Make that threat again and your bitch ass gets sued by more lawyers than your simple mind could count. Wash your face and get back to work."

Nautilus backtracked to the restroom. Another observation.

37

"Stoned," I said, still reeling from Ava's supposition.

We were back at HQ, me pacing the room, Belafonte going through Darlene Hammond's life, mostly documented in arrest reports. We were looking for a link outside of the hard life of runaways and the fall into prostitution and drugs. There had to be something.

"It fits, Detective," Belafonte said. "Anointing oil, fire, the wrapping in wool – the 'flesh of the lamb', if you will. You said unbalanced religios use a mish-mash of symbols."

I sat and pulled close a stack of files, the lives of three women reduced to symbols on paper. I'd been through them a dozen times, nothing. After five minutes I heard Belafonte clear her throat.

"Here's something interesting. When Darlene got

busted for hooking, another woman named Vera Garrido went down with her."

"So what's the big deal?" I asked. The MDPD didn't tend to bust single working girls, preferring sweeps that net a dozen or more at a time. They'd pick a corner or an area, pack a wagon with hookers – some screaming and swearing, others giggling at the absurdity of it all – and haul them to the station. They were back at work within a day.

"Garrido . . . she's got the same address as Darlene. They were roomies. Maybe Garrido could add some input. Maybe the perp targeted the girls when they were on the street and Garrido saw something."

"Track down Garrido's whereabouts," I told her. "See if she's been busted since. Bet she has."

Belafonte went to the computer and linked to MDPD, ticking at the keyboard. After a minute she shook her head. "Nothing. And before you ask, I just checked the obituaries."

I called Letha Driscoll, Darlene and Vera's former apartment manager. "You didn't tell me Darlene had a roommate," I said, not happy.

"You didn't ask and it weren't no big deal." I could almost hear the ashes tumbling as she talked.

"You happen to know where Vera is now?"

"I saw her a month back, she dropped by to crow on her new job." A dry and humorless cackle. "She's in the bright lights, a marquee girl."

"A little more information might be nice, Miz Driscoll."

"She works at a place called Red Flash Productions. And when you ask for Vera, ask for Amaretto Fyre. F-Y-R-E. How's that for a name . . . hot, huhn?"

The building was in Model City, an old stucco monstrosity from the forties, plaster crumbling away, lathe visible like rusting bones. The windows were barred, and the door was black-painted steel, looking strong enough to withstand cannon fire. A postcard-sized sign proclaimed Red Flash Productions. The letters rode atop a red lightning bolt.

There was a buzzer and intercom. I buzzed.

"*Yeah?*" crackled a voice. Whatever happened to *Hello*?

"We're here to see Vera Garrido. Or maybe Amaretto Fyre."

"*Who the fuck is 'we'?*"

"The FCLE."

"*What's that?*"

"The Florida Center For Law Enforcement."

"*We're not doing nothing wrong.*"

"If you don't open this door, the next sound you hear will be . . ." I leaned against the wall and counted. I was at seventeen when the door opened and a gorilla appeared.

"Be *what*?"

I held up my badge to a guy maybe six-four in a

244

wife-beater tee, hirsute, as they say, not so much body hair as fur . . . arms, shoulders, neck, ears. Mr Fuzzy was muscled like a power lifter, wearing tight cut-offs straining at the quads. He had his eyes set on Tough, probably to disguise his confusion. I've gotten to the point where I can detect stupidity by smell, and this guy was reeking.

"Whaddaya want here?" he growled.

"We'll ask the questions, bucko," Belafonte said from behind me, smelling it too.

"Who is it, Kevin?" called an imperious voice from above.

I started past Mr Fuzzy – or Kevin as I now knew him – but he put a hand on my arm. I tend to give the preternaturally moronic a bit of leeway.

"That can land you in jail," I said. "They'll shave you there, you know. Lice control."

"Hunh?" he said, but the hand came away.

"*Kevin!*" the voice repeated. "Who is it?"

Belafonte and I climbed the creaking stairs. A hall turned left at top and we saw a slender guy in jeans and a pink linen jacket. He was in his early thirties and wore a hipster goatee, a porkpie hat, and had a movie-director lens strung around a pencil neck. For some reason he had painted the nails on his index fingers black. I miss all the trends.

The guy stood in the center of the hall. Further down was a door and I saw bright light streaming out. I flashed the brass pass. "We need to talk to Vera Garrido."

"She's busy. Come back in two hours."

"We're here now."

"I take it you have a warrant?"

"It'll take a while to track down a judge, get a warrant issued, have it run over here." I patted my mouth in a fake yawn. "We'll wait. Can your people fuck with cops looking on?"

"I'll run for popcorn," Belafonte deadpanned, getting into the game.

C. B. DeMille sighed and rolled his eyes. "Break time, everyone. Amaretto! Unwanted visitors here to talk to you."

The light died in the room as the crew trooped out, sound and lighting, cameraman, and a guy I took to be the star, since he wore only a towel. The guy seemed to like being a celebri-stud, grinning as he passed and – I swear – shooting a greasy wink at Belafonte.

We entered the room, a half-dozen lights angled down at a bed. A boom mic was near the ceiling. The place smelled like sweat and sex. The bed was dressed with two frilly pillows and a huge pink teddy bear. A small table in the corner held vibrators and sexual lubricants. A woman with a mane of wild blonde hair was sitting on the bed, pulling a white silk robe around her, sort of. Her eyes were like little green rocks.

"Wha' you want?" she said, sounding three-quarters fried, the extra-crispy version. Amaretto Fyre, neé Vera Garrido, weighed about ninety-five pounds. That was without the silicone, however, which added ten. She had more tats than open skin: two rows of stars encircling her neck, a tiger climbing one thigh, a spider's web on the other, a row of Oriental characters on the left shin. A tangle of roses entwined with skulls fell from a shoulder to her right nipple. She saw me looking.

"Like 'em?" she said, probably thinking I was having sexual thoughts. She wasn't my type. I'm not sure whose type she was.

"Just admiring the art, Vera," I said. "You're a Louvre on legs."

"Hunh?"

Belafonte moved closer. "We won't take much of your time, Miss Garrido," she said gently. "We just want to ask a few questions about your old roommate, Darlene Hammond."

"Dar?" Life flickered in Garrido's lithic eyes. Her hand clasped Belafonte's forearm, as if needing to touch another human being. "Nothin' happen to Dar, did it? She's OK, right?"

Belafonte turned to me. "How about you let me talk to Miss Garrido? Alone, I mean."

"I'll be down the hall with my buddies."

C.B. was in the next room down, a dirty mattress on the floor, the walls painted with fake graffiti. I figured it was a rape set, some men having fantasies about women taken against their will in filthy surroundings, though I use the word *men* only to denote gender. C.B. and Kevin and a camera guy were looking at a monitor and watching scenes shot earlier in the day, the star working on Vera, who made high-pitched squeals every time starshine thudded into her.

"*Eeee . . . Eeee . . . eeeee . . .*"

They glanced up when I entered, then looked back to the screen. Down the hall Vera Garrido started crying. It was almost the same sound as the squeals.

"You about done?" C.B. said without looking at me, unconcerned with Garrido's despair. "We're behind schedule."

"*Eeee . . . eeeeeeee . . .*" The sounds of sex mixed with Garrido's weeping and my stomach was churning. I walked to the monitor and turned it off. A rat used in a Hollywood-style production had more protection and rights than a porn performer, especially the women, who were debased and degraded and used like porta-johns. I'd met one who'd performed in so many anal sex scenes that she'd lost control of her sphincter and wore a diaper. She was twenty-three.

C.B. glared, but I gave him a smile. "So . . . a graduate of the UCLA Film School, right?"

"Fuck you."

I crossed my arms and leaned the wall as the others studied a script and ignored me. Several minutes passed and I heard Belafonte calling.

"Detective Ryder? You back there?"

Finished. As I started out the door I heard Belafonte utter an expletive followed by a howl of pain. I sprinted to an anteroom near the stairs, the director and crew on my heels. We found star stud curled into the fetal position on the floor, towel at his feet, face tight with pain and hands cupping his meal ticket.

"The bitch hit me in the balls . . ." he gasped. "With a fucking stick."

Belafonte was folding the baton back to purse-size. "He exposed himself to me," she said.

C.B. went ballistic. "Police brutality! My lawyers are going to eat you alive!"

"Really?" I said. "In one bite?"

"I'll have your badge! I'll have her in jail! I'll *sue*!"

I leaned against the wall and stared into C.B.'s eyes, my hands in a weighing motion. "Let's see, Director Boy . . . the word of a respected police officer, or the word of a porn actor? Which will a jury believe?" I gave him my most charming smile. "Plus, C.B., when the suit hits the news, your mama's going to find out what you do." I smiled. "What do you tell her . . . that you make dog-food commercials?"

A blind shot that hit something. C.B. looked down at his stricken star. "Just leave," he whined. "You've ruined a whole day's shooting."

I declined praising a splendid double entendre, and we headed out into air untainted by sweat or stupidity. "He really exposed himself?" I said to Belafonte as we crossed to the Rover.

38

I felt diseased after being in an enclosed space with pornographers and needed fresh air and sun to burn porno-bacteria from my soul. I suggested that before we got into Vera's back-story, we pick up some chow and take it to Morningstar Park on the upper east side, not overly distant.

"That sounds splendid, Detective. I forgot to eat brekkie. I had some files on my kitchen table. I sat down to think about eating . . ."

"And got caught up in the case. Been there."

We stopped for carry-out Cubano sandwiches, heading to the bay shore and finding a picnic table under a spreading jacaranda tree. Vivian Morningstar and I joked about the park being named after her, and they shared attributes, like packing so much natural beauty in a small space. We spread out our meals as a group of kayakers paddled by in bright boats. At our backs a quartet of Lycra-clad bicyclists whizzed past. Across the lawn a young couple sat a few feet apart as their new-to-legs toddler practiced walking between them.

I took a bite of sandwich and turned to Belafonte. "So what's the skinny on Miz Garrido?"

"Vera and Darlene spent four months together, mostly in a druggy haze. When their pimp got shot, Darlene went one way – exotic dancing – and Vera met up with Kevin, who promised he'd make her a rich film star."

"And introduced her to Director Boy. I'll bet she's not rich yet."

"She's still paying off the money he lent her for the breasts. I took some insight into the religious stuff. According to Vera, Darlene was from a strict religious family in Arkansas. We're talking church four times a week, all day Sunday, no dates in high school, made to kneel and pray for hours for various infractions, beatings for others. She ran away the day she turned eighteen. When she first came to Florida she ended up at a place called Hallelujah Jubilee. Vera wasn't sure what kind of work it was, except that Darlene dressed up in various costumes. Vera said, and I quote, 'It was like those soldiers that act out old wars, except from the Bible'."

"Civil War re-enactments, I think she means."

"When Vera asked Darlene more, like exactly what she did, she'd always change the subject."

"From there?"

"She left the Jubilee place after a few months and headed to the bright lights of Miami. We know what happened here – hooking – then she lifted herself up a rung into dancing."

"And now dead. How about you give this Hallelujah, uh . . .'

"Jubilee. It's southeast of Kissimmee. I'll call and find out what she did and when."

After their lunch, Harry Nautilus and Rebecca Owsley continued through the park, Nautilus noting the kid craning her head to take in every detail, as if absorbing sights and scents and colors, and he realized she was emulating him.

They were walking through the mock Bethlehem, past a rough-hewn wooden manger scene populated by actors portraying Joseph and Mary and the Magi. A camel grunted near the rear of the scene, its bridle firmly in the hand of one of the Magi. A tethered goat stood beside the crib holding the infant Jesus, a lifelike doll mostly hidden under rough cloth. The actors were mouthing scripted lines as cameras clicked and guests looked on with joy or wept.

Nautilus again noted how young the actors were – late teens or early twenties – Joseph and the Magi made up with huge dark beards to disguise their youthful skin. *Makes sense*, Nautilus thought. The pay was probably little above minimum wage, but budding actors got a line for the résumé and the gig had to be more fun than flipping burgers at Micky Dee's. Nautilus wondered if the kids had to get their own lodging or the park carried that expense.

"Some of these actors aren't much older than you, Rebecca," he said as they passed the Nativity scene. "Maybe you could get a job here in a couple years."

"I'd rather go to Disney World and be Cinderella. She escaped, right?" Rebecca saw the look on Nautilus's face and gave him a sly grin. "Just joking. You don't have to ask if I want an ice cream."

The cobbled road ended at a sign saying *Watch Your Step, Maintenance in Progress*. A pair of uniformed maintenance men were kneeling and replacing stones in the road, a wheelbarrow of orange-sized cobblestones beside them.

"Looks like hot work," Nautilus commented to a man sifting gravel between newly installed stones.

The guy wiped his brow on his shoulder. "Someone snuck into the park last week and pulled up two square yards of stones. Probably sold them on E-bay as holy relics."

"Takes all kinds," Nautilus said, turning back. He looked at his watch, then at Rebecca. "Ready to call it a day?"

"Can you watch me again tomorrow? This was cool."

"Depends on what your parents need," Nautilus said, thinking today beat driving Celeste Owsley from store to store as she filled the trunk with purchases, or ferrying Richard Owsley around, either ignoring Nautilus to talk on his phone or expounding on his religious views.

They reached the gate. Nautilus heard a voice over his shoulder.

"Did you have a great day with us? I bet you did!"

Tawnya of the bouncy curls. The all-smiles and fuzzy words Tawnya, not the face-slapping, threatening Tawnya.

"We had an interesting time," Nautilus said. "Both of us."

Tawnya accompanied the pair to the parking lot. "You employ a lot of actors here," Nautilus said, making conversation.

"Over a hundred. Some are characters, others sing and dance in the shows."

"They seem so young."

"The average age is about twenty-five. The characters are younger, the regular show people are older."

"Where do the kids stay? Rents have to be high in the area."

"Dormitories. They stay free as our employees. We also provide meals at very low prices."

"Got to keep the workers happy, right?" Nautilus said.

"Everyone's happy at Hallelujah Jubilee," the good

Tawnya chirped, her smile verging on beatific. "It's Heaven on Earth."

After our respite we headed to HQ to write reports and jump on the phone inquiries. Belafonte started to call Hallelujah Jubilee just as Roy walked by. I ran to the hall.

"Menendez?" I asked. "Tell me MDPD's got a lead that's not in the papers." I worried about Vince living the Menendez case twenty hours a day.

"Not that I've heard. How about you, Carson? Anything on the burned hookers?"

"They were likely stoned to death, Roy."

A confused stare until it sunk in. "Like with rocks? You're keeping this one far from the press, I hope."

"They're fixated on Menendez. It's our only break, if you could call it that."

Roy blew out a breath and looked at Belafonte, lowering his voice to a whisper. "How's she handling the hooker angle . . . holding up OK?"

An odd question. "Fine, I guess. Why?"

"I checked out her vita last week, under the radar. Her mother died years before and she and an older sister were raised by Papa, a cop. You know that's no guarantee against bad stuff, right?"

"What happened?"

"The sister fell into an ugly crowd, got hooked on smack and ended up in the life to pay for the habit. It wrecked the father's health, he had a breakdown, was sent by the doctor to Miami to get help from a specialist

256

at the U. Miss Belafonte came to be with her father and watched him decline over four years."

"The father die?"

"He's in an institution, hopeless. A political family friend back in Bermuda greased the citizenship papers. Belafonte had been looking at a law-enforcement career, put it on ice until her father was basically a vegetable. Started back up a few months ago."

I recalled talking to Belafonte about her history at our initial meeting, how she'd changed the subject. Now I knew why.

"The sister?" I asked.

"In a grave in Hamilton. OD'd years ago."

I shot a glance at Belafonte and wondered if Vince had installed her as liaison solely due to the Sandoval connection, or if he saw something in her and wanted to see if I saw it, too. I did, and in retrospect realized Vince had done me a favor.

"Keep pounding, Carson," Roy said, patting my shoulder. "It's always darkest before dawn."

"I'm not sure we've gotten to midnight, Roy."

He headed to the elevator and I turned back as Belafonte hung up the phone. "That was odd."

"What?"

"Hallelujah Jubilee. I got human resources and asked about the employment dates of Darlene Hammond. The first thing out of the woman's mouth was, '*Oh*! There's no one by that name ever worked here.'" Belafonte changed her voice on the *Oh*, going up a register.

"*Oh?*"

"Like she was chirping. I said, ma'am, we have it on pretty good authority that Miss Hammond was employed at Hallelujah Jubilee. "'*Oh!*' she says. 'I may have misspoken myself.' Then I said, '*Oh! . . .* could you please check your records?' She said she would, but it would take a while and she'd have to get back to me."

"Any idea when?"

"She's not sure they can give out personal information. She'd have to check."

"*Oh!*" I said. "Hand me the phone."

I got a nice lady named Molly, who sounded young and I used a pleasant voice. "Hi! This is Detective Carson Ryder, Senior Investigator at the Florida Center For Law Enforcement. You just spoke to my assistant."

"Oh! *I did. I told her we might have employed someone of that name, but then I told her I'd have to check with—*"

"To every thing a season, right?" I interrupted.

"*Excuse me?*"

"A time to reap and sow? A time to talk and a time to listen? It's now time to listen, Molly: I need to talk to someone way above your pay grade. Have someone in authority – not your boss, maybe your boss's boss – get in touch with me before the end of the day. Write this down . . ."

I gave her my number and had her read it back.

"*Oh!*" I said. "Perfect. I'll be waiting."

We returned to the investigations, checking recent prison releases of sexual offenders, talking with parole officers, then tracing offenders and verifying whereabouts at the time of the crimes. Eleven releases in the last six months, eleven alibis that checked out.

Dead end again.

39

Roland Uttleman was sitting in the deserted kitchen of the Schrum home, bored and passing time by sifting through the daily mountain of mail sent to the Reverend. Most offered prayers or homilies, or spoke of how the writer had been touched by Schrum at some point in his long career. Many cards and letters were from churches and signed by the congregation. Some writers – conditioned by Schrum's years of entreaties for cash for his various projects – sent cash or checks. Uttleman set aside the checks and pocketed the cash.

He was alone in the downstairs, lesser employees of the network in the leased house, the low-wage worker bees and volunteers writing donation requests, updating program schedules, or praying for their spiritual leader, often for twenty or more minutes, which Uttleman was beginning to suspect was a form of malingering.

Uttleman cocked an ear upwards and heard singing, Andy Delmont with Schrum. Delmont had not done a single performance at COG since Schrum had sent himself into exile. The dim-bulb man-child was getting a salary of a hundred-twenty grand a year to perform, peanuts compared to what he made from record sales. It was time for the kid to go back to work at the studios in Jacksonville. The only problem was the singer relaxed Schrum. Uttleman recalled a newspaper story about high-strung thoroughbred horses made less skittish when a goat was in their stalls, a "calming goat" it was called.

Andy Delmont, calming goat.

Still, the songs were driving Uttleman nuts. And the room-rattling thumps when two-hundred-sixty pounds of Schrum would drop to his knees above, praying with Delmont.

Uttleman opened another letter and a twenty fell to the table. He gave a cursory glance at the page, pencil on yellow notepad.

Dear Reverent Schrum – I am sorry you are sick and I pray four you a hundret times ever day. I now you will git well like you did the last time Praise God!!!! I have the sugar reel bad and the docters have to take off my other leg. Pleese sir If you have the time to pray for me I would apreciat it. I inclose an offering.

Uttleman sighed. The halt and lame were always wanting Schrum to send prayers their way, like the guy

261

could beam them on demand. He pocketed the bill and pitched the letter into the trash as Hayes Johnson came in the back door, his face pensive.

"What is it, Hayes? You look distracted."

"I just got a call from Tawnya. An agent from the FCLE called, asking about Darlene Hammond."

"Who answered the phone?"

"Molly Holcomb. Since it was about employees, Holcomb told Tawnya."

Uttleman forced his face to remain calm. "What were they asking about Hammond for?"

"The cop, a woman, said it was an inquiry into former employment, wondering if she'd ever worked at Hallelujah Jubilee. There was a second call. A man, a senior agent. He wanted to be called back today."

"What will you do?"

"Tell him the truth: Darlene Hammond worked with us for a while over two years ago. That she was, uh . . . a fine employee who decided to move on."

"I wonder what the little bitch got herself into?"

"I don't want to know," Johnson said.

Uttleman sat quietly as Johnson tapped out the number, said, "Detective Carson Ryder please. Oh, it's you? I hope I'm not bothering you, sir, but this is Hayes Johnson from Hallelujah Jubilee. How are you this fine day? Excellent to hear. I got word that you were looking for some information on a former employee, a Darlene Hammond . . .?"

Uttleman couldn't hold in the smile; Johnson's sincerity was glorious, the voice of a man born to sell.

"I had the records sent to me. It seems Miss Hammond worked for the park for just over five months. Yes, the dates were . . ."

Uttleman tiptoed to the fridge and retrieved a Coke. He would have liked something stronger, but with the low-level park employees in and out all the time, soft drinks were the choice. Some idiot kept making pitchers of Kool-Aid, the most noxious concoction Uttleman had ever tasted. He sat back down as Johnson continued to schmooze the cop.

"No, sir . . . she wasn't with us very long, not unusual, many employees are here as a summer job. No, I never met her personally, or if I did I don't recall. We've had hundreds of employees over the years. Her position?" Johnson shot a look at Uttleman. "Let me see . . . um, she was a character actor. That means dressing up as various women from the Holy Book: one day she might be Mary, the next she might be Eve, or Ruth, or Miriam. Or perhaps not a character, per se, but color, as in wearing period garb and populating our biblical settings. It's an easy task, walking around and interacting with our guests. You get your photograph taken a hundred times a day."

Johnson winked at Uttleman, secure in his salesmanship, his schmoozing, his polished sincerity.

"No, no . . . not a problem, Detective. We're always happy to do anything we can for our fine friends in law enforcement. I hope I've been able to . . . pardon me? Who?"

Uttleman saw Johnson's face go from pink to ashen in the span of a heartbeat. "Uh . . . I don't have that information. I only requested records on Darlene Hammond. I can certainly do that. Um, let's see . . . it's past five now and the office staff have left. I'll call in the morning and let you know as soon as possible. Certainly, sir, no trouble. Goodbye."

When Johnson's hand hung up the phone it was shaking.

"What it is, Hayes?" Uttleman said.

"The cop wanted to know if two other women had been employed at the park."

"Who?"

"Kylie Sandoval and Teresa Mailey."

"Jesus," Uttleman whispered. "Why?"

"He didn't say and I didn't ask," Johnson said.

"What are you going to do?"

Johnson looked at his watch. "Fly to HJ as soon as I can. I've got to get rid of a few files."

"Will it be hard to make them, uh, disappear?"

"They were cash employees, remember? No official records, no tax forms or anything like that. I'm not even sure their names are anywhere, I just have to make certain."

Harry Nautilus stood on his balcony, beer in hand. Celeste Owsley had returned an hour back with enough packages to fill Santa's sleigh. He'd picked her up at the airport, relating that the day at Hallelujah Jubilee had been a delight.

264

"Becca wasn't snarky?" Owsley had said as Nautilus unloaded packages from the Hummer. "I swear . . . some days that girl goes outta her way to jump on my last nerve. I love her dearly, and thank Jesus every day for sending her, but can't wait for this phase to get past."

Shop less, communicate more, Nautilus thought, the Owsleys seeming like three disparate worlds jammed under one roof, each spinning in its own orbit.

The sun was fading fast, the luminous western sun turning a cirrus-rumpled horizon into a bouquet of orange and purple. The park would be shutting down, animals turned out to pasture before tomorrow's performance. Nautilus turned to the strange building at the far south edge of the park, the lone and slender tower strident against the pastel sky. What did the pastor from Mobile do every day in a tall and rickety-looking structure on the scruffy edge of a Christian theme park?

Maybe a little ride was in order. Some air to clear his head.

Nautilus drove past a small motel down the road, nondescript, two wings of rooms with scarred doors facing toward the road, one wing obviously closed, the windows boarded. The other – a half-dozen rooms – seemed open. A station wagon sat outside one room. There were trash cans in the lot, refuse piled to the top. The small swimming pools still held water. Someone was still making money from the place. The sign, unlit, said *River's Bend Lodge*, though whatever river once there had probably been diverted to make way for the park.

Nautilus continued until seeing the turnoff to the structure, unmarked save for a *Private Property* sign. He pulled down the road a quarter-mile, past a bend that would hide him from the highway. A tingling crawled across the pit of his belly.

Just a quick look. Was it possible?

Probably. With a proper subterfuge.

Nautilus drove another quarter-mile past another lane branching to the south. He followed it to a dead end of sand and scrub brush and an old dumping ground, rusting appliances, old tires, molding cardboard. The fast-food bags and scattered beer cans suggested the locale was a party spot, local teens, probably. He climbed atop the Hummer and got his bearings. He couldn't see the structure for the trees, but the thrusting cross of the park gave him an orientation.

He paused and thought, then nodded at a decision made.

Daylight fading fast, Nautilus upended an old washing machine, finding a rubber input hose inside. He pulled his pocketknife and cut it off inside the metal connectors, almost a meter of hose. His next step was piling together some small lengths of lumber, dried and brittle cardboard, and tossing a tire atop it.

He opened the fuel cap on the Hummer and dipped the tube inside, putting his thumb over the end before retracting it. It gave him a few ounces of gasoline, all he needed. He held the tube over his pile of refuse and lifted his thumb. Finally, he pulled out his lighter and touched the edge of the assemblage, a soft *whump* as the gasoline turned into bright flames.

He resumed driving and headed toward the structure, pulling to the guardhouse as a lone security guy exited, hand up in halt. It was the same guy Nautilus had seen when dropping Owsley off.

"This is a private road, you can't . . . oh, it's you. Harry, is it? Whaddaya want?"

"I was driving back to the motel and saw smoke from the woods. Far side of the enclosure. Don't know if it's park property over there."

"It is. Restricted."

Nautilus did nonchalant. "Yeah, well, I thought you should know, we both being in the protection biz and all."

In the distance a trickle of black smoke climbed into the windless sky.

The guard scowled. "What you think's causing it?"

Nautilus shrugged. "I'm just a driver."

"Shit. I should probably check it out. But I'm not supposed to leave here."

Nautilus nodded. "I hope it's not some kind of forest fire starting up. Do you think the wind's blowing this way?"

The guard looked between Nautilus and the smoke, now almost lost against the darkened sky.

"Be right back."

The guy jumped in the security van and roared down the road. Nautilus gave it a five count, then slipped into the guardhouse, one door outside the gate, the other inside. He saw the lock control pad, pressed *Open*. Nautilus entered the inner compound, moving quickly over the fifty feet to the door of the towering metal structure. The entry door beside the huge equipment door wasn't locked, the guardhouse the main protection. The door opened to darkness and Nautilus pulled an LED penlight from his pocket, scanning the area inside the door and finding a bank of switches.

He pushed the door shut and flicked the first two. The nearest half of the room illuminated, the lighting dim, most of the space in shadow. Nautilus started to flick on the other switches but caught himself . . . what if one turned on outside lights?

And whatever was in here, he just needed to know why everything seemed as hush-hush as Oak Ridge in 1943. He glanced at his watch: Ninety seconds elapsed. As his eyes adjusted to the low illumination, shapes emerged from the dark: Heavy-duty welding equipment, a forklift, a stack of heavy stud-link chain, the kind used in ship anchors. A track ran the length of the floor. At the far end of the building, deep in shadow, stood a heavy-duty crane body. Beside it, in section, the boom waited, not yet assembled.

Whatever needs lifting here, it's big.

Nautilus checked his watch: two minutes gone. He had maybe five. Nautilus scanned the penlight over the area. It was too small to penetrate the depth, so he strode forward while beaming it toward the walls and corners.

There . . . huge-ass boxes.

In a far corner sat a quartet of wooden containers, duplicates of the one that had come on the semi. They were about twenty feet long and eight wide, a fourth box as long, but only six feet in width and breadth. Checking his watch – two and a half minutes – Nautilus jogged the dirt floor to the containers, dodging wiring and debris scattered over the floor. The massive boxes were two feet taller than he stood, three of them bolted shut. But the smaller one was lidless, its top leaning against the corrugated wall. Still, it was too high to peer into.

Nautilus saw a meter-square crate a dozen feet away labeled *Brackets-1025-M - 10-count*. Nautilus pulled it to the container, glancing at his watch: Three and a half minutes gone.

Nautilus jumped atop the crate, leaned into the yawning opening and shone his penlight inside.

40

The jezebel had made a mistake, Frisco Dredd thought, sitting in his van on the downtown Miami street. Maybe it was because she lived just a few blocks from the hotel where she was now doing filthy and unspeakable things to a man, but she had parked her little red car in a lot two blocks away.

No taxi tonight. No stepping from the bright lights of a hotel with people on the street or looking out from restaurant windows. She had driven her own little car and parked it in a lot two blocks away. A lot that had but two lights, one now gone from a single shot with Dredd's Crosman CO_2 pellet gun, the same one that had knocked out streetlamps along the stretch of road Teresa Mailey would travel.

Tick was the only sound the rifle made, and half of the lot went dark. The rest was just the waiting.

Dredd's hand drifted to his shirt, making sure the top

three buttons were undone. Jesus needed to see why the vixen had to be punished.

Harry Nautilus stared into the box, perplexed. Before him was the front segment of a rocket: four feet in width, tapering over its fifteen or so feet of length to a rounded point. It was burnished on the outer surface, sleek and beautiful and almost serene, like a Brancusi "Bird in Space" sculpture.

Nautilus aimed the light toward the tapered end, as round as an orange. He checked his watch: Four minutes gone. He startled to a horn honking stridently in the distance and retreated across the floor to the lights, retracing his route.

By the time the guard returned, Nautilus was sitting on his hood, drumming his thigh and whistling Ellington's "Take the A Train". He gave the guard a *what's-up* eyebrow as the man jumped from the vehicle.

"Kids drinking, I expect. Found a buncha beer cans and trash. They'd built a fire. There's over a hundred acres of scrub out there, old roads crisscrossing, and all sorts of drinkin' and make-out spots. They musta seen me coming and took off. I flat-out mashed that horn to let 'em know I saw 'em."

"That's the way to handle it," Nautilus said, thinking, *What a yokel*.

"Anyway, thanks, buddy. I'm gonna tell the honchos they gotta block off that side road."

"Have a good one."

Nautilus faked a disinterested yawn and climbed into the Hummer. Twenty minutes later, back in his digs, he grabbed a beer and sat on his balcony, staring toward the dark building.

A rocket in a biblical theme park? It made no sense. Illogical from every angle.

Conclusion: *not a rocket*. Something that resembled a rocket. Theme park, tapering, pointed steel assembly. Welding equipment. Tracks in the floor. A big-ass crane waiting to lift heavy pieces into place.

It was a *ride*. Some kind of monorail maybe. No, given the twin tracks, a train . . . a sleek aerodynamic train. Or . . . was it the front segment of some newfangled roller-coaster, the hoist waiting to build the support system?

That made sense.

But so did a restaurant, like the Gatlinburg or Seattle space needles, the elongated cone in the building forming the spire atop the restaurant. That made sense as well.

Whatever it is, Nautilus told himself, it had something to do with a ride or a restaurant and, like everything else in the strange land of Hallelujah Jubilee, was created to inform, entertain, and make money.

Nautilus blew out a breath. He'd risked his job to discover the park's next big audience attraction. He put his feet up on the railing and leaned back, looking out over the pasture behind the motel. There, four hundred feet away, an elephant grazed slowly in the moonlight, beside it a donkey and a dromedary camel, off from their shifts in Ark Land. The camel lifted its head and called across the fields, a quivering moan that seemed to linger unnaturally long, as if trapped inside the air.

Though the night was warm, Nautilus suppressed a shiver.

Two hundred bucks a day, he reminded himself.

41

Roland Uttleman sat in the dimly lit kitchen of the Schrum house reading a medical text. The project was in the increasingly capable hands of Richard Owsley, soon to have his own program on the Crown of Glory network, an electronic store, so to speak, where he could sell taped sermons, books, branded bibles, tout upcoming live appearances. Owsley would soon be living the life he espoused, Paradise on Earth. Manna from every direction, including Eliot Winkler, who had more manna than Croesus.

But with the miracle of 1025-M nearing completion, it was time for Amos Schrum to have his own "miracle": A healing. The next few days would bring cautious advisories from the COG PR staff – engineered by Johnson, no one from the staff allowed near the holy man – saying Schrum seemed to have been touched by God, his physical condition improved. The faithful wouldn't need any medical information, God's will that a great leader continue living, but there had to be a plausible explanation for the medical types who'd be yammering on news outlets.

Uttleman would be asked to comment, and was speaking possibilities into a pocket recorder, trying to be as authoritative as Hayes Johnson.

"Initially thought to be a cardiac event, but tests revealed a severe reaction to a medication Reverend Schrum had been taking . . ."

Nice, Uttleman thought, listening to the playback. But it couldn't be purely medical, there had to be a sense of divine intervention. He expanded on the theme.

"An initial cardiac event followed by intense and recurrent bouts of arrhythmia with cardiac stress and enlargement suggested the worst scenario. I discovered the possibility of a toxic interaction between two of the many medications being administered to my oldest and dearest friend, and arrhythmia ceased. But I'm not sure even that discovery . . . no, that revelation, can explain the Reverend's rapid recovery, nothing short of . . ."

Miraculous.

Perfect, Uttleman thought. Medical *and* mystical. There'd be the usual cynics and scoffers, but screw them . . . they didn't fill the coffers.

Uttleman startled to the sound of breaking glass from upstairs. He bolted to the elevator, pressing wildly at the button as outsized footsteps thundered across the floor toward the front. *He's going to the window*! Uttleman sprinted the stairs to Schrum's room, seeing a weaving, lurching Schrum pulling at the balcony door. The twenty-four-hour vigil was below on the streets, two hundred or more, many camped there.

"Amos!" Uttleman yelled, crunching over a piece of broken glass, a shattered quart of vodka on the floor. "What are you doing?"

Schrum seemed perplexed by the doorknob, his white hair fallen forward on his head, the eyes glazed and darting. "I have to tell the truth, Roland. I . . . have to regain my soul."

Uttleman advanced slowly, hands up. "You can't do this, Amos. It might destroy you."

Schrum nodded toward the crowd. "Look at them, Roland. They believe in me."

"Because you've been a force for good, Amos. All your life."

Schrum's knees buckled, but he wrenched himself upright. "You of all people know that's a lie," he said.

"You're drunk, Amos. Think of what you're doing."

"I have to unburden, Roland. I have to witness before God."

Uttleman was frozen into immobility as Schrum turned the knob, the door swinging open. He began to stagger outside.

"Don't do that, Reverend," said a quiet voice behind Uttleman. "Stay inside."

The doctor turned to see Andy Delmont framed in the

276

door, wearing blue pajamas with indigo piping, his feet bare and pale. The singer stepped into the room, his eyes steady on the wavering Schrum.

"Don't step out there, Reverend," Delmont said. "It's the Devil moving your feet."

Schrum paused, rubbing his eyes as though trying to bring them into focus. "Andy . . . my heart says I should—"

"Your heart's in a dark cloud, Reverend, like we've talked about before. Come away from the door, sir. It'll pass."

"Andy, I don't know what to do."

"It's demons, Reverend. They'll leave you soon enough. They always do."

"You know me, Andy," Schrum nodded. "You're my best counsel when I'm . . . like this."

Schrum pushed the door closed and lurched back across the floor. When his feet tangled and Schrum pitched forward, Delmont was there to catch him, half guiding, half dragging the drunken Schrum to his bed.

"There you go, Reverend," Delmont said. "You get yourself some sleep."

Schrum muttered something incomprehensible and rolled his head to the pillow, passing out. Delmont gently pulled the covers over Schrum, tucking them around the man's shoulders.

"You've done this before, Andy," Uttleman realized.

"The Devil wants Reverend Schrum to confess his sins to the world so his enemies can tear him down. We're

277

all sinners, Doctor, ain't none of us perfect 'cept for God and Jesus. Reverend Schrum hisself told me that."

"Where were you?"

"Sleeping in the back bedroom. Reverend Schrum likes me close in case he needs singing and comfort and other stuff."

Uttleman said thanks and good night and crossed the yards to his car as his adrenalin subsided and he replayed the incident in his mind. The kid sure seemed to know which words pulled Schrum back from the brink.

"Reverend Schrum likes me close in case he needs singing and comfort and other stuff . . ."

Stuff meaning protection? Uttleman wondered. Like keeping Schrum from making a fool of himself when drunk?

Had the wily Rev figured that one out as well?

Frisco Dredd sat low in the seat in the parking lot, watching shapes on the bright-lit street a half-block distant, pedestrians, traffic, bustle. But the small lot was tucked between two towering buildings, like in a shadowed valley.

Yea though I walk through the valley of the shadow . . .

Three times Dredd had to duck low, people crossing the lot to enter cars after their meal or picture show.

"Was it this dark when we left the car, Paul?"

"Looks like a light burned out."

Dredd sipped from his bottle of water. He'd been in

278

the van for hours, almost two in the morning. Waiting was easy because he could sing songs in his head and make the time disappear.

> I heard an old, old story, How a Savior came from
> glory,
> How He gave His life on Calvary, To save a wretch
> like me;
> I heard about His groaning, Of His precious blood's
> atoning,
> Then I repented of my sins . . . And won the victory.

Then, backlit in the lights of the main street, a woman's shape, moving swiftly, long legs scissoring toward the lot. *Sparks . . . the whore*, leaving some man drained half-dead on a bed and reeking of sin and perfume. She moved closer and Dredd made out the motion of her hips and the backlit silhouettes of her long legs, hair swinging as she walked.

Come on, harlot, come on . . .

She'd have to pass behind the van to get to her little white car and Dredd was coiled to spring out and slap his hand over the Jezebel's wet mouth, feel her hot scream beneath his palm, the tender lips opening and closing as her spit soaked his fingers, her mouth like a . . . He moaned as his animal strained against the wire but the blessed pain kept his mind on his holy task. Dredd put his hand on the door handle and started to push down . . .

"*Excuse me, ma'am?*"

A voice from nowhere, like the soft voice of a child. Dredd ducked low and eased his eyes above the dashboard, seeing someone walking to his quarry.

"Jesus, kid," the Sparks-whore said. "You scared the fuck outta me."

"*I'm sorry, ma'am. I didn't mean to. I, uh . . . do you have a little money? Some spare change?*"

"Lemme look. You new to town?"

"*I, uh . . . just got to Miami this morning. I hitchhiked.*"

Dredd could have grabbed the whore and tossed her in the van, hit her until she was still, but the other one would be screaming her lungs out. The main street was a half-block away, people walking, cops patrolling. Too dangerous.

"Hitchhiked from where?"

"*A town in Arkansas – you'd never know the name, nobody does. I got a ride most of the way. But the guy who picked me up, uh . . .*"

"Wanted payment," the jezebel said. "And it wasn't money."

"*Yes, ma'am. I jumped out and ran and got another ride here. I'm sorry to have to beg but . . . I ain't had nothing to eat since I left.*"

"Here's fifty bucks."

"*WOW, thanks. I really mean it.*"

"No prob. So what are you gonna do in Miami? You got somewhere to live?"

A pause. "*I never thought about anything more than getting away.*"

"So you got nowhere to sleep tonight?"

"*There's bridges.*"

"You like being raped?"

"*NO!*"

"Then don't sleep under bridges. You got a job?"

"*I, uh, not yet.*"

"What can you do . . . you got a diploma?"

"*I figured maybe I'd get a job first and then get a GED down here.*"

"You got it in reverse, girl. GED gets the job. Hey . . . you like fucking for money? Sucking the dicks of wrinkly old guys?"

"*WHAT! Eeww . . . no.*"

"That's about the only job left open. Listen, there's a place you should go see. Butterfly Haven. It's where you can be safe."

"*That's a goofy name.*"

"It's because crawly worms change into butterflies, something like that. And so what if it's stupid if it keeps you safe, right?"

"*I don't know if I . . .*"

"Go to Butterfly Haven, tell them where you came from, why you left. The guy that runs it is a priest or one of them things. But he won't give you a bunch of bullshit. And you'll have a roof over your head while you figure out some solid moves."

A pause. The girl said. "*Ma'am . . . can I ask how*

you know so many things? Did you, I mean, were you ever . . ."

"I'm a . . . an airplane pilot," the whore told the girl for some reason. "I fly across the ocean and all around the world. Airplane pilots know a lot of things because we see so much stuff. Good stuff and bad stuff, we see it all."

"A lady airplane pilot," the girl said, like she was low on breath. *"That's so cool."*

"Get in the car and we'll go get something to eat, then I'll drive you over to the Haven. Hurry . . . this place gives me the fucking creeps."

42

The next morning took me straight to the DA's office, a final meeting on the upcoming Shockel indictment. Waylon Jay Shockel was a serial rapist who drove a pilot car for overloaded semis. When overnighting at truck stops, Shockel went on the prowl. The legal proceedings had to be tight and by the book with no chance for a successful appeal. I'd spent two months tracking the rapist and if all went right, he'd spend the rest of his life prowling the confines of a cell.

I was sitting with prosecutor Miles Billingsly when my phone rang, Belafonte. "My partner," I said. "Got to take this."

I went to the hall. "*When are you coming in?*" she said. "*I found something interesting.*"

"I'll be another hour with the attorneys. You find something major?"

A pause. "*I guess not, not really. You're gonna find it out anyway when Hayes Johnson calls. I just wanted to be the first to tell you, that's all.*"

"Who's Johnson?" My mind was on Schockel.

"*The CEO at Hallelujah Jubilee. I'll only confirm what he tells you.*"

"And that is . . ." I looked up, saw DA Miles Billingsly looking my way and tapping his watch. "Gotta go," I said. "Whatever you're doing, keep it up."

Seventy minutes later I was back at HQ and heading to my corner office until Bobby Erickson called my name. Bobby was a retired Florida State Police Sergeant who worked the phones. He unfailingly wore his beloved dress blues, but had foot problems, so Roy let Bobby wear slippers, big suede pillows with fleece puffing around his ankles. Erickson was short and rotund and seemed perpetually concerned, lips pursed, eyes frowning over half-glasses.

"S'up, Bobby?"

He blinked at a pink call slip. "You had a call from a guy named Johnson. Wants you to call him back." Bobby frowned at the note. "Haze Johnson? Who names a kid Haze?"

"H-A-Y-E-S, Bobby. But yes, the homophonic confusion does tend to confirm your point."

He retreated on the fluffy pillows, shaking his head. "Confused homos? Some day I'll understand what you're saying, Carson. This ain't the day."

284

"Belafonte around?" I called to his back.

He pointed through the floor. "She went to the atrium to grab a yogurt."

I hung my jacket on the peg behind the door and sat. The call slip had Johnson's number and I tapped it out.

"Hello," a deep and confident voice said. "This is Hayes."

The CEO of an influential broadcasting network and attendant enterprises had given me his private number? No long-distance management here. The guy was hands-on.

"This is Detective Carson Ryder, Mr Johnson. Sorry I wasn't here to take your call – a meeting."

"No problem whatsoever, sir. I'm happy to be of service in any small way possible."

"I take it you spoke to your people about the women in question, Teresa Mailey and Kylie Sandoval?"

"I had them check records going back ten years. I assure you, Detective, neither woman has been in the employ of Hallelujah Jubilee."

"What I need to know. Thanks for your prompt response, Mr Johnson. I wish more folks were as attentive as you."

Confirmed: I hadn't figured on any connection, and now knew for sure.

Also confirmed: Outside of the religious aspect we were back to zero.

* * *

Belafonte was back in ten minutes, spooning yogurt. "I just heard from Johnson," I said. "Neither Teresa nor Kylie ever worked at Hallelujah Jubilee."

The spoon froze in mid bite. "What?"

"No connection to the park. Neither victim."

She stared, as if my words were in Swahili. "I don't quite . . . this is what he told you, the CEO of the network?"

"Si, Señorita Belafonte. I wish we'd found a connection, anything. But I like this Johnson guy, he got right on—"

"Meeting room," Belafonte said, tossing the yogurt cup into the trash. "I think now would be appropriate."

I was up and on her heels. She pushed aside the sprawl of files to accommodate her laptop. "You ever get so you can't sleep?" she said rapidly, like she couldn't get the words out fast enough. "The damnable pictures racing through your head, and they go faster at night? That was me last night and I needed to do something, but I've been through the cases a thousandtimeseachand—"

"Calm down, Belafonte. Talk slower."

She took a deep breath, let it out, continued at normal speed. "I started thinking about what Johnson said yesterday, about the employees in biblical roles. How they get their pictures taken constantly?"

"Yes?"

"There are photo-sharing sites all over the internet: Shutterfly, Reddit, Flickr, Picasa, Photobucket . . . tens of thousands of birthdays, vacations, weddings, bar mitzvahs, reunions . . . I entered the search words 'Hallelujah Jubilee'. There are hundreds, maybe thousands of photographs. Johnson was correct about one aspect: people love being photographed beside actors in biblical garb."

Belafonte ticked keys to call up a file and angled the laptop my way.

"Do you know who this is, Detective?"

I saw a half-dozen tourists beaming for the camera as they flanked a young woman in a rough gray robe, a cowl over her head, hands clasping a baby lamb. I knew the face, though I had seen it in death.

"Teresa Mailey," I said, staring dumbfounded as Belafonte scrolled through a half-dozen saved shots. Teresa Mailey in varying costumes, with different people.

"Kylie?" I said. "Was she also . . .?"

Belafonte showed me five photos of Kylie Sandoval, ending with the girl in a brown coarse robe, a thick scarf over the amber tresses. She was posed before a bus, its side saying *Possum Valley Baptist Church of Murfreesboro, Tennessee*. A dozen hefty ladies flanked Kylie, all beaming like they'd just won the Betty Crocker Cookie Open. Kylie Sandoval was smiling as well, her mouth at least. The eyes looked sad.

"Remember the coarse cloth I found hidden in Kylie's closet?" Belafonte said. "Look at the scarf she's wearing."

It was brown and rough-loomed and the same fabric Belafonte had shown me a few days ago. I heard Hayes

43

A sudden sizzle of energy had me pacing the room.

"Johnson had me hook, line and sinker," I said, rounding the table a fourth time. "But he called, not a park employee. That was the only thing nagging me: People of Johnson's stature don't make calls about low-level employees."

"Unless they want to make sure the denial carries weight."

I nodded. "Damn, Johnson was good. I wanted to reach through the phone and shake his hand."

"Should we confront him with the photos?"

I circled three more times, tumbling the situation through my head. "It'll tip him off. For now we sit tight and think. You handed us a huge lever, Holly. Now we have to figure out how to use it."

"Holly?"

"You prefer Belafonte?" I said, looking into the brown eyes that had spent hours scanning through photos in the dead of night. She'd listened to what Johnson had said, honed in on one sentence, turned it into gold. "I don't care what you want to be called, I'm calling you a professional. Incredible work."

She reddened and looked toward her lap. "Thank you. And Holly will be quite fine."

I felt buoyed, suddenly alert, renewed. I didn't know what we were looking at, but we saw *something*.

"Let's put a microscope on Hallelujah Jubilee," I said. "Can you do that quickly and quietly?"

"I'm on it. What will you be doing?"

I turned to the window and gazed high into a blue sky brightened by sudden promise. Ever since Ava had proposed stoning and the method of death, I'd been considering going to a well I'd used sparingly but effectively.

"I'm thinking I'll consult an expert in the field," I said.

"An expert in religion?"

"In madness."

I jogged to my office. During my brother's institutionalized decade he'd known several homicidal religious maniacs, including Preaching Bill Barton. Barton was an ordained minister in a small Ohio church who'd had visions of children in his congregation possessed by demons ("I saw them tiny little eyes light up with hellfire") and had stealthily abducted and murdered three of them. Police were stymied by the disappearances until

290

one Sunday morning when Barton's sermon included pulling the eyes of the children from his pocket to demonstrate how they glowed in the dark.

Jeremy didn't answer the landline so I tried his cell phone. He answered and in the background I heard a jumble of voices talking, yelling, singing.

"You're out in the street, right?" I said. "In front of Schrum's house?"

"It's party time here, Carson. Schrum's press office just released a statement suggesting the great man might be on the mend. The statement was a mix of medicine and mumbo-jumbo, but it's got the crowd in an ecstatic frenzy. A rumor's circulating that Schrum appeared at his balcony door last night, as if ready to step out, but turned away at the last moment. The throng is taking it as a sign that he's up and about, which, as I've mentioned, has been since his arrival."

"Maybe it's a sign I'm supposed to call you. I need a bit of insight on a case."

"*Bit* as in minuscule portion?" he said, amused. "You never need a bit of anything, Carson."

"I simply need observations on religious psychopaths. You've known a few."

"Yes, indeedy. I liked them."

It threw me. "Weren't they hard to control . . . being in the service of the divine and all?" For ten years in the Institute my brother had made a study of the shattered minds around him and turned it into a game: Seeing how fully he could enter their skewed landscapes and make

291

them do his bidding. It was fiercely dangerous and more than once he'd been infected by their madnesses.

"Not that hard, Carson," he said. "The trick is to figure out their personal symbology and use it to speak their language. Once you know that, you always find them governed by very strict rules."

"How about you go someplace quiet and call me back, Jeremy. We can talk."

"How about you send me candy and I'll munch a while?"

I almost groaned. By *candy* my brother meant case files, reports, photos. He especially enjoyed photographs of crime scenes.

"No need, Jeremy. It's just a broad question about—"

"You know I have a sweet tooth, Carson," he said softly. "Feed it or you're on your own."

"They'll be there in an hour," I growled. "Stay by your damned computer."

I checked on Belafonte, gathering all the low-hanging fruit on Hallelujah Jubilee, so absorbed in her work she didn't see me. I sent Jeremy thirty or so pages, plus a dozen photos. I figured my brother would need several hours to start making conclusions.

After a half-hour I returned to see what Belafonte had unearthed.

"Here's what I have from the internet, Detective. Hallelujah Jubilee opened eight years ago. It had a rocky financial start, loans coming due before much income was generated. It now seems a moderately successful enterprise. The park is a non-profit overseen by the Crown of Glory broadcasting network, headquartered in Jacksonville."

"What's Schrum's part?"

"He and his wife started the network operation almost forty years ago from a tiny thousand-watt station in the middle of nowhere. She died several years back, cancer. Schrum's chairman of the board . . . the front man for a big band."

"But Johnson runs the whole show?"

"The business side at least. I don't think Schrum goes near it: he's the spiritual leader, the holy centerpiece."

Bobby Erickson pushed open the door. "Gotta call, Carson. A Doctor Faustus."

"Thanks, Bobby," I said. "I'll take it in my office."

I trotted the hall to my office, closed the door and sat, looking at my watch. "Forty minutes, Jeremy? I expected it would take longer."

"You have an afflicted fellow out there. A very religious upbringing, the word *severe* comes to mind, like being beaten senseless while Mummy or Daddy told him how diseased and evil he was. Do you know the effect that can have on a young mind?" He paused, then screamed, "WHERE ARE YOU HIDING, YOU MISERABLE LITTLE BASTARD?"

I froze. It was my dead father's voice. Jeremy could mimic it perfectly. For a split second I was nine years old and hiding in a closet while our father raged through the halls, his insane anger like black lightning blasting apart our house.

"Jeremy—" I rasped. "Don't start with the—"

My brother cut me off with, "I TOLD YOU NO GODDAMN ANIMALS IN THIS HOUSE!"

Words from my tenth birthday, our father clutching the pet hamster I'd kept hidden under my bed, slamming it into the wall as if pitching a baseball.

My palms were sweating as I found my voice.

"Stop it, Jeremy, or I'm hanging up."

My brother's normal voice resumed. "I was simply setting the stage, Carson. You've been there, I've been there. But as nasty as dear ol' Da could be, he never made us dirty in the eyes of God. He must not have thought of it. We both escaped relatively intact, mentally speaking. This unfortunate fellow didn't. He's been so soaked in religion all he sees is good and evil, God and the Devil. It's Manichaean, the world a constant struggle between dark and light, expressed in Christian symbolism. Your burning boy has a thing about women, making me suspect it was Mommy who sparked his torments. I think he sees women as evil, but not condemned to hell, not if he can help it. Maybe he's saving Mommy."

"What do you mean?"

"He's killing the women's evil powers with the stonings. But it's akin to an exorcism, their redemption coming when he wraps them in the lamb – how's that for fun? – consecrates them with sacred oil, splashes them with the biblical magic-fire of naphtha, and flicks his Bic. I'd bet my next week's stock profits he has an altar somewhere. He'd need the ritual aspect."

"Wasn't it Jesus who said let he without sin cast the first stone? If the perp's so Bible-driven . . ." I let the question hang.

"He'll have a mental construct to bypass it, Carson. A justification, some sort of special dispensation from God or Christ. He is, after all, saving women from their evil natures."

"Thanks, Jeremy. That might be a help in my—"

"Now," he interrupted, "what aren't you telling me?"

I paused. "What, uh, do you mean?"

"I saw the data and the pictures. Give the forensics photographers a huzzah from me, Brother, excellent composition. And you did happen to notice the faint cross in the sand under the one body, correct?"

"Yes."

"Excellent. But what little details aren't in the reports?"

I thought it out; no harm done to tell him the latest. "We have a link between the cases: the victims had all been employed at a religious theme park up by Lakeland, Hallelujah Jubilee."

A pause so long I wondered if we'd been cut off.

"Jeremy?" I said. "You still there?"

"You realize, Carson, that the fellow who founded the enterprise is supposedly dying down my block?"

"Schrum's based out of Jacksonville, and the Crown of Glory network operates the park as a non-profit. I can't see a—"

"Maybe you should ask your old partner what he knows."

"Harry? Why Harry?"

"There's a house behind the Schrum edifice that seems rented by folks in the righteous Rev's entourage, comings and goings at all hours. Limousines, Hummers. Stern-faced men carrying bibles and briefcases. The Winklers. Attractive young people I assume to be staffers. A goofy and ever-present fellow dressed like Gene Autry. That's a classical allusion to a—"

"I know who Gene Autry is. The point being?"

"Your Mr Nautilus is part of the proceedings. I saw him at the house three days ago."

Jeremy had never met Harry. My brother was either deluded or jerking me around. "What makes you think that?"

"He was in the neighborhood and reading a newspaper. He offered it to me, points for civility."

"No way. Couldn't have been Harry."

"Does Nautilus have some form of chauffeurly duties? He was leaning against a Hummer as he read, as if the vehicle was his charge."

I stiffened. Only a handful of people knew Harry was driving for the Owsleys. And he'd joked about the Hummer and the hush-hush nature of the job. Was my brother telling the truth?

"You talked to him?" I asked.

"He was quite polite and hid his confusion."

"Confusion at what?"

296

"You favor Mama, looks-wise, I favor sweet old Da . . . but there is a resemblance between us, *n'est pas*?"

"He recognized you?"

"He's never met me. He saw a ghost in my cheekbones, my jawline. We both have rather sturdy jaws, right? And dazzling smiles, like the one I'm wearing now."

44

I called Harry's cell phone. He answered on the sixth ring. "You don't usually call when working, so I expect you have the day off."

"Nope, I'm working. Tell me what you see."

"Uh, what?"

"What you're looking at, Harry. Your vista."

"Is this a game?"

"It's dead serious, accent on dead, which is why I'm so serious."

"What's going on, Carson?" His turn to be serious.

"Are you in Key West, Harry? I know you were there a few days ago. Something to do with that old preacher who's giving up the ghost – Schrum."

A pause. "How do you know that?"

"My crystal ball. And if you don't 'fess up I'm going to send the flying monkeys after you."

"I'm not in Key West, Carson. I'm in Central Florida."

"How are things at Hallelujah Jubilee?"

A perplexed pause. "OK, Carson. What the hell is going on?"

"Remember what Clair used to say about synchronicity?"

"There are no coincidences," he recited, "because everything links in a fantastical web so far beyond human knowledge it'd be like an ant walking across Einstein's calculations on special relativity. The ideas are supporting the insect, but so far beyond the ant's comprehension that—"

"We've got a freaky situation here, brother, and you being at Hallelujah Jubilee has dropped another ant on the calculations. Wanna get together for a drink in a few minutes?"

"Where are you?"

"Miami."

"A few minutes? We're two hundred miles apart."

"Where you want to meet?" I looked at my watch. "Let's say in forty-five minutes."

I'd banked on luck and got it: the departmental chopper was free and twenty minutes later I was watching the Everglades sweep past a half-mile below, green and blue and blazing with reflected sunlight. In no time I was over farmland and roads and clusters of housing developments, close enough to earth to see heads crane upward as we roared northward in the Bell chopper.

Harry had suggested a bar-restaurant in St Cloud, about ten miles from where he was staying. There was a small airstrip in town, and I jumped from the chopper, jogged fifty paces, and was in the mighty bear hug of my amigo.

"You're on a case that has to do with the park? Jeez, Carson, what the hell—"

"First let's get somewhere I can grab a brew and a burger. A nap would be nice, too, but I don't think that's in the plan."

We jumped in a big bright Hummer and five minutes later were in Joker's Lounge, a single-story block building with knotty-pine walls, tables steadied by matchbooks, a television playing sports over a Formica-topped bar, swiveling stools that creaked, a pinball machine beside a jukebox . . . Plato's original form for the American roadhouse. The grilled cheeseburgers were in the concept, too – thick and dripping and if you ate more than two a week you'd need your veins flushed with muriatic acid.

When beef and grease and beer had refreshed my brain, I laid out the details to Harry.

"Stoned?" he said, eyes wide. "Jesus. You mean like—"

"Pelted with rocks large enough to break bones, crack skulls. The pain would have been excruciating."

"All of the women worked at Hallelujah Jubilee?"

"We have proof, though the head dog lied about two of them. I think he would have lied about all three, but we were ahead of him on one vic."

"What did the women do, Carson?"

"Part of the park's schtick is having actors in period costume. Robes and sandals and whatnot. People take pictures . . . a lot of them."

He popped a fry in his mouth and nodded. "The phones and cameras never stop. But how do you know?"

"Some of it came from a guy named Hayes Johnson. For the rest Belafonte and I took a trip on the Google express."

"Johnson? Never heard of him."

"Johnson's the CEO of the network and seems awfully camera-shy for a business leader, but Belafonte dug up a shot from an annual meeting three years back."

I pulled my iPad and called up a photo of a big guy behind a podium, smiling like his racehorse just cinched the Kentucky Derby.

"Saw the guy once." Harry nodded. "But was never introduced. He was present when I first dropped Owsley off in Key West. How'd you know I was there, by the way?"

I'd never told Harry about Jeremy's Byzantine trip to semi-normalcy in Key West; as far as he knew, my brother was still hiding in Kentucky. Now wasn't the time to get sidetracked.

I said, "That's one I'll have to hold close for a bit."

Harry looked into my eyes and nodded, knowing I'd have a reason. "What do you need from me?" he asked without losing a beat.

"You seeing anything, or are you always behind a wheel?"

"I'm seeing stuff that doesn't make a lot of sense. There's a building, about five stories tall, lashed together quickly. Owsley goes there every day. I think it's some form of religious gig." Harry told me about the Owsley guy's talking-in-tongues act with the big box.

"Weird. What's in the building . . . you know?"

A grin, but only in Harry's eyes. "I'm not supposed to."

"You creeped the place, right?"

"Last night. It was too much to resist."

"You found something interesting?"

He shook his head. "Nothing but parts for a ride, some streamlined thing. Track. Usual construction equipment."

"Owsley's doing all that ritual stuff for a damn ride?"

Harry closed his eyes and held his hands together as if in prayer. "May God in Heaven fulfill abundantly the prayers which are pronounced over you and your boats and equipment . . ."

"Ah," I said. "Got it." Harry was reciting from the Blessing of the Fleet, an annual event in Bayou La Batre, Alabama, the shrimp boats gathering for an invocation against harm, the blessing delivered with much pomp and majesty by a Roman Catholic priest. Harry was saying different strokes for different folks, just in his own inimitable way.

"I also saw a bit of curiousness a couple days back," he said. "There's a park worker named Tawnya – you only get first names here – who's all smiles and sunshine

302

and happy days forever, but I saw her bitch-slap a low-level worker and dole out a mean-ass cussing."

"Low-level like what . . . janitor? Landscaper?"

Harry leaned forward, his voice low. "No, brother . . . get this: the person she was kicking around was one of the role players."

I stared. "Like my three victims."

"Seems so."

"Can you keep your eyes open, Harry? Maybe even get a little, uh, proactive."

"I don't have the shield," Harry said, meaning no law-enforcement membership, and thus no protection from getting caught in places he shouldn't be. Still, he followed his final bite of burger with a wink. "But I'll do what I can."

"Amos nearly went outside, Hayes." Uttleman pinched his thumb and forefinger a half-inch apart. "It was that close."

The pair stood on the back porch of the Schrum house, the security guard sent to fetch sandwiches, more to keep him away than for hunger.

"You said he was drunk?"

"Plastered. He wanted to confess." Uttleman closed his eyes. "He said he was burdened."

"Andy stopped him?"

"He stood there in his little-boy pajamas and convinced Amos to stay inside."

303

Johnson shook his head and watched a gull flick through the blue sky above.

"How?"

"You ever see how the kid's eyes light up when Amos steps into the room? Andy worships Amos."

"So do a lot of people," Johnson scoffed. "Donations are up thirty-seven per cent."

"True, Hayes, but it's like it's . . . different with Andy. He never wants anything back. I think Amos looks at Andy like he's a clean spirit". They're confidants, they pray together. Uttleman paused. "Maybe it's what's holding Amos together."

Johnson leaned the porch rail, arms crossed and looking down a head's-height to Uttleman. "You think singer-boy can keep Amos together another four days?"

"Four days?" The physician's eyes widened. "It's happening that soon?"

"It's what Eliot wants, no way around it. He's pouring money into the project like water, had the fabricators working three shifts. The bottom assembly's arriving tomorrow, the last piece. It'll take two days of crane work to fit everything together."

"And Owsley?"

"Our Mobile pastor's come to, uh, understand Eliot. And conform himself to that understanding. In return, he's the newest member of the COG family, soon to receive a daily show in mid-afternoon. I expect much of our new brother."

Uttleman cleared his throat. "Pastor Owsley's wife seems kind of . . . chilly. Think he might be one to join our little—"

Johnson raised his hand. "Plenty of time to gauge the man's needs. But that aspect is going to be curtailed for a while."

"Because of the police questions?"

Johnson nodded, unconcerned. "Best we take a hiatus of a couple months, Roland. Rid ourselves of the current choices. A clean start come fall."

Uttleman sighed dramatically and falsely. "Just when I thought Greta was starting to like me."

Johnson smiled and gave Uttleman a reassuring pat on his shoulder. "We'll have a final party, Roland. The night of the event. When the roof is drawn back on the tower and the stars are shining down on the event, we'll be miles away, savoring our own, uh, spiritual moments. When Amos's rash promise becomes reality and he's free, he'll become the Amos of old. Can you imagine what his second escape from death will do to attendance at Hallelujah Jubilee?"

"You said Eliot needs it to happen in four days . . ." Uttleman said. "Any special reason?"

"You've been out here too long, Roland," Johnson grinned. "You've lost track of time. What's special about that day? And why will it please Eliot?"

Uttleman ran the calendar in his head. He slapped his forehead in an *Aha!* moment.

"Damn, Hayes. It's Pentecost."

* * *

Harry Nautilus dropped Ryder at the airstrip, shooting a thumbs-up as the noisy gizmo shivered improbably into the sky. He hated choppers, damn things had the glide path of a brick. Bird and bees had wings, not rotors, which was the design nature intended.

Feeling an odd sense of renewal, he headed back to the motel to formulate a plan. He could be Carson's eyes up here, but given the deadly events in Miami, he'd have to look close and fast.

His return path took him near the structure and he felt its gravity pulling him close. *Just another look . . . see if anything new is up*. Owsley was there and working, whatever the hell he did, and though he'd been brought back to his digs by someone from the crew on the structure, Nautilus had an excuse to visit.

He turned on to the rutted lane to the building. Rounding the first bend he saw a crew of three guys bolting a heavy steel gate to freshly installed stanchions. It was a natural choke point, scrub forest crowding one side, a steep drop-off into the drainage ditch on the other. One of the men glared and waved for Nautilus to stop, but he smiled and waved nonchalantly as he blew by, a cloud of dust and cursing in his wake.

The first thing he noticed on his approach was two bright new Chevy Suburbans – black and cobalt – parked by the guardhouse instead of the beater truck driven by the yokel Nautilus had lured from his post. The second was an empty semi rig parked beside the fuel and water tanks. Seemed another big piece had been delivered.

Nautilus looked past the semi and saw a Towne Car with a trailer. The cranky old fart was here.

A hard-eyed block of meat and muscle was out of the guardhouse before Nautilus was in Park. Gone was the forest-ranger outfit, the new guy wearing a suit as black as his scowl. The breeze caught his jacket and displayed a shoulder rig carrying a Glock 17, major firepower.

"How'd you get past the gate?" Black Suit said. "The road is closed."

"Gate?" Nautilus said. "I saw some guys working when I drove in."

"What's your business?"

"I'm Pastor Owsley's driver. I wanted to see if he needed a ride back to his lodging."

"Don't leave the vehicle," Black Suit said. "I'll phone inside and ask."

It took a few seconds before he returned. "He's coming out. Stay inside your vehicle."

Two *stay-in-your-vehicle*s within a minute and spoken like a mantra. Black Suit had been rehearsed, Nautilus knew, and all cordiality had disappeared.

"Where's the regular guy?" Nautilus asked. "With the Ranger Rick uniform?"

"Not your business."

Owsley exited the building, tie off, shirt sleeves rolled up, a man distracted from his work. Behind Owsley the old guy in the wheelchair rolled to the main opening, beside him a pair of security types, more meat packed into suits. The old groper scowled at Nautilus as he side-mouthed words to security. All three squinted toward the Hummer like staring down a rifle sight.

Owsley arrived. There was no smile. "What is it you need, Mister Nautilus?"

"It's about the time you usually get done, so I thought I'd see if you needed a ride back to—"

"I told you my return is taken care of. Please stop disregarding my instructions and go back in case Celeste or Rebecca need you."

"I checked before I left and they didn't—"

But Owsley was already walking away. Seized by a thought, he turned. "I heard that you were here last night, Mr Nautilus. Why?"

"I was bored at the motel and took a drive. When I came down the main road I saw smoke and thought I'd alert the guard."

A long stare. "That's all?"

"What else is there?"

"I don't think you need to be here any more, Mr Nautilus."

It was almost a dismissal. Back in the Hummer and driving away, Nautilus came to the road crew, one of them shaking his fist. He stopped beside three men, two young and skinny guys who looked straight from the turnip truck, and a man in his mid-thirties with square shoulders, thick arms and a black sweat-drenched sleeveless T-shirt with a Harley-Davidson logo. He strode to the Hummer with thick fists clenched.

"I fuckin' told you to stop. You got dust all over me."

308

"It's a dusty road. And you're not a stop sign."

The man brandished his fist at the window line, his spit spraying Nautilus's face. "I'm gonna bust your goddamn black—"

Nautilus grabbed the man's fist in an iron grip and dove to the passenger side, pulling his assailant's face into the roofline, *Thump*. Nautilus released the arm and it followed its owner to the ground. Nautilus resumed the driver's seat and shot *And?* looks at the other two laborers.

"We ain't lookin' for no trouble, mister," one said, staring at his prostrate companion. "Gabe's just a hothead is all. An' he's hung over."

Contemplating the various natures of idiocy, Nautilus retreated to his motel room, sat on the balcony with a brew, contemplating the sudden change in tone in the security staff and the unhappy looks aimed in his direction. He ran a potential conversation in his mind, the former guard talking to his superiors . . .

"*I had to run out last night and chase some kids off the prop'ty.*"

"*You left the guardhouse?*"

"*That guy drives Pastor Owsley around, Harry Nautilus? He showed up and pointed where a fire was, some burning tires and shit. I wouldna left the guardhouse 'cept Nautilus said he'd watch things while I took a quick look. He's a cop an' all so I figured it'd be fine.*"

Did they suspect a ruse? Or had the event simply revealed a breach in security resolved by putting hardcore gunslingers in charge. Or, the most interesting possibility, did Nautilus's history as a cop mark him as more than just a guy who turned a wheel . . . and somehow a threat?

Questions, questions . . .

One thing was for sure, just like that the hayseed had been replaced by hard-eyed pros with heavy-metal thunder strapped to their chests. It was more than coincidence.

Also seeming more than coincidence: the glossy black Suburban currently crawling the parking lot below, pausing behind the leased Hummer, like making sure Nautilus wasn't out roaming the night.

I'm up here, Nautilus thought, *watching you watching me.*

He smiled. This gig was suddenly getting interesting.

45

Frisco Dredd pulled in front of Sissy Sparks's apartment building. After missing her in the darkened parking lot, he'd come back to his room and had a revelation: He could do no wrong. He was on a holy mission backed by the Lord Jesus Christ, King of all Heaven.

His thinking in the darkened parking lot had been addled. What he should have done was grab a hammer from the toolbox, smash the head of the runaway girl, then grab Sparks. His mission was pure and beyond worldly laws, the only law the Law of Heaven. The woeful whore Sparks would be atoning for her sins and the interrupting girl would be a lamb in the arms of Our Lord, him petting her and thanking her for letting Frisco kill her in His holy name.

Thank you, Lord for sending this revelation . . .

In the morning Dredd had visited a sign shop and

paid a rush fee for two simple cardboard signs saying, *Singer's Carpet Cleaning*, followed by a fake phone number. A few strips of double-sided tape and Dredd was ready.

The time was perfect, shaped by the hand of God . . . just past dark, so no one could see much, but still early enough a carpet cleaner could be making a pickup. Dredd had received another revelation in the afternoon: get a used area rug, carry it to the trash bin beside the whore's building.

Dredd wore green pants and a green shirt picked up for a few dollars at a uniform store, and as he crossed to the trash bin, he sang a hymn beneath his breath:

"*I have learned the wondrous secret, of abiding in the Lord,*
I have tasted Life's pure fountain, I am drinking of His word . . ."

It wouldn't do for prying eyes to see a man take a rug to the apartment and come back still carrying it, but he walked empty-handed, a simple man on a job. He passed a slender man in tight white shorts walking a little brown dog, the man's small high buttocks pressing the fabric – a faggot, you could tell, gonna burn in hell. The man looked at Dredd and nodded *good evening* and Dredd felt his animal strain at the wire, the queer's filth trying to drag Dredd back into sin. He paid the sinner no mind and continued on his way.

> ". . . *I have found the strength and sweetness, of*
>   *abiding 'neath the blood,*
> *I have lost myself in Jesus, I am sinking into God.*"

He reached the bin and gathered the carpet to his shoulder, plodding the final fifty feet to the whore's door. He knocked, knowing by the lights she was in there. She left different ones on when she was out whoring.

"Who is it?"

"Got your carpet here, miss. All cleaned and ready to go."

There was an eyehole on the door and he knew he was being watched.

"I didn't have any carpet cleaned," a woman's voice said, hard and soft at the same time, like buttermilk mixed with buckshot. "You got the wrong place."

"Apartment 22-A? That's what it says here on my delivery slip, miss. At least I think so. I, uh, busted my glasses this morning. I cain't see too well." Dredd moved a piece of paper in front of his eyes, like a man with a visual deficit. "It sure looks like 22-A."

He waited. Two seconds passed, five . . . The sound of deadbolts slipping free. The door opened and the whore stood framed in light. She was so beautiful Dredd couldn't move, couldn't breathe.

"Gimme that delivery thing," she said. "I'll read it for you."

As Dredd stared with his mouth open, the Jezebel pulled the strip from his hand and looked at it.

313

"There's no address on—"

But Jesus arrived to push Dredd across the threshold, the carpet falling as his hands reached for Sissy's throat.

Ten minutes later, Dredd crossed the street to his van, the carpet heavy on his shoulder, the weight and nearness of the unconscious woman – wet mouth open with wide pink tongue drooling out – making his animal squirm and burn against the slender wire. A patrolling cop car rolled by and Dredd kept his face low as he aimed a weary smile and nod at the darkened occupant, just a workman making a late pickup. The patrol car continued down the avenue, no brake lights. Dredd opened the side door and slid the carpet inside. He could smell the vixen's perfume and the pain in his animal made him gasp as the carpet cleared the opening.

He was closing the doors when he saw a pair of headlamps approaching . . .

The cop car had reversed direction. A whoop on the siren. Hidden by the open door, Dredd pulled a heavy masonry hammer from the toolbox and set it beside the carpet. He turned as the cruiser stopped.

Keep me safe in your arms, Lord. It's in your name I toil . . .

He leaned into the light, pushing a broad smile to his face. "Hey there, Officer . . . I fin'ly get to go home. Hate these late pickups."

Nothing from the darkened cruiser. After a few seconds the door opened and the cop from the other day got out, setting his hat on his head. "You've been here before," the cop said, eyes wary.

"I wouldn't think so, Officer. I usually work north of here."

The cop's hand went to the grip of his pistol. "Please keep your hands where I can see them, sir, and step away from the vehicle."

"Just as soon as I get this carpet inside I can—"

"Hands out NOW!"

Though it was dark in the van, an angered Lord put the handle of the hammer in Dredd's hand and spun him around so he stopped right in front of the cop, taking two steps and bringing the hammer down into the center of his forehead.

Jesus hit the cop two more times and threw the tool into the bushes of the whore's apartment.

46

"Carson, it's Vince Delmara. Where you at?"

"Heading to the Palace, Vince. I'm bushed. You?"

A long sigh, like the last air escaping from a balloon. "I'm looking at an MDPD officer dead in the street. You should hear what I just heard."

Minutes later I was in Wynwood, a tough neighborhood until relatively recently, cheap rents and interesting housing stock attracting young hipster types and a host of trendy dining and drinking establishments.

I roared off Biscayne on to 29th Street, went a couple more blocks and turned a corner. The scene was a nightmare I'd seen too often: cop cars crowding the block, lights beating blue and white against houses and apartments, terrified onlookers restrained by uniformed officers, two ambulances, another half-dozen command vehicles and unmarkeds. The air was a crackle of walkie-talkie chatter. I heard barking and saw a pair of hounds from a K-9 unit being leashed up by a handler.

I parked as close as possible and jogged to a circle of cop cars in the middle of the street, Vince at the epicenter. I excused my way past a female officer wiping tears from her eyes and saw the sheeted form on the pavement, Vince standing above and talking to a pair of MDPD detectives, Frank Bowling and Leandro Basquiat. Vince said, "Give us a minute here, guys," and the pair nodded and retreated.

Vince bent and pulled back the sheet. I saw a young and handsome face from the closed eyes down, above the eyes a hideous wreckage of blood and bone and brain. Vince replaced the sheet.

"Why am I here?" I said.

Vince nodded to an ambulance fifty feet away, pulled on to the sidewalk. "We got a lady that caught the last of the attack, dialed 911. It's why I called you, given what you told me about the religious weirdness with the burned girls. The witness is pretty shaken, but I'll let her tell you what she told me."

We approached the ambulance as white lights flickered like fireflies in adjoining yards, cops and tech people searching with flashlights for a murder weapon, a pipe, a tool, anything. Two K-9 units were working the scene, one on either side of the street.

A red-eyed woman sat inside the ambulance, mid twenties or thereabouts, black leggings, a blue silk T-shirt to mid thigh, bright beads encircling her neck, her hair a bouffant of braids dangling to her shoulders. She would have been pretty, but crying had melted mascara down her cheeks and her pink lipstick was smeared. She wore black fingerless biking gloves, which explained the sleek Orbea bicycle in the grass beside the vehicle.

"This is Wenda Bronstein," Vince said gently. "Miss Bronstein, I know you've told your story to me, but could you please repeat it to Detective Ryder."

She nodded and swallowed hard. "I was – I was biking home, one block down. I couldn't make out what was happening, it seemed so weird. I got closer and saw the police car and the . . . the policeman lying in the street under the streetlamp. A man was standing over him, saying words. It was like he was praying. I heard 'Jesus', and 'Accept this sinner.' Then he bent over the policeman and did that hand thing. Like in church."

She made the sign of the cross. I shot a look at Vince.

"Th-then he got inside a white van," Bronstein continued. "Not fast, but like he didn't have a worry in th-the world. I swear he was grinning."

"How close were you?"

"When I saw the blood I freaked and ran up on to the sidewalk. My feet came off the pedals and it took a second to get them back. He sp-spoke to me, just one word."

"What was it?"

"'Whore.'"

"What was he driving, did you see?"

318

"Just . . . a white van. There was some kind of sign but . . . I'm sorry, I was too scared, trying to get away."

"We've got BOLOs out on white vans with signage," Vince said, unnecessarily. A lot of white vans were going to be stopped tonight. I was thanking the young woman when we heard a yell from a yard two houses down.

"Over here. OVER *HERE*!"

We bolted past a pair of howling dogs, their handler pulling them back, leashes straining. I slipped on suddenly wet grass, Vince grabbing my arm to keep me from going down. "Easy," another MDPD detective said. "There was a lawn sprinkler running. Everything's soaked."

We walked the last few steps to see legs beneath a stand of purple bougainvillea fronting the porch of a yellow duplex. I feared another death until the bushes flashed white and I heard the clicking of a camera, relieved to realize it was a forensics tech beneath the bougainvillea.

"I've got the shots," the tech said. "I'm bringing it out."

The tech was Martin Petitpas, a rail-skinny black guy in his early thirties who'd grown up in South Louisiana and whose nickname was Pittypat. He reminded me of a younger version of Wayne Hembree back in Mobile, same dry humor, same moon-round face. But there was no humor in Petitpas's face as his wet clothes cleared the thorns and he displayed an evidence bag containing a rubber-handled masonry hammer, the label denoting an Estwing Big Blue, twenty-two ounces, forged steel, one face a hammer, the other a chisel curved like a fang, its four-inch length smeared with blood and cerebral tissue.

"Jesus," Vince whispered. "Can you get prints, Pittypat?"

"Composite handles can be tough, Vince," Petitpas said quietly, anger printed on his normally jovial features. "And it's been soaking. But if this SOB wasn't wearing gloves, we'll get you prints."

We retreated from the sodden yard as Officer Jason Roberts's body was loaded into an ambulance, grim-faced cops watching the second of their own to die violently in under two weeks, first Menendez, now Roberts.

"What do you think, Carson?" Vince said. "Any connection to the burned girls? The religious thing you talked about?"

"Our boy has a thing about women, Vince. If he's targeted a male cop it's a . . ." I paused, a weary mind suddenly making connections.

"What?" Vince said.

"Get your people to knock every door in the area," I said, almost yelling. "Wake everyone up. If no one answers, find out who lives there."

Vince was a fast study. "You think your perp made a grab and got caught in the act?"

"Knock those doors," I said. "See if a woman is missing."

Vince hustled away and I found a support group passing out Styrofoam cups of coffee, grabbed one and went to the Rover to escape the surging, angry cops. A half-hour later I heard my name being barked from a bullhorn.

"*Detective Carson Ryder! Detective Ryder . . . you're wanted at the front of the white apartment building!*"

I sprinted the distance, found Vince looking for me. He gestured to follow him down a wide hall to apartment 22-A, a pair of thirtyish males outside the adjacent unit.

"We've got an empty here, Carson. No one's answering. Her neighbors, these gentlemen, say the occupant is a medical-equipment salesperson named Sissy Carol Sparks."

"We thought we heard Sissy earlier," the nearest male said. "Her door. But she's out a lot on business."

"Thanks, guys," Vince said. "You can go back inside."

The pair nodded and retreated into their unit. When the door closed Vince turned to me. "I ran the name, Carson. Miz Sparks may be selling something, but I doubt it's medical equipment."

"Prostitution?"

"Remember Madame Cho's house of horrors? Sparks was a masseuse. She went down in last year's bust. She also had a possession arrest a month before that, heroin, but skated because it was her first."

"Since then?"

"Nothing. Clean record."

We heard footsteps and saw a pair of uniforms flanking a plump and bespectacled man in his mid forties, a brown jacket over khakis, the apartment manager bearing keys.

We stepped inside. A blind person would have known it was a woman's space, the smell of female lotions and potions thick in the air. The living area was furnished sparsely, but with an eye to color, the couch and flanking chairs a roseate pastel, the walls a soft blue. There were a dozen framed photos on the walls, sky-heavy landscapes, vast tracts of blue over lonely, unpopulated beaches or flat plains of desert.

"Got blood on the carpet," I said.

"And a picture on the floor," Vince said, lifting a decorative photo of a seascape. "There's where it came from," he said, tapping a bent hanger on the wall as a possible scenario unfolded: the perp gains entry, punches the occupant to chill her out, as she spins backward her flailing hands knock the photo from its hanger.

"It's my guy," I said, stomach churning. "He's got another one."

47

Vince added the Sparks woman's name and description to the van BOLO and scurried back to his department to monitor the search. I was too charged with adrenalin to sleep. Back in Mobile Harry and I would have headed to the Causeway, an eight-mile-long stretch of low road traversing upper Mobile Bay, sipping beers and staring into the dark water lapping at the reeds, or watching the lights of a freighter angling into the Port of Mobile. The Causeway was where we could retreat into ourselves as the stars wheeled above and the nightbirds called from the trees.

But my partner had retired and the Causeway was now just a place to visit in memory.

With no Harry and no Causeway, I followed the hammer to the forensics lab, passed hand to hand like an Olympics torch, the bearers hoping it could light the way to Officer Roberts's killer. Martin Petitpas handed the hammer to Dr Arun Chandrakant, the Acting Director, who passed it to Dean Hogue, the specialist in latents. When I arrived Hogue had the hammer from the bag and was studying it stem to stern with a high-powered loupe as Petitpas looked over his shoulder.

"Water gonna be a problem, Dean?" Petitpas said. "Thing got soaked."

Hogue was fifty, a laconic ex-Texan who wore cowboy boots, hand-tooled belts, and Western-style shirts under his lab jacket. Like me, he spent a lot of time outdoors either in a kayak or with a fishing rod in his hands, and his long and angular face was tan in the dead of winter. His gray eyes studied the hammer and I knew he was making calculations.

"Water shouldn't be no problem, Martin," Hogue said. "Problem's the composite surface of the handle, shitty for holding prints. Plus the handle's dimpled with holes. I'm thinking we'll fume with cycrocrylate and use a gelatin lifter. We'll fluoresce the tool and hope this fucker was too crazy to think about wearin' gloves."

"How much time?" I asked.

"I'm cooking long and slow, Carson. Like brisket. It'll take two hours at least. I'll set up now."

There was nothing I could do for Sissy Carol Sparks but hope and pray that a cop saw a white van and the cavalry got there to find the woman alive. "I'll be in my usual spot," I said, walking the hall to a storeroom that had a cot. In my two years in Miami I'd bagged out there often enough that the cell-sized enclave had been dubbed "Ryder's Room". I reclined on the cot and fell into a doze, burned out by too many days of starting before dawn and ending deep into dark.

I was dreaming of a black fire when I heard my name and sat up to see Vince above me and shaking my shoulder.

"Hogue raised prints," he said.

I jolted up and glanced at my watch. Almost three hours had passed and it was two in the morning. "When?"

"Fifteen minutes back. I let you sleep while we ran them through the databases. You looked like you could use it."

I saw the sheets of paper in Vince's hand. "You got a hit."

He nodded. "A guy named Frisco Jay Dredd."

"Dread?" I said, wondering if I was still dreaming.

"One E, two D's. Thirty-six years old. He's a mental with a record going back years."

"Tell me you've got an address . . . anything."

"That's the shit. His last-known address was in Alabama at the Institute for Aberrational Behavior. You know the place, right?"

More than Vince realized: After my brother had been sent to prison for life, the ferocity of his supposed crimes and mental acuity drew the attention of the IAB's then-director, Evangeline Prowse, who managed his transfer, studying him for nearly a decade. I'd also been there on other cases, in particular a madman named Bobby Lee Crayline who I'd tracked several years back.

"I know the Institute," I said. "They do important work. When was this Dredd there?"

"Five years ago. He beat up a woman after having sex with her, got sent to Holman, but was too freaky for them to handle, ranting religious stuff all hours of the day and night. The IAB took him in for study. When his sentence was up, he was released."

"What else you got?"

"Petty shit starting in his twenties, but increasing the past few years. Vagrancy. Shoplifting. Drinking and drugging busts. And general weirdness."

"Like what?"

"Preaching hellfire and brimstone on street corners, drunk and ranting and scaring the bejeezus out of citizens. He once stormed into a church, pushed the minister aside and delivered his own sermon. The last entry is a petty theft rap, eighteen months ago. He stole vegetables from a storefront bin in south Alabama and took them to his digs under a bridge. When the cops arrived he was singing hymns and masturbating."

"At least we have a name," I said, trying for glass half-full. "And a description."

"The bastard's used to living in the shadows, Carson. Dredd could be anywhere."

"You, uh, gonna broadcast the news that Dredd's the killer?"

Vince backed out the door, looked up and down the

hall, fearful of ears. "I do that, every cop in this city will want to put a bullet in his center ring. For right now, I'm saying he's a person of interest. It'll give us time to get more background, maybe put a net over him. Listen, Carson, I already foresee a problem with this Institute place . . ."

"Getting into Dredd's records."

Vince nodded. "I take it this is a medical facility, doctor-patient privilege and all."

"I know the current director. I'll see what I can do when morning hits."

"Get some sleep, brother," Vince said "We need you to hit the ground hard come the sun."

I sat on the cot and leaned back, smelling that I needed a shower. I was too beat to head to the Palace, not with a ready cot under my ass.

"Tell Hogue I need a wake-up call at seven," I said, and was probably asleep before I was horizontal.

48

Nautilus awoke at eight in the morning and checked his messages. Celeste Owsley needed to go to a Kissimmee hairdresser at one, Rebecca wanting to go to a nearby mall at three, something about shoes.

He took his coffee on the balcony, the cross shining in the east, the fresh sun waking the world as Nautilus pondered his options. *I'm Carson's eyes*, he thought, gazing across the empty pasture, the beasts undoubtedly packed within the Ark. Nautilus figured park employees arrived a half-hour beforehand to get into costume and position. The employee lot was toward the rear, definitely not Joshua-level. He knew he could be an intimidating figure, especially for what he wanted to do. It could all fall flat. Unless . . .

He thought a moment and pulled his cell. "Howdy, Rebecca," he said when the kid answered.

"Hi, Harry," Rebecca Owsley said, sounding buoyed.

"Harry? How about Mister Nautilus?"

"You call me Rebecca."

A sigh. The kid was a trip. "Listen, Rebecca, I'm going back over to the park this morning. Wanna go?"

"With you, Harry? Cool."

"Best tell your mama."

"She sleeps until around ten and if she gets up before that she's like soooo bitchy. She'll be all happy that we're going back." A pause. "And she won't have me around all day."

"I gotta shower, eat and get dressed. You in or not?"

The pair were at the park twenty minutes later and pulled into the employee lot, three acres of asphalt surrounded by sand and scrub.

"Why here?" Rebecca asked. "This is where the workers park."

Nautilus adjusted the air conditioning and turned to Rebecca Owsley, wearing a brief white skirt and a red tank top, pink loafers on her feet. "You know I used to be a cop, right?"

"Sure."

"I saw something last time. One employee hit another when she didn't know anyone was watching. It interested me. I'm wondering if the employee who was struck might be frightened of the other, because that's how she looked. I want to see if I can talk to the employee who was hit."

"Why?"

"It might be a simple spat, or it might be something worse. It's the way a cop thinks."

"You said *she*, Harry," Rebecca said. "Was it Tawnya who hit the other girl?"

Nautilus fought to keep his jaw from dropping. He'd left the kid at the restaurant on the far side of the restroom. No way she could have seen the confrontation.

"Why do you think that, Rebecca?" he asked.

"Because Tawnya's a mean bitch."

"Uh, pardon me?"

"I can tell by the way she talks to me. She thinks I don't pick up on it, but I do. Once I saw her looking at me like she'd like to spit in my face. She thinks I think I'm special because I get a Joshua pass and you drive me around."

"You saw all that?"

"I *observed* it," the kid clarified. "But Tawnya didn't see because I was looking sideways through sunglasses. I don't think she's real smart, but I'll bet she makes up for it in nastiness. Hey . . . you know she's got a tramp stamp? That's a tattoo above her butt. They're called tramp stamps because sluts get them."

Nautilus had noted the ink on Tawnya's arms, but the kid seemed one step ahead of him. Maybe it was the similarity in ages, Rebecca able to spot duplicity where Nautilus saw unctuous politeness.

"How do you know Tawnya has a tattoo there, of all places?"

"It was sunny the other day and she had on a white blouse, remember, kind of sheer? When you turn just

330

right light goes through and you can see skin. I saw a dark shape sticking up from her skirt. Either it's a real big birthmark or a tattoo." Rebecca grinned mischievously. "But since it's Trampy Tawnya, I'm betting tattoo."

Nautilus didn't know what to say, so he sat back within the sanctuary of smoked windows and watched the incoming parade of staff. You could tell the local employees – landscapers, electricians, maintenance types – from the part-timers, the former tossing out last-minute smokes from their cars and trucks as they entered the lot, the latter fresh-faced and younger and often arriving in groups. To the former it was a job, the latter saw a mission.

Nautilus looked in the rear-view and saw a blue Toyota van enter the lot, Tawnya at the wheel. The van pulled up to the employee entrance and a quartet of young women exited before the van pulled away. Nautilus scoped out the faces as the girls angled toward the back gate.

"That girl . . ." he said, nodding at a twentyish woman in tattered jeans and a tight gray tee, brushing back shoulder-length brown hair as she walked with her head down. "She's the one Tawnya slapped."

"Are you gonna go talk to her?"

Nautilus continued scoping out the girl, looking anxious, somehow frail, even in her youth. "I'm afraid she'll get spooked. Especially if a guy comes up out of nowhere—"

"And has a voice like *this deeeep*," Rebecca said, dropping two octaves, "and is about ten feet tall."

331

Nautilus nodded. The kid not only saw things, she saw into things.

"Lemme do it," Rebecca said, pushing on the door handle. "I'll talk to her."

"No way, stay here and we'll—"

But Rebecca Owsley was out the door and moving across the parking lot.

Ten minutes passed and Nautilus was about to go after the girl when he saw Rebecca striding from the employee entrance, her face pensive. He opened the passenger door and she jumped inside.

"Rebecca, you can't just go on your own like—"

"Her name is Greta. She's scared to talk to you. She's kinda weird."

"Weird how?"

"Like she's not all there, like maybe sixty per cent of her brain got turned on this morning. Anyway, I told her a friend of mine saw her get slapped and was wondering if she was OK. She got all scared and owlish, y'know?"

"Owlish?"

Rebecca widened her eyes to imitate fear. "Going, *who? Who?*"

"And you said?"

"You weren't with the park, but a guy who took care of people, like a protector. She'd been all like *go away*, but when I said protector, she said, *How*? It was a good thing."

"*Who* to *How* is good?"

"*Who* was scared, *How* was hopeful, at least just a little bit."

332

Nautilus stared at the kid. She was sixteen?

"What happened then?"

"Greta got all schizo because some other workers were getting closer. I gave her your number and said call you, just to talk. She said she didn't have a cell . . . she wasn't allowed. I gave her my phone."

Nautilus refrained from shaking his head. "You said you did other things in there. Like what?"

"I walked around to see if I could see Trampy Tawnya. No luck. Maybe she was busy slapping someone."

49

When awakened I had the energy to head to the Palace, grabbing a shower and change of clothes. At eight I had called Belafonte and given her a quick overview of what was happening, telling her to continue her research on Johnson. I next left a message for Dr Nancy Wainwright to call as soon as she arrived at work.

Dr Wainwright had been the director of the Institute for Aberrational Behavior for six years. I had last been there five years ago on the Bobby Lee Crayline case, Wainwright calling me out of the blue when the sociopath's legal team had wanted to hypnotically regress Crayline to his childhood, part of a defense strategy. Both she and the former director of the Institute, Dr Prowse, were terrified that the regression would blow the hinges off whatever final door kept Crayline in limited restraint.

The procedure went ahead anyway, and to disastrous effect, but I had answered Dr Wainwright's summons and driven to the Institute to try and forestall the hypnosis. In my book she owed me one and it was time to collect on the chit.

Her call came at 9.45, and I was on it in a single ring. "Detective Ryder," Dr Wainwright said, her voice pleasant and familiar. "It's been a while. You're still in Mobile I expect?"

"In Florida, Doc," I said, picturing Wainwright, a slender woman now in her mid-fifties with penetrating and intelligent brown eyes behind round-framed glasses. She'd proven to be an excellent steward of the Institute founded by Dr Prowse, so much so that the former Alabama Institute for Aberrational Studies was now the National Institute for Aberrational Studies. "I'm an agent with the Florida Center for Law Enforcement."

"Still specializing in the disturbed cases?"

"We all have a calling," I said. "Listen, Dr Wainwright, we've got a problem here."

"Miami? The Menendez woman? Have they found anything yet?"

"No, but I'm calling about another case. A former patient of the Institute has been killing women here. He stones them to death, wraps them in cloth, douses them with olive oil and accelerant and sets them on fire. Two of the three were still alive when he set them alight. Last night he killed a cop by bashing in his head with a hammer."

"My God," she said. "Who?"

"Frisco Jay Dredd."

Seconds ticked by, followed by a soft exhalation of breath. "Not unexpected, Detective."

"I need to know more about Dredd," I said. "Anything you can tell me . . . and more."

"You know I can't go into—"

"Bobby Lee Crayline, Doctor Wainwright. You needed me, I came running. I need you now."

"It's different. That wasn't—"

"Did I mention that Dredd has another woman? She's probably alive . . . for a bit."

Another long pause. "I'm, uh, not in a good place. Let me call you back. Fifteen minutes."

It took seventeen, me staring at my phone, waiting.

"I drove off the Institute grounds," she said. "I'm parked a half-mile down the road. I don't know why . . . it makes me feel better about, uh, talking."

"I understand. What can you tell me about Dredd?"

"Frisco Dredd is reality-challenged, Detective. Sometimes he seems normal, gentle. Other times he's delusional, and can be completely under the sway of his delusions."

"Religious delusions, unless I miss my guess."

"Frisco Dredd believes himself a battleground between Good and Evil. One night an attendant heard moaning in a shower stall. He found that Mr Dredd had somehow managed to strip a length of hollow plastic conduit from a wall, a tube. He jammed one end into a faucet, inserted the other end deep into his bowels and turned the hot water on full."

"A high-powered enema," I conjectured. "Trying to wash the evil away."

"He nearly died from a perforated intestine and later explained Satan had crawled up his anus while he was sleeping and needed to be flushed out. There were psychological aspects at play, Detective. Dredd is bisexual, and it wasn't Satan that had violated his anus."

"It was other men," I said, not in my brother's league but still no stranger to the symbolisms of a tortured mind.

"In Dredd's upbringing, homosexuality and its practice was a mortal sin against God and Nature. Dredd also manifests Hypersexual Disorder. You're acquainted?"

"Sex often starts as impulsive in earlier life, ramps up to compulsive, all-encompassing. An addiction as desperate as a heavy heroin jones."

"The victim is driven by libido," Wainwright affirmed. "Masturbation a dozen times a day or more, sexual fantasizing beyond the normal range, countless anonymous sexual partners. The victims are often terrified by the intensity of their drives, but it would affect Frisco Dredd even more."

"The harsh religious upbringing," I said, recalling my brother's analysis.

"Dredd didn't want to talk about his early life, but I told him if he wanted to trade prison for the Institute, he'd have to answer our questions truthfully, we were a

337

research facility. He gave me little, and perhaps was lying, but it seems he was part of a larger family who had a transient lifestyle. Poor. Often made fun of by other children. Their religion was fundamentalist in nature, extreme, involving harsh punishments for minor infractions like talking back . . . beatings, made to kneel and pray on concrete for hours on end. Being told he would burn in hell for his sins. You know what this sort of thing can do to a young mind?"

"All too well."

"Two months after the hose incident a guard noticed Dredd walking oddly, gingerly. A search found that he'd jammed the entirety of his genitals into a can fished from the trash. He said it was the only way he could keep his animal locked up."

"Animal?" I said, shaking my head.

"In Dredd's mind, his sex drives are the spawn of the Devil, sinful and disgusting, and yet the feelings suffuse every aspect of his being."

"Was there an issue with his mother?" I said, cribbing from my brother's analysis.

"Damn, Detective Ryder. If you ever quit the FCLE, we could use a mind like yours at the Institute."

You've already had one, I thought, saying, "Tell me about Mama."

"Dredd refused to speak of her, becoming agitated when she was mentioned, singing or praying loudly when I'd try to go there. He'd subconsciously squeeze his genitalia whenever the subject came up, pinching. I can't help

338

but wonder if she was hypersexualized as well, trying to beat the same feelings from her son, the sin. Making him ashamed of his drives, his genitalia. It would explain a lot."

"What about job history? Education? What work has he done?"

"Home-schooled, but all that meant was daily Bible lessons. He spoke of odd jobs, driving construction equipment, working on ranches, painting ships, farming chores, roustabout at carnivals. He'd work a while, then fall into drink and drugs, get fired. His whole life was itinerant, the only constant being a bleak and joyless vision of the Bible."

"Itinerant," I sighed. "He knows how to live off the grid."

"He's lived his life as a member of the underclass, and knows how to move in that stratum. I hate to say this, Detective, but Dredd's resourceful. Not bright in an IQ sense, but canny, cunning. He knows how to manipulate us – us being the regular folk – and since sees us as Godless heathens consigned to Hell, he doesn't care."

"You had to let Dredd loose on to the streets?"

"He'd served his time. Plus we observe, Detective, remember? We don't offer therapies, save for helping patients try to understand their drives and control them. But to Frisco Dredd, the world is Good and Evil and that's all he knows." Wainwright paused, as if wondering on what note to end our conversation. "I have to go back to the facility," she said, her voice suddenly tired and saddened by the news I'd brought. "I hope you catch him, Detective. I pray you do it fast, because from what you tell me, Frisco Jay Dredd is now totally controlled by his demons."

50

Harry Nautilus was revisiting the park in his head when a knock came to the door. He opened it to find Richard Owsley in a dark suit, his features darker still, the bright smile now a thin-lipped frown.

"Mr Nautilus, I'd like to talk to you."

Nautilus waved entry. "Step inside, Pastor. You're paying for the room."

"Actually, I'm not," Owsley said. "At least after today. I'm here to tell you your services are no longer needed."

"Might I ask why?"

"I've made other arrangements."

"Did I do something wrong?" Nautilus gave it three beats. "Like go to the facility on my own the other night?"

"Your unheralded appearance was rather surprising. The, uh, others wondered why you were there."

341

"I saw smoke and reported a fire, Pastor." It was, Nautilus knew, fully true, though he refrained from mentioning that he had set the fire.

"I also heard that you went to the facility again yesterday and assaulted a man on a work crew."

"Nope," Nautilus said. "The guy was irritated that I'd gotten dust on his shoes and approached me with intent of doing harm. I disabused him of that notion, rather gently, given the circumstances. What really happened was—"

A raised hand from Owsley. "I don't want to get into who did what, Mr Nautilus. I've accepted a position with the Crown of Glory network and my family is moving to Jacksonville. Your services are terminated as of today."

Nautilus nodded. The weirdness was continuing. "In that case I'd like to say goodbye to Rebecca, Mr Owsley. She's a fine person."

"Becca is grounded, Mr Nautilus. She lost her cell phone, worth over five hundred dollars and has to learn consequences."

Owsley turned for the door, his brief sermon over, not so much as a *thank you for your work*.

"Pastor?" Nautilus said.

Owsley paused, hand on the door knob. "Yes, Mr Nautilus?"

"Who did I piss off?"

"Pardon me?"

"It was that sad old fuck in the wheelchair, right?"

Without a word, Owsley left the room, pulling the

342

door shut behind him. Nautilus went to the balcony, stepped outside, and thought for several minutes. He returned to the room, packed, and departed for the airport.

"I know someone's there!" Sissy Carol Sparks shouted. "I hear your goddamn breathing!"

The hissing of breath. The sound of something touching the floor, a clicking, like stones bouncing together. Though her eyes were open her world was like the bottom of a mine, black as black ever was. When she breathed she felt the hood moving out and back, held in place by a knotted cord.

Steps circling to her right. She swung a fist and struck only air.

"Take this goddamn thing off my head. Have the balls to let me see you!"

"*Flth . . . jzbel . . .*"

"Stop mumbling and talk!"

Sissy's mind raced as her hands scratched the emptiness, the footsteps dodging and weaving, cat and mouse. *Think!* What advantage did this pervert have? Everything. He owned the situation. What did Sissy have?

Nothing.

No, that was wrong. From the top of her shining auburn hair to the tips of her pink and perfect toes, she was Sissy Carol Sparks. She had the mind, she had the machinery . . . and she had never met a man able to stand up to it. She heard an object swish past her ear, smack a wall a split-second later. *What the fuck was that?* She heard something rolling on the floor, nudge her foot.

It felt like a goddamn rock. Was this loonie throwing rocks at her?

"*For he is the servant of God,*" the voice said like a chant, "*an avenger who carries out God's wrath on the wrongdoer . . .*"

"What are you saying, you pervert!"

She heard her captor grunt with effort and the sound of another object hissing past, so close to her right wrist she felt its passing breath. Sissy swallowed and took a deep breath. She was a performer and the performance of her life had to come right now.

"*And the great dragon was thrown down, that ancient serpent, who is called the devil and Satan, the deceiver of the whole world . . .*"

Hearing clicking of stones and knowing her captor was going for a third shot, she stood straight, cocked a hip and stared through the mask toward the muttering voice. "I know you're playing with it," she said, trying to keep her voice from trembling. "Your dick."

"*. . . he was thrown down to the earth, and his angels were thrown down with him . . .*"

Another grunt of effort. Fierce pain in Sissy's thigh as a rock slammed home. She stifled the scream and fought to keep her hand from the pain. *Don't give him the satisfaction.* The rocks clicked again.

"You're scared of women," she said, knowing she was

344

throwing her last spear. "That's it, right? The bag over my head thing? It's the shame."

The clicking stopped. "What did you say to me, harlot?" The voice was a ragged whisper.

"You know what I do for a living, right? Now and then I get guys want to fuck me with a bag over my head. They're ashamed, that's why. They know I can see them and they're scared of what I can see. What are you scared I'll see?"

"*For he is the servant of God,*" the toneless chant continued. "*An avenger who carries out God's wrath on the wrongdoer . . .*"

The clicking of stones. A grunt. Something slammed the wall at her back and rolled away. Sissy made herself giggle. "Oh sure . . . throwing rocks at a girl with a bag over her head. Did your daddy teach you that one? Was your daddy scared of girls, too? Or is it more a mommy thing with you?"

Every sound ceased. The chanting. The footsteps on the floor. The clicking of the rocks. Hands surrounded her neck and the room exploded into light, Sissy blinking into eyes inches from hers, a mouth twisted in a hideous snarl, the hood in a brown hand that looked like a claw.

"SHUT YOUR FILTHY MOUTH, WHORE!"

He back-handed Sissy into the dark concrete wall, a high heel snapping off as she fell. The man stared from a dozen feet away, his hands balled into fists and his eyes like pinpoint jets of gray flame.

Sissy's skirt was hiked high and showing sleek lengths

of silken leg, one foot bare. She brought a hand to her face to push back a fallen lock of hair, using it for cover, the other hand undoing a button on the sheer black blouse to display additional cleavage and the frilly top of her black bra. Pretending to be dazed, Sissy pushed herself to sitting, taking deep breaths to let the boobs press against the silk.

Look at them, monkey man. They have more power than you do.

I hope.

Sissy stood unsteadily, feeling the man's eyes across her as she leaned the wall. She was in a goddamn barn, wood walls, heavy wooden supports, windows boarded over. At the far end was a concrete bench with its top scorched black, beside it a pile of cloth strips, a half-dozen bottles labeled Naphtha, and a gallon jug of oily-looking shit.

Sissy shook back her hair, gave her captor a hit of the eyes. She let her mouth droop open as the pink tongue traced her lower lip. Her captor stood motionless with his mouth lolling wide, gray eyes drinking in every glorious inch of Sissy's body, a man who'd crawled a hundred miles of desert to suck from a sweetwater oasis. He looked more dazed than Sissy as his hand fell to the front of his pants and clutched. He winced and moaned. Sissy's eyes looked past the fondling hand and saw something glistening on the faded blue denim.

Jesus God . . . is that blood?

51

Nautilus sat on the balcony of a Knight's Inn a half-mile from his previous lodging. He'd driven to the airport and surrendered the leased Hummer, renting in its place a blue Jetta. The room was smaller and lacked the amenities of Jacob's Ladder, but Nautilus needed only a place to sit and plan. Carson had asked him to keep an eye out and though his unemployed status made that a bit more difficult, it was also a challenge. Harry Nautilus found challenges exhilarating, perhaps why he was whistling.

He was about to run to the store for a supply of snackage and brews when his phone rang. The caller ID said, REBECCA.

Not Rebecca. The call was the phone she'd given to Greta. "Hello, Greta," he said, his voice warm and friendly.

"I was t-told to call this number," the girl said. "Th-that maybe someone could help me."

"My name's Harry Nautilus. Did Rebecca tell you anything about me."

"She s-said you were a protector. Like Spider Man or Superman. She said you saw me get slapped the other day."

"Do you get slapped often, Greta?"

"I . . . I don't want to talk about it."

"And we shouldn't," Nautilus crooned, the girl as jumpy as a kangaroo on meth. "Not on the phone – in person. To see each other's faces and get to know one another. Can you do that, Greta . . . meet me somewhere to talk?"

A long pause. "I want that girl there, too. Rebecca. She's . . . nice. And smart. I don't know you. You might be one of them, like a test. You might be a lawyer."

Lawyer? Greta wasn't making a lot of sense, Nautilus thought. But Rebecca had said the girl seemed a bit loopy.

"Rebecca can't come, Greta. She told her parents she lost her phone and they grounded her."

"I'm not coming without her. I trust her."

Nautilus blew out a breath. "Where are you, Greta? At the park?"

"I-I'm in Bethlehem today. It's break time and I'm in the bathroom. I can't be seen with a phone, I'll be punished."

"Let me see what I can do, Greta. We'll talk again when—"

348

"YOU CAN'T CALL! THEY'LL HEAR!"

"You'll call me," Nautilus said. "Keep the phone turned off until then. When's your next break?"

"In, um, about two hours."

"Call me then. I'll see if I can't change things."

The phone died on Greta's end. Nautilus went to the Jetta. With the sun nearing zenith and beating down like a ninety-degree hammer, Nautilus flushed the vehicle with cool air and cruised by the motel holding the Owsley family, wondering who was in the room. Rebecca surely, Celeste a fifty per cent likelihood – half her time spent shopping – with Richard Owsley a good bet to be at the structure, waving a bible and ululating at giant boxes.

He parked in the lot and slipped the Joshua-level pass around his neck. Owsley had forgotten to divest him of the amulet, and perhaps – if Nautilus was lucky – had been too distracted by his project to inform the motel staff that Nautilus was now *persona non grata*.

He strode nonchalantly to the door just as a young bellman was rolling a cart of luggage out to a waiting taxi. The bellman stared at Nautilus.

Come on, magic . . . Nautilus thought, nodding at the man. *Be there.*

The bellman's face lit in a beatific smile. "Mr Nautilus . . ." he said, almost genuflecting. "I hope you're enjoying your stay."

"A fine visit," Nautilus said, hiding his relief.

"Just the girl's in the suite, Mr Nautilus." The bellman winked. "We're keeping an eye on her."

"Excellent," Nautilus said, wondering what *that* meant. "I have to pick up some papers for the Pastor."

The bellman wished Nautilus a blessed day and proceeded to the cab. Nautilus caught the elevator to the Owsley floor, knocked on the door.

"Who's there?" Rebecca's voice, glum.

"Harry."

The door opened, the kid wide-eyed, wearing stone-washed jeans and a pink sleeveless blouse, her hair tied back in a ponytail. She held a can of Dr Pepper in her hand. "Daddy said you had to go back to Mobile. You took another job."

"An unfortunate rumor. I'm still here it seems, though now in the Knight's Inn, a few blocks east."

"I *knew* Daddy was lying. Whenever he lies his voice sounds like fur feels."

"I hear you got grounded."

An eye-roll from Rebecca. "Daddy told the ogres on the staff here – all those happy-faced goofs in the lobby? – to make sure I didn't leave the motel. If I did I'd be grounded all summer."

Which explained the bellhop's words about keeping an eye on the girl. Nautilus looked inside, checking out the expansive suite of rooms.

"Where's your mama, Rebecca?"

"My aunt came from Tampa and they went to Orlando. Mama said they're going shopping but I'll bet they go to Disney World. It's a lot better than that crummy old park here. And I'll bet it doesn't smell like goats and camels."

350

"Your father?"

"He's been gone since I got up. He's almost finished with some project, then he wants to talk. Something about our future."

The move to Jacksonville, Nautilus figured. "Listen, Rebecca, Greta called. She's scared and doesn't trust me, but she trusts you. She's afraid I'm setting some kind of trap, or a test. She's going to call in about ninety minutes. I'd like to stop back then and have you answer the phone and convince her to trust me and meet with me."

Rebecca crossed the floor in thought, spun back to Nautilus. "I don't think Greta's going to trust me over a phone, Harry. She'll need to see me, right? To be . . ." the kid puzzled for the word, said, "*assured* that everything's all right."

"Not in the cards, Rebecca. You can't leave the motel."

The kid held up the bottle of soda. "I'm not allowed soft drinks. You know that convenience store down the street? I just got back from there. I put on sunglasses, tucked my hair up under a scarf, and went down the back stairway. I made myself walk like I'm older . . ." the kid straightened and crossed the room with choppy steps – the gait obviously stolen from her mother – and turned back to Nautilus. "See?"

It was a masterful ploy, Nautilus had to admit. Seen from the lobby as she crossed the lot toward the c-store, none of the busy staffers would make Rebecca as the sixteen-year-old sequestered upstairs.

He shook his head. "You have to stay here. I'm not going against your parents' wishes. That's final, girl."

A pout started to cross Rebecca's face, a look Nautilus hadn't seen since they'd made the trip to the park. But like a thin cloud passing a bright sun, it dissolved into radiance.

"OK, Harry. We'll do it your way. When you coming back?"

Back on the balcony of the motel, Harry Nautilus looked at his watch, ninety minutes had passed since he'd spoken to Greta, meaning it was time to return to Rebecca. He patted his pocket for the Joshua pass and headed to the second-floor walkway, stepping down to the lot when a voice came from behind him.

"Hi, Harry. Jeezle, it's hot out here."

He spun to see Rebecca Owsley leaning against the doorframe of the room where the soft-drink, snack and ice machines were located, dramatically fanning herself with one pink hand, the other clutching a can of Dr Pepper.

"What are you *doing,* girl?"

"I wanted another Dr Pepper, but somehow just kept walking." Her amused eyes scanned the parking lot, weeds growing from the asphalt. "This place is kind of a dump, isn't it?"

"You can't be here with me, Rebecca. It's a motel. You're sixteen. It doesn't look right."

She grinned. "We'll tell people you're my father. They'll believe that, y'think?"

Nautilus sighed. "Get in the car. I'll drive you close to your digs and you can sneak—" His phone rang. He pulled it from his pocket. The screen said REBECCA.

"Hi, Greta," he said, his voice as creamy as a chocolate. "I'm happy you called back."

"I . . . I'm on break, they told me to go early so I can work later. I've only got a minute."

"Like I said, Greta, we need to meet, to speak."

"Is she there? Rebecca?"

"She can't be with us, Greta . . ." Nautilus started to explain. "It's gonna be impos—"

The phone disappeared from Nautilus's hand, snatched by Rebecca Owsley.

"Give me the phone," Nautilus said, fingers making the gimme motion. But Rebecca Owsley danced away, talking as she moved across the parking lot. Nautilus started after the kid, but glanced toward the small swimming pool to the side, two scruffy palms shadowing a pair of hefty ladies in one-piece swimsuits, stern and suspicious eyes turned on the big fiftyish black man and the petite teenager, the women probably about to dial 911.

Nautilus put his hands in his pockets and approached the pool, putting on his warmest voice and most benign visage. Carson had once said that – when he wanted to – Harry Nautilus could charm the milk from a coconut without leaving a hole in the shell.

"Howdy, ladies," he said, putting his elbow atop the fence surrounding the pool. "This looks like the place to be today."

A look between the women, wondering whether to respond. "Yes," the one on the right finally said. "It's hot today."

"Down to visit folks, or just enjoying our fine Florida weather?"

Another pause; wondering what his angle was. The one on the left said, "We come down every year and visit Hallelujah Jubilee."

"Don't you love the Ark?" Harry said. "It's so real. I think it's like being there at that blessed time."

A pause. A large black man was speaking their language! The smiles widened and became real. "I love the rides, too," said the lady on the left, nodding to her sister. "But they make Thelma dizzy."

"I've got the vertigo," Thelma said. "It's in my ear."

"There's still so much to see," Nautilus said. "Bethlehem, Jerusalem, the Passion play."

"We see the Passion every time we're here. We cry and cry."

"Where are you girls from? Up north?"

A tinkle of laughter. *Girls*. The women were in their mid sixties, but probably saw girls in their mirrors, bless mirrors everywhere.

"Pittsburgh. We're sisters."

Nautilus turned and saw the kid approaching, phone away from her cheek, a happy smile on her face, a portrait in innocence. "Well, ladies, it looks like my stepdaughter is finished with her call or text or whatever. I can't understand how those fancy phones do so much."

354

"They confuse me no end," Thelma's sister said. "I wish I had my old Princess phone back."

Harry did a courtly semi-bow. "Nice meeting you fine folks. Enjoy the park."

Twin smiles on the chubby faces. "And wonderful meeting you, sir. Have a blessed day."

Rebecca stood before Nautilus and handed back the phone.

"Don't ever grab my phone away ag—"

"We're meeting with Greta, Harry. You and me. She says there's a motel on Conway Street with a small woods behind it, a path that goes inside. We're supposed to wait in the woods and she'll meet us."

52

When I returned to the department, I found Belafonte huddled in conversation with Clinton Monroe, a former IRS agent and a crack forensic accountant whose primary duties were tracing drug money through its laundering and making cases against launderer and launderee alike. I was happy to see the brilliant Monroe, sixty-two, pudgy and balding and looking like a guy whose twin hobbies were bridge and bird-watching, which they were.

"We've been checking out Hayes Johnson, as you requested," Belafonte said. "Which brings in the whole Crown of Glory network, including the Reverend Amos Schrum."

I sat and asked a question I always wanted to ask about famous televangelists. "What's Schrum make? My guess is a million at least."

"Fifty grand," Monroe said.

"*What?*"

Monroe chuckled. "The COG Foundation owns Schrum's fancy house and furniture and leases it to him for a dollar a year. The Foundation provides a car and driver. There's a plane at his beck and call. All his meals and living expenses are picked up by the Foundation. I imagine there are other perks, like Foundation-supplied insurance and medical plans. Basically his life is funded by the Foundation, and I expect it's a nice one."

"It's splendid PR," Belafonte said. "The relative pauper's salary looks like Reverend Amos Schrum has been called to service by God, not Mammon. And I expect it curtails potential problems from a staff that's four-hundred strong."

"Problems like what?"

"The network pays crap," Monroe said. "A lot of the work is done by unpaid volunteers, the low-level stuff at least – handling the mail, deliveries, working the phone lines for donation. They offer a full page of internships, unpaid or with a minimal stipend. The median salary for a television studio cameraperson in the US is about seventy grand a year. The COG network pays its camera operators an average of forty-one grand."

I once had a girlfriend who worked for a TV station and recalled the various unions attendant in the operation of the station. "They don't have to pay union scale," I said.

"Because COG is not a television network, it's a church. And a foundation. And various subsets. It's actually a very ingenious set-up."

357

"So if a cameraperson or a singer or a stage electrician complains about the shit salary . . ."

"An administrator steps in and says, 'Look, buddy, Reverend Schrum himself only makes fifty G's. He's grateful for the chance to serve God and all his angels.'"

I nodded. "And, of course, when you're always asking for donations . . ."

"It looks great on the books. The folks at COG work there because they're called to service. Plus the park, Hallelujah Jubilee, is run as a non-profit educational entity. It barely breaks even."

"Breaks even?" I said, perplexed. "Harry tells me the park is a money machine . . . forty-buck admissions, four-hundred-dollar bibles, fifty-buck Ark posters. Unless they have heavy debt, it's like owning a casino."

Monroe shook his head. "No debt load there. The Hallelujah Jubilee Foundation didn't pay for the land. It was bought for the sum of sixty-seven million dollars and donated. The benefactor was an Eliot Winkler. Anyone heard of Winkler besides me?"

"A crabby old fart in a wheelchair, according to Harry," I said. "Seems to have some intense religious feelings."

"Winkler's worth about four billion dollars. His high-level managers are required to attend prayer meetings."

"I'm more interested in Hayes Johnson. He's rolling in the dough, right?"

"Johnson makes the princely sum of two hundred and twenty thousand dollars a year."

"To run a whole network?"

Belafonte tapped at her laptop and turned the screen to me. I saw a palatial three-story pink-brick home on a waterway, a fancy motor yacht moored in the background. "I do love Google Earth," Belafonte said. "Johnson's domicile. Does that look like two-twenty a year to you?"

"I checked real estate records," Monroe said. "Johnson bought the place for two-point-seven million four years ago."

I turned to Belafonte. "Didn't you tell me Johnson built a shaky company and sold it for eleven mil? That explains the Taj."

"There's a fly in the ointment." Monroe grinned. "It seems three million dollars went to an ex-wife who divorced Johnson eight years back, a problem Mr Johnson has with women not his wife. Several million more went to settle suits with franchise owners who felt Johnson's sales pitch had been deceptive. The amount is hush-hush, but a *Wall Street Journal* article speculates it was around seven million. Between the wife and the legal problems, Mr Johnson is no longer a wealthy man."

"So where's the money coming from?" I mused.

53

Greta was kept in the broken-down motel Nautilus had seen while driving, and wanted to meet behind the unused wing, in an acre of cane and scrub brush. He brought Rebecca – Greta's condition for appearing – and they parked a block distant and walked to a thicket of vegetation less than two hundred feet from the motel. The pair sweated in the hot sun for ten minutes until hearing a rustling through leaves and feet over sand, Greta.

The girl looked beaten down and frightened, eyes darting every way but at Nautilus.

"How did you end up at Hallelujah Jubilee," Nautilus asked. "Can we start there?"

Hands with chewed-to-the-quick nails pulled a rumpled pack of Marlboros from her jeans, lit one. It took three deep sucks of smoke before she could talk.

"My step-dad, in Bratton, West Virginia. We . . . didn't

get along. He was . . ." her eyes closed and Nautilus thought she was fighting back tears. "I *hated* him. So I run off for Florida. I saw an ad in the paper that they had jobs here. I didn't have but one set of clothes and when I came in to apply I smelled like it. I figured they'd spray me down with bleach and throw me out, but it was Tawnya I talked to and she was real nice. I didn't know that she was on their side, and after a month got some of us to start doing things. I mean more than working at the park."

"Like what, Greta?" Nautilus prodded gently.

A long hit on the cig. "They make us give shows. Dance and things like that."

"Who makes you do this?"

"Two men, sometimes three. It's like a party."

"Are there drugs there? Drinking."

Greta looked away.

"If it's just a party, Greta," Nautilus said, trying to pry loose more information, "and if you're happy with it, then I made a mistake. You and Tawnya were just having a spat."

The girl hit the cig, finger nervously tapping the filter. "They make us do more than dance, mister. We . . . have to touch one another."

"Do you have your clothes on, Greta? When you're touching?"

Greta swallowed hard, like fighting nausea. Rebecca stepped in and took the girl's hand, pulling her over to a far section of the clearing. "Come with me, Greta,"

Rebecca said. "Harry . . . why don't you take a walk for a few minutes. I'll meet you back at the car."

No way was Nautilus leaving the girls alone behind the Florida version of the Bates Motel. He shook his head. "I'll be on the other side of the cane. But out of earshot, so you ladies can talk."

Ten minutes later Rebecca pushed through the green stalks. "Greta got scared she was gone too long and they'd come looking for her. She's back inside."

They walked to the Jetta in silence. Nautilus turned on the AC, but stayed parked. "The men make the girls kiss and make out, Harry," Rebecca said. "It's gross. The men do it to the girls. They put their things in them and other stuff. Don't give me that look, I'm sixteen."

"Why doesn't Greta leave?"

"This is where she can have a place to live and eat. But if she ever tells, the men will have their lawyers attack the girls."

"The lawyers?"

"Greta says the lawyers can make it look like the girls are lying. The girls will get put in jail."

Nautilus suddenly understood. The legal realm was a complete mystery to most poor folks, a realm of absolute power and privilege. To folks from the underclass, lawyers seemed to know everything, control everything – and he expected the girls had been screened for just such a distinction. Naive, poorly educated, prone to shame about their situations . . .

"Why did Greta get hired?"

"It's like there are two kinds of workers. Most are real churchy and love the place. The others are Greta girls . . . they're in trouble, or don't have anywhere to go. If they leave, they can't ever come back. Or tell about what happened."

"If they tell," he said, "the lawyers will get them."

Rebecca nodded. "They're *super* mean, the lawyers. No one will believe the Greta girls."

"Tawnya. She's in charge, right? In control?"

"She comes to the parties, too. But more to make sure the girls do like they've been told."

"Did Greta talk about drugs?"

"Tawnya gives the Greta girls pills and stuff to drink. Greta says it makes her feel all floaty and she hardly knows she's at a party."

Drugs for compliance, Nautilus thought. Plus they blunted memory, the girls barely able to recall what happened. Nautilus heard a lawyer bloviating in his head: "*The women making these scurrilous allegations, Your Honor? They're drug users, outcasts from their own families. The park gave them jobs and a fine place to live and these tragic women repay kindness with lies and ridiculous allegations. I demand this senseless case be thrown out of court, a slander on the reputations of fine men . . .*"

"Has Tawnya been here long?" Nautilus said.

"For about a year. One of the Greta girls is named Deely . . . she's been here the longest. Greta says Deely remembers another boss girl before Tawnya. I think her name was Sissy."

363

"These men? Do they have names?"

"Bobby and Stevie and Tommy. They're old. One's real fat. Greta hates them."

Bobby, Stevie, Tommy . . . Nautilus figured he was hearing pseudonyms.

"Just the three men?"

"Greta says there used to be another one. She never saw him, just heard from one of the girls before her. He was real old, like a grampa. His name was Teddy, but the girls called him Whitey behind his back."

"Whitey?"

"Yeah," Rebecca nodded. "Because of his hair."

54

Amos Schrum was staring at the floor as if it might rear-range itself into the solution to a problem. He blew out a breath and pushed back a shock of overhanging hair, turning to his visitor.

"Tomorrow's Pentecost, Andy. It starts at midnight."

Delmont was sitting beside Schrum and strumming chords on his guitar. Above the white slacks he wore a red-and-white checkerboard shirt with a blue paisley bandana around his neck. He set the instrument aside.

"Yessir, I know."

"That project I told you about? It's scheduled to happen as Pentecost opens. I'm supposed to be there, which means slipping from Key West shortly, at least for a few hours."

"Don't go, Reverend," the singer said, taking Schrum's

hand. "You yourself told me it was wrong, and it's more than wrong, sir, it's evil and dangerous."

Schrum patted Delmont's hand and stood. He walked to the window and peered outside. The signs had shifted from *Bless you* and *You are my light*, to *Praise Jesus for healing, Hurry back,* and *See you on TV*. He let the curtain fall back into place. "I gave my word, Andy."

"To Mr Winkler. He's a man. What about your word to God?"

Schrum turned toward the door. "Is that the elevator I hear?"

"I figure it's Mister Johnson and Dr Uttleman. I think they're coming to take you to Pentecost."

"Could you leave us, Andy? I need to talk to our friends."

"I'm not sure they're always your friends, sir."

"I'll keep that in mind, Andy. Are you still going back to the mainland tonight?"

"I haven't been home in days, Reverend. And now that you're going to heal, it'll be good to be back singing on my show again." The singer started for the door, turned, concern in his eyes. "You're staying here, Reverend? Not leaving tonight?"

"Let Hayes and the doctor in, Andy. Then please close the door."

The singer departed. Seconds later Johnson and Uttleman appeared. They looked anxious, trying to hide tension behind expansive smiles.

"Sit and have a drink," Schrum said. "Roland has a

couple bottles in the desk. He's been saving them for my complete recovery, but I'm feeling pretty feisty right now."

Uttleman poured and the men sipped quietly until the doctor cleared his throat. "Uh, we've been hearing from Eliot, Amos. It seems Pastor Owsley has exceeded all expectations."

"He's sprouting angel wings?"

"Eliot now feels Pastor Owsley has the capabilities to launch the event."

"Eliot doesn't need me?" Schrum said, looking over the top of his glass. "Is that what you're saying?"

"The Pastor has blessed the pieces as they've come together, and has done a splendid job of being a spiritual intermediary. He has . . . uh, a potent magnetism, especially as he's explained his particular theological stance to Eliot, his thoughts on rewards in the here and now. How the world is supposed to operate when the Bible is correctly translated. Eliot and Pastor Owsley have become . . ." Uttleman frowned, struggling for a term.

"Co-dependents?" Schrum said.

Johnson stood, set his empty glass on the desk and gave Schrum a sad smile. "You've benefited greatly from Eliot's munificence in the past few years, Amos. I hope you're not sorry to see him shift allegiances."

"Not at all," Schrum said, reaching for the bottle and pouring another three fingers. He lifted his glass as if in toast. "I expect the new arrangement will be perfect for both men. Heaven-sent, so to speak."

"How so, Amos?"

"Eliot and Owsley are both hungry men, Roland," Schrum said, a wisp of smile crossing his lips. "It's a blessing that they can now feed on one another."

I left Belafonte and Monroe to write up their findings and assigned myself the daunting task of tracking down the religious maniac named Frisco Jay Dredd. Florida-wide BOLOs had turned up nothing and I figured the van had been ditched, hidden or disguised.

Belafonte followed me out the door of the meeting room. "Mr Monroe can handle the reports," she said. "I want to go after Dredd."

I sighed. "I need you here and ready to handle something, Holly."

"What?"

"Sissy Carol Sparks, Dredd's last abductee. If he follows pattern, the woman is dead and waiting to be found. When the victim shows up, I need you to follow through."

She nodded softly. "I understand. I'll be ready."

I sat in my office and scanned the reports on Dredd and replayed my conversation with Wainwright. I couldn't figure out a handle on the monster: the man was a drifter, a loner, taking cash jobs and moving around like the human equivalent of a neutrino, invisible, virtually undetectable.

My eyes tripped on the police report detailing the time Dredd had barged into a small Baptist church in Satsuma, Alabama, two years ago, pushing the minister – a

Reverend Harold Tate – from the pulpit and proceeding to shriek about devils and damnation until the county cops arrived. The report mentioned it took three cops and two Taser darts to subdue Dredd. It also noted that the minister declined to prosecute, saying Dredd was "a sad case with a sadder history".

I felt my pulse quicken: It sounded like Tate had known Dredd. Hoping against hope for some small tidbit, I dialed the church.

"Hello," a gentle and countrified voice said. "This is Reverend Tate."

"Reverend Tate, this is Detective Carson Ryder with the Center for Law Enforcement over in Miami."

"Oh my . . ." Tate said, puzzled. "That sounds important."

"Not such a big deal, sir," I said. "I'd like to ask you a couple of questions if I may. I understand there was a man named Frisco Dredd who commandeered your church one morning."

"At night, actually. Evening service on a Wednesday."

"Could you tell me about it?"

"Not much to tell. Mr Dredd banged open the doors in the middle of my sermon and started yelling about all sorts of things . . . sin, redemption, Jesus. He was obviously drunk or on drugs, not making any sense. He called several of the women in the flock whores and I asked him to leave."

"I take it he didn't."

"He ran down the aisle like a mad bull and pushed

me from the pulpit and continued his yelling from there. I was fearful for the people in the church and called the police. They came and hauled Frisco away, still ranting at the top of his lungs. I felt sorry for him."

"It sounds like you knew Dredd."

"The Dredds were originally from Satsuma, Detective. They lived in a broken-down gray house on the edge of town and a poorer, scruffier lot you never saw. The household was mother, father, three children and Frisco, who the family took in when Frisco's mother died in childbirth. He never knew his father. I'm a religious man, Detective, saved by the blood of Christ. But I know I'm a sane man. I'm not sure I could say that about Mrs Dredd."

"How so?"

"She was a zealot – is that the right word? Crazed by religion, excessive. But by *religion*, not by God, who I see as merciful and loving. To her, religion was a set of absolute rules and processes. She was a cruel woman, punishing. I heard that she used to tell Frisco that he'd killed his mother by being so full of sin when he was born."

"My God."

"The problem was – well, one problem was – that Retha Dredd was a woman of strong desires and excesses. Particularly when it came to men. She couldn't stop herself from, uh, taking up with them."

"Nymphomaniacal?"

"I don't know much about that. I do know she often took up with more than one at a time. A sick, sad lady."

"What about the father?"

"Tinker Dredd. He died early, alcohol. When alive he seemed to look the other way, though he couldn't not know what was happening. I also heard that he, um, didn't much care for women, and that maybe Mrs Dredd brought in some men that, um, he might, uh . . ."

"I understand, sir."

"This was a horribly dysfunctional family, Detective. There was pain and suffering and the children were witness to the whole spectacle. But that was behind the scenes, the home life. There was the other side."

"Excuse me . . . other side?"

"Just as the creator inexplicably gave Retha Dredd one side that claimed allegiance to the Lord and another that made her lie down with any man she saw, the family had ugliness on one side, beauty on the other."

"You're losing me, Reverend."

"They were all musical, Detective. They traveled from town to town as the Dredd Family Singers, a gospel group. What a rough life that must have been for the children – living out of an old bus and performing like puppets at revivals and country fairs. The family never made any real money; there were a lot of little gospel groups competing for the same dollars, and the Dredds weren't anything special . . . except for the one."

"You mean Frisco?"

"Andrew Dredd. You wouldn't know the name. But he went on to make a name for himself on the Crown of Glory Network."

371

I felt my breath freeze in my throat. "Crown of Glory?"

"He's a big singing star there. Of course, Andy couldn't use a name like Dredd in big-time show business. These days he goes by the name Andy Delmont – much nicer. Andy's a personal favorite of the Reverend Amos Schrum, who I hear is on the mend, bless his soul."

55

I stared out the window, trying to stay calm and think. We had a blood connection between the COG network, the girls, and Frisco Jay Dredd, a connection named Andy Delmont, a man whose adopted brother had killed three women; no, four, the Sparks woman almost certainly wrapped in charred wool and beside a roadway or waterway. I shook my head over the destruction and pulled my laptop closer, Googling *Andy Delmont, images*.

The screen filled with dozens of photos of an attractive, baby-faced man ranging from twenties to thirties, almost all in what I took to be stage costume, white or sky-blue suits with a Western cut, some with glittery music notes on the lapels, some where he was wearing a matching cowboy hat. In some he was on a stage, a golden crown in the background underscored by the words *Crown of Glory* in shining, metallic gold. Delmont was smiling in every shot, either his default look or he showed the pretty teeth whenever he saw a camera.

Delmont looked eerily happy, like he'd buried the childhood of travel and travail, and I recalled Jeremy's description of a man he'd seen several times at Schrum's Key West outpost: "*A goofy and ever-present fellow dressed like Gene Autry.*"

Delmont, I figured. The constant smile was a bit goofy. Maybe even spooky. The question was, where was Delmont now? And how soon could I aim questions at his unsettlingly cherubic face?

I picked up my phone and dialed. "Baby brother," Jeremy crooned. "I'm afraid I'm in a spasm of artistic creation, painting, so I'll have to ask you to call back in—"

"I need to know if Gene Autry is still at the Schrum house."

"*Pourquoi est-ce, mon frère?*"

"Have you seen him today?"

"I've walked twice around back of the place, just because it gives me a thrill to be so close to a miracle. The Crown of Glory network says the old boy's ticker seems to have been touched by the Almighty, and requests donations to continue the healing. I'm not quite sure what God does with the money, but maybe the upkeep on Heaven is—"

"Have you seen Delmont, Jeremy?"

"He's often on the back porch twiddling on a guitar. Not today."

374

"Shit," I said. "I don't suppose there's any way you could . . . no, guess not. Thanks, Jeremy. By the way, how's Ava?"

I held my breath. *Come on, Brother, take the bait.*

"No way I could what?" he said, curiosity in his voice.

"Find out if he's in there – Delmont. Like you've said, the place is cordoned off, security front and back. Can't be done. I'll call back when this is over and explain why I'm so—"

"Give me a half-hour, Carson," he said.

Nautilus and Rebecca had started pulling away when his phone rang.

"It's from you," he said to Rebecca.

"Greta."

He turned on the phone. "Hi, Greta. Thanks for talking to us."

"They was looking for me when I got back. The other girls. I don't think they know anything."

"You girls, the four of you . . . you don't look out for each other?"

A grunt. "Be nice if it worked that way, mister. But it don't. Someone'll snitch. And get something for it. A day off, some cool dope."

Nautilus recalled the girl's blunted eyes and understood, figuring the girls had been expertly selected for their vulnerabilities: rejection by family, abuse, chemical dependencies, lack of self-esteem. When you have no worth, words like *integrity* and *honor* were just wind off a tongue.

Greata said, "The reason the others were looking for me . . . there's a party coming. We're supposed to clean up and put on our party clothes."

"When?"

"Tonight. They're usually late. But time don't mean nothin'."

"Where are these parties held?"

"At some fancy house by that lake . . . Tokalikea or somethin' like that. The east one."

"Tohopekaliga?"

"We get driven out there and party. We can spend the next day, too, eat up all the fancy food leftovers. Then we have to come back."

A question had been nagging in Nautilus's mind. "You girls at the special motel. You don't, uh . . . you're not like the others, the, uh . . ."

"The ones that come with the big smiles and always blessing everything?"

"Yes. What's the story there?"

"Pretty much the truth, I guess. That we're like a special mission of Hallelujah Jubilee: sinner girls brought there to meet Jesus and git saved. People leave us alone. The ones that don't hold their noses, that is. Gotta go, someone's coming. And anyway, that's all I got to tell."

My brother called back in forty minutes.

"Delmont's not there, though old Schrum's still in residence, God's hand massaging the old ticker or whatever. No one's quite sure where Delmont is, though he's scheduled to play at the network tomorrow morning. It's Pentecost, you know."

"How did you find out about Delmont?"

"*Assez facile, mon frère.* I trotted to the local music store and bought a guitar case, a very nice one. I took it to the door of the Schrum abode and said I had a delivery for Mr Delmont . . . his new custom-made guitar? There was a *soupçon* of commotion as pretty young people and stern-faced guards yelled back and forth inquiring as to Mr Delmont's whereabouts, an important delivery at the door and all. Consensus was that Rodeo Boy recently decamped for the airport, probably heading home to rest his hat before tomorrow's show."

"Thanks, Jeremy, masterful work. I'll pay you for the guitar case."

"Not necessary, Carson. It's the perfect size for my hedge trimmer. And by the way . . ."

"Yes?"

"You don't need to try and trick me into these things. You might simply ask."

56

Sissy Carol Sparks felt like crying. She hadn't cried in years and had almost forgotten what it felt like. The crazy man was going to kill her, burn her alive. That's what he'd said.

An hour ago she'd had his mouth drooling open, his eyes riveted on her as she'd crawled to him, breasts swinging, hair swaying, the ache of the rock in her thigh, but a soft and wanton smile on her lips. "C'mon, mister," she'd purred. "You don't want to hurt me. I can do things to you that'll leave you seeing stars for a week."

"Can you fix me?" he'd whispered, a man in a sexual trance. "I need it so bad."

If I can wear him down, fuck him senseless, I might be able to run outta this hellhole . . . he even left the door open a crack . . .

"I can fix you up perfect, mister," she'd promised. "I'll make you right."

The man stared down, a moan escaping his lips as Sissy moved to him. She'd unzipped his stained pants and slipped the underwear down over a bulge; not standing out, but she could fix that. Her fingers moved tantalizingly slow as she eased the saggy yellow boxers down his thighs . . .

Gasping. Staring. Disbelief.

Everything was swollen like a purple balloon and crusty with blood and pus and she could see what looked like bright pieces of wire sticking out. Her nostrils flooded with a stench remembered from when her grampa had the diabetes and his toe rotted off.

Gangrene, they called it.

"Fix him, girl," the man pleaded, grabbing Sissy's hair and pulling her face close to the reeking, dying organ. "Put your mouth on him and make him better."

Sissy had recoiled, pulling her head back. The man had put his hand behind her head, trying to drag her into him. "FIX HIM!" the man screamed. "MAKE HIM WELL!"

Sissy had puked her guts across the floor, driving the man even crazier, shrieking about whores and sin and beating her with hands swinging like windmills. She rolled across the floor as he kicked at her, screaming in his own pain as she screamed in hers. He'd cornered her beside a big concrete bench thing with burn marks across it but when he moved in Sissy punched him in his crotch. He'd wailed like an animal and dropped to the floor.

Sissy bolted through the door, finding a woods, trees and vines and bushes and a house in the near distance. She had run to the house and pounded on the door, screaming for help. The door was opened by a pretty-faced man in a cowboy hat.

"Help me . . ." Sissy pleaded. "There's a crazy man in that barn over there. He's trying to kill me."

"I know," the cowboy had said in a pleasant voice, his eyes glittering like hot little stars. "You need to pay for your sins, Miss Sparks."

The cowboy grabbed her neck, Sissy's strength used up in the fight with the crazy man . . .

Who limped up to the house two minutes later, punched her senseless, and led her back to the barn on a rope.

"No Sissy Carol Sparks?" I said to Belafonte.

She looked disconsolate, sitting beside the phone and leafing through reports. "The others were found within hours of being dumped. I expected something by now."

"Sparks could still be alive," I said.

"So you believe in fairy tales?"

Belafonte had the tight-eyed stare of someone about to either scream, throw things, or both, and I set her on finding out all she could about Andy Delmont, né Dredd. And fast. I mainly needed to know where he lived. Mr Delmont and I were overdue for a long talk.

My phone rang: Harry told me about a girl named Greta, and parties, and men with diminutives for names.

"Suggestions?" I asked, feeling I was tumbling back in time, the single-word question one I'd asked my senior partner a thousand times before.

"Put a watch on the motel. Tail the bastards to their hole by East Tohopekaliga lake. It's about fifteen miles from the park."

I established the availability of the chopper, then phoned authorities in Osceola County and told them to set a table for the FCLE tonight.

"Did you say Osceola County?" Belafonte said when I hung up.

"Harry thinks Hallelujah Jubilee bigwigs are taking some girls to a party house tonight. Why?"

"Mr Delmont-Dredd has property in Osceola County, a farm. He also has a house in Jacksonville."

"How did you get that info so fast?"

"Mr Monroe taught me a few things," she blinked. "Like back-door entries to various state agencies when those agencies are closed."

I ran several scenarios through my mind. "It sounds like Osceola County is where the action is tonight. The chopper's coming for us in minutes. We gotta book fast, a storm's rolling in from the Gulf."

"Chopper for us? Both?"

"I need someone to supervise a stakeout at a motel and then, hopefully, a bust. Harry can't, I don't know

381

the Osceola cops, so you're in charge, Holly. Better go powder your baton."

Lightning from the incoming storm quivered in the western sky by the time we hit the Osceola County Police HQ. Most senior staff were in Atlanta for a convention and we inherited Sergeant Eddie Baskins. He was in his late thirties, a big, baby-faced, loud-voiced good ol' boy, over six and a half feet tall and belly-centric. I figured he'd once been a standout on the local football team, probably by falling on his opponents.

I was a bit less certain of his cop credentials. Maybe it was the mother-of-pearl grip on his sidearm and uniform pants tucked into red, hand-tooled cowboy boots. I doubted he wore them when his superiors were in town.

"Of course we can handle your stakeout, Detective," Baskins affirmed, tapping the glitzy semi-auto and studying a wall-mounted map of the county. "There's a team stationed at a park by the lake, extra manpower to assist in the operation. The secondary unit is our SWAT team."

He picked up a Dixie cup and spat a saliva-glistening wad of tobacco sludge into it, wiping his lips with the back of his hand. Three Osceola officers were in attendance, all in their twenties. One winced, one rolled his eyes, the third stared at the floor. I got the feeling they hoped the Atlanta convention would be brief.

Belafonte eyed Baskins warily. "Do you think perhaps the SWAT unit is a bit of overkill, Sergeant?"

Baskins frowned. "I believe I'll be the judge of that, little lady. Who did you say you were again?"

"Holly Belafonte," she said. "I'm handling your stakeout."

"She's handling it?" Baskins said, head snapping to me. "I thought you and *him* were in the lead." Baskins jabbed a finger toward Harry, leaning the wall with arms crossed. I'd introduced Harry simply as *Detective Nautilus*, omitting that *Detective* was a former title. Another demerit for Baskins, who should have checked Harry's ID.

"Detective Nautilus and I are going to Cypress Lake," I said. "We'd appreciate a couple of your people coming along."

Baskins narrowed an eye, like we were city slickers trying to pull something. "First you needed assistance on a stakeout . . ." he groused. "Now you're adding things."

Belafonte stepped up. "May I inquire if that costs additional?"

Baskins turned to her. "What?"

"Like when you get a scoop of ice cream and it's two dollars," she said, elegant fingers mimicking dropping sprinkles into ice cream. "But if you add chocolate jimmies, it's two-fifty." Belafonte clicked opened her purse and pretended to root around inside. "If it costs more to add an expedition to Cypress Lake, how much will it be?"

Baskins stared down a foot at Belafonte, sure he was being either used or mocked. "Where the hell are you from, lady?" he challenged. "That stupid accent sure as hell ain't Miami."

"I'm from Bermuda," Belafonte said, hand still in her purse.

Here we go, I thought.

"That's in South America," Baskins growled. "What the hell you doing here?"

In a microsecond the baton was out and extended and whipped an inch under the Sergeant's nose to *thwack* the map on the wall.

"What *we* are doing here," Belafonte said softly, "you, me, your officers . . . is conducting a surveillance operation." The baton tip repositioned with another *thwack*. "Here is where we are, and" – *thwack* – "here is where we are going. That's what *we're* doing here, Sergeant," she said. "But what *I'm* doing right this instant is wondering if you're *professional* enough to conduct a proper surveillance, and can your people tail another vehicle without DRIVING UP THEIR BLOODY ARSE?"

The room went as silent as a tomb. Baskins swallowed hard and nodded.

It was twilight as most of the cops charged off in Belafonte's wake, Harry and I and two Osceola officers speeding to Andrew Delmont's southern hideaway. A mile west of the Florida Turnpike by Cypress Lake, it was tucked into several tree-dense acres, a heavy gate barring a gravel lane that snaked into the overgrowth. The Osceola guys were a bit nervous since I had no warrant, but I told them we were just going to ring the doorbell, like bible salespeople.

The cops pushed the gate open and we headed through, the night now dark and streaked with lightning to the southwest. I smelled rain in the stiffening wind, the tree-tops dancing as we drove two hundred yards to a pair of buildings in a clearing. The scene was not what I'd have pictured for a successful gospel artist, the house small and gray and desperately needing paint, shutters hanging askew, the sparse grass studded with weeds. There was no light in the house.

I climbed the steps to the listing porch and pounded the door. "Mr Delmont? Andy Delmont? I'm from the Florida Center for Law Enforcement and I need to ask you some questions."

Not so much as a creak of a floorboard inside. I backed away, staring at the house until hearing words from this afternoon, Pastor Tate: "*The Dredds were originally from Satsuma, Detective, a broken-down old house on the edge of town.*"

Was Delmont, consciously or subconsciously recreating a childhood home?

"No one's here," I said. "Anything down the lane?"

The county mounties aimed their headlamps down the dusty trail, revealing a barn in the distance, half sunk into overgrowth. "Might be a place to hide a van," Harry said.

I nodded. "Gotta look. Then we'll head to Delmont's home in Jacksonville. Bet it's fancier than this wreck."

Harry and I drove the five hundred feet to the barn, the slats of a one-time corral rotting on the ground, connected by tangles of barbed wire. We got to the door as rain started. I heard Harry sniffing the air.

"Yeah," I said. "I've been smelling rain for an hour."

"Not rain," he said. "I smell smoke. And . . . is that gasoline? Kerosene?"

I suddenly smelled it, too. "I think it's naphtha," I said. The door was unlocked and swung into a wall of black. The smell became overwhelming.

"There's gotta be a light," Harry said, patting at the wall. "There."

The barn flooded with sickly yellow illumination. I saw a brown-dirt floor littered with round stones the size of oranges, a stack of torn fabric, and at the far end sat a concrete bench, charred, reeking of oil and naphtha.

Atop the bench lay a woman, naked, bound by ropes, her bruised head hanging off the side. Dead, but not yet wrapped. I felt sickened as we crossed a floor studded with orange-sized stones. Getting closer, I saw none of the expected tissue damage from being pummeled with rocks. I picked up speed, running the final feet.

The woman's eyes flickered open and her head turned our way.

"I never thought I'd be happy to see cops," she said, her voice a dry rasp as her mouth fought to make a brave smile. "You guys *are* cops, I hope?"

* * *

"What did Dredd say?" I asked Sparks as she was loaded into the ambulance ten minutes later. She had a hematoma on her thigh and various facial contusions, but seemed in good shape, considering. "Did Dredd tell you where he was going or when he'd be back?"

The medic handed her a cup of water and Sparks refreshed her voice. "The bastard was screaming about blasphemy and needing to leave, but that he'd be back to kill me. He was real pissed off by something about Pentecost. I mean, even for a lunatic with a rotting dick. It was crazy . . . like he was yelling into the scar in his chest."

"The man in the cowboy garb," I said, "Delmont. Any idea of his whereabouts?"

"I heard a car leave. It was still light out."

"Just one vehicle?" I asked.

"It sounded like it. But mostly what I could hear was my heart."

"Suggestions?" I asked Harry, twice in one evening.

"Dredd is a big package of weirdness, Delmont seems a big package of weirdness. The only other weirdness I know is whatever the hell Owsley's doing in that building behind Hallelujah Jubilee. Maybe the weirdnesses are coming together."

57

The Osceola guys stayed on scene, Harry directing us toward Hallelujah Jubilee as the storm arrived in earnest, low, roiling black clouds delineated in hard flashes of white light. In the distance I saw a cross so tall it seemed more of the sky than the earth, invisible until lightning flashed, then gone.

Harry cut down a side road and drove a quarter-mile until we came to a locked gate.

"They just built this. Hang on."

Harry had brought his .45 Colt, a big and powerful pistol that looked small in his hand. He blew the lock into component parts, pushed open the bar, and we continued, cutting south and no longer seeing the spectral cross. Instead, I saw a vertically oriented structure about a hundred feet tall, like a square silo, fifty feet a side or thereabouts. It pushed from a long and low two-story structure. The thing looked like it had scales until I realized they were corrugated panels slapped together in willy-nilly fashion.

Harry pulled to what appeared to be a guardhouse. It was dark.

"No security types?" I said.

"I figure the locked gate was supposed to keep folks away. And maybe the fewer eyes, the better."

I peered past the guardhouse as shapes resolved against the dark: two large SUV's and a dark Hummer. The main gate was open.

Harry nodded at the Hummer. "Owsley's here."

I studied the turf as we exited the car: stacks of construction refuse, battered barrels, upended crates, bales of wire. Two big silver tanks sat side by side against the wall of the building, behind them a big Cat 'dozer with a blade.

"What's in the tanks?"

"Usual construction stuff . . . water and diesel fuel."

I kept up my scan, looking into the flashes of lightning. "Over there," I said, "parked back in the trees – a van."

We trotted that way and peered into the van, Harry shining a penlight. It looked recently cleaned. "Wasn't Dredd in a white van?" Harry asked.

"The van was repainted," I said, looking closer. "Probably with spray paint. Dredd's around here. What time is it?"

"Almost midnight. Almost Pentecost."

We turned back to the structure as lightning flashed,

showing a square cannon pointed at the sky and illuminated in slow strobing. We went to the main door and
tried the handle. "Locked," I said.

Harry nodded to our left. Another jagged white line
sizzled through the rain-smelling air. I looked down the
horizontal wing of the building, fifty meters of windowless corrugated metal.

"*Testing,*" said an amplified voice inside the structure.
Then louder, "*Testing!*" We heard a fingernail tapping
the mic, a squeal of feedback.

"It's Owsley," Harry said.

"*Test . . .*" Owsley said as if in confirmation. "*Give
me more echo. Test . . . testing. OK, that's good.*"

We jogged to the far end of the structure. The door
was unlocked and hanging open. We entered a dark
cavern, blocked by looming, spectral shapes. Harry flickered his penlight over sections of crane boom, construction
timbers, sheets of corrugated metal, spools of cable. We
crept forward, dodging and ducking construction equipment, tripping over bolts and wires and other detritus,
our sole light the pale circle of Harry's penlight. I watched
it shine over timbers, an acetylene tank, a Bobcat loader
. . . a small face.

"Hi, Harry," the face said. "Who's this?"

"Rebecca?" Harry hissed. "What the hell are you doing
here?"

The kid slipped out from behind a box large enough
to hold a pickup truck. "I wanted to see where Daddy
worked. He drove over and I hid in the back."

"Dammit, Rebecca," Harry said. "There may be a dangerous man in here."

"Then it's good I'm with you guys. Are you Carson?"

"*Mr Winkler's coming,*" Owsley said, the enhanced voice booming over the amplification system. "*He's pulling up outside. Places everyone.*"

I said, "What the—"

Harry grabbed the kid's hand and we continued forward, the main room a hundred feet distant. We could see nothing of that section of the floor, blocked by a mountain of large rectangular shapes. We heard a door open, the one in front. A light snapped on and we crouched behind a donkey engine and peered forward, seeing a man in a wheelchair whirring into the main room. Someone in the rafters had trained a spotlight over the man, like he was a major celebrity. A dozen steps behind a scowling woman was at the edge of the spotlight, arms crossed, pacing like she'd prefer to be anywhere else. I heard her say, "Give it up, Eliot. Let go."

"*Welcome, Eliot Winkler,*" Owsley's voice boomed over the PA system, the words echoing in the structure. "*It's a blessed day . . . A heavenly day!*" A dramatic pause before Owsley boomed, "*Bring me the animal!*"

We crept forward, stopping behind a huge wooden crate. "These are what the semis were delivering," Harry whispered. "There must be a half-dozen of the things."

"*The time approacheth, Eliot,*" Owsley's voice thundered, then shifted to a softer voice, as if reading: "*The disciples were amazed at His words. But Jesus answered again and said to them, 'Children, how hard is it to enter the kingdom of God!'"*

"I know that verse," Rebecca said, "It's from Matthew—"

"Shush," Harry said. "I've got to get you outside."

Another spotlight snapped on in the upper reaches of the tower. I looked up and gasped, seeing the top twenty feet of a rocket gleaming in the light.

"Jesus, Harry. It's some kind of missile."

Another spotlight flared on, aiming high, but below the first, illuminating another twenty feet of tapering missile shaft.

"What's that sound?" Rebecca Owsley asked, looking up toward a metallic grinding. "A plane flying over?"

It was the roof being retracted, gears straining high above as cloud-to-cloud streaks of lightning illuminated the inside of the tower.

"*God's looking down on us, Eliot*!" Owsley roared. "*We have his blessing!*"

The roof opened fully to reveal a sky rippling with electrical energy, the clouds boiling black and purple and lit from within.

A countdown began. "*Ten*," called Owsley's voice.

"What's going on?" the kid asked.

I yanked at Harry's arm. "They're going to fire the thing."

"*Nine*," Owsley intoned, followed by "*Awalalcaba-halladadamashuasu . . .*"

"What the hell?"

"Talking in tongues," Harry said.

"*Eight . . .*"

We stumbled ahead as a third spot snapped on, illuminating twenty more feet of gleaming metal thorn. Only the base remained in the dark. What would happen when the rocket fired?

"*Seven . . . Ishnohisadocodocaballaha . . . six . . .*"

"Maybe it's a suicide thing," I said, heart pounding in my chest. "The flames will fry everyone."

"*Five . . .*"

Harry tripped over something on the floor and went down.

"*Four . . .*"

"Come on," I said, pulling on his arm as the kid ran in to grab the other one. "We gotta run."

"*Three . . .*"

Harry yanked at his ankles as Owsley yelled *TWO*. "I'm wrapped in baling wire or something . . . Run, Carson . . . get the kid out the—"

"*One!*" Owsley shrieked, followed by . . . "*LET ME BE YOUR VEHICLE OH MIGHTY GOD!*"

Too late. Harry and I froze, bodies tensed against an explosion. Seconds passed with no explosion, no rocket lift-off. Harry stripped the wire from his feet and peered around the final crate into the main room, now lit as bright as daylight.

He whispered, "I don't believe it."

58

I followed Harry to his vantage point and saw the object in full, illuminated from tip to base. But the base wasn't a rocket engine, it was an opening about eight feet high and five wide.

The object wasn't a missile, it was a gigantic needle. As in sewing.

It got stranger. I saw Richard Owsley standing at the needle's base in a snow white suit and holding the tether of a Dromedary camel. Owsley was twitching like he was being jabbed with cattle prods and ranting like a madman into a wireless microphone.

"*Arabacaddahasheem . . . Thank you for this miracle, oh Lord . . . Alacacabadelonayamayah.*"

"My God," Harry whispered. "I understand it now."

"Please tell me."

"From Mark 10:25," Rebecca Owsley said. "'It is easier

394

for a camel to pass through the eye of a needle than for a rich man to enter Heaven.'"

"*Baracbadaceemandadada* . . ." Owsley continued. "*We implore you ALMIGHTY GOD TO aragagdabena-pana* . . ."

The man in the wheelchair was twenty paces from the base of the needle and in either the throes of ecstasy or madness, arms above his head, twitching and shaking and screaming "THANK YOU, GOD!" almost as loud as the amplified ululations of Owsley and the growing thunder, the storm crossing directly above. The woman was shaking her head in disbelief as Owsley led the camel toward the needle's eye. Rain poured through the open roof and Owsley's face turned to meet it.

"*Bless this mighty symbololahhheeeegagawashae, oh Lord, and thank you for giving it us and ahhahgagmel-bethashaloma* . . ."

The three of us were spellbound as Owsley stepped into the needle, yanking the rope. The camel balked, perhaps spooked by the thunder, and stopped dead. Owsley strained at the tether.

"HARDER!" the old man howled. "PULL HARDER!" He turned to the shadows, screaming, "HELP HIM, YOU FOOLS!"

Two burly security types ran from the dark, one helping Owsley with the tether, the other putting his shoulder to the camel's rump, causing it to buck and jump.

"GET IT DONE!" the old man raged.

Harry and I stood transfixed until a bolt of lightning

seemed to explode inside the building, followed by the shrieking of metal being torn. We turned to see a huge section of the wall crash inward. Support timbers tumbled to the floor in a cloud of dust. The walls shook.

"What the hell?" I said.

"A bulldozer just pushed in the wall," Harry said. "It's pushing a . . . Jesus!"

"What?" the kid asked, staring at the mayhem.

"About a thousand gallons of diesel fuel," Harry said, eyes wide in horror.

I saw it through the settling dust, the big Cat bulldozer from outside, its wide blade rolling a silver tank over fallen timbers and sheets of corrugated metal. "BLASPHEMY AGAINST GOD!" a voice howled. I saw a man standing at the controls, shirtless, a horizontal slash across his chest and madness in his eyes.

Frisco Dredd.

"BLASPHEMERS!" Dredd screamed, shaking his fist, his face a rictus of anger. "YOU CANNOT CHANGE THE LAWS OF GOD!"

The scene was so unreal that no one moved. Lightning exploded. The lights shivered and went out, returned seconds later. The camel had dropped to the ground, its last defense. No way the men would move the beast. They turned and ran, competing with Owsley for the lead. Three others appeared in their wake, probably the crew who'd been handling spotlights and audio. The woman was beside Winkler, trying to pull him from the building. He spat at her and swatted her away.

"Get the kid out," I yelled over the pounding of thunder and the roaring of the 'dozer.

Harry tossed the kid over his shoulder like a sack of meal. "Run, Carson," he shouted, heading for the door. I watched the bulldozer pivot, aiming for the needle. Eliot Winkler, his face a mask of fury, seemed to take it as a challenge and rolled his wheelchair before the oncoming bulldozer, holding up his hands in a Halt motion. I pulled my weapon and drew a bead on Dredd, but smelled fuel fumes and held the shot: Sparks from my gun could ignite the air and turn us all into Dredd's sacrifices.

Was that what he wanted?

A crack of lightning and the lights died for several long seconds. They flickered on, dimmer, the interior now a land of shadow. I didn't see Winkler, and then I did . . . the crushed wheelchair a dozen feet behind the 'dozer, the tank torn open by the blade and leaving a trail of diesel fuel over Winkler's flattened remains, the thick fumes now burning my eyes.

I scrambled for the door as lightning found the metal roof and sparks tumbled from five stories up. I saw the camel rise and run toward the door as the 'dozer approached the needle, Dredd standing erect, screaming toward the sky like a man possessed by the Furies.

"AND HE CARRIED ME AWAY IN THE SPIRIT INTO A WILDERNESS AND I SAW A WOMAN SITTING ON A SCARLET BEAST . . . FULL OF BLASPHEMOUS NAMES AND HAVING SEVEN HEADS AND TEN HORNS . . ."

Lightning again flashed as I dove through the opening followed by a second flash and a thudding *whooomp*: the sound of hundreds of gallons of fuel igniting in a closed space.

59

"Eliot's been obsessed," Vanessa Winkler said, sitting in a conference room borrowed from the Osceola County Police Department. "He got MS and started throwing money at everything and everyone, looking for a cure. Then he found Schrum, who did a laying on of hands and pronounced Eliot clean. Eliot suddenly got better. It was a remission, not uncommon."

Two hours had passed. There was little left of the structure. Even less of Eliot Winkler.

"Eliot figured Schrum hot-wired him to God," Ms Winkler continued. "Even when Eliot got sicker, he was convinced it was Schrum keeping him alive. 'Look at you, Eliot,' I'd say. 'You're getting worse.' He'd snarl that he'd be dead if it wasn't for Schrum."

"Your brother got sicker still."

She nodded. "When Eliot realized he was gonna get

stuck in the ground like everyone else, he became obsessed with Mark 10:25, camel and needles and all that. He started blubbering about saving his soul by giving the money – every fucking cent – to charity. Then Amos says 'Maybe it doesn't have to be that way, Eliot . . .'"

"The project began," I said. "1025-M, Mark 10:25. Put a camel through the eye of a needle and your brother could go to Heaven."

"Madness," Winkler said to herself, then turned to me. "Is Amos here? I want the joy of telling that asshole the Winkler gravy train died tonight."

"Schrum never left Key West," I said.

Disgust filled Vanessa Winkler's face. "He sets the idiocy in motion and finds someone else to do the work. That's Amos Schrum, Detective. I predict he'll be back on stage within three weeks."

I let Ms Winkler return to a life that had probably improved considerably and moved to the cell holding Andy Delmont. He'd been outside the Ark at Hallelujah Jubilee, singing songs in the dark and waiting to pick up Frisco Dredd, no doubt so they could complete the Lord's work on Sissy Carol Sparks.

I passed another cell on my way, seeing three men inside, the larger of the two trying to look tough, barking at the older and bespectacled fellow. "Man up, Roland, the lawyers are on their way." The larger one was Hayes Johnson and I resisted the urge to tell him we'd spoken on the phone.

A guard opened Delmont's cell and I entered to find the singer not on the cot but sitting on the floor beside the toilet, arms around his knees. When he looked up I saw the same eerie smile and empty eyes noted in the online images. Delmont was in the room with me, and yet wasn't.

"Andrew Dredd?" I said.

"Not any more," he said amiably. "It got changed to Delmont 'cos Dredd wasn't a proper name for a praise singer. The Reverend Schrum helped me make it my official name."

I sat on the cot since Delmont seemed content with the floor. "Frisco Dredd was your cousin, right, Andy?" I said. "A member of the family band."

Delmont looked pleased that I knew his family's history. "Frisco's mama died when he was born so we took him in, the Christian way. He became my brother an' we spent all our time together when we was little. We never seemed to stop trav'lin' . . . had an ol' bus we lived out of. Me an' Frisco was best buddies and did ever'thing together."

"Everything?"

He stared, an eerie and enigmatic smile on the baby face. I felt a sensation of cold on my back, there and gone. "Who was in charge of your family, Andy?" I asked.

"Mama. Daddy died from drinkin' when I was twelve. Mama said the demons ate him from the inside out."

"Did your mama have any demons inside her, Andy?"

401

Something flashed through his eyes so fast I couldn't peg the meaning, then his face went blank.

"Andy . . ." I tried again. "Did your mama—"

He reached up and pressed the flush button on the toilet, producing a howling five-second *Whooooosh*. He gave me a polite smile, like he didn't hear the question.

"Come on, Andy. Did your mama have any—"

Whooooosh. The toilet again, followed by the *I-can't-hear-you* look. Delmont wasn't going there.

"Who's the Prince of Lies, Andy?" I asked, going somewhere else.

"The Devil, sir," he said easily, back on a topic he could deal with. "That's one of his names."

"Do you lie?"

"Lots, when I was younger. But since I got saved by Reverend Schrum there's no need to lie. It's a sin to be false."

I took a deep breath. "You helped your cousin kill three women, didn't you, Andy?"

Delmont stared at me with his head cocked as if the question was perplexing. "We saved the ladies, sir. They was fallen and was gonna pull the Reverend down with them . . . they'd have told on him because it's the way of whores and Jezebels. The Reverend has holy work to do here on earth."

"It was just those women who, uh, tempted the Reverend, Andy? The four of them?

"The Devil took Reverend Schrum to Mister Johnson's

sinful lake house seven times, sir. But the Lord interceded and made the Reverend stop his downfall."

Or . . . I thought, Schrum wised up, realizing getting caught would put a big damper on donations. Or maybe it was delayed or sublimated guilt . . . I'd seen that as well.

"Tell me, Andy . . . was silencing the girls – I mean, dealing with the whores – your idea? Or was it Frisco's? I guess what I'm asking is . . . was any part of it from Reverend Schrum?"

"The Reverend and I spent a lot of time together, sir. The last few months he would drink spirits and confess to me about how he'd fallen to temptation. I protect him when he's like that, sir. And no, weren't no reason to tell Reverend Schrum what Frisco and me were doing. He'd a just worried more."

"Frisco had been tempted by Jezebels himself, right, Andy?"

"Women like that have powers from Satan. Satan tempted Frisco with dirty thoughts even when we was little. His soul was filthy sick for years. But last year I got him to come live with me on my farm. He read the Bible all day an' most nights and figgered he was deep in debt to the Devil and hell-bound fer sure . . . spending all eternity on fire. Frisco needed a holy task to buy back his soul. God gave me the message to use Frisco to save Reverend Schrum."

"Who came up with the idea of stoning the women?"

"The Bible told Frisco how it worked, sir," Delmont

403

said with a beatific smile. "He pulled the whores from a path to Hell and sent them to Judgement in the righteous manner. The Lord is merciful."

"What about the needle? You knew about that?"

A frown crossed the radiant face. "Mr Winkler was scared for his soul because he had so much money. The Reverend told Mr Winkler if a camel went through a needle, things could change. It was supposed to be like a parable, but it was all Mr Winkler could think about. He started building things on his own. Reverend Schrum used to say Mr Winkler was getting on his nerves, but it was his heart he meant. He came to Key West to get away from Mr Winkler, but that man just wouldn't go away."

"You told Frisco about the needle, right?"

"I'd never seen Frisco so mad. He said it was a blasphemy. When God says something, you can't make it change."

I recalled Harry telling me that Owsley had started receiving anonymous threats when he came to Florida, took the shot: "It was Frisco who called Pastor Owsley, right, Andy? Made threats?"

A head bob. "The Pastor was trying to help Mr Winkler go against God's laws."

"Would Frisco have killed Pastor Owsley if he got the chance?"

Again, the beatific smile. "Yes. To save him."

I'd spent enough time in Delmont's broken world. I stood and looked down at the mad singer, smiling at me like I was a momentary swirl in a wide and ancient river.

"You know you've broken laws, Andy," I said. "You'll have to go away for a very long time."

"Man's laws and Man's time, sir. I have all eternity with Jesus."

60

It was four in the morning. Since it was a big operation and I'd alerted Roy what we'd be doing, he was up and waiting for news.

"I'm heading in, Roy," I said on my cell. "I'll give you the full report tomorrow. You won't believe it, but I swear it's true."

"I want to hear this story tonight. Or I guess it's morning, isn't it?"

"I have to track down Belafonte and find out what—"

"Belafonte's here at HQ, Carson," he said. "She's been here for hours."

"She drove to Miami? Why?"

"She wanted to bring us a gift."

"Pardon me?"

"Just come in, Carson. We'll have a parade." Roy was being cryptic, but he also sounded oddly happy, like he had a lobster dinner on his desk. The night was still producing oddities. "Hey . . . you bringing Nautilus?" Roy asked.

"I figure Harry'll hang out on Matecumbe for a few days."

I rang off. All the guys who'd accompanied Belafonte were gone and I spoke to the desk officer as we headed out. "What happened on Tohopekaliga?" I asked.

"We got the three guys in custody," the DO said, meaning the Johnson half-brothers and the doctor. "The other one went with the tough lady back to Miami. She's from Bermuda. It's a British protectorate. I just learned that tonight."

"Other one? What other one?"

A shrug. "Some Hispanic dude. She jammed cuffs on him, locked him to the D-ring in the back of a cruiser. She said a lot of people were looking for him."

I was shaking my head as Harry and I headed to the waiting chopper. Would the weirdness never end?

We were in the air minutes later, the storm dissipating, the night sky clearing to the south. The world below sparkled with lights of small towns and vehicles strung like chains of white-eyed insects on the roads below our beating rotors. Speech was difficult with the noise and helmets with microphones, but Harry and I managed a bit before shutting into our own worlds.

"The girl," I said, "Rebecca. What's gonna happen there?"

"Rebecca's the only adult in the family, Cars," Harry said, looking down on a dark plain studded with light. "She starts college in a couple years, wants to study science, probably biology. I expect Rebecca will get her way. She's good at that." He paused. "Cars . . .?"

"What?"

"That was fun tonight, y'know? Like old times."

"Yeah," I said. "Like old times."

In what seemed scant minutes, we hit the Clark Center as day dawned in the East, the long and lonesome blue of the ocean dappled with the pink and orange glitter of sunrise over waves, iridescent and glorious and hopeful all at once.

The Center was quiet as we stepped from the elevator. "Hello?" I called. "Anyone here?"

"Back here in your office," Belafonte's voice called.

We headed down the hall until stopped by Roy's voice at our backs. "You hit the mother lode, Carson. It's over. You deserve a parade."

"Parade? What's over? What are you talking about, Roy?"

He winked. "Go see Belafonte for details."

We entered my office. Belafonte was sitting on the couch and I did introductions. "The desk guy at Osceola said you hauled a prisoner back, Holly. What's that about?"

Roy appeared at the door. He nodded to Belafonte and she put her arms behind her head and leaned back on the couch. I'd never seen her so relaxed.

"We followed the Johnson limo to the house on the lake," she said. "Three men and the girls went inside and the chauffeur parked at the head of the drive. I wanted the man silenced before he pulled his cell and alerted our rascal boys. I crept behind the limo, yanked the door open, and flashed my badge."

I heard a chuckle. Roy.

"The chauffeur's name was Hector Machado," Belafonte continued. "An ex-gang member who got religion and hired on at the Hallelujah ranch as a groundskeeper. He was promoted to driver for Johnson after a month."

"I don't need every detail, Holly. Did the girls get pulled out?"

"Oh sure, we handled that little job rather quickly." She smiled. Was that *coy*? Laughing *and* coy . . . who was this woman?

"We entered the home and found four young ladies in shorty gowns and negligees. There was enough liquor to start a pub, plus various pills and marijuana. Hayes Johnson, his brother Cecil, plus a buggy-eyed gent named Uttleman were lounging about in their undies. The latter stated that he was a doctor and had rights. I told him he had the right to get handcuffed first, which didn't seem the effect he was hoping for."

"Great that you got the girls out of that hellhole," I said, thinking it was, unfortunately, an easy rap to beat ". . . *the women were all over the age of consent, Your Honor,*" a high-priced lawyer's voice said in my head, "*and willingly accompanied the men to the house for drinks and dinner, bringing illegal drugs, unbeknownst to the gentlemen* . . ."

"Don't you want Belafonte to finish her story?" Roy said.

"I thought she just did."

"You've forgotten Mr Machado," Belafonte said. "When he stepped from the limousine, the first thing Machado saw was the Osceola unit in tac gear: rifles, helmets, full body armor, knives strapped to thighs, night-vision glasses . . ."

Roy said, "You're gonna love this, Carson."

"It seems Mr Machado thought he was the target," Belafonte said. "He dropped to his knees and commenced bawling like a baby, saying he'd confess if we kept his sister in the home. I said, 'What are you bloody talking about?'"

"Need a drum roll, Officer Belafonte?" Roy said. "This would be the time."

Belafonte stood and leaned against the wall, arms crossed and a look of grand amusement on her face. "Mr Machado confessed, Detective Ryder."

"Confessed to what?"

"The killing of Roberta Menendez."

I stared, dumbfounded. Roy sat on the front of my desk, though I should have been the one to sit, the world spinning.

"You'll need the backstory," Roy said. "Miz Menendez, a religious lady, visited Hallelujah Jubilee recently, part of a church group. A frugal woman, she was a bit dismayed by the expense. She went home and did due diligence on the park, finding its paltry reported income at odds with her experience. When she found there were no huge debts – like land payments – our numbers lady suspected proceeds were being siphoned off before they hit the books."

Belafonte said, "Hallelujah's accountant is Cecil, Hayes Johnson's brother. Somehow Johnson discovered the intrepid Menendez suspected skimming, which turns out to have been exactly right: three tax-free million a year, one-point six mil a year to Johnson – who probably set it all up – eight hundred G's a year to Cecil, six to Doctor Uttleman. Roberta Menendez knew a member of the park's board and approached her. It probably got back to Johnson that way."

My head was topsy-turvy. "How do you have exact figures?"

Roy's turn. "Three hours ago Jacksonville agents raided Cecil Johnson's office with two FCLE forensic accountants in tow. They found a set of duplicate books in a safe you could have opened with a penknife. They also recovered emails between the three men saying something had to be done about Menendez before, as one poignantly put it, 'this bitch destroys our retirement fund'."

"What about Schrum?" I asked, recalling that he'd created the park.

"Clean. No payouts in his direction," Roy said. "I think Johnson saw a chance to turn HJ into a personal profit center."

"Machado," I said, shaking my head in disbelief. "Bring me back to him."

"Machado has a thirty-five-year-old sister with early-onset Alzheimer's. Machado's dirt-ass poor, had to put his sister in the cheapest care he could find, a dump. Johnson made Machado an offer. Care to guess what?"

It took me five seconds. "Eliminate Menendez and the sister gets upgraded."

Roy nodded. "The sister's now in a high-class place in Orlando, with the bills paid by Hector, who went from a salary of thirty-five grand a year to eighty-five. Oddly enough, the care in the new facility is about fifty G's a year."

"Where from here, Roy?" I said, pretty much knowing the answer.

"I think we can find a way Machado's sister stays in decent care." He winked. "Contingent on Hector's spilling everything he knows. As far as the FCLE breaking the Menendez case, well . . ."

"Miami-Dade was instrumental in solving the case," I finished, knowing how the script would be written. "The FCLE was happy to assist in any small way possible."

"Menendez was theirs. Officer Roberts was theirs. They need it."

"When the reports are written on this one," I said, "I want it noted that key findings in the Menendez case were—"

"—the result of splendid police work by Officer Holly

Belafonte," Roy said. "Already handled." He smiled at Belafonte. "I expect a gold shield is in your future, Officer Belafonte. Congratulations."

She reddened as we gave her a round of applause. Roy thanked us for our hard work, then started back to the hall, now streaming with incoming sunlight. He stopped in the threshold, head cocked, like a sudden thought had arrived. He turned and looked at Harry.

"Can I see you in my office for a few minutes, Detective Nautilus?"

"Sure . . ." Harry said, following Roy into the hall. "But it's no longer Detective."

"I guess that depends on how much you're enjoying retirement," Roy said, clapping his hand on Harry's shoulder and angling him down the hall, voice diminishing as the pair trod the carpet to his office. "I've got a couple odd ideas I'd like to bend your ear with . . ."

61

The pink Adidas cross-trainers of Sissy Carol Sparks padded down the sidewalk of Little Havana, past a used clothing store and a bodega. When she'd pushed her feet into the Ferragamo slings this morning the things had hurt. Maybe it was because the six-hundred-dollar shoes had been bought from a Chevy parked in an alley off of Flagler Street for a hundred-twenty bucks, stolen, or maybe the damn things were fakes. It didn't matter: she'd dropped them in the trash as she'd left the apartment. She'd jammed her three cocktail gowns in after them, and was now dressed in loose slacks and a nondescript yellow blouse. Her hair was pulled back and held in place with a red rubber band.

Sissy had been thinking about her life. All the way from sprinting from her drunken uncle in Hicksville to a crazy-eyed looney chucking rocks at her head and yelling about sin.

Damn, but those shoes had hurt.

Sissy had a small suitcase in her hand: a couple pairs of underwear, some blouses, jeans, T-shirts. Her cosmetic case slimmed down to basics.

"*Get over here, girl,*" her uncle called from the back of her mind, unshaven for four days, staggering on squishy legs, a bottle of Jim Beam in his hand. "*I wanna give your pretty face a kiss.*" Her uncle's voice was replaced by the voice of a music teacher in high school, the pair sitting on his shabby couch in his apartment at the edge of a corn field. "*You're so much older than you are, Sissy . . .*" a tongue licking her neck as fingers crawled up her thigh. "*You wanna know what I mean by that?*"

Then to the great big guy at Hallelujah Jubilee, Mister Johnson, called in to meet Sissy on her second interview at the park and staring at her like she was a big, juicy steak.

"*We could use someone like you, Miss Sparks – may I call you Sissy? Someone to help us find and help special girls like yourself. To be their leader, so to speak. A mentor. Do you know what that means?*"

She'd never left Hicksville. It was stuck inside her wherever she went, whatever she did, carried around like a disease in her heart. No matter how high she thought she was flying, she was still a worm crawling in the dirt.

Until everything changed, nothing changed.

The pink Adidases of Sissy Carol Sparks stopped on the pavement, the sun blazing like a golden torch in the sky. Sissy took a deep breath, tightened her grip on the suitcase, and turned to a walkway leading to a large and brightly colored two-story house set back into palmettos and blooming jacarandas. There was a small sign on the front of the house, a cross framed in a pair of sun-yellow wings. Below the image were the words *Butterfly Haven*.

THE DETECTIVE CARSON RYDER SERIES

J.A. Kerley

THE HUNDREDTH MAN

In Alabama, Detective Carson Ryder is on the hunt for a disturbing killer. Famous for solving a series of crimes the year before, Carson has experience with psychopaths. But he had help with that case – from a past he's tried to forget. Now he needs it again...

THE DEATH COLLECTORS

The portfolio of a psychopathic artist thirty years dead sends Detective Carson Ryder and his partner Harry Nautilus into the chilling and hidden world of those who collect serial-killer memorabilia...

THE BROKEN SOULS

Carson and his partner Harry are up to their necks in a harrowing investigation, where all clues point to a powerful family whose strange and horrific past is about to engulf everyone around them in a storm of violence and depravity. And Ryder's right in the middle of it ...

BLOOD BROTHER

Detective Carson Ryder has a secret. His brother, Jeremy, is one of America's most notorious killers – now imprisoned. When Jeremy escapes, he becomes the chief suspect in a series of horrifying slayings in New York – and soon Carson is pulled into a dangerous game of life, death and deceit...

IN THE BLOOD

Detective Carson Ryder must put his personal problems aside when he takes on a bizarre new case involving an abandoned infant, a murdered S&M-loving televangelist, Neo-Nazis and satanic rituals. It seems that the baby fighting for its life has powerful enemies. Can Ryder save the life of an innocent child?

LITTLE GIRLS LOST

Children are disappearing in Mobile, Alabama, the latest snatched from her own bedroom. There are no clues – and, as yet, no bodies. Carson is brought in to the investigation, and discovers that the answers lie closer to home than he could have imagined...

BURIED ALIVE

Carson Ryder's vacation is interrupted when he's summoned to a grisly murder scene. With more savage killings, and the FBI inflaming the situation, Ryder sifts through the increasingly bizarre clues. Is there more than one killer involved? And how does Carson's clinically insane brother, Jeremy, now on the run, fit into the picture?

HER LAST SCREAM

secret network of crisis centres helps abused women escape their tormentors. But now someone is killing hem before they reach safety. Carson and Harry need an undercover cop to pose as a threatened woman, drawing the killer out. Harry's niece volunteers, but Harry promised to keep Reinetta safe. Suddenly he's unsure if he can even keep her alive...

THE KILLING GAME

After a humiliating encounter with a cop, Gregory Nieves launches a vendetta against the Mobile Police Department, Alabama, and one man in particular: Detective Carson Ryder. Carson doesn't know it yet, but he is caught up in a sadistic game of life and death. And there can only be one victor...

THE DEATH BOX

A specialist in twisted crimes, Detective Carson Ryder has barely started his new job in Miami when called to a horrific scene: a concrete pillar built of human remains, their agony forever frozen in stone. The case drags him into the sordid world of human trafficking, where one terrified girl holds the key to unraveling a web of pain, prostitution and murder. But Ryder's not the only one chasing the girl. And the others will kill to keep the secret safe.

THE MEMORY KILLER

A series of brutal assaults in Miami leaves Detective Carson Ryder, specialist in bizarre crimes, mystified.

None of the victims can recall their ordeal, but evidence reveals the predator's name, height, age and colouring. Carson knows exactly who he's after – so why can't he find him?

With each abduction the violence is escalating, and it's only a matter of time before torture becomes murder...